THE CANDLESTICKS
AND THE CROSS

THE
CANDLESTICKS
AND
THE CROSS

A Novel by

RUTH FREEMAN SOLOMON

G. P. PUTNAM'S SONS
New York

DEDICATION

*To my family: to those who were, in gratitude;
to those who are, in love; and to those
who will be, in profound hope.*

THE CANDLESTICKS
AND THE CROSS

I

THE morning air hung breathless over the vast von Glasman estate, as somnolent as if it were still August instead of October. In the garden of the white manor house, yellow leaves drifted from maple trees, and great beds of chrysanthemums and dahlias blazed, but the lawns were browning, and needed to be trimmed. Not an able body, male or female, could be spared for house or garden chores, however, until the grain was safely in.

Into the windless air, vegetable, cutting and herb gardens released a potpourri of scent. Sharper odors rose from cavernous dirt cellars where provisions were stored: crocks of dill pickles, tangy apples and hard green pears, marinating lettuce leaves, herrings in wine and spice, sour green tomatoes, smoked meats and fish, jugs of black caviar and many wooden barrels of aging brandy, alongside bottles of wine on racks.

Mellow and spent, the orchards covered acres; colonies of chicken coops and ponds where ducks and geese preened lay beyond the gardens. And still farther on stood the famous Pirov stables, renowned from border to border of Russia.

By right of descent from one Aaron von Glasman, who had claimed it from Tsar Peter, Ronya von Glasman Pirov was mistress of the great white house and the surrounding lands. But not of the stables. These had been a princely gift from her father to Boris Pirov on the day she married that gigantic, blond Tartar.

She first saw him in St. Petersburg in 1881, when she and her

9

father, David von Glasman, sat in the reviewing stand above the huge square where the royal guard paraded. The Dowager Empress was in the adjoining box, taking the salute from line after line of horsemen, the cream of the cavalry. Never had there been a handsomer assemblage of young males, and, Ronya thought contentedly, she could have her pick of them as partners at the palace ball that night. Which one to flirt with? She shaded her eyes with one small hand, contemplating the faces as they passed. Then there was only one man on the parade grounds.

"Who is he?" she demanded.

"Who is who?" David spoke absentmindedly, unaware that there was only one.

Ronya pointed. "That man," she said, "the great blond one."

"For all his blondness, Ronya, his mother is the Tartar Queen. His name is Boris Pirov."

"Good," said Ronya contentedly. "You know him."

"I know his father," he said.

She raised her voice over the beat of passing hooves. "I want him. I want to marry him."

"Whoa, little daughter! Not so fast." Her father's full attention was on Ronya now. "Are you serious?"

"I was never so serious about anything in my life," she said.

"We'll see." David's attention seemed to return to the ranks of the regiment. "It might be arranged," he added slowly. "You could do worse."

Ronya and Boris had been married for several years before she learned how it had been possible for her father to give her Boris, and then it was from her sister, Katya, Countess von Brusilov, that she heard most of the story. The threads of all their disparate lives, of the past and the future, the very skeins that made up the complex of Russia, ran through the delicate fingers of Katya's husband. An observer rather than a doer, Alexis von Brusilov had the gift of perspective, an ability to set pieces in place and to weigh their relative importance.

Like David, he knew the elder Pirov, a colonel of no consequence at court who had, however, attracted attention by his inability to support an extravagant taste in women on his meager pay. He would not be a problem. The Empress, on the other hand, regarded his son, Boris, with affection. As her guardsman,

Boris was not free simply to resign his commission and go to live on the von Glasman estate in the Ukraine. She must grant her permission, and release him. This was a delicate matter.

David held high cards in any negotiations, for he served his sovereign well as her most respected financial advisor and had her ear at all times. Nevertheless, he delayed bringing the matter up. Ronya was young. Her fancy might light on another handsome man. She had not seen Boris again, for he had failed to appear at the ball. Might she not change her mind? For six months David waited, but his daughter showed no sign of a change of heart.

Then David talked with Ronya in the library on a gloomy fall day. A fire was burning on the hearth, but his hands were cold as he took hers and, sitting beside her, told her a hideous story.

Boris' mother, she now learned, was the woman to whom the Odessa Tartars, a clan whose hatred for Jews ran deep and implacable, owed allegiance. She was the descendant of a Greek princess who, centuries before Odessa was a city, came with her troops to conquer the wild Tartars of the hills. When it became clear that the Greeks were no match for the powerful hill men, the princess, according to ballad and legend, seduced the Tartar leader, and gave her handmaidens to his followers. From their seed there issued a new breed, the Arghun, among whom the blond, or "Golden Ones," were considered royal. Legend also claimed that at death these Golden Ones must be carried on a white stallion to burial on a Tartar hill above the Black Sea, and there rest beside a Tartar woman.

Ronya's eyes widened as she listened to her father tell this tale, and they began to blaze as he went on to say that Boris' mother, a fiery Arghun, having heard of the possible marriage between her son and the Jewess Ronya, had already struck against the Jews. Claiming to have witnessed the ritual murder of a Jewish boy, she reacted with such fury that she had roused her Tartars to an orgy of murder. They had killed a hundred Jewish children, all male, and thrown their mutilated bodies into the Black Sea.

"Will you marry the son of such a mother?" David asked sorrowfully. And after an anguished moment, Ronya answered, equally sorrowfully, "I must, Father."

11

They never spoke of it again, but joy seemed to go out of David von Glasman. Now the negotiations proceeded.

Colonel Pirov's fortunes improved and his career prospered. He was soon well on his way to becoming a general and could afford to indulge his appetites. The alliance was his salvation. Only his son, Boris, a proud man despite his youth, felt burning humiliation at being sold like fodder for horses. Nevertheless the date of the wedding was set.

Everyone, even Katya, her sister, thought that Boris had seen Ronya for the first time when she walked between her father and mother down a velvet rug toward the wedding canopy made entirely of white roses and sprays of lilies of the valley. Forever after the guests reminisced, "What a marvelous spectacle! A golden giant towering over his tall, good-looking father, waiting to lay eyes on Ronya, the most beautiful Jewess in Russia."

Only Ronya and Boris knew that this was the second time, not the first, they had faced each other. Hours before the guests were due to arrive, David and Ruth von Glasman and Colonel Pirov rode off to escort Rabbi Levinsky back to the house. Katya and Alexis, themselves newly wed, had cut short their honeymoon to be at Ronya's wedding. Because they were tired from their long journey, they had been given rooms in a guest cottage some distance from the main house where they would be entirely undisturbed. The servants were busy with last-minute preparation, the peasants and gypsies were already celebrating.

Confined to her room, according to custom, Ronya was thoroughly bored. She sent Lydia to the gypsy camp on some nonsensical errand, preferring to be quite alone.

Two hours before he was expected, Boris arrived. Ronya heard the front door slam and his voice cry out. She was on her chaise longue, wearing nothing but a thin robe, when she heard him, and the word that drifted up to her was "Mother!"

On bare feet she darted to the top of the great, curving double stairway and started down. Halfway, she stopped. Below were two people, their backs turned toward her.

They were dressed alike—high black boots, tight black breeches, bright tunics open at the neck. They were of almost equal height, equally flat and hard and narrow-hipped. Except for the slight swell of her breasts and the long strangely blond

12

hair plaited, in the Tartar fashion, in many braids which streamed down her back, the woman was as masculine as the son.

Boris put out his arms like a child reaching for its mother; he bowed his head, then straightened and said, "Stay for the wedding. Give me your blessing, Mother. Please."

The woman's voice was surprisingly high, but strong and resolute. "Marry the Jewess and I give you no blessing but my curse! *Limbs rotting, may you die alone.*"

Boris seemed to turn to stone.

"Choose," the woman intoned.

That was when Ronya spoke. "Yes, Boris Pirov, choose!"

Startled, they turned and looked up. It was a magnificent moment. The hatred that gripped mother and son faded from their faces. All the rest of her life Ronya was convinced that in that instant the Tartar woman, the murderess of Jews, had loved her. Her eyes lit and the taut lines around her mouth softened.

Her voice fluttered up through the vaulted hall. "Come to the Tartars," she said. "Be my daughter then, lovely one."

Trapped between his mother and his past, his bride and the future, Boris gave Ronya a look so steadfast and tender that her heart raced. She turned back to her room without a word, so caught in the wave of passion that swept over her she scarcely heard the mother's screaming threat, "The Golden Ones never escape!"

Now in the autumn of 1900 Boris Pirov, champion horseman not only of the Ukraine but of greater Russia, bred and trained mounts for the Imperial cavalry. In the stables he ruled undisputed over barns and carriage house, blacksmith shop and corrals, horseflesh and a troupe of attendants.

The grooms and stableboys, like the field hands and house servants, lived on the property in a cluster of houses constructed from local clay, whitewashed and plaster-trimmed. Behind each cottage was a vegetable garden. Nearby, in a meadow where buttercups, daisies and wild hydrangeas bloomed, was their stone church.

Except to go hunting, peasants seldom ventured beyond the open fields into the dark forests that edged them. There the gypsies lived and since Aaron von Glasman's day they had been

13

under the protection of the manor house, though their ties to the land were tenuous. In their veins flowed the blood of Cossacks from the steppes, adulterated by Mongolian Tartars, Jews and passersby. They rarely entered the stone church but called themselves Christian, while still practicing magic and witchcraft.

Gypsy houses, like peasant houses, were stout, but tents were pitched around their encampment and the tongues of their painted wagons rested on wooden blocks. Overnight they could hitch up the blooded Pirov horses and be gone. Allegiance to the von Glasmans seemed short in their long history; allegiance to a chieftain went much further back. At present, they acknowledged a queen, a woman named Tamara, whom they would follow wherever she commanded.

Tamara—dark, volcanic and sensuous—bore an exotic resemblance to Ronya von Glasman Pirov. Though she stood a head taller and was coarse where Ronya was fine-grained and chiseled, their eyes betrayed their kinship. Aaron had been the first but not the last of the von Glasman men to consort with gypsy women.

Since early morning, church bells had been ringing up and down the valley to proclaim the harvest festival, the deepest notes coming from the gilded campanile of Saint Sophia in Kiev. By afternoon the taverns were filled with men already drunk on vodka. The more seemly, and the women, crowded the domed churches and even the Jews worshiped unmolested. Ronya had sent a rich gift to the general of the Ukrainian army, and on the strength of it the general had ordered: "Let the Jews feast." Without fear old men lit candles in the synagogues and chanted their thanks for the wheat.

At sunset Boris Pirov cantered his favorite white stallion along a deserted trail, enjoying the ripe smell of autumn. Good weather for the harvest day's riding competition, good too for the great public feasting and wild dancing that would follow.

As usual there were entries from the Pirov stables in each event. Boris' horses regularly swept the field because he knew how to train them as well for sports as for battle. This year, however, for the first time, his elder son, Igor, would wear the Pirov colors. The youngster was a heavy favorite and his father had

14

worked him relentlessly for weeks and wagered hundreds of gold coins on him. Igor, he knew from gossip in the officers' club, had also bet recklessly on himself.

Slowing down, the big man on the big horse dismounted in the driveway of the manor house, threw the reins to a waiting groom and swung up the steps to the front door. Candles were already burning in the great central hall lined with heroic Belgian tapestries. Lighting a cigarette, Boris lingered for a moment to enjoy a feeling of repose; Aaron von Glasman was an architect with an unerring instinct for proportion and style. Through the decades since he had completed his house, other von Glasmans had added treasures to it—luminous paintings and Chinese rugs, baroque silver and French porcelains, rare books and bronzes.

When the house became Ronya's, after her father's death, she replaced heavy damask hangings with printed linens and chintzes in the English manner, painted the walls warm, becoming colors. With her own hands she arranged the bouquets of flowers for every room. And, like each mistress of the estate before her, she trained country girls to serve the family unobtrusively with more than country elegance.

Boris dawdled over his bath, then shaved and dressed with care. He looked in the mirror, adjusted the fresh stock he had put on, and sauntered across the hall to his wife's bedroom door.

"Ronya!" he called. There was no answer but he went in and opened a cabinet where, to please him, she kept a bottle of vodka and glasses. Boris poured himself a drink. Lacking the original to toast, he gravely raised his glass to a photograph of Ronya that stood in a gold frame by his side of the bed. It was, he thought, quite the best picture she had ever had taken. The photographer had caught the arch of the dark brows (often referred to as "Gothic") and the completely beautiful mouth, lips parted eagerly. Damn it, where was she? He drained his glass and set it down. She would probably be in the kitchen at this hour, for she was, to Boris' never-ending amusement, a woman who loved to busy herself with chopping boards and rolling pins against a background of shelves stacked with spices. Her cooking was as famous as his horses.

The subject of the photograph was so absorbed in climbing

15

up a stepladder to fetch a crock from a top shelf that she did not hear Boris enter the kitchen. He caught her trim waist in his big hands and pulled her down, spun her around and kissed her mightily on the mouth.

It was nearly twenty years since he had first seen her, at the top of the stairs in the great hall, and there had been endless storms between them since. If these years had altered her, it was to underline the strengths of her face. The eyes were as expressive, dark and deep, the skin as milky, the mouth as volatile as ever. No gray diluted the brown hair brushed up into a high knot, burnished copper when sunlight struck it. Only the jaw was not the same. Her chin had been a child's on that long-ago spring morning. Now it betrayed a forcefulness that would have been disturbing in a less feminine woman. For the thousandth time Boris marveled at her loveliness and at how, while his appetite for other women came and went, his hunger for Ronya was never appeased.

Settling into a capacious rocker, he cradled her in his lap. There was silence between them in the stone-flagged, wood-paneled kitchen he had built himself to be her province and plaything. His wife ran her fingers through the golden mane of his hair.

"Mmmm—you smell good."

"*You* smell like cinnamon and apples."

"The samovar is hot and I just took the strudel out of the oven," she said. "Do you want a piece?"

"Wonderful," he said. "I'll put off leaving for an hour. Why don't you tell Lydia to serve us in the library?"

Ronya rose and shrugged in exasperation.

"I should have noticed." Her lips were suddenly thin. "You *are* dressed for a night in town."

Boris heaved himself out of the chair, turned and started for the kitchen door. No sooner had he passed through it than Ronya darted out into the hall, bolted up the stairs and slammed her bedroom door.

It was Boris' turn to shrug. In the library he sat down on a sofa before the enormous stone fireplace and waited for Ronya to relent and reappear. He waited for half an hour, soothing his mounting irritation with vodka. Then he pulled a velvet cord which hung beside the door.

The call was answered by Lydia, a lively old woman with a face like a winter apple. When Ronya was a girl, Lydia was her friend and confidante. Now she was housekeeper as well, in charge of the rosy wenches who churned butter and made beds and polished the brasses and washed the linens. Nothing went on in the house that Lydia did not know and from her privileged position she interfered shamelessly in family affairs.

"Order my carriage," Boris commanded.

Tough peasant that she was, Lydia was unafraid of Boris, who could be an intimidating man. Instead of obeying she put on a defiant face and stood, firmly planted, hands crossed over her round stomach.

I'll be damned, thought Boris, if fat old Lydia doesn't want to talk. Aloud, he said, "Go ahead!"

She did not move. "Count Alexis and Countess Katya arrive tomorrow on the afternoon train from St. Petersburg," she said.

Amusement diluted Boris' annoyance. "I know that, Lydia."

"I know you know, Boris, my master."

"Lydia," he said, "you're doubtless a well-meaning woman. You are also a damned nuisance. Now get the hell out of here and do as you're told."

Her point made, Lydia said, "Yes, sir," and departed.

Boris shook his head in unwilling admiration and fixed himself another drink. Katya and Alexis—Ronya's older sister and brother-in-law. Possibly Lydia was right. Possibly this trip into town was ill-timed. He was debating the point when the door opened. Ronya was wearing a jewel in her hair which sparkled less brilliantly than her furious eyes.

"I've come because I'm out of cigarettes," she announced. Inwardly Boris chuckled as he solemnly lit one of his and gave it to her. She inhaled and looked up at him, her dark eyes still angry. "We lost Smolny today," she said. "There's not a tutor left in Kiev who will take on Georgi. He outwits them all."

Boris laughed. The abounding and destructive energy of his younger son entertained him. "I share his contempt for the mealymouthed teachers you engage. The boy ought to be at the cavalry academy."

17

"I can't bear the thought." Ronya's voice was mournful.

It was a familiar argument. "After all, he'll have his aunt and uncle to keep an eye on him in St. Petersburg," Boris said.

Ronya was not to be comforted. "I know. It's just that I can't bring myself to send him away so young. Besides, it's brutal to expose a child to nobody but men, especially military men who care nothing about education—just drill and discipline—and whose only real enthusiasm is horses."

To a point, Boris agreed. "All right," he said. "I'll give you another year. But for heaven's sake, let me pick the next tutor. I'll find one who's man enough to handle the young imp."

Despite her relief Ronya returned to the attack. "You push both Georgi and Igor too hard."

"Come now, Ronya. I counted on a pleasant hour with you!"

"And I counted on a whole evening of pleasant hours," she blazed. "What a Tartar you are!"

"You knew that when you married me," he said.

"But you don't *look* like a Tartar," she said. "No Tartar has a right to be blond."

"This one is."

Ronya was not beguiled by his reasonableness. "You never have understood Igor. He'll win your miserable championship for you but even you can't make him the rider you are. He'll break his neck or he'll break his heart. Igor has no real toughness."

"Have you any more to say?" Boris was roused now.

"Yes, I have. It was stupid to let Igor leave the university."

"Oh, Ronya." Boris threw up his hands. "You know as well as I do Igor is shrewd. He's good with horses. He is *no* good with books. What's the sense of a university degree for a boy like that?"

It was true enough but still she was vexed. "You set your sons a rotten example," she said.

He did not deny it. "Let's get this straight," he said. "I was and still am a lot of things I don't want Igor to be. Believe me."

From the driveway horses' hooves sounded. Boris said nothing as he gave Ronya a quizzical look, bowed slightly and walked gravely out of the library.

He climbed into the light carriage and gathered up the reins slackly, shoulders sagging. His team of matched geldings caught his mood and ambled dispiritedly. The thought of a night with Vera, who was certainly an accomplished trollop, was no longer alluring. Even in her anger Ronya was incomparable. Boris really wanted only one woman and that woman was his unpredictable, mercurial wife, who utterly captivated him. The trees along the road passed in steady succession as he argued with himself. To return, to humble himself and have her crow over him—should he give Ronya that advantage? Minutes passed before he reined in sharply. On whatever terms, this night he would spend with Ronya.

As he turned the team, his head went up and the sagging lines seemed to disappear from his rugged face.

"Giddap," said Boris softly. The geldings did not need to be urged. They were already settling into a swift trot. By the time he reached the house Boris was once more in high good humor.

There was no one in the library. He vaulted up the staircase, words forming on his lips—I'm taking you out to dine, my love. It's a long time since Kiev had a look at the most beautiful girl in Russia.

Ronya's room was empty.

Again it was Lydia who answered the bell. She looked up at Boris. "Father Tromokov came right after you drove off. My mistress has gone to supper with him. They spoke of attending a meeting afterward."

"Where are they dining?" Boris asked.

"They did not say," Lydia replied smugly.

"Where is the meeting to be held? What kind of a meeting?"

"I don't know, sir, I'm sorry."

Deflated, Boris dismissed her with a nod. The house was suddenly forlorn and he returned to his carriage and drove to the stables. His thin, dark son Igor and a bowlegged groom with mournful eyes under drooping lids sat in the tackroom playing two-handed pinochle. Boris watched the playing out of the hand before asking, "The Blond One been here?"

Igor said, "Gone hunting."

"I'm sleeping here for him tonight, sir," the groom said.

"Come outside, son," he said to Igor. "I want to talk to you." But when they stood together in the light of a lantern, Boris

19

could find nothing to say except, "Go have supper with your brother Georgi. Get a good night's sleep." He put an arm across his son's shoulder. "We'll work the four-horse team tomorrow."

"All right." Igor's voice was cool.

"I'm going to town."

"All right," Igor repeated and moved away.

Cursing under his breath, Boris climbed back into his carriage and drove to the officers' club of the local barracks.

The morning was clear and sunny. Boris, who had slept in his own room lest he waken Ronya when he came in late, stretched contentedly and stood looking over the treetops at the freshness of dewy turf and distant hills. A slight sound made him turn. Ronya, carrying a tray, was coming through the doorway. Boris took it from her and put it on his bedside table. "My morning tea," he said. "Kind of you, little dove."

Ronya kicked off her slippers and climbed into his bed. "*Our* morning tea," she said. "Why are you laughing?"

"Happy," was all he said.

"Boris Pirov, you look absolutely ridiculous—standing there stark naked with your socks on." He remedied that by pulling them off and getting into bed beside her. Ronya's voice was subdued. "Did you have a long and thirsty night?"

"Yes," said Boris and she turned her face away.

"I went to the officers' club," he added quickly, "and drank a lot and bet a lot. On Igor. Gave tremendous odds. I had to. No one wants to bet against him."

Ronya put her hands on Boris' face. "Thank you, darling, for—sweetening my day."

What went on behind closed doors was no mystery to Lydia. She brought Boris a man-size breakfast when he appeared in Ronya's kitchen. Her mistress was still asleep. After he had finished, he went into the small morning room and wrote a letter to the dean of the university, who had advised him to withdraw Igor:

September 7, 1900

Dear Sir:

Would it be possible for you to engage a suitable tutor for

my second son, a high-grade hellion, who could exhaust Hercules?

I have nothing further at my command to recommend my son Georgi.

Yours truly,
Boris Pirov

This missive he dropped onto a silver salver in the hall on his way to the stables.

After an early lunch the coachman drove Boris and Ronya to the railroad station in Kiev. Everywhere there were crowds and an air of immense excitement. Fine carriages, like the Pirovs', waxed and glistening in the afternoon sunlight, were flanked by droshkies, lumbering wagons with long narrow benches for passengers, peasant drays and mule-drawn carts. Dust and laughing voices swirled through the air. From all over the Ukraine people were converging on Kiev. Soon the city would be filled with delicate, fair-skinned women from St. Petersburg, olive-skinned women with almond-shaped eyes from Moscow, Amazons in high black boots from Odessa, with portly gentlemen, gold watchchains draped across their bellies, and shabby soldiers with Slavic cheekbones, Cossacks, Tartars, young riders from everywhere. The celebration of the wheat harvest belonged to them all since the wheat fed them all. And many Jews—the ones who could obtain travel permits—came because the son of Ronya von Glasman was to ride.

When the train slowed to a stop, Ronya and Boris saw Count Alexis Brusilov waving from the window of a first-class compartment. "We shall have a happy visit, Katya my dear. Boris is with Ronya and the wild eagle looks tame and contented. Not Tartarish at all."

"Thank heaven," said Katya. "I've prayed that some day those two would stop tormenting each other."

Hand in hand the Brusilovs walked to the end of the car corridor, where the door stood open. While Alexis tipped the conductor, Katya, who seldom hurried, jumped down from the train and ran to Ronya. Alexis followed her, shook hands with Boris, and the two men stood watching the reunion of the sisters.

21

After a moment of hugs and greetings, Ronya said, "I always make a fool of myself at stations," and threw her arms around Alexis. Boris stooped to kiss Katya's hand and told her gallantly, "You look adorable. If I'd met you first, Alexis would still be a bachelor."

"Don't be silly, Boris," Katya said, half in earnest. "I couldn't cope with you for a day. Ronya's a marvel."

Suddenly serious, Boris put out his hand to her. "Let's be friends, Katya," he said.

Before she answered, his sister-in-law looked into the crowd to make sure her husband and Ronya were out of earshot. "I lie awake at night, Boris, worrying about Ronya."

"No need, Katya," he said and gave her his arm.

The front door was already open when the carriage bearing the Brusilovs and Pirovs rolled up to the house. Out plummeted Georgi. Not because his uncle was a man of great power in St. Petersburg and his aunt a favorite of the Empress Mother, but because they doted on him, Georgi adored them. He bounced like a rubber ball, exploding with excitement, babbling news and getting in everybody's way as the maids carried luggage from the cart that followed the big carriage. His delight was so contagious that even saturnine Igor was grinning, and Lydia's face shone.

At length the commotion subsided and the family proceeded to the library, where a samovar was bubbling. For an hour they chattered, interrupting one another to deliver a present or some bit of news or gossip. Igor alone fell silent under the barrage. Not so Lydia. She surfeited "her" family with attention—just one more cake? Another glass of tea? And she had comments on everything. When at last she could stuff them no longer, she rang for the maids to carry away the trays and, reluctantly, followed them from the room.

With some semblance of peace and quiet restored, Alexis opened the chessboard. "A game, Boris?"

"No thanks, my friend." He glanced at Igor. "We've only twenty-four hours left. . . ."

His brother-in-law chuckled. "A final workout? Having myself placed a wager on the future champion of the Ukraine," he inclined his head toward Igor, "I might, if invited, watch a wild gallop around the ring and a jump or two."

Georgi went to the stables with the men, dancing all the way.

That night, Ronya and Boris gave a reception for the Brusilovs, an annual custom which varied not at all from one year to the next. Guests arrived punctually at six, would leave punctiliously at nine, in order to give the race committee time to meet. Rich aristocrats and poor, solid provincial landowners, military men in gold-decked dress uniforms, patricians in power and climbers who desired to be—all eagerly found their way to the Pirovs'.

The priest, Father Tromokov, like a rusty crow among peacocks, gravitated toward the table where vodka was being served, his voice booming out above all the others. If the women thought him uncouth, they gave no sign. His popularity with their husbands was second only to Boris', just as he was second only to Boris as a horseman, a consumer of vodka and a man of the world.

And no bejeweled woman in the room carried her head higher than the gypsy queen Tamara, who, like Father Tromokov, was an invariable guest at Pirov parties. Conscious that her décolletage drew the eyes of every man present, she flirted with them all, indifferently. Her real attention focused on Boris. He turned away from her, sullen and angry.

Ronya seemed oblivious to the duel between her husband and Tamara; she moved from group to group, joining in conversations that centered on horses and the outcome of tomorrow. At eight-thirty, with a skill born of long practice, she began to bring the party to a close. For another half hour farewells and compliments eddied in from front steps to hall. "The most delicious whisper of dill in your greens, Ronya darling. . . ." "Georgi's growing into such a charmer!" "Igor does get handsomer every day." "You must be proud of them."

When the door had closed behind the last guest, Boris, saying, "With your permission, gentlemen," herded the judges into the library. These men, a motley group, were all friends, nevertheless. Vladimir, a coarse brute of a man, loved Boris to the point of sentimentality. The Cossack chief, known to be a terrible enemy of the Jews, was a willing guest of the Jewess, Ronya von Glasman. Mischuk, chief of police for Kiev, astonished Ukrainians by being incorruptible, and an exemplary judge of horses, as well. There was a Tartar whose bald head and flowing beard bespoke the hordes of Genghis Khan. He paid tribute to Boris' Tartar mother. The last member of the committee was popular Father Tromokov. Alexis sat with them ex officio. The men liked him for his sharp wit and sound judgment.

Usually the business of the meeting was confined to a few rounds of vodka, a few friendly skirmishes, settled with bets, and the reelection of Boris as chief judge.

Tonight promised to be no different. Drinks were poured, men found easy chairs or settled on sofas. It was so warm the fire had not been lit, the windows were open and the scent of flowers drifted in from the garden. Tromokov was sprawled in a huge armchair, half-drunk, heavy-lidded and, for the first time all evening, quiet. Boris alone remained on his feet, pacing a little, brows pulled together, cogitating. Suddenly he spoke up in a voice that commanded attention from them all.

"I cannot serve as a judge tomorrow," he said.

It was as though a bolt of lightning had been loosed in the warm room. Protests rang out.

"How in hell do I fire the starting gun and cheer for my son Igor, if I'm a judge?" he asked rhetorically, holding up his hand to still the objections. "I'll be my own master tomorrow, standing by my boy and feeding him every trick I know."

"Excellent," Alexis said.

"My money rides on Igor," the Cossack insisted, adding with mock candor, "Must I, then, as a matter of honor, resign, too?"

The Tartar, slower to grasp the situation than the others, suspected Cossack trickery and advanced menacingly on his hereditary enemy. "Cossack rides," he said scowling, "and *you* bet on Igor?"

In mock terror, the Cossack fell on his knees. "I love money!" he protested.

As sole outsider, Alexis alone had the right to intervene in this horseplay. "Gentlemen!" he spread his hands. "There is among you one just and honorable man. What says Mischuk?

24

Does a man undress before he takes a bath or after? Tomorrow Boris is father and horse-owner."

Mischuk did not hesitate. He stood and raised his glass as he spoke. "It is unthinkable that we accept the resignation of Boris. Since he was nineteen he has been Russia's national champion and in all those years his sportsmanship was above question. My soul is untroubled. He will judge fair."

Vladimir dropped his glass with a crash, leaped at Mischuk and kissed him on both cheeks, shouting, "I love you. I love you." To Boris he said solemnly, "How does Igor look? I mortgaged my house."

Boris clucked, pretending dismay. "Fine!" he said.

Father Tromokov began to sing a rowdy song in a raucous voice. Soon all except the Tartar joined in the final stanza. He sat, very drunk, like a sphinx.

Alexis fell into a chair, fanning himself, and said, "Tell us your decision, Boris. I refuse to stay up any longer."

"I'll sleep on it," Boris said, "and give you my answer when we meet at the races." He moved toward the door. "Comrades, there are bedrooms ready for any of you who wish to remain."

His eyes uneasily fixed on the Cossack, the Tartar said, "We are a crowd. Let us go."

The men shook hands. Vladimir embraced Boris. "Tonight I am a monk," he said. "I dream only of money."

Alexis and Boris said goodnight outside Katya's door; then Boris walked down the hall to Igor's room and went in quietly. Looking down at his son's slender form, he pulled the blanket over a bare shoulder. "Be an eagle tomorrow, Igor," he said gently.

II

BORIS on his white stallion led the way to the sports field, early in the morning, followed by Igor and Georgi, each of whom led extra horses. Behind lumbered two large carriages; in the first Ronya, Katya and Alexis; in the second Lydia with her favorite relatives. A procession of trainers, grooms and stableboys, some whistling or singing, trailed after. The master blacksmith drove a droshky filled to overflowing by his fat wife and squealing progeny. The Pirov servants were on foot, carrying hampers of food and wine, rugs and parasols. Peasants jolted along in hay wagons. Brushing back their drooping moustaches, the men tilted jugs of vodka to their mouths. Buxom girls shrieked with laughter and enjoyed wet kisses and hot hands that reached under wide skirts as a prelude to nightfall. The harvest was a time of fertility. Old women stared ahead at nothing. Their flesh no longer hungry for love, they dreamed of hot roast potatoes and strong warm beer.

At the end of the long line came the gypsies, their caravan led by Tamara. Her blouse was embroidered with an eagle fitted over magnificent breasts. Behind were her people in their painted wagons, the men strumming two-string guitars, the women dressed in passionate red or green, snapping their fingers rhythmically, their black braids beating time. Last of all came Tamara's son and heir, called "The Blond One." Like Boris he was golden. Like Boris he was tall and beautiful and he, too, rode a white horse.

The Pirovs made camp on a knoll from which they could view all the day's events. By tradition the judges sat with the Pirovs until time for the races. Above the noise of snorting horses and barking dogs, Boris had a few final words of advice for Igor. "Turn Peacock over to his groom. I want him to memorize every turn, every obstacle, every pebble on the course. Remember: No reins on the first jump—just your knees. Lady will sail up to the sky for you. Get ready, son. And good luck!"

Amid a chorus of good wishes, Igor, dashingly handsome in red tunic, black breeches and boots, took his leave.

"You see, gentlemen," Alexis said to the judges, "you must accept Boris' resignation. Today he is all father. It would be unsuitable, even unnatural, for him to try to act impartially."

Vladimir answered for them all, saying firmly, "No Boris, no judges. No judges, no contest. That's final. What do you say, Boris?"

Before answering, Boris turned to Ronya. "You hear that?" he asked her. "Have I any choice?"

She smiled up at him. "What rubbish you do talk, Boris Pirov. You are the fairest, most honest man alive. It is your duty to judge. And may your son do you proud."

Alexis chuckled. "A typical Russian decision. No different from the ones made at court."

"Listen," Ronya said when Boris had left them. The crowd was giving him a wild ovation. Men smelling of horses and saddle leather crowded around to shake his hand and pound him on the back. His golden hair shimmered in the sunlight and they loved him, this man so indissolubly part and parcel of the land.

At last their hero, by habit soft-spoken and slow to invoke his strength, had to force his way through the mob. In the center of the field the horses were assembled and the judges inspected them, one by one, recording their condition. At Boris' signal the mounts were returned to the grooms and the riders called together. He briefed them: "Remember that in a country of fine horsemen, you are the finest. These animals were bred and raised and trained for this day. Good luck!"

Boris fired his pistol and the games began. The crowd waited for Igor. His father's people, the Tartars, backed him as one of their own. The Jews, too, had a stake in Ronya von Glasman's son.

Three gaited horses trotted briskly into the ring. Igor's mare,

27

Lady, carried her head high, nostrils sucked in, ears pricking forward. Igor was calm and sure, the communication between man and beast perfect, and there were cheers from the crowd.

When the riders had gone through their paces, the judges came back into the ring and the ringmaster ordered, "Line up!" Again the judges inspected the mounts, checking each point— legs, shoulders, curve of necks, quarters. At a further command from the ringmaster the three riders went through their performances once more and the judges conferred.

"Lady," came the announcement, "handled ably by Igor Pirov, places first." The watchers waved and yelled.

Igor ran away with the next two events, as well. In the fourth the audience went crazy. This was an obstacle race and Igor left the other contestants far behind. In seconds he had retrieved a white handkerchief from the ground, then slid under the belly of his horse while it galloped at top speed, emerged on the other side and reseated himself in the saddle. A roar went up. "Bravo young Pirov! Bravo Pirov!" The Cossacks swarmed onto the field and surrounded the boy while his own people shouted.

Boris, glowing, let the demonstration go on for several minutes, then fired four times for the last event.

At the signal a stranger, recognizable as a Crimean Tartar by his dark, stony face, rode into the ring, standing with each foot on one of a team of horses. A Cossack and two other contestants followed. Igor was last, riding two and controlling two other horses. His eyes were fixed straight ahead, his left hand uncharacteristically tense on the reins, his right hand thrust out for balance. The young man worked his horses competently but for the first time he was cautious and insecure, offering no challenge either to the Tartar or the Cossack, who were performing feats of suicidal daring. As their riding accelerated in speed and bravura, Igor brought his own horses to a halt.

Like a black hawk, the Tartar closed in on the Cossack's terrain, a predator moving in to the kill. The Cossack challenged him with equal fury, and death entered the ring. Igor and the two other riders had retreated to a far corner of the arena, their faces streaked with dust and sweat. The crowd was silent.

Before this bizarre battle could end in tragedy, Boris ran to the corner where Igor sheltered. "Give me your horse, son," he said. Igor, his eyes hooded, handed his father the reins.

Hands steady as a statue's, Boris proceeded to the center of the ring, crossed in front of the Cossack and rode straight on, to the Tartar. The dark man reined in and the two faced each other, immobile. Boris turned for an instant and gestured to the Cossack to leave the ring, then touched his horse's flank and moved forward until the two beasts' noses touched each other.

"Black Tartar!" Boris challenged. "Choose! Fight me now or go back to Odessa and tell my mother my answer. Tell her I made my choice a long time ago. Tell her that my son Igor rides for the Jews today."

The other man's glance flickered and fell. He raised an arm in salute, like a soldier obeying the order of a superior, wheeled and rode out of the ring, and down the road toward town.

It was over, leaving a numbed stillness around the field. Few onlookers had understood the short, violent encounter, but there was a lingering sense of dismay. Into the hush Boris rode again, this time on his own white stallion and treated the crowd to so staggering a display of horsemanship that they were soon clapping and yelling and contented again. They broke the necks of vodka bottles, threw silver coins recklessly into the air, grabbed and pummeled one another and sang: "Long live the King! Long live Boris Pirov!"

Boris dismounted, made his way back to the judges' box and fired the final shot that signaled the official end of the games. Ribbons and prize money were distributed, with every contestant receiving a share. Igor was champion of the day.

The first Pirov to reach Boris was Georgi. "You were great!" he bellowed. "But why didn't you lick that black bastard? I bet Mother would have."

Boris tousled the golden head of his youngest. "Don't say 'bastard.' Your mother wouldn't like it."

"She says it all the time."

Boris grinned. "A lady's privilege, Georgi."

Georgi extricated himself from his father's hand. "The Blond One wouldn't have let the Tartar force him out of the ring— neither would I," he said confidently. "Why did Igor?"

29

His father turned on him. "Georgi! Never compare your brother to the Blond One again!" His voice was cold with anger, and Georgi quickly put a respectful distance between himself and his father.

A moment later, Ronya, looking up into her husband's face, was puzzled to see how withdrawn he seemed.

"Are you tired, Boris?" Ronya asked.

"Not particularly," he said gruffly. "Hell, I've lost my cigarettes." She lit one of hers and gave it to him.

"Ronya," he snapped, "you know I don't like you to smoke in public."

Irritated, Ronya stood up. "I'm going for a walk. Will you come with me, Katya?"

"I'd love to."

"You're not going to wait and congratulate Igor?" Boris had suddenly come to life again.

"Igor's been and gone," Ronya said. "He was in an agony of impatience to find his friend Duvid and be deluged in flattery. He'll join us for supper and the dances."

Boris and Alexis sat silent for a few minutes. Then Boris reached into a straw basket and pulled out a bottle of vodka. He uncorked it and drank. The smell of food cooking in the fairgrounds' stone ovens drifted toward the knoll. He took a second drink before handing the bottle to his brother-in-law. Alexis put it away, saying gently, "What's troubling you? Come on, tell me, Boris."

At the sound of his name Boris turned. "Igor was timid with the black Tartar."

"You're hard on him, Boris," Alexis said slowly. "The lad is not yet eighteen and he acquitted himself well. I'm proud of him. You should be proud of him."

As though he had not heard, Boris went on, "Alexis, the Tartars tested Pirov mettle today. That fellow was a killer and he was an emissary from my mother. Once again she has tried to force me to choose between her people—my people the Tartars —and Ronya's people. Well, she got her answer."

Alexis was puzzled. "Your mother? Don't tell me she's still alive!"

"Yes," said Boris, "she's alive. It isn't enough, damn her, that she cursed me. She has to hound me, too."

He took the bottle out of the basket again and stood up. After they had each had a drink, he said, "I'm tired of talk. Let's find the von Glasman girls. It's still a fine day."

That evening there was a chill in the air and the servants stoked the fires. In the red glow of burning logs, Pirovs and Brusilovs sat apart from peasants and gypsies to eat supper from hampers. Light wicker chairs were ranged in a semicircle, forming an island in the midst of, yet apart from, the gigantic crowd. Even vodka failed to raise Boris' spirits and he sat, heavy-browed and saturnine. Ronya was deliberately cheerful, chattering to Alexis and Katya.

As fires died down, torches were lighted and shed eerie, salmon-colored light on the clearing which would be the stage for the rest of the night's celebrations. With much shy giggling, the peasants moved into the open space and started dancing, pantomiming the ancient rituals of planting and harvesting. They were followed by the hunters and trappers, who mimicked the sounds and movements of birds with uncanny accuracy, and then the Tartars strode into the ring of light and danced a bawdy takeoff on feasts and weddings.

Noise gave way to the sighing song of balalaikas, moody then increasingly wild. Boris and Georgi joined the performers, in their element in the *gopak*, leaping to crazy heights with a natural, inborn rhythm, their fair hair tossing. But now it was Georgi who captured the audience. In his youth there was magic, and the movements of his body were poetry. *Gopak* finished, he danced alone to the minor wailing of the balalaikas, weaving a pattern of steps of his own imagining, so flawless that people wept. There was no applause. Silence was the tribute paid to Georgi.

From under the dark trees, softly, insolently, the gypsies came at last into the flickering light. Violins began to play, as though from a long way off, music of meadows and unknown seas, of ferns and pastures, heaven and death. The gypsies stood motionless in a wide circle and into it walked their queen, Tamara,

31

head back, hair flowing to below her waist, each arm coruscating with gold bracelets. For a moment she stood, eyelids lowered, mouth drooping sullenly, then snapped her fingers. At once the violins broke into an angry lament and she danced the tribulations of her people.

Again Tamara snapped her fingers. The violins soared, hot and sensuous. The queen became the seductress. Naked feet skimming the bare ground, she improvised an erotic, contorted fantasy, stomach working under her brilliant skirt, nipples of her full breasts hard and dark, bracelets jingling. Boys watching—ashamed, curious and fascinated—sweated and moved uneasily from one buttock to the other as they sat on the ground. Men stared with unwavering eyes, mouths hanging open, howling at her as she asked them all with eyes and tongue and movement to accept her invitations. Vodka bottles were emptied, trancelike, while women blushed or snuggled closer to their men.

Tamara snapped her fingers for the last time and the violins fell silent. With much ribald joking the crowd began to disperse.

Lydia seized Georgi's hand and started to drag him toward the Pirov carriages. Over his shoulder he called back, "Come *on!* It's over." But no one moved.

Boris sat, as stony-faced as the Tartar, sweat on his brow. While the last of the onlookers loitered in the darkness, he turned to Ronya and there was grief in his eyes. She looked beyond him, locked in a personal solitude born of jealous agony.

"Look at me," Boris said.

The sight of her sorrowing face unleashed such a flood of love and remorse in him that, unaware of anyone else, he scooped her up, petticoats flying, her pretty legs exposed to the knee, and strode down to where a groom was holding the reins of his white stallion. There some of the crowd lingered, admiring the horse and gossiping with the stablemen. In front of them all Boris gave Ronya a long, impassioned kiss.

"Boris!" she cried, trying vainly to pull down her skirts. Then, under her breath, "How beautiful you are!"

Igor was near when his father vaulted into the saddle, lifted his mother up and galloped away with her. He watched them through eyes blinded by fury. His own failure and his father's victory that afternoon had swelled jealousy into hatred. In Ronya's protest he heard what he wanted to hear. His ears were closed to her words of love.

A great, lecherous eagle was outraging his adored mother. He turned away, distracted, until the Blond One grabbed his arm.

"God damn it to hell!" Igor said, wrenching himself free. "He made your mother a whore and you a bastard. He forced himself on my mother—you saw it! Everybody saw it. Why do you love him? Why?"

Without waiting for an answer Igor jumped onto a strange horse, gave the nag a savage kick and rode off recklessly.

There was a lump in the Blond One's throat as he watched his beloved half brother disappear. To himself he mourned, "Will he never understand? My mother was born a whore."

It was past midnight before Alexis and Katya were at last alone together in Katya's bedroom.

"Alexis, my darling," she said, turning away from her dressing-table mirror where she had been brushing her black hair, "why doesn't Ronya take a whip to Tamara? Why will she go on cherishing her in spite of everything? And how *can* Tamara make"—she raised her hands in distaste—"love to Boris and at the same time cleave to Ronya?"

Alexis smiled. "That's a lot of questions, my Katya. But perhaps there's a single answer. A very ancient one, at that.

"You know as well as I do how the von Glasman men have cherished the gypsy queens ever since they took title to this land. And begotten children on them. Now there is no male who bears the name of von Glasman. Boris, through his marriage to Ronya, assumed their role. Like von Glasman men before him he fathered a gypsy child, the Blond One." He shrugged. "This distresses you. It distresses Ronya. But the thing is done and has to be lived with." He took Katya's hands in his.

"Tonight you saw a miracle. Boris really broke the hold Tamara has had on him. In sight of us all he rejected her and claimed Ronya.

"You know that Ronya inherited Tamara as much as this house, the peasants, the cattle, the fields and the crops. Tragic and troublesome, I grant you, but the inevitable price she pays for being David von Glasman's heir.

"In all this I am the gainer. When your father gave you to the Empress and to me, you were freed from heavy Jewish tradition, with its terrible penalties, to become a member of my house and a Christian. And so I can only be grateful, my love. Grateful—and tolerant."

Igor, tormented, rode through the darkness to Kiev on the horse he had appropriated. He went from tavern to tavern until, very drunk, he drew up at the last house on the hill where a woman named Vera waited for his father. He knocked at the door and she opened it to him.

III

"THE Countess Katya wants you to come to her sitting room," Lydia announced to Ronya the next afternoon.

"Later," Ronya said. "I'm in no mood for the Countess and her high-minded advice." She picked up a bunch of wild grapes. "Sit down, old hen," she said. "Where is the Blond One? I haven't seen him since the races."

"He's back, Ronya, my mistress."

"Back from where?"

"Back from wherever he goes. Who knows where?"

"What I've been wondering," Ronya said, putting a grape in her mouth, "is whether his fanatical attachment to Igor is wearing off. He hasn't seemed to be playing shadow so insistently lately."

"He's a good, sweet boy," Lydia commented.

"Who, Igor?"

34

"No!" The old woman sounded indignant. "The Blond One. How such an angel could come out of such a she-devil, I'll—"

"Shut up, Lydia!" Ronya took another grape. "I hear the gypsies are cutting timber. Do you know why?"

Lydia's eyes narrowed and she said nothing.

"Tamara building another house?" her mistress prompted.

Lydia thawed. "Yes. Soon she'll have more houses than the Tsar."

"I shall send her a present for her new one," Ronya remarked agreeably. "That Dresden chariot." She pointed to a delicately wrought piece of porcelain that stood on a small table. "See it?"

"Yes, my mistress. I've been seeing it all my life."

"Wrap it up and deliver it to Tamara. There'll be a note with it. She'll understand that however rottenly she behaves I still recognize her as a queen."

Lydia stood up and grumbled, "If it was me I'd give her a good taste of my whip, not my mother's fine chariot."

After a bath Ronya put on the dress the maid had laid out for her, then went down the hall to the room where Katya was waiting.

"I expected you sooner," her sister said tartly.

"Sorry. A headache."

"I'm tired of your stalling." Katya was obdurate. "We're going to the library and we are going to discuss Georgi."

Ronya preceded Katya into the corridor and paused outside Georgi's closed door.

"He's not there," Katya said. "Alexis had some business with the Cossack chief and took Georgi with him.

"There is *no one* at home *and* I've ordered Lydia not to let anyone interrupt us."

Ronya dropped her a mock curtsy. "Thank you, Countess."

In the library Katya seated herself very straight on a carved, high-backed Queen Anne chair. Ronya wandered to a window and stood looking out at the garden. Neither sister spoke.

Katya's eyes roved restlessly around the room which, from earliest childhood, had been her favorite part of the house. Here were gathered together the most cherished of the von Glasman possessions—a Constable, a Rembrandt etching, a superb Russian primitive, ivory figurines, carved furniture made priceless by time, and rugs that glowed against wide-boarded, dark polished floors. Her eyes came to rest on her father's white jade chessmen in an open silver-gilt box engraved with lotus flowers, gift of a Mandarin prince he had known in Manchuria.

"You've always loved that." Ronya had turned from the window. "Take it home with you, Katya."

"Thank you, Ronya," Katya said dryly. "It belongs here. Sit down, please."

"It's such a lovely day, Katya. I'd rather be outdoors."

"Sit down, Ronya!"

Ronya sighed and settled herself on the sofa.

Katya scolded: "You have the most incredible talent for evading an issue when you choose to."

"I am not aware of an issue," Ronya said.

"Ronya, stop looking everywhere but at me. I am prepared to sit here all day and all night, if need be. You might as well make up your mind to hear me out right now."

Again Ronya sighed. "I know you, Katya. When you're set on anything, you're positively valiant. And a damn pest. Suppose *you* hear *me* out.

"You love Georgi. Alexis loves Georgi. Excellent! That pleases me. You have no child. Alexis has no heir. That's sad and I am sad for you. However, Georgi is mine. I haven't the slightest intention of giving him away—even to you. So you see, Katya, my dear sister, there is no issue. Nothing to argue about."

"It's not all that simple," Katya said reasonably. "Georgi isn't the only person we're talking about. There's Igor, too. If his young brother were Alexis' adopted son and inherited the Brusilov title it would solve many future problems for both boys."

"Surely, Katya"—Ronya was affronted—"you can't believe that I'd use Georgi to protect Igor?"

"Why not? Our father did the same thing for you. Gave me to the court and to Christianity so you could live here without fear. If you want the rights you enjoy to go on to Igor after your death, you'll have to part with Georgi."

"Our father didn't—consciously—*use* you, Katya!" Ronya was on her feet again.

"Of course he did."

Ronya's hands were clenched so tight the knuckles showed

36

white. "No!" she cried. "The Empress forced him to give you up. It was her way of punishing him for refusing to be converted and not accepting the title she wanted to give him. She made him bring you to court. Commanded it, to remind him he was a Jew."

"Why can't you face facts?" Katya asked. "Why *will* you be such an incurable romantic? You think Father was so devoted to Judaism? Then why did he stay here? Mother loathed Russia. He had connections all over Europe and was rich in a currency that was good all over Europe. He could have gone at any time. Russia wasn't a life-and-death love for him, the way it is to Alexis and Boris. But with your marrying Boris he knew your life was here. And as long as you stayed in Russia you had to be protected. Marrying me to Alexis did that."

"Katya von Glasman Brusilov! You aren't telling me that you regret having married Alexis?"

"Of course not. But you have your memories of Father; I have mine. What I am saying is simply that he gave me away deliberately. To make you safe. He manipulated the Empress into asking for me. A Christian for a Jew. It was his way of remaining an empire builder and of guarding you. David von Glasman was a charming man *and* a ruthless man. Alexis, whom I love, has given me many of these facts—and we both know that he would not lie."

"You talk about facts," Ronya protested, "and the facts disprove what you say. Father did leave Russia, soon after my marriage. He and Mother went back to her people in Vienna. You know that."

"Oh, Lord, Ronya." Katya's voice was weary. "You pride yourself on your honesty but you see only what you want to. You were dead set on having your Boris and Father never refused you anything. He didn't mind because he wanted your sons to inherit the power he'd built up. They were to give him immortality. But he underestimated Boris, thought he was just a handsome stud for you, who wouldn't stand in his way. That was his first mistake. He also underestimated you. That was his second mistake. He didn't know anything about your kind of love. He couldn't bear it and he fled."

Ronya felt suddenly cold. Though the afternoon sun still

37

streamed warmly into the room, she lit the fire. "Would you like tea, Katya?" she asked in a small voice.

"Not unless you would."

"Finish what you have to say, Katya."

"Have I hurt you, Ronya darling?"

"You have a right to say what you believe."

"Do you understand that I love you, little sister?"

"Yes."

"When you come down to it," Katya said slowly, "I suppose I want the same things for Igor that Father wanted for you. But more than that I want to protect Georgi. He has in him the makings of a wonderful person, with Alexis to harness all that energy. I want him to be the next Count Brusilov, so the Tartars can't claim him."

"The Tartars!"

"Yes, Ronya, the Tartars. You know the legend. He's the Golden One. The Golden One belongs to them. That's why Boris' mother cursed Boris for deserting them. It's less that I want him given over to Catholicism than I want him to be saved from the Tartars. Alexis is a powerful man. Even the Tartars would be incapable of laying hands on *his* son."

Ronya exploded. "This is the most ridiculous nonsense I ever heard. The Tartars indeed! You're as superstitious as Boris if you believe in the Tartar woman's silly curse and the Tartar legend. Really, Katya—"

"The Tartars, I'm sorry to say, are no joke," Katya insisted. "They're pagans still and they still eat Jews. One way or another they collect tribute. They take what's theirs as well as what isn't. One day they may even take the throne."

"If they want an uncrowned king, let them take the Blond One," Ronya said.

Katya looked her sister straight in the eye. "They don't want him. He's only Boris' bastard."

Ronya flinched. She wanted to run out of the room but knew her legs wouldn't carry her. Katya waited for the lines of pain to leave Ronya's face, then got up and pulled the velvet bell cord. "I'd like tea now, Ronya," she said.

Again the two women sat silent until after Lydia had bustled off. Ronya shook her head impatiently as if to dispel the shadowy aftermath of a nightmare and inquired, conversationally, "How are things in St. Petersburg at the moment? I can't believe a thing I read in the papers." She lit a cigarette.

The door opened just wide enough to allow Alexis to show his face and to say, with mock meekness, "I just met Lydia going for tea; she said I was *not* to disturb you, but I'm *so* thirsty!"

"Oh, come in, darling," Katya urged. "We need you; I need you especially, for Ronya is asking for news of the court, and you know what a botch I'll make of it."

"Georgi?" Ronya asked, looking nervously past Alexis, into the hall.

"I left Georgi at the stables; he and the Blond One are giving one of the yearlings a workout." Alexis, who could sometimes look both dignified and roguish, crossed the room, pressed Katya's hand to his cheek, but sat down on the sofa next to Ronya.

"I know by your question and your face that you have been discussing Georgi's future," he said gently. "And I know it is painful—but so necessary!"

Ronya's reply was prevented by the arrival of Lydia with the tea and a young maid assistant, whom she directed in a cranky voice. She was annoyed because Alexis had got past her protective barrier around the sisters and, since he had, that a mysterious and very high level conference was obviously in process. She began to fuss with the teacups, preparing to pass them and catch a clue to the discussion, but Katya cried, "Oh don't bother, Lydia, I'll do that!" and Lydia's "Yes, Countess, certainly, Countess" was almost a hiss. Ronya managed a smile and a fond command. "Shoo, old hen and chick," she said.

Half a cup of fragrant tea had warmed her before she spoke again. "Painful, yes," she said turning to Alexis, "but more than that, puzzling. Katya tells me that at court conditions are terrible and prospects ghastly, with the Tsar torn between the hounding of his mad wife and the urging of his wise but domineering mother. And she insists that the Tartars are going to eat us and that Boris' mother's curse is not a lot of nonsense—oh, Alexis, what *is* happening?"

"A great change is coming over Russia," Alexis answered somberly, acknowledging the honest question behind Ronya's

39

childish tone. "And leadership is sadly lacking. The Tsar, whom I revere for his good qualities, is not a man who can hold for long to his own more liberal principles, and his mother's, against the influence of that extraordinary fanatic, his wife. Really extraordinary!" He shook his head, for a moment abstracted, lost in the problem of the Tsarina's anti-Semitic mania and mad religious frenzies, a problem that had absorbed much of his energy for months.

"But the Tsar depends heavily on you, Alexis, and yet you say there is no leadership!" Ronya protested.

"That dependence on me is, shall we say, fitful." Alexis smiled ruefully. "But even if it were steadier, dear Ronya, I am not willing to assume—if I could—a position of obvious power. I have the interests of those dearest to me, and their people to protect, and this must be done quietly, with a strong and trusted premier to work with me. And with a strong and trusted man to take my place—a Brusilov heir." He paused and met Ronya's eyes, and because of that exchange there was much he did not need to say, but he added, "There is deep jealousy of you, my dear, of your wealth in land. And the Tartars, who would as soon eat the Tsar as you, nevertheless in their hatred of Jews, work for those intriguers at court who back the Tsarina."

Ronya cast an almost shy glance at Katya, and rose. "Katya, forgive me," she said. "I didn't realize how understanding and really kind you were being . . ." But before she finished her sentence, Katya, too, was on her feet, her arms around her sister.

"Now, now," admonished Alexis, "no tears. Just some straight thinking."

Ronya drew back, and her smile flashed. "Straight thinking and *life*, Alexis. I don't care what we lose, if we keep that, if we keep on loving life, and living it, somewhere—here preferably, but with Boris, my children, their children, and you and Katya —oh, I could be happy on an ice cap." Her laugh bubbled. "I'll talk to Boris. He's a very straight thinker, and a straight shooter!" Alexis grinned. "But not today. He and Igor are delivering horses to headquarters tomorrow, you know; they'll be back the next evening."

When the door closed behind Ronya, Alexis drew Katya down on the sofa beside him. "She could be happy on an ice

40

cap," he mused, "and I believe she could. But Boris and I are bound to this strange land, this Russia, my darling. And I need you with me!"

IV

RONYA leaned against the stable wall. Morning sunshine lit red glints in her dark hair and added brilliance to the embroidery of her white blouse. In one hand she held a whip and idly swung it at pebbles on the ground. With uncalculating accuracy she sent one after another catapulting high into the air.

In a few minutes Boris and Igor would set out to rendezvous with a cavalry detachment encamped some forty miles south of Kiev, taking along an additional hundred mounts from the Pirov stables. While she waited to say goodbye, Ronya watched Boris supervise the saddling-up, stooping to tighten a girth, gentling a skittish animal, giving instructions and, from his great height, dominating the bustling scene. Except that his rugged face was more deeply etched, he looked little older than the day when she lost her heart to him forever.

Boris swung up onto his horse, then catching sight of his wife, slid to the ground again. Pretending to trip, he caught hold of Ronya's whip.

"I can't go," he wailed. "I'm hurt!"

"Prop yourself against the wagon," Ronya mocked him. "Be careful your stallion doesn't trample you. I'll run for a doctor."

"An hour in bed will cure me, Ronya."

"Full evidence, Boris Pirov," she said judicially, "of the extent of your injury."

Boris took Ronya's arm and led her away from the stable door. "Let's go back to the house," he said, "and confer about my health."

41

"Describe your symptoms! I don't want to risk catching your fever."

"They are too complicated to describe. Take a chance," he implored.

Choking with laughter, Ronya said, "Turn your head away."

Instead his hands slid over her breasts. "The horses can wait," he said.

"So can you!" Suddenly she saw Igor and was serious. "Stop. Your son!"

Boris grinned. "I guess you're right."

"I've been thinking of my father," Ronya said. "I love him, Boris. He gave me you." Suddenly her eyes filled with tears. She touched his face and fled toward the house. Boris followed her with a quizzical, not unhappy gaze, and turned to Igor, who waited on his horse, sullen and impatient; his visit to Vera had left him weary, resentful and guilt-ridden. He and his father led the horses into the forest road, and for several hours exchanged not a word.

It was still and warm. Wolves seldom hunted until the cold settled in, so when Boris discovered he had come unarmed, Igor made light of it.

"The fault was mine," his father apologized. "My thoughts weren't in the saddle when we took off."

"Oh, it's really too hot for wolves," Igor reassured him. "Besides, *we* can handle them!" His eighteen-year-old spirits were rising again.

Boris smiled happily. Since he was thirteen Igor had ridden with him to deliver horses, and now worked as an equal, each of them enjoying the other's skill.

At dusk they made camp by a stream. Igor watered the horses while Boris strung ropes around tree trunks to form a corral. Together they unloaded food for themselves and grain for the animals from the pack horses, and Boris singled out three lead horses to hobble. Together they fed the herd with the competence of long practice, then built fires along the corral fences.

The dawn was crimson and peaceful when they broke camp and by late afternoon they reached the cavalry unit. As the men were fond of Igor and idolized Boris, dinner was a celebration.

42

Around huge campfires toasts were drunk, racy stories told and songs sung.

To get through the forest and home before nightfall, Boris and Igor should have left at cockcrow. But when the sun rose, vodka fumes still suffused Boris' brain and Igor slept on, as the young do, dead to the world till he was shaken awake. It was noon before the last farewell was said and the two, on fresh mounts, cantered off.

They rode straight through the afternoon and into the crisp evening. Gradually the trees and bushes blurred in the bronze and lavender afterglow. Boris was thinking that the time had arrived to find a convenient campsite when over the hushed forest came a sound, cold and lonely, high and aloof as a star. The call was answered by other calls, the cry of wolves.

Boris, who had slumped in his saddle, straightened sharply. "Rein in, Igor," he commanded, pulling his own horse to a sudden stop. "The ax!" From its leather sheath Igor stripped their sole weapon and found his hands wet with the cold sweat of fear.

The stealthy silence of the forest was ruffled by a snort. Boris' horse, ears pricked forward, had cleared his nostrils to smell the danger he could not yet see. Boris saw the wolf first. It stood perfectly still at the edge of a small clearing, studying the riders, eyes calculating and terrible. An instant later the horses bolted. Boris and Igor pulled them up within a few yards.

Boris had just time to gain an impression of many wolves before one leaped for the muzzle of his horse and two others attacked its hindquarters. The wounded gelding sank beneath him and Boris, half jumping, half flung from its back, rolled clear and grabbed the tail of Igor's mare to pull himself off the ground. The panic-stricken animal lashed out with her hind legs and Boris went down again. He slid away shouting as he fell, "Jump, Igor!"

A strong odor of tarry musk rose from the wolf that streaked in to assault the man on the ground. Boris grabbed wildly at the slippery fur, fighting to evade the rapid snap of fangs. In one rolling bundle man and wolf tumbled free from the hysterical drumming of the horse's hooves. As he reached down, seeking the vulnerable portion of the male anatomy, Boris experienced

43

the wrenching ache of teeth sunk into the flesh below his armpit. With furious, reflex strength, he tore off the brute's testicles, then flung the dying body from him, his roar drowning the animal's shriek.

Lurching to his feet and howling obscenities, Boris grabbed a stout bough from the ground and brought it down on the back of a second wolf, breaking its spine, while Igor charged in and cut out the rest of the pack, swinging his ax and bellowing curses.

The wolves made short work of bringing down Igor's horse, which lay dying beside his feet, so close that the young man slipped on its entrails. A huge she-wolf sprang, hurdling with such force she crashed through his defenses and toppled him off his feet. Boris yanked the ax from Igor's hand and chopped into the attacker.

The sound of shattering bone and the smell of spurting blood paralyzed the pack for an instant. In that fraction of time they faltered and lost the initiative.

Without warning every animal turned tail and fled into the forest while Boris scrabbled up pebbles and hurled them at the underbrush into which the pack had faded. Silence closed in again.

"They're gone. How's your arm?" Boris was panting heavily.

Igor flexed his muscles. "It's all right," he said, though he winced with pain.

"Can you finish off your horse, son?"

As Igor raised the ax, the quivering animal gave a last sigh and was still. Lowering it, Igor said, "You hurt?"

"Not much." Boris bent to his saddlebag and hauled out a slim-necked earthenware flask, tore the sleeve from his lacerated arm and had Igor pour vodka over his wounds.

"Let's get out of here," Boris said, reaching for the flask. He raised it to his lips and took several hearty gulps, and passed it to Igor, who swished the alcohol around in his mouth and spat it out. Boris grinned.

They walked steadily in comradely quiet, always listening, though reason suggested the wolves would not hunt again that night. There was no sound but the crunching of their boots

44

over the forest trails and reaction set in. They began to talk a little, cockily.

"I must remember to take you along whenever I'm likely to meet wolves," Boris said.

"I like wolves," Igor swaggered, very pleased.

"I must admit I respect them," Boris said.

"They couldn't have been hungry," Igor mused, "so why attack us?"

"Probably a pre-adult pack." Boris spoke soberly. "Males and females running together. It's not just humans who feel frightened and lonely when they're young. Well, pretty soon they'll mate—they're monogamous, you know—and turn into model parents. The grown ones kill only to survive."

Again they lapsed into silence, Igor considering his father's parable, Boris brooding over his son. How courageously he had handled himself and what a contentious, difficult child he was! Imitating his father, leaning on his mother, victim of his own bad temper, already prodigiously promiscuous yet capable of gentleness and affection.

An hour later the men found themselves at the end of a rough village street. The moon silvered the Greek cross on a small stone church. Thatched huts were dark and no smoke drifted upward from the chimneys. Not even a dog crossed their path as it led past shuttered windows behind which peasants slept. At the outermost edge of the village they came upon an ugly brick building. A flicker of light showed through imperfectly fitted shutters. Boris knocked softly.

The door opened wide at once.

"Do not be frightened, Madame."

"I am not frightened," a voice said. "Trouble does not knock. Come in."

They found themselves in a warm workroom that smelled deliciously of baking bread. The woman, blinking in the light, was tall, handsome and bore herself proudly.

"We ran into a bit of trouble in the forest," Boris explained. "Forgive the way we look. I am Boris Pirov and this is my son, Igor."

The woman smiled. "I know who you are, Gospodin Pirov. You have been well described."

45

"May we ask for a night's lodging? In the morning we'll arrange to hire horses and get back to Kiev."

"You are welcome," she said. "I am Sara and this is my husband, the baker." She motioned toward a man at the far end of the room.

He looked up briefly and frowned, disconcerted by the size of Boris and the disarray of Igor, then turned back to his kneading.

"My husband means no offense," said Sara, leading the Pirovs into the next room. "He must bake many loaves before morning."

The main room of the house was sizable and simple with a round center table and chairs, of which one was big and comfortable. On the sideboard were brass candlesticks under a mottled mirror and in front of a small sofa was a low chest. In an alcove-kitchen pots and pans of burnished copper hung neatly on the wall.

Boris stopped to take his boots off so he could stand erect under the low ceiling. Sara led the strangers to a door. "I'll bring you hot water," she said, "and after we've eaten, Igor can give me that shirt. I'll clean it and mend it as best I can."

"You are very kind," Boris thanked her.

He and Igor poured warm water from full pitchers and lathered themselves with unscented soap. As he rubbed himself dry on rough, unbleached cloth, Boris said, "That's a real woman, my boy. Good-looking and no questions. No fuss."

The young man gave his father a distrustful look. "She's nice," he said. "Leave her alone."

"Hold your tongue, you young puppy," said Boris in a harsh whisper.

When they came back into the sitting room, candles were lit and charcoal burned in the samovar. A young girl was laying a white cloth on the table. She was incredibly, angelically lovely, with long shining black hair, transparent white skin and small, pouting lips. When she lifted her cornflower blue eyes, Boris stopped short.

Sara spoke. "This is Julie, my niece and foster-daughter. Julie, this is Gospodin Boris Pirov and his son, Igor."

Julie gave Boris a shy smile, then looked into Igor's dark face. The two of them were transfixed. Between the girl of fourteen

46

and the eighteen-year-old boy there was an instant communication so profound that the foster-mother of the one and the father of the other were startled into silence. It was a magical moment.

Fright welled up in Sara. Even in this lonely village the Pirov men had a name for licentiousness.

"Julie! Serve the tea, while I get supper." Sara's voice was sharp.

Standing by the alcove, Boris watched with admiration as Sara's hands flew from one pot to another. Tension, he knew, underlay her darting movements and before she could protest he took the spoon from her hand and began stirring the thick bean soup. Sara looked up curiously and he smiled down at her. "It's ready. Let's eat," he said, "and don't worry, Mistress Sara. No harm will come to your Julie. I give you my word."

Neither Julie nor Igor noticed that it was Boris who served them with herring slices, onions and potatoes, that it was he who spooned sour cream over the cucumbers and radishes. Sara shook her head in perplexity and, distracted, forgot to call Isaac to the table and to ask Boris and Igor to cover their heads before eating.

When they had done, Boris got up. "I don't know when I've enjoyed a meal more. Now, with your permission, Mistress Sara, Igor and I will step outside for a smoke."

The men went out into the darkness through a door so low that Boris, who neglected to duck, bumped his head. When they returned, Julie was gone.

After a large breakfast next morning, Boris excused himself. Sara directed him to a stable where he engaged horses, then loitered, inspecting the place and talking to the owner. He was giving the boy time with Julie. On his return he found Igor in front of the bakery with Sara and Julie. "Say goodbye, son," he said, and smiled at Sara. "Thank you, Mistress Sara."

Boris and Sara stood looking at the boy and girl. What they saw told them that Igor had managed a few minutes with Julie and that he had told her whatever it was that he wanted her to hear.

"Goodbye, little Julie," Boris said, put his hands around her waist and lifted her up. She leaned her head comfortably against

47

the big man's shoulder. The gesture was so uncharacteristic Sara's eyes widened in surprise. Boris set the child down gently and raised the woman's hand to his lips.

"We came as strangers," he said. "We leave as friends. My respects to your husband. In a few days Igor will return the rented horses. If you permit, he will call on you and Julie."

Against her better judgment, Sara found herself granting consent.

V

AT dinner, that evening, Boris was just telling about the meeting with Julie when Ronya broke in. "I feel sorry for the silly wolves. You really maltreated them."

Alexis seconded her. "Upon my return to St. Petersburg I shall appeal to the Tsar to introduce a law granting wolf packs an annual Pirov to eat."

Georgi interrupted and, though his father held up a hand and admonished him "Whoa!," plunged on. "I can tie a horse so that he can still reach green shoots to feed on and I can keep watch and I'm a dead-eye shot."

Boris winked at Igor. "We need another good man along when we make deliveries. Do you think he'll do? If so, Georgi, you've got the job."

Completely taken in, Georgi was so jubilant he all but patted himself on the back. He beamed at Igor. "All right with you?"

Igor smiled, revealing a deep dimple. "Sure," he said. "You might as well learn now. When I go into the cavalry, you'll have to take over for me here."

Georgi's face clouded. He had plans of his own—he meant to escape from his mother's watchful eye. It was his firm intention to go to St. Petersburg, be a cadet and spend his spare time with his uncle and aunt. Katya, whom he had let in on his secret, gave him a slight signal to be quiet, in deference to which Georgi held his peace.

Igor was talking and Georgi, half listening, caught a name. Julie.

"What?" he said.

"I said I'd take you to the village and introduce you to Julie."

"Who's she?"

"My girl," said Igor.

Georgi knew about Igor and girls. He suppressed a yawn and said to his mother, "Can I go now?"

Much to his surprise, his mother answered, "You may."

He leaped from his chair and was off to plot ways and means to get rid of his current tutor.

The instant the door closed behind him, Ronya said, "Boris, what's all this about a girl?"

"Ask Igor," he said. "Julie's his girl, not mine."

He looked across the table at his son. It was a long, appraising look and it said: Stand up to your mother. Fight for your girl. It'll make a man of you.

No one in the room, not Ronya or Katya or Alexis or Igor misunderstood that look. In Ronya it roused warring emotions— gratitude to Boris and a fierce determination to place every possible obstacle in the path of a romance between her noble son and a little nobody from a ghetto village.

"Speak up, Igor," she challenged him. "We're listening."

All eyes were fastened on Igor who, enjoying himself hugely until then, was now uncomfortable. His mother, to whom he always turned for understanding, seemed remote, critical. If they had been alone, he could have poured out his feelings about Julie but in this gathering he felt naked, exposed.

"There isn't much to tell," he said. Boris turned his face away and Igor rushed on. "Except that I love Julie!"

No one moved.

"I'm going to marry her and I've already told her so."

Katya said quietly, "And what did Julie say to that?"

"She said—she said"—Igor was floundering—" 'Your family has to want me, too, especially your mother. Pray, Igor.' "

49

Boris saw temper on Ronya's face and put a hand on her shoulder. "Don't say it, Ronya," he advised.

She jerked away from him and drew a deep breath, preliminary to delivering a cutting remark. Alexis intervened.

"What you have told us," he said magisterially to Igor, "is scant evidence of anything. If that's all you know, let's hear from Boris. Tell us what really happened, old man."

Boris shrugged. How to describe the miracle he had witnessed in the baker's house? "I saw Julie," he said slowly, "fall in love. I saw Igor return her love."

"Fall in love!" Ronya snorted. "Go on, Boris. You—you jackass!"

"There's nothing more to say." Boris was totally unperturbed.

"Well I've got something to say." Ronya slammed her hand down on the table upsetting a glass of wine. A slender red trickle spread on the damask cloth. "Let me remind you, Igor, my son, that you are heir to this estate. After you have done your military service, you will make a proper marriage with the daughter of one of the great Jewish houses of Europe. Until that time you are not to play games with a decent Jewish child. Stick to the peasant wenches if you must."

Igor was on his feet, even more furious than his mother. "Don't you tell me how to treat Julie. She's better than you are." His voice became suddenly controlled and deadly. "You chose your husband but you'll not choose my wife. And I don't give a—" Boris' hand shot out and Igor winced with pain.

"You will *never* be insolent to your mother again!" he bawled. "Now get out!"

The door slammed behind Igor.

Boris' lips tightened. "Anything more to say, Ronya?"

"I made him miserable enough," she said. "You didn't have to hurt him."

"Oh, God!" Boris put his head in his hands.

"I suggest," said Alexis, "that we rinse the bad taste of this little scene out of our mouths with wine."

Boris righted Ronya's glass and poured the wine silently, then raised his own "To Julie." Ronya stared at him and her expression changed. She drank his toast without demur, then raised

50

her glass again. "To us all," she said solemnly. "To love and happiness. To life!"

Katya threw back her head and laughed delightedly. "I'm blessed if I understand either of you but I have a horrid feeling you've reached some sort of agreement."

As though he had been following a separate train of thought, Boris said, "I'm pretty sure she's illiterate. She spoke Yiddish with her aunt and Ukrainian to us, and that rather badly, searching for words."

Ronya's famous eyebrows went up. "Good heavens, is the girl stupid?"

It was Boris' turn to laugh. "Not at all," he said. "Unlike you, Ronya, my dear, Julie has the wisdom to know that with two ears and one tongue it's as good to listen as to talk."

"Very original!" Ronya rose. "We've been at this table for two hours. Let's let the servants go to bed."

An hour later she left Katya at the piano and Boris and Alexis at the chessboard and went to Igor's room. He was not there.

The next morning, after her first cup of tea, Ronya went again to Igor's room. The bed had not been slept in.

Back in her room, she rang for Lydia and, when the old woman appeared, commanded, "Send someone to the stables at once. I want to know if the hired horses are still there."

Although the Brusilovs were leaving within the hour, she waited for the answer. On the strength of it, Ronya went to a chest and selected an embroidered silk shawl, a lovely thing, then rummaged through several drawers and found a jewel box. From it she took a gold bracelet, wide and heavy and free of all ornamentation. To go with these gifts Ronya wrote a formal note to Sara, ending, "My husband was deeply impressed with your niece. I hope you will allow me the pleasure of giving her a bracelet I wore when I was her age." Having signed and sealed the letter, she left it with the gifts on the bed for Lydia to wrap, with scrawled instructions to put them in her top dresser drawer.

Then Ronya sat down and waited until the time for Katya and Alexis to leave for the station, when she put on a robe, ran down the stairs and burst into the room where the Brusilovs and Boris were finishing breakfast.

51

"Why didn't you wake me?" she scolded Lydia.

"I—I forgot, Ronya, my mistress."

"Never mind explaining. Lay my clothes out at once!"

Katya smiled. "I've never known Lydia to forget anything before. I assumed you were breakfasting in bed."

"I won't be a moment," Ronya insisted.

Boris said, "There isn't time, Ronya. Say goodbye now."

Ronya sighed. "I can't imagine why I overslept."

When she went back to her room Lydia was tying a bow on the package. "What was *that* about?" she asked.

"Lydia, you were wonderful," was all Ronya told her.

She dressed quickly, took the package and hurried to the stable. Igor was not there but the Blond One greeted her.

"Have you seen Igor?"

He shook his head.

"Can you find him?"

The Blond One nodded.

"Good. See if you can have him home before his father gets back. But first arrange for the hired horses to be returned to the village at once. And have this package delivered to Sara, the baker's wife. Tell the men to waste no time in getting started."

All afternoon Ronya waited for Boris and Igor but neither one appeared. After supper with Georgi and his new tutor, she went to the library and was reading there when Lydia came in and told her Igor and the Blond One were eating in the kitchen. Ronya put away her book, wrote a couple of letters on estate matters, then went up to her own room. She had bathed, brushed her hair and had just about decided that Boris was spending the night elsewhere when he strode in.

"Boris," she said, "I—"

"Hold it, Ronya!" he commanded.

"Let me finish," she said.

"You talk too damn much," said Boris furiously.

"Boris, I—"

"You will *not* give orders in the stable again, ever, without first consulting me!"

"I'm sorry."

"No, you're not," he roared. "You're a scheming, interfering female. I told Sara that Igor would return the horses."

"But how could I know that, Boris?"

"It doesn't matter. You did. Igor will ride to the village the first thing in the morning with gifts from me."

He started for the door but his anger seemed to have drained out of him.

"Going to bed, Boris?" Ronya inquired sweetly.

"Yes," he said.

"In your own room?"

"Would you like me to stay here?"

"Yes."

"All right," he conceded. "But *no* talk!"

She held out her arms.

VI

TWICE that winter Boris asked Ronya to invite Julie to Kiev. The first time her answer was to go to St. Petersburg and visit Katya. The second time she took Georgi and his tutor to her dacha at Odessa.

To his elder son, Boris said, "Bide your time. Your mother will come around."

Igor rode almost every day to the village in a sleigh. There he would wrap Julie in sheepskins, tie her shawl over her hair and take her out driving in the white world. Some afternoons he pulled her on a sled, snow crunching under the runners. White flakes blew into their faces and the sun glared on ice and half blinded them. At night, under thin, pale stars, he took her home to the warm hearth and the smell of supper cooking in the little alcove-kitchen.

When spring came they walked, hand in hand, into the woods and sat on clumps of wild mustard while she sang to him. No bird had a sweeter voice and she poured out the melodies of her

53

people with such purity that Igor's heart melted in him. For the first time he gave his full trust to another human being, telling her his dreams and aspirations.

Sara, seeing the bright color in Julie's cheeks and how her eyes shone, doubted Igor. After each of the boy's visits she tormented Julie with questions and pestered her with accusations. Though Julie protested her innocence, Sara carefully counted the days of Julie's cycle and if the girl were a day or two late, turned frantic with worry.

"The proud peacock has robbed you of your innocence," she stormed. "Why should he marry you now? For your great dowry, perhaps? Let us go to the river and drown ourselves before the village hears of your disgrace." Then she would raise her arms to heaven. "I beseech thee, oh my Lord, come to the aid of Julie. Purify her heart. Destroy Igor. Destroy his father. Punish me. I was powerless to resist his charm. For the sake of worldly vanity I opened my door to him and my heart."

As each day grew lovelier, Julie became more frightened. When first Igor took her to the woods, she felt safe and warm, filled with happiness while they made plans for the future. But now she was self-conscious and ashamed. If Igor stroked her hand or tried to kiss away her melancholy, she froze. "No. Don't. Stop." She ran from him like a frightened animal.

For a time Igor defended Sara. "She's a good woman who knows her responsibility," he said. "She has every right to suspect me. How can she understand that I'd rather die than hurt you?" And once he almost confessed that he felt no passion, only love. His lust he satisfied in Kiev.

Finally, exacerbated by Sara's admonitions and Julie's gloom, Igor was reduced to the age-old question, "Don't you love me?"

"I just don't know. I'm so mixed up."

"Trust me, Julie."

"Why should I? Perhaps you'll never marry me," she mourned. "Why should you? Your mother won't let you. You're too handsome and too eligible to be the husband of an ignorant village girl with no dowry."

"Don't judge my mother." Igor was torn between two loyalties. "You don't know her."

54

"She judges *me*, and she doesn't know me. To her I'm just the penniless ward of the baker's wife."

At the end of his patience, Igor said, "All right, Julie. We'll marry. Now. The hell with everything and everyone except us."

"But your birthright? How will you make a living?" Julie was even more frightened than before.

"Horses! Wherever there are horses I can earn money and take care of you."

"Igor Pirov! The devil himself has robbed you of your senses. You're too foolish to be anyone's husband yet. You'd not like being poor. Nor running from village to village. You'd hate me for it." She sighed. "We'll just have to wait."

Touched, he gathered her into his arms, though she turned her mouth away from his. "Stop being frightened," he said. "Sing to me again."

"I can't."

"Why on earth not?"

"Because I'm—scared."

"But *why?*"

"Because I love you. Because I want to be part of all the things and people you're part of and that are part of you. Not—" she wailed. "Sara warned me!"

After each visit to the village, Igor confided what had happened to the Blond One. On a warm summer night in the still darkness of the pine trees, he poured out his heart for the hundredth time. "She's an angel and she's so unhappy," Igor said.

For months the Blond One had thought constantly of Julie, when he strummed his guitar, when he went into the forest and when he cared for Boris' horses in the stables. He longed desperately to help.

"Do you want to get married now?" he asked, his blue eyes troubled.

"No."

"If you wanted to, you could, you know. I've got more gold than I can count. It's yours. I don't need it. Never will."

Igor laughed. "How do you know? Some night a girl will follow you into the forest and you'll learn what fun it is. Then

55

you'll meet one like Julie and get married. She'll want a house and a carriage and you'll be damned glad of your money."

"Not I, Igor," the Blond One said with dignity. "I'm a bastard. I don't want a bitch in heat and I have no name to give a girl like your Julie. You love Julie and yet you spill your sperm all over Kiev."

"I'm not married," said Igor.

"But you don't really want to be. Why?"

Igor shrugged. "Lots of reasons. I hate the idea of going into the cavalry a married man and missing all the fun. Besides, Julie's such a baby. One evening in the woods I was sitting with my back against a tree, the way we are now. Her head was in my lap. I was stroking her hair and she was singing. When she finished I leaned down and kissed her gently on the lips. It was the one and only time I ever got carried away with Julie. When I started giving her hard, passionate kisses, she tore at my hair and scratched my face. Poor little Julie! She thought for a month she was going to have a baby."

The Blond One smiled. "Well, what *do* you want, Igor?"

"It's mainly what I don't want. I don't want Julie miserable. I don't want to pretend to be a pious Jew and sit in that stinking synagogue of theirs. I don't want my mother acting like a stranger and I don't want to be beholden to my father. And I am sick and tired of riding through that damned forest, back and forth, back and forth."

"That covers what you don't want. Now, what do you want?"

Igor poked his fist affectionately against the Blond One's shoulder. "Christ! When you do talk, you sound just like Father."

"Sorry," the younger boy laughed. "You want Julie here, don't you?"

"More than anything. I dream of it."

"Are you ready to be engaged?"

"I'm engaged already."

"You know you *can* get her here?"

"How?"

"Ronya doesn't know how Sara taunts Julie. Does Boris know?"

"I can't tell him."

"But, don't you see? He'd tell Ronya and insist that she put an end to it by bringing Julie here."

Igor pondered. "It's no use. She'd twist him around her finger, somehow." However, he brooded over the Blond One's advice and half decided to talk to his father. The next morning, when he had the opportunity, the impulse was gone and he said nothing.

But Boris no longer needed to be told. He already knew. Early that morning as he stepped out of the front door, he found the Blond One waiting for him. Silently the boy handed him a note, then turned and went down the path while Boris read what he had written:

> Julie needs you. She waits for Igor every Friday an hour before sundown at the edge of the forest.

Boris lit a match and set it to the paper, then followed the Blond One to the stables. He took the boy aside and said, "Can you delay Igor Friday night so he doesn't get to the village till an hour after sundown?"

The Blond One nodded.

As summer ripened into August, Boris was never at home in the evenings and Ronya chafed increasingly. One night, just as he was about to leave the house, she waylaid him in the hall.

"I have decided," she said, "that Igor really does love Julie. I am ready to receive her."

Boris eyed her warily. "When, Ronya?"

"As soon as I can discuss the situation with Rabbi Levinsky. Since I've waited this long, I don't want to make a mistake. You have no idea how proud poor Jews can be."

Boris took his hand off the shining brass doorknob. "What are we having for dinner, my predictable Ronya?" he said.

"Predictable!" It was as though the front door had blown open and a great gust of wind had cleared the heavy atmosphere. She laughed joyously. "There are pieces of sausage in the bean soup.

A stew is simmering in a copper kettle. The wine is cold and I have baked apples and cheese to go with it."

Much later that night Boris lay, his small Ronya blissfully soft and warm, cuddled in his arms. In the after-pleasure of drugged senses and satisfied loins, he thought her asleep until her fingers stirred over his face. "Go to sleep, little dove," he said drowsily.

Ronya stirred. "I want to talk."

On the edge of a dream, he hesitated before answering, and could not find it in his heart to stop her. Her capitulation in accepting Julie had been gallant and she had foreborne to tax him with his continued absences.

"What is it, darling?"

"Julie."

After waiting more than half a year, Ronya could not wait until morning.

Her words came in a rush. "What if I've waited too long? What if she is truly wounded? But I couldn't bring myself to uproot her and move her into this strange new world where she'll have so much to learn, until I was positive Igor loved her. What if she resents my relationship with him, and fails to see how carefully I've planned my treatment of her? I had to be convinced that she was the one girl for him. After all, he's had plenty of passing fancies before this."

Boris, his recent visit to Julie fresh in mind, could find no sympathy for Ronya's rationalizations. The child had been taken aback at sight of him and was obviously, though she was polite and friendly, in a state of real distress. He talked nearly two hours, patiently, and at last thawed her reserve until she seemed, once more, to trust him and what he said. When he got up to leave, Julie had said, "Thank you, Boris, my father."

He resented the agony she had suffered. "You've tried to outwit destiny, Ronya," he said testily. "Can't you learn that even you have to give in sometimes?"

Ronya pulled away from him but he held her tight in his arms. "You took one look at me," he said, imperturbably, "and that was that. But for Julie and Igor you set up an obstacle course."

"You talk like a fool." Ronya was undaunted. "Can't you see the difference? I was *born* ready for Boris."

He let it go. She was drifting into sleep when he spoke again. "I have seen Julie."

"Tell me," she said.

"Her bruises will heal. That's all." Boris got up and went into the bathroom, returning with a glass of cold water for Ronya. When he held it out to her, she murmured like a fledgling bird and he drank it himself, stretched out beside her, kissed her lips and tucked her body into his before falling asleep.

The next morning Ronya opened her eyes to find Boris gone and a note on his pillow.

> I have sent a message to Rabbi Levinsky. He will expect you around three o'clock.

It was already midmorning when she rang for breakfast and got out of bed. She opened the shutters and stood looking out over her world of grass and boulders around which flowering shrubs tossed gently in the breeze. Slipping out of her nightgown, she let the air cool her skin while she thought earnestly about what she would wear.

A quarter of an hour later, surveying herself critically in the mirror, she removed a jeweled brooch, then rearranged her hair, plaiting it into thick braids and pinning them around her head, in an effort to look mature and serious for the interview.

The coachman came for Ronya at two o'clock and an hour later she was standing facing Kiev's foremost rabbi.

"It is good to see you, Ronya von Glasman," he said in the musical voice that was so famous. He added, half shyly, "You are still the most beautiful girl in Kiev."

"No, dear Joseph," she shook her head, "but it is nice of you to say so."

He helped her out of her light coat and motioned her to a cushioned chair, pulled another opposite and sat down himself. "I've waited for you a long time," he said, sighing.

"Whatever do you mean, Joseph?"

59

"Almost a year," he said. "You have come about Julie Brodsky, haven't you?"

"You know about Julie?"

"Oh, yes. When I heard your Igor was courting her I went to see the village rabbi. I had reason to be concerned, I think, but he told me Igor had made friends with the people who rise early to earn their daily bread—even the water carrier. I was surprised, as well as pleased, to hear that Igor sometimes goes to the synagogue with the baker." Ronya was so startled she dropped the gloves she was removing and Rabbi Levinsky concealed his mirth as he bent down to retrieve them for her. "For the sake of a Jewish maiden, the son of Boris Pirov sits on a bench, breathes fetid air and endures long prayers. I saw no reason to interfere!" He paused. "Retribution, Ronya?"

Nonsense, thought Ronya to herself, but she said, "Good for Igor."

Rabbi Levinksy's manner changed. Authority was in his voice when next he spoke. "Have you decided to accept Julie Brodsky, Ronya?"

"Yes, Joseph."

"Why have you changed your mind?"

Ronya considered. "My mind was never made up," she said. "Igor is wild and impulsive. I wanted to be sure Julie was more than an infatuation with him. They're both terribly young still and Julie's background presents difficulties."

"But you *have* decided now?"

"Yes. I am ready to announce the engagement. I want to take Julie home to educate and prepare her for her future. And I do not want Igor to rush into marriage with a child. Do you approve?"

"I have a disturbing feeling, Ronya von Glasman, that you still shape your methods to serve your purposes."

"Is that wrong?"

"That depends on your methods and your purposes."

"Joseph Levinsky! You know that no matter what my shortcomings I am incapable of hurting or shaming the child."

Even as she said it, she became aware that she was no match for this Jewish sage. With honeyed words he was drawing her into a labyrinth. True, his father had performed her wedding

60

ceremony, but there was a score to settle. He had no wish to give a Jewish daughter to Boris; rather he wanted to give Boris' son to the Jews. Solomon built the temple strong.

Watching Ronya, Joseph Levinsky sat remembering the girl he had loved long ago and delighting that she had changed so little.

"Why do you continue to call me Ronya von Glasman?" she shot out at him.

The rabbi answered softly. "I do not recognize your marriage."

"How dare you, Joseph Levinsky! Your own father married me to Boris."

"Yes," his voice was mild. "He was widely censured. By me, too."

Puzzled for a moment, she then said deliberately, "I mean to take Julie with or without your consent, with or without your help. However, I know that you have power to sway public opinion. I'll make a pact with you. If you . . ."

The rabbi interrupted with a commanding gesture. "I will enter into no pact. I believe in the brightness of your soul. Now, answer my questions."

Ronya held her tongue and nodded.

"Do you plan to give one son to the Christians so that the other can remain the richest and best-protected Jew in Russia?"

"No."

"Will Georgi's father stand with him during the ceremony of the bar mitzvah?"

Ronya's heart sank but she answered steadily, "Yes." Then she added, demurely, "And I shall give a great feast and you will be the only Jewish male present except Igor."

The rabbi was not amused. "There will be Jews in the synagogue during the services and for the religious ceremonies." She bowed her head.

"During the years you have sent me large sums of money for my charities, for years responded to appeals for help from persecuted Jews. You have used your influence in high places, paid fines and bribes. These same Jews whom you have saved deny you. Why do you continue to help them?"

"They are my people."

61

"You understand that Julie Brodsky will never outgrow her heritage? That she is part of her past?"

"I know."

"Do you, Ronya von Glasman, believe in God?"

Ronya looked straight into Rabbi Levinsky's eyes. "To me the dogma and ritual are simply part of occasional beloved ceremonies. Yet I have kept the miracle of faith. Yes, Rabbi Levinsky, I believe in God."

He returned her look with an openness that matched her own. "You may have Julie Brodsky," he said. "I will make the arrangements."

"Thank you. Joseph? Will you marry Julie to Igor?"

"You know I will, Ronya."

The labyrinth had dissolved; the antagonists emerged, each with a measure of victory. "Tea, Ronya?" Levinsky offered.

"Please, Joseph."

While he went to ring for it, she stood up and stretched her arms above her head, feeling suddenly light and relaxed.

Ronya drew the tea when it came and as they sat with the samovar between them, a nice intimacy replaced their former tension. The conversation was desultory, familiar. It was Ronya who returned to the reason for her visit.

"How do you happen to be so interested in Julie? Is it just on account of Igor?"

"Julie's story," he said slowly, "began millennia before she was born. And in it there is a miracle. I want to tell it to you in order, from the beginning."

Ronya settled herself and, uncharacteristically, said not one word.

VII

THE village where Julie was born was older than the ancient city of Kiev. Its Jews bore the lineaments of their history, some mixed in coloring, like Spaniards, others dark-eyed with Roman features and still others with white skin and blue eyes.

Inbred, rebuffed, denied schools, forbidden to travel, they were deprived politically and socially, victimized by plundering Cossacks (and revitalized by Cossack rape). They lived in a vacuum and struggled to keep alive some vestiges of the things they held most dear—freedom, learning and culture.

Abraham Brodsky, father of Julie, was a skilled craftsman, a goldsmith who rarely worked at his trade. A fine Hebraist and student of the Talmud, he took refuge from the present in the past and the future, studying signs and listening for voices to tell of the time and manner of the Messiah's appearance. His spirit was untroubled as he devoted his days to holy conjectures.

Though Abraham was pious and poor, learned and foolish, his pretty wife Rhea considered her man a gift from God. This plump and appealing woman was unconcerned that he neither toiled nor provided for her and their children.

Loaves of bread she had in plenty, enough even to trade, for her sister had married the baker. The peasants gave her hens and eggs. Fish abounded in the forest streams; woods were full of nuts, wild berries and edible greens. The well gave cool, pure water. She dug other people's potatoes and picked fruit from her neighbors' trees. Rhea lived in abundance. And was herself abundant.

Married at fourteen, her first baby was born as she turned fifteen, and each year after that brought another child. Julie, born on December 25, 1886, was the eleventh daughter.

Neither Abraham nor Rhea made any bones about it. Another girl was a burden, but they did not repine. Abraham, Rabbi Levinsky suggested, smiling, probably drank a schnapps and consoled Rhea with some such speech as, "You are still young and God has a generous heart." And Rhea comforted Abraham, "She has two eyes and one nose, two ears and one mouth. She has both arms and legs. It could be worse."

"*Taka*," Abraham agreed. "Let us not complain."

For the first six months of her life Julie was happy. Wrapped warm in rags, suckled at her mother's breast, she was safe.

Rhea herself never understood what happened when she became pregnant again. She knew only that she began to dislike this girl child and was incapable of keeping her feeling to herself. It showed in her face, in the tone of her voice and the way she let the baby's head loll when she gave it the breast.

Julie responded as babies do. She cried.

When she was fourteen months old, Julie was completely abandoned. Rhea had borne a son. Subsisting on crusts of bread smeared with chicken fat, the little girl was an outcast.

Eight older daughters had survived and they turned away so as not to see Julie's large, reproachful blue eyes. They never took her with them when they went to fetch water from the well or into the woods to gather pine cones.

In winter she crouched under tables and chairs, at night hid under a bed, and when she was only three she began to toddle off by herself through the village to the woods. When she was tired she sat down under a tree, and one day a bird perched on a low branch beside her. The bird was her first friend, for when she returned she gave it crumbs from her crust and it sang to her.

"How did you find this out?" Ronya spoke for the first time.

The village rabbi, Joseph told her, was a simple man but sensitive and a mystic. Julie's beauty—her brilliant eyes, transparent skin and narrow, delicate nose—seemed to him a miracle in that village, and her treatment a shame. He learned from the peasants of Julie's friendship with first one bird, then all birds, and he heard their claims that she charmed the birds and that dogs never barked at her.

"Pogrom!" said Rabbi Levinsky. "You know what that means, Ronya. Julie was five years old when she heard the neigh of Cos-

64

sack horses, the yells of Cossacks on the rampage, the shouts of friendly peasants, 'Hide, Jews! Hide!' "

Rhea tumbled first through the trapdoor to the cellar of their house. The older girls grabbed younger ones and two by two dove after Rhea into the cave. Julie was forgotten.

A peasant neighbor chanced to be passing and went in to see that all was well with the Brodskys. He found Julie in tears, picked her up and carried her to his house.

There he stuffed cloth into her small mouth, bound her hands, shoved her into a chest and slammed the lid. It was the only way he could think of to hide her and be sure she kept quiet.

He stood in his door and watched the Cossacks who, he soon realized, had ridden into the village on a lark. They set a few fires to haystacks, and when the priest ordered the villagers to put them out, the Cossacks lent a hand. It was obvious that nothing was to be gained by keeping Julie concealed but he didn't trust Cossacks. Not until the dust had settled and the clatter of hooves died away did he lift the lid. The child was unconscious. With trembling hands he untied and ungagged her, laid her on his bed and put hot bricks wrapped in rags at her icy feet and a cloth soaked in cold water around her feverish head. Then he ate his supper and fed his dog. Together they sat by Julie and the peasant sang her Ukrainian lullabies.

At daybreak, seeing her stir, he said, "How do you feel?"

Julie lifted her head. "I'm hungry."

The peasant fetched stale bread and dampened it with milk. He gave her a lump of sugar and a dried fig. When she had eaten, she licked her lips and asked, "Are you my friend?"

He scratched his head and ignored her question. "It's time for you to go home now, Julie," he said.

"I don't want to go home. Will you be my father, please?"

"How can I?" he said. "I haven't got a wife."

"Let's go find you one," Julie said.

"I'll tell you what, little blue-eyed pigeon. I'll wait a few years; then I'll marry you."

"I am a Jewess," Julie said. "A Jewess does not marry a peasant."

65

Ronya nodded appreciatively. How well she knew! This was Jewish pride.

The peasant, annoyed that Julie—who was an object of pity in the village—rejected him, scratched his head again and pondered. Stroking his nose with one finger, he decided Jewish people were funny, but they were God's problem, not his. His business was to plow fields, get drunk and frolic a bit, go to church on Sunday. It was more than enough. "Go home, Julie," he said.

The village talked of nothing the next week but how Julie had been hidden.

On Saturday the rabbi mentioned the peasant in the synagogue and the *rebbetzen* sent him a gift of smoked whitefish and wild cherry preserves. On Sunday the priest praised him from the pulpit for his Christian deed. Several women brought him small gifts and a ruble or two found their way into his pocket.

Indignantly, the women of the Christian congregation proposed that Julie be made a ward of the Jewish community. Sara, the baker's wife, went numb with shame when she heard of it and stormed off to Abraham's house, which she had never entered since her sister's marriage.

The door was open. Abraham sat at a crude square table of unsanded boards, peering intently into a book and running a finger along a line of Hebrew text, rocking while Rhea rocked, too, her butterball son in her lap.

"Monsters!"

Abraham raised his eyes, but Rhea gave no sign that she had heard except to clutch little Simon tighter. As Sara walked toward Abraham, he put down his book and stood up, saying amiably, "You have finally set foot in this house. We are grateful."

Sara scoffed. "You used to be a man. My sister turned you into a mouse."

"So," said Abraham, "if it is to be that I am a mouse, don't expect me to roar like a lion." He took Sara's arm. "Sit down, please."

Sara looked at the man and saw that he was still handsome, however seedy. She sat down.

"We have not been close friends for quite a long time," Abra-

66

ham said to both women, "but we are still relatives. We shall drink a glass of tea together and talk."

Rhea put her son into a wooden cradle and went to the samovar, fetched a teapot, three glasses, six lumps of sugar and a plate of *gribbenes*. As she fed the boy crisp pieces of this rendered poultry fat, a delicacy he loved, she took quick peeks at Sara. Her sister, she could not deny, was imposing with her dark rich hair, firm skin and youthful carriage. Herself as round as a dumpling and as doughy-skinned, she was stung to retaliate against such injustice.

"It is a pity that you have no manners. What *chutzpah*—to burst into a house and shriek 'Monsters!' "

"Perhaps," said Sara, "but I repeat: you are a monster."

Abraham looked at the sisters patiently, and addressed them slowly. "On the one side you are both right. On the other you are both wrong. It can only be that Sara came to chastise us because the girls forgot to pull Julie through the trapdoor.

"However, the fault is also Julie's. She should have followed. Heaven knows she has been cautioned about the Cossacks often enough. So of that we'll make no more. Once the dog has run off with the meat, what good is brandishing the meat cleaver? We shall, therefore, proceed to another level of logic.

"For many years Sara has sent bread. It does not matter that Sara has not spoken one word to us in all that time. We remembered that she is our sister and we did not make her wretched by exercising false pride. By receiving we did not deny her as our kin. That makes us equal."

Abraham held out his hand to Sara. "You should not have called Rhea, your sister, a monster. A kind word is better than bread."

He held out his other hand to Rhea. "You should have anticipated that Sara still hides loving kindness under a sharp tongue and extended understanding to her."

Sara glanced at the man bleakly. Her voice harsh, she said to Abraham, "Is Julie not your child?"

"Her father I am," Abraham answered. "Whose child she is only God knows. But this I *do* know. To this house and to this village she does not belong—she with eyes bluer than the sky,

67

and a voice sweeter than a nightingale's." He lifted his palms in a prayerful gesture. "How did she come to us? What will become of her?"

Rhea's face was sullen. "Tell her about Julie's nose, too," she mocked. "Tell her how it sticks up like she is above the rest of us—like God meant her for a palace and sent her to us by mistake."

Sara waited for Rhea to finish, then said to Abraham, "I want Julie."

For once, Abraham made a decision. "Go where the birds are. There you will find Julie. May she fill your heart and you hers."

Early on the morning of Julie's eighth birthday, as he did every morning, Isaac, Sara's husband, pulled out the last long-handled slablike implement stacked with loaves from the oven and shuffled off to sleep. Sara and Julie tiptoed around the kitchen getting ready for the birthday supper. Together they carried out the prune-and-apple compote and buried it in the winter snow to chill, dusted and swept the sitting room and laid a fresh cloth on the table, polished the copper pots and in the afternoon went for a walk in the woods, where fresh snow hung like tinsel on the branches. On the way home they left a loaf of bread and a pot of honey for the peasant.

As the sun dipped over the horizon, they woke Isaac and, by way of celebration, he drank a tumbler of *bronfin* instead of his customary glass of tea. They sat down to a merry meal, but Julie was in an agony of impatience for it to end so she could open her present.

The first knock was faint but it startled her. Sara had just lighted the candles against the early winter dusk. Isaac's face looked pale in the yellow glow.

The second knock was louder. He rose and started for the door.

"Don't answer," Sara said. "We're closed. We have the right to enjoy the child's birthday."

The third knock was a bang.

"Please, Sara," Isaac said. "Maybe a neighbor has trouble."

He came back from the door with Rhea, bundled in a long black shawl, by his side.

68

Rhea shivered and lifted her hands to warm them at the flame of the candles. Sara ladled out a steaming bowl of soup and set it before her. She pushed a spoon into her hand. "If you come to wish my Julie health and happiness, you are welcome. Sit down and eat."

"I came to take her home where she belongs."

Wild with panic, Julie slid off her chair, kicked at her mother and then tried to run away, Rhea grabbed her. "Stand still, you troublemaker!"

Sara stood stunned. "Why, Rhea?" was all she could manage to say.

Rhea looked insolently at her sister. "Julie was a loan, not a present. Now I want her back."

"What cruel joke is this?" Sara moaned. "Why do you frighten Julie? Let go of her arm."

Instead Rhea gave Julie's arm a jerk. "Get your things, stuck-up one. To the peasant you run with presents. Your mother you do not come to visit—not once in three years." Julie stared at her blankly. "Don't look at me like a dumb animal!"

Isaac pushed back his skullcap, opened his mouth and sucked in air. Feeling dizzy, he picked up his glass and drained it. "Dear, good, generous Rhea," he said in a tiny voice, "do not make a scandal."

"Shut up, mouse!" said Rhea contemptuously.

Issac winced and sat down, peering at Sara uncertainly, waiting for her to make a move. Sara managed to keep her voice calm. She said, "The past is past. Do not spread one stain on another. Leave Julie to me. She is all I have. You have so many children to love—"

Rhea cut in. "That is my good fortune." Then she delivered the final insult: "Barren one! God made you a freak."

Sara bit her lips so savagely she tasted her own blood. Forgetting Julie, she was possessed by an old hatred and sobbed: "Abraham was mine but *you* married him. Fourteen years old you were and you stole him from me."

"To talk so before your own husband and a child! It's sickening," Rhea said self-righteously.

Sara sprang from her chair and flung herself on Rhea, tearing at her sister's face with her nails. Isaac tried to separate them,

69

but the strength of fury was too great for him and he cried, "Run, Julie, as fast as your legs can carry you. Fetch help."

Her hands on Rhea's throat, Sara herself began to suffocate and she let go. Standing tall and terrible, she intoned, "My curse on you. May Simon, your son, die a hot quiet death. Soon. Very soon."

By then there were neighbors in the room and two of the women led Sara away. In the dark they undresssed her and put her to bed. A little later, looking in to see how she was, they found her feverish. "Pack Julie's things," she said in a low voice. "Then leave me alone." The women did as they were told, then helped Rhea and the silent child home.

The next day Sara tore her garments and strewed ashes on her head. In her empty house she draped the mirrors with black. On the seventh day she went to the rabbi and said, "I have killed Rhea, my sister."

"Rhea is not dead," the rabbi said. "However, even here in Russia where crime is condoned and murder committed in the name of the Tsar, your attack on Rhea is an unforgivable sin under Judaic law, and that is the law by which we live. But since Rhea pushed you into the pit where the devil seized your hand, and since women have come to me to say they do not censure you because in desperate circumstances one commits desperate deeds, I shall intercede for you with God so that your place in Paradise will be reserved."

In the Brodsky household Julie lived under a cloud. Her sisters blamed her for their mother's scratched face. Rhea could not contain her loathing, and whenever she looked at the child, she prayed, "Dear God, put aside Sara's curse. Take Julie instead." Abraham felt compassion for Julie but withheld sympathy rather than anger Rhea.

January, February and March passed and Simon was as plump and rosy as ever. Gradually Rhea lost her fear and the girl's mute stillness started to distress her, so she coaxed the child out of her corner, insisted that she tuck in at night with one of her sisters. Julie responded hopefully and even hummed a little. In all things she was obedient to Rhea except one. Each night she crept into the narrow space behind the stove to sleep.

70

On the first of May, Simon was restless. The next day he was droopy. By the third he was gravely ill. Rhea tried every remedy she knew, all unavailing. That night she called Julie. "I need your help," she said. "Simon is very sick. Sing to him. A song is often the best medicine there is."

Julie turned up the kerosene lamp, bent over the small boy and said sadly, "A bird has the same look when it is dying." She sat down on the side of the bed, took Simon's hot hands in hers and began to sing. Rhea, watching in terror, saw her son grow quieter.

Outside the narrow window, day was breaking. Rhea covered the two children, took down her black shawl and whispered to Julie, "Stay with Simon. I'll be back."

The synagogue was built of tree trunks, laid up on a rock foundation. Its dim interior was furnished with benches and a central rostrum on which stood the Ark that housed the Torah, draped in velvet trimmed with sequins. Stairways to the right and left led to a small balcony where the women sat during services.

In the foyer Rhea filled a dipper from the pail and spilled water over her hands, reciting "Blessed art thou O Lord of the universe who commandeth us upon the washing of hands"; then she went to find the rabbi.

When he saw her, the rabbi was surprised. "Rhea Brodsky, what are you doing here at this hour?"

She started to tell him, but the rabbi interrupted, "I know about the curse."

Rhea wailed, "Simon is grievously ill. He does not vomit. He does not hurt. But he is dying. Read the scroll of parchment and tell me how to save my son."

"I have no words of solace for you, Rhea."

She flushed. "I shall not go away from here until you promise to rescue Simon from the Angel of Death." Then she wept.

The rabbi let her cry for a long time. "Now," he said, "you know sorrow. Do you think of the anguish of Sara? Do you, perchance, also grieve for having abandoned Julie?"

"No," said Rhea truthfully. "I think only of Simon, my son. I tremble for Abraham, my husband. If God takes Simon, who will say Kaddish for him after he passes on to the next world? Who will recite the mourner's prayer in the synagogue?"

"A good wife must also be a righteous woman, Rhea. You have transgressed divine law. The whole truth of the Torah is, 'Do not unto others, what you do not wish others to do unto you.' You, blessed mother of many children, took from your only sister the child who is her life. Now God threatens to punish you for your sin. Give back the girl, Julie, to Sara. Ask her forgiveness. Let there be peace between you. Then and only then will God spare Simon."

When Rhea came running into the house, Abraham was at breakfast with several of the girls. They all looked dejected. Flinging herself into the chair opposite his, she asked, "How is Simon?"

"Very sick. Julie is with him. He cries if anyone else comes near."

She shook her head, then told them everything the rabbi had said.

Abraham pronounced, "The rabbi is the voice of our Lord on earth. Obey him."

Rhea reached for a roll, broke off a piece and popped it into her mouth, saying nothing.

"Why aren't you on your way to Sara's? Why do you hesitate?" Abraham asked. "Sara is now our only hope."

His wife sighed. "I am willing to give Julie back but to ask forgiveness, to fashion words of apology—"

"Do you want pride more than your son?" Abraham said. "Remember, Rhea, the rabbi has spoken. Do as he commands or Simon will die."

Rhea went into the bedroom and laid her hand on Julie's head. "Go eat, child, while I gather your belongings. You are going back to Sara, your aunt."

His night's work finished, Isaac was already asleep when Rhea and Julie arrived at the bakery. It was Sara, dressed in the unrelieved black of mourning, her hair covered with a black kerchief, who opened the door. Silently she stepped aside and motioned them into the living quarters, where she pointed to chairs and seated herself on the sofa. Julie threw down her small bundle and went to stand by her aunt.

"Please," Sara said again, pointing to a chair, but Rhea remained standing while she recited everything the rabbi had said to her and admitted her reluctance to beg for pardon. As she talked, Julie slipped her hand into Sara's.

"I recant my curse," said Sara, her heart overflowing with emotion. "Simon will live." She stood up. "I'll make tea. Go to our bedroom, child. Put away your things and rest. You look tired."

For over an hour Sara and Rhea ate and talked. At last Rhea rose to leave. "Sara," she said, "the hate began before Abraham. How did it start?"

"What difference? It is ended. I promise that you will never regret that you gave Julie to me. I shall give silver-plated candlesticks to her for a wedding gift."

"Plated with silver! Why, Sara! Are you rich?"

Sara smiled. "No. But I shall manage." She went back to her kitchen and returned with six fresh eggs, almost a pound of butter, a whole chicken and two bottles of wine. "Come into the bakery, Rhea," she said. "I'll wrap this and give you bread."

Rhea said, "It's too much, Sara."

"We are one family now. We share."

At the door the sisters embraced. "Sometimes will you bring Julie to see me? Lately I got fond of her," Rhea said.

"Of course. And you will all come here. We'll celebrate the Sabbath, dance at weddings, eat matzos on Passover, feast on Purim and fast on Yom Kippur. We'll do all sorts of things together. But remember, Rhea, for my Julie a little honey. She doesn't like chicken fat."

Rhea was greeted by a rejoicing family. Abraham ran to her and, in front of the girls, who blushed and giggled, he flung his arms around her and kissed her. "The miracle has occurred! He is well. A few hours ago Simon is dying. Now he sits in bed munching a soupbone."

Rhea dumped the food Sara had given her on the square table, except for one lone twist of bread and two eggs, and started out again.

"So, *nu*," said Abraham, "where are you going now?"

"To trade," Rhea answered. "I need a large jar of honey."

It had been midnight before Ronya left Rabbi Levinsky's house to drive home, but she was the first of her family down for breakfast. When Igor and Georgi put in an appearance, she briskly informed them that they were to be moved from their pleasant quarters overlooking an oak-shaded balcony on the second floor up to small attic rooms.

"What's the hurry, Ronya?" Boris hid a smile.

"Thanks for trusting me," Igor said with clumsy, youthful sarcasm, then reconsidered. "Perhaps you're right. Julie is very old-fashioned. I'll move."

"But the roof slopes and you can't see a thing except trees," Georgi protested. "There isn't even a toilet up there!"

"I had no idea, Georgi, that toilets and running water were so important to you. Move up with Igor," Boris commanded. "You can have the smallest, darkest room and from now on I want you at the stables before *and* after your lessons."

"Now what did I do?" demanded Georgi, outraged.

Ronya disregarded his indignation. "The attic rooms are really charming, Georgi. You'll love yours. I'll have the beams painted, shelves built for your books, the floors carpeted." She reached out a hand for the honey pot.

"Nothing of the sort," snapped Boris. "From now on Georgi's going to get a foretaste of life at the cavalry academy."

Georgi brooded. It was going to be a nuisance to get out of the house through a third-story window and a narrow one at that. He spoke bitterly. "On account of Julie nothing is ever going to be the same again."

No one denied it.

VIII

DURING the succeeding weeks men with ladders and buckets of paint and brushes tramped in and out of the house. Brawny fellows removed heavy Germanic furniture from the wing which had been occupied by the Pirov boys, and while they worked Ronya spent whole days in Kiev. When she returned, wagons full of goods followed her carriage. Even her own kitchen was at sixes and sevens because of alterations she was making in the pantry.

Boris tried to resist change to the house which he considered quite perfect as it was.

"Why the devil are you turning the whole place upside down for one little girl?" he demanded.

Ronya only replied placidly, "The family portraits can go up to the attic hall, I think. All those gloomy von Glasmans might depress her."

But when Ronya finally invited her three males to see her handiwork, Boris was astonished at her understanding of what would be appropriate for a girl she had never laid eyes on. The banished von Glasmans had been replaced by watercolors of country scenes, of birds and flowers. Formerly dark walls were now a lilting blue. The new furniture was simple, painted eggshell white and upholstered in blue and white striped taffeta, except for the massive mahogany bed now canopied in toile. When Ronya and Katya were born in that bed, the hangings had been somber velvet.

Igor was frankly delighted. For the first time he really believed his dream was coming true, that Julie would actually be here.

"How did you know her color is blue?" He marveled at his

mother's intuition and rewarded her with a happy smile, chin dimpling, face alight with rare pleasure. Throwing open the French doors to the balcony, he took a deep draught of air. "I've just thought, though. Julie's never had a place all to herself and she might be frightened at night alone. Could you have a lock put on these doors?"

Ronya eyed her son speculatively. Was Julie so timid? she wondered. Ah, well, she'd know soon enough but Igor's mother had no stomach for namby-pamby girls. "I'll see to it," she said evenly.

"What about fresh air?" Georgi asked virtuously.

"Julie still thinks night air is unhealthy," Igor informed his brother. Then, turning to Ronya, he surprised her with a noisy kiss. "Thank you for all this," he said. "Julie is going to love it."

Not to be outdone, Georgi hugged his mother, too.

As soon as Boris was alone with Ronya, he put his hand on her waist and said, "There are exactly three things I want in all the world." He released her to tick them off on his fingers. "You. You. And you."

"Get along with you," said Ronya. "I've a thousand things left to do."

For another week Ronya busied herself with planning and ordering materials for a wardrobe for Julie, and Boris was occupied in the stables. Only Igor was restless.

"When are you going to get Julie?" he importuned his mother.

"The minute I hear from Rabbi Levinsky," she said patiently. "Matchmaking takes time, you know."

"Why?"

"I don't really know and it is a bother. I've rushed everybody and here we sit. The village rabbi is probably making mountains out of molehills. He may be fussing because I don't serve kosher food and raising a lot of other foolish objections."

"I'm going to the village."

"I promised Rabbi Levinsky you wouldn't."

"But why, in heaven's name?" His young jaw was set.

"Because, Igor, the situation really is odd. Both rabbis are acting as marriage brokers and tradition compels us to be patient and courteous to the *shadchonim*."

"All the same, I'm going to the village and I'm going to bring Julie back. The hell with the damn rabbis!"

Thus confronted with delay in the village and rebellion at home, Ronya sought a course of action and found a solution in an essay her father had written years before—*On Conflict and Harmony*. "Attempt a compromise," he had advised, "by introducing an entirely new idea. Link it with your purpose in such a way that your antagonist does not comprehend the hold in which you have engaged him. Let him think that he has emerged, at least qualifiedly, the victor."

Ronya introduced the new idea and, because he trusted her, Igor fell into her trap. He agreed to leave at once to visit the Brusilovs, taking his mother's word that by the time he returned Julie would be waiting for him.

The day he left, the morning post brought Ronya a parcel. Lydia carried it up to Ronya's room. It contained the gold bracelet, the shawl and even the ribbon with which Lydia had tied up her gifts to Julie. There was also a letter.

High-born Ronya von Glasman, the Jewish goya:
Your blond devil brought your son to my door. They looked admiringly at my Julie and Igor edged his way in with lies of love, with false promises of marriage, with smiles, with presents, with rubles of silver for the children of the village, with gold pieces for the rabbi to distribute among the old and the feeble. So the people made room for him, I, too, and he stole my Julie's heart.

The fault is mine also. The Tartar said, "We came as strangers. We leave as friends." My Jewish heart believed him. Can you imagine!

At you, daughter of an illustrious Jew, I am surprised. To ill treat an innocent girl is a worse sin than what you did. At least I think so.

Now my Julie, deceived, is abandoned. Before your son came she scorned the decent Jewish sons of the village. Now they will scorn her—God forbid!

Perhaps it is not fitting for a Pirov and the nephew of a countess to marry the niece of the baker's wife. However, it is also not fitting for a good Jewish girl to marry the son of a Tartar who publicly maintains a mistress. Gossip flies with the wind. My quarrel is not with you.

One last thing I say. Igor came. He refreshed himself in my Julie's purity. Now he has stopped coming. Good! Do me a favor. Keep it like that. Let the fancy girls in Kiev have him. Like father, like son.

With respect,
Sara Baker

P.S. It is with great restraint that I keep myself from saying, "May ill *mazel* be yours with Igor."

Lydia had stood while Ronya read, fingering the shawl. "The insult of gifts returned!" she grumbled indignantly. Ronya ignored her.

"Send a runner to the stables," her mistress ordered. "I want the Blond One at once. Bring him to my room yourself." Lydia gathered up her skirts and ran.

While she waited, Ronya dressed in sturdy riding clothes and packed a small suitcase with a change of clothes, the shawl, the bracelet and the ribbon. Finally she went to Boris' room, took a pistol from a drawer, and belted it on.

When the Blond One and Lydia entered her room, Ronya was ready. Lydia eyed her costume with disapproval. The boy looked quizzical.

"I am going to the village," Ronya said, "to fetch Julie. I need a covered wagon and a team that knows the forest and that I can keep in line. Borrow everything from your mother, Tamara. I shall take nothing from the stables, not even my own whip. If anyone asks you anything, you know nothing. That applies to you, too, Lydia."

"I am going with you," said the Blond One. In his voice Ronya heard Boris' voice.

"No, son," Ronya said. She had never called him "son" beforefore. "The weather is clear. I'll be out of the forest before dark. You needn't worry about me."

"The forest changes all the time and it's a lonely place. It's fair now but may storm later. Let me come."

"I would like to have your company," Ronya said, "but it's not possible. I must go alone. You must stay here."

He yielded and proceeded to detail the route: an hour into the forest and she would come upon a stream from which many trails branched. The one to the south led to the village. That was a shortcut and she was not to take it. Instead she must ride straight ahead until she came to a creek. If she followed that, she would find herself on a wagon road marked by wheel ruts. There she was to turn south. It was, he said, the longest way but the safest.

Ronya had the gift some small women are blessed with: she could make herself tall. Arching high onto her toes, she touched the tall Blond One's face with her lips. His "Thank you, Ronya, my mother," sounded like a song.

"For the pleasure of seeing Tamara's face," said Lydia, as soon as he was gone, "the first time she hears him call you 'mother,' I'd gladly spend ten years in purgatory."

"So would I!" Ronya laughed, glowing.

Lydia folded her arms across her ample bosom. "Suppose my master returns before you do. What shall I tell him?"

"Tell him to go to the devil."

Lydia beamed. "He'll tear my heart out."

Ronya brought the wagon to a stop in front of the bakery, jumped down and hitched the horses to a post. With a rifle in one hand and her suitcase in the other, she managed to knock on the door.

Isaac opened it but remained cautiously behind it, eyes glued to the rifle. "I am sorry about the gun," said Ronya, aware that she had frightened the man. "I was afraid to leave it in the wagon. I am Ronya, mother of Igor."

"Sara!" called the astonished baker. "Sara! Company! Igor's mother is here."

Standing on the threshold, Ronya concluded the man was an idiot. She put down her suitcase to wait but Sara came out at once. If she saw Ronya's weapons her eyes showed no surprise, only admiration for the woman who had dared the forest alone to come to her house.

"Come in and be welcome," she said, picking up Ronya's suitcase.

Ronya, looking at this tall, immaculate woman, felt a rush of

79

pity. That such a woman should have a—*thing* for a husband. She reached out her hand and gave her a smile that began in the eyes and spread to the lips.

That smile convinced the anxious Sara that Ronya could be a friend. At once everything was surprisingly clear and easy. "Come in back, Ronya. You must be hungry. There's a pot of noodle soup left over from supper and parsnips in real meat sauce. Come! While you clean up, I'll heat the food."

"I'm starved, Sara, and I've heard about your cooking. But I must see to the horses first. I drove them hard."

"Isaac will attend to it. He'll get somebody from the stable to fetch them."

Emerging from behind the door, Isaac uttered the only gallant sentence of his life. "It is an honor and a pleasure to oblige the lovely mother of Igor," said he. Sara could hardly believe her ears. She had no idea that he could reach such heights of etiquette and was delighted by Ronya's thanks, which implied no social distinction between bakers and Pirovs.

"After the stable, go fetch Julie," she said. "But don't rush. And don't hurry back from Rhea's."

"Sara—the bread!" he wailed.

"Tonight the devil can take the bread. For all I care the whole village can fast."

After he shuffled off, the two women measured each other. Both were sensible, both schooled in the art of bargaining. Matchmaking was a moral business with a practical purpose, transacted according to rules established by tradition. Sara knew that Ronya would weigh her side of the scales with her charm and her power and conceded her that right. No matter. Her Julie would be wife to the Pirov heir, the inheritor of the von Glasman fortune. That fact eliminated many awkward questions.

Sara heated water so Ronya could wash while supper was prepared. Ronya ate with concentration and a gusto that was the fashion in Sara's world. She waited until the table was cleared to mention the real purpose of their meeting.

"How is it," Sara asked when they were sitting together on the small sofa, "that neither your husband nor your son nor an escort of male servants rode with you on your journey through the forest?"

"Boris and Igor are not in Kiev right now," Ronya replied. "Your letter demanded immediate action. I came without servants to avoid gossip."

"About the letter." Sara looked down at the hands folded in her lap. "Excuses are like cupping a corpse. I can't say that I am sorry that I dictated it because I'm not. It brought you here.

"I take back the hard things I said. There is an old Jewish saying, Ronya: The whole world is one town. I heard the rumor that Ronya von Glasman refused to accept the girl from the village—nothing travels faster than gossip. I confronted Igor with this. He didn't exactly deny it. So my nightmare began. I saw my Julie ravished, deserted, dying more of shame than of a broken heart. Some nights I couldn't sleep. Some mornings I never wanted to wake up again."

"The wall of misunderstanding encircled us both," said Ronya. "I am here to open the gates, Sara. Do you know the story of the rabbi with the open mind?"

Sara sighed. "Of course. What Jew does not? You make the point. I've got my side and I am right. You've got your side and you are right. Both sides can't be all right and that is right, too."

Ronya spoke of the arrangements she had made with Rabbi Levinsky and ended by saying, "I'm worried about him. He's not a man to break his word or fail to keep a promise. If he were ill I should have heard."

Accepting this, Sara felt called upon to talk about Julie. "That she cannot read or write or speak pure Russian is not entirely my fault. Her father is a great scholar and I pleaded with him to teach her. But he had no interest in educating a girl, and Rhea objected too. Julie wanted to learn but was refused by Abraham in the house of her parents.

"What could I do besides what I did? I taught her all I know. She has her numbers; she solves problems in her head. She is clean and polite, eats nicely, speaks softly and never sits with her legs apart. Julie is intelligent—she learns fast. She'll not shame you, nor will Rabbi Levinsky ever regret that he is sponsor to Julie."

81

Ronya's only comment was, "I find it difficult not to feel bitter toward the Brodskys. Thank God, Julie had you, Sara."

At this moment Rhea bustled into the room, followed by Abraham and Julie.

"I am Rhea, the *real* mother of Julie. A pleasure to meet you. Make the acquaintance of Abraham, my husband."

Ronya smiled but looked only at Julie, who lingered in the background like a frightened child. She rose and opened her arms to the girl, who brushed past Abraham and Rhea and slipped into her embrace. "Julie, my daughter," she said.

"She has no dowry," Rhea announced defensively.

Sara bent down and lifted the lid of the low chest that stood in front of the sofa. From it she took out two candlesticks that shone in the firelight and held them out to Ronya. "Julie has these. She does not go to Kiev with empty hands."

"They're beautiful, Sara, and dowry enough. Give them to Julie yourself. It is your right."

Outwardly Julie's sweet young face was grave, but Ronya sensed that its quiet veiled a complex of emotions, pride and gratitude, tinged with embarrassment.

Rhea took charge of the situation in her own bossy way. "Julie, Sara your aunt gave the candlesticks with both hands. I see that you took them the same way. That's nice. Now sit down on the other side of the sofa by your future mother-in-law and listen, because my mother's heart compels me to speak."

Instinctively, Julie protested, "No. Don't." But her voice was little more than a whisper.

"Julie, my child," said Ronya, "now that you have thanked Sara, go pack your lovely candlesticks and whatever else you need. We must leave early tomorrow morning to get through the forest before dark."

"So soon?" Rhea complained. "Then we must settle everything at once."

Julie subsided onto the sofa, candlesticks clutched to her immature bosom. Ronya turned toward Rhea.

"I shall be glad to hear what you have to say."

"The wedding. When will it be?"

Abraham added in a conciliatory voice, "These things have to be settled, gracious lady. Perhaps it would be more fitting to al-

82

low the rabbis to make the decision and conclude the final arrangements."

"I make my own decision," Ronya replied tartly. "I shall also make my own arrangements. At present I can give you no wedding date."

Rhea did not attempt to hide her displeasure. "I'm not satisfied. We insist on a definite answer. Put meaning in your words, Ronya von Glasman."

Ronya and Sara exchanged glances as revealing as shrugs. "Rhea," Ronya said, "my name is Pirov. I suggest that you remember that."

"Furthermore"—Sara interrupted firmly—"Rhea and Abraham demand no further. Julie belongs to Igor's mother now. I have given her. Just be grateful to God for showering his blessings upon her."

It was not easy to quiet Rhea. "It is indeed a dark time when a mother can't get a plain answer to a plain question."

You can't help admiring her tenacity, Ronya thought. She laughed. "All right, I'll give you a plain answer. Tomorrow I shall take Julie, the candlesticks, a few provisions, and we will travel some thirty miles. But for Julie the distance is far greater. She is moving to a new life. To prepare her for it, I shall nurture her into womanhood. When she understands her responsibilities as future mistress of the von Glasman estate and wants Igor as a woman wants a man, there will be a wedding. Not before. Julie is mine now and I swear to you that she will wear virgin white for a bridal gown."

Abraham raised his hands. "O Lord, lift up Thy countenance upon Julie. Be gracious, O Lord. Recast her fate. Lead her, O Lord, to a place where her bright color, her rich song, will wake response. So shall I, your servant, be shorn of guilt. Thus shall I enjoy the blessings of peace."

And Julie, who at the age of fifteen still feared a man's touch, felt born again. Ronya, her mother, had given her the greatest of gifts—time. At that realization Julie was filled with a delight so overwhelming it flooded up into her face, lighting her eyes and suffusing her clear skin with color. Seeing this transformation, Sara sat stunned, for the first time fully comprehending that the one person she truly loved was leaving her forever. Julie would change under the tutelage of Ronya and her heart would be alone.

Rhea broke the spell. She pounced on Ronya and gave her a juicy smack on the lips. "That's what I call a plain answer! *Mazel tov!* Welcome for a relative." She took charge. "Abraham, get Isaac. Tell him enough already with the bread. Together run, bang on doors, say, 'Julie is engaged. We are host. Come! Rejoice! Bring guests.' Then hurry and fetch the other children and fetch Julie's peasant, too. Off with you!

"Sara, quick, prepare for the party. Fill the decanters with wine. Cut honey cake. Julie, put away the candlesticks. Help!"

Years later the village still talked about the party at the baker's house that night. Everyone came, even the rabbi and the *rebbetzen.* Toasts were made to Julie, the Kaleh, wine glasses crushed in *mazel tov,* bread pulled from the ovens and eaten hot.

The village fiddler played as never before and Ronya, her skirt lifted high, danced first with Abraham and then with the peasant, executing the lively steps of the *kazatska* she had learned from the gypsies. The women clapped their hands in approval and the men shouldered one another aside for a chance to dance with Ronya.

When the fiddler stopped to have a drink, Ronya asked Julie to sing. The shouts, the jokes, the laughter ceased as she led the girl to the center of the room. At first Julie's voice was almost too faint to hear, but as her heart began to flow into her music, no one moved or made to leave. The voice was angelic and the child was lovely as an angel, her shining hair flowing free over her shoulders, her face radiant with joy. She has not only worked a miracle, Ronya thought, Julie *is* a miracle.

Suddenly it was time to go, and as the men and women crowded out of the house, the sky was streaked with dawn. At the instant of parting Julie clung to Sara while around them good nights and goodbyes rang out, to Julie and to Ronya von Glasman. Her people were not yet ready to call her Ronya Pirov.

IX

LYDIA clucked and cooed over Julie. "Come, pretty one," she said, indicating the stairs and inviting Julie to follow her. "Your eyes are full of sleep. I'll bring warm milk and put you to bed." Ronya concealed a smile. Lydia had adopted Julie along with the rest of them. Poor Julie.

In all innocence Julie resisted being bundled off before she had a chance to see this wonderful house. "I'm not a bit tired," she said. "All the way from Kiev I was fast asleep."

"Just the same, you had better rest, young mistress." Lydia was obdurate. "You'll have no peace for days to come what with Georgi wearing you out taking you all over the place and the peasants celebrating your coming."

Ronya intervened. "Come see the library and *then* you can take a nap, Julie. I'll leave you there to look around for a few minutes. There are a couple of things I have to attend to."

The instant the door closed behind the child, Ronya followed Lydia into the kitchen, where they were well out of earshot.

"Talk fast, Lydia."

"Yesterday, late in the afternoon Boris pranced into the house yelling, 'Ronya, my love, I'm home. I rode all night.' I'd sent all the servants away so no one answered him. While he looked for you, I ran to my room, locked the door and waited to see what would happen. It happened. He kicked in my door, got hold of me by the shoulders and bawled, 'Where in hell is Ronya?' I began to bawl. Then he let go, said 'Sorry, Lydia,' and stormed out of the house. He hasn't been back since."

"Take care of Julie," Ronya said. "Tell her I've been called away and will see her in the morning."

At the stables Ronya woke the groom on duty and had him

85

hitch her team to her carriage. From a hook on the wall she took her whip.

Although she had never seen the house where she was sure she would find Boris, she knew where it was, halfway up Kiev's steepest hill and hidden from the street by a high wall. It was not, she discovered, a large house. The front garden was small and in back there was none, just a straight drop to the river. On one side a stable contained stalls for two horses and room for one carriage.

Boris had bought it with Ronya's money long ago, before he made the stables pay, and had installed in it a succession of women, some common, some well-born, with whom, when he was angry at Ronya, he took out his fury, always scornfully. There were times when he was so obsessed with his wife that he could not even accomplish this revenge.

Ronya hated his seedy affairs but was too proud to make an issue of them. Tonight, however, she resolved to put an end to Boris Pirov's philanderings. He would never visit this filthy house again, she promised herself.

At the precise moment when she pulled up in front of it, Boris walked into the bedroom at the back where Vera waited, lying naked in an erotic pose. Surveying the woman, the room with its clutter of silk pillows, ostrich feathers and boxes of chocolates, he felt nothing but weary disgust. "To hell with you," he said.

"You're joking," Vera laughed. "I'm the most adept practitioner of my trade in Kiev and not above sharing you with your wife."

It was then that they heard Ronya's step. Vera caught her breath as she saw the woman approaching the open door, whip in hand.

"Turn over, harlot," Ronya ordered the woman.

Vera was not given to panic. Surely Ronya knew of her existence. But what if she had found out about Igor? Sheer terror gripped her.

The first lash fell across her generous thighs.

"On your belly, strumpet," Ronya said furiously, "or I'll cut you to ribbons and rub salt into your wounds." The whip lashed mercilessly.

"Scream!" Ronya commanded.

Vera screamed.

Boris, seeing the line of welts across his mistress' buttocks and knowing that Ronya would soon draw blood, caught her wrist. "That's enough."

"Shut up!"

Boris grinned. "Let's get out of this place."

Lowering her whip, Ronya preceded him through the door, her earrings dancing in her ear lobes. Not even a whimper came from the woman on the bed.

Boris could not sleep. He rolled out of bed and lit a cigarette. What a woman! By the time he had mounted his horse she was gone. Catching up was easy, getting her to stop another matter. "Steady, steady," he cajoled her horses, at which she belted them with the reins and urged them on. He felt foolish at the equestrian acrobatics he was forced to perform to the tune of the tinklink of harness bells. However, he brought his stallion alongside one of her pair and leaped from horse to horse. Bringing the team to a halt, he joined Ronya in the carriage. They drove home silently, and at the top of the stairs, she went into her room, still without a word.

Now, the first rays of the sun lit the painting of his wife that hung at the foot of his bed and Boris had an uneasy feeling she was laughing at him. He threw back the sheet and his feet thudded to the floor.

In Ronya's room the curtains were drawn and the air was sweet with the scent of white roses in apple-green jars and of violets in lavender-blue porcelain bowls. Ronya lay asleep on her back under a silken coverlet. He studied her elegant mouth with its sensual lower lip.

"Ronya, my love!"

She opened her eyes, dark pools of sleep, and saw the fire in his, their hazel flecked with green and gold, as he leaned over to kiss her. The sensuous lips stiffened and she turned her head away.

"I love you, Ronya. Only you," he pleaded.

"I know, Boris." Her voice was a cool whisper.

"I shall never be unfaithful to you again," he said.

"I know that too, Boris. But I want something else."

87

"What, Ronya?"

"I want you to be a Jew. To stand at your son's side in the pulpit of the synagogue for the ceremony of bar mitzvah. To have compassion for the weak and exiled. Help them, Boris. Their hearts weep and they are too proud to beg. Respect and serve my people. I want the Jews to call me Ronya Pirov."

"I will stand with Georgi," Boris said slowly. "I will do—what I can. But my mother is a Tartar. Can I escape from that? What can I promise?"

"You have promised enough, Boris my husband."

Never had they made love together in such harmony, understanding and unity. In the warm aftermath, Boris stretched and murmured, "I feel glorious!"

Ronya laughed. "I know something that will make you feel even better—Julie is asleep in her room."

"Well, I'll be damned." His bewilderment was genuine. "Not a horse, not a wheel missing from the stables but you and Igor drove to the village!"

"I sent Igor to Moscow," Ronya said complacently, "and went alone."

He whistled. "And how," he tousled her hair, "did you get into the house on the hill?"

"Through the cellar window. You *are* obliging to carry a metal bar in your saddlebag." Her voice was smug.

"No wonder the Jews still call you Ronya von Glasman! They remember your father. He stole Manchuria from the Chinese."

"He had his reasons." Suddenly, Ronya was serious. "He served his Empress and Russia. I serve my family. Do you want to hear why?"

"Go back to sleep, little field marshal." But it was he whose eyes closed. Ronya pulled the sheet over him, got up, tiptoed to the bathroom and softly closed the door.

Down the hall Julie was wide awake, enjoying a voyage of discovery around her new room. She sat on the chair at her ruffled dressing table and touched the enameled mirror and brush and comb, moved to the window seat and gazed dreamily out over the trees. She fingered petit point and vermeil, stroked the silk and velvet of cushions, peered at pictures and, finally, examined herself in the mirror.

"Yes, young mistress"—Lydia had come in without knocking—"take a good look."

Utterly obedient, Julie stared at herself in a simple white peignoir, a blue ribbon in her hair, and wondered how she could have gone to sleep one girl and waked up quite another.

"Here's your hot chocolate, child," said Lydia. "Drink it up. Ronya, your mother, will be here in a minute."

When Julie opened her door to a light knock, it was not Ronya but Boris who stood outside with Georgi. She thought she had never seen a more remarkable pair than the golden man and his golden son. Laughing and bouncing around his father, Georgi blurted excitedly, "You sure are skinny." When she said nothing, he added, "But you sure *are* pretty!" Georgi had fallen in love.

Boris swept Julie off her feet. "You 'sure' are!" he said, then put her down gently. "Be happy, daughter of my choice."

For a moment they were silent. Julie's voice was tiny but clear as she said, "All the happiness in the world is in this house."

Boris touched her hair for an instant. "Ronya's on her way," he said.

Alone again, Julie returned to her chocolate—and thoughts of Igor. Why had she never been able to persuade him to tell her about this house, so that she would be prepared? And how wrong he was about everything and everyone except his mother! How could he possibly care more for the Blond One than for the adorable Georgi? How doubt his father?

"Good morning, Julie!" Ronya stood in the door, looking radiant. "Did you sleep well?"

"I was too excited. It's all—so new."

"I know," said Ronya, "but you'll soon learn your way around."

"I love this house," Julie said ardently. "It's as if—I don't know how to put it—it's as if all my life I'd been homesick and now I'm home."

"This *is* your home, darling." Seeing Julie so moved she was close to tears, Ronya drew her out onto the balcony to distract her. "Have you looked at the garden?"

89

Below them an ancient figure of Buddha was dappled with light from the morning sun.

"What is it, Ronya, my mother?"

"That's Buddha, the Indian teacher and saint. He taught in Burma and China. The statue came from Harbin, a city in Manchuria. After breakfast I'll show you where it is on the map. This Buddha stood at the edge of a lake that was covered with lotus flowers."

"Lotus?"

"It's a kind of water lily which opens in the morning and closes at night and has the most delicious fragrance."

"Imagine! I had no idea the Chinese had their own saints and their own flowers. Do you mind questions, my mother?"

"Boris says even birds stop chirping at night, but not me! I love any excuse for talking." She led the way back into the bedroom.

"Did Lydia show you the conveniences?"

"She brought me a washbasin and a chamber pot."

"Come along, then. It's time for your first lesson."

"No, my third! I've already learned about Buddha and the lotus flower."

The bathroom astonished and awed Julie, but when Ronya asked if she wanted to take a bath, she slipped out of her peignoir without embarrassment and was in heaven over being able to sit up to her chin in warm, scented water. When Julie asked Ronya to wash her hair, Ronya felt that already she was sliding comfortably into the role of daughter.

Julie dressed herself again in the clothes she had brought from the village and Ronya made no comment. A wardrobe would come later. "I don't know about you," she said, "but I'm ravenous."

Together they did justice to the baked fillet of whitefish with parsley and melted butter Lydia served them, and helped themselves generously to steamed peas and mushrooms broiled in wine, which were followed by creamy cheese, crusty bread and oranges.

Julie had never seen an orange. "It looks like the full moon."

"And it's called an orange."

90

"I have heard the name," Julie said gravely. "Once a stranger came to the bakery and told us that he was from a land where the sun is hot all year and snow never falls. We gave him bread and he gave us stories. I liked the names and made up a song about them." She stopped to reach for an orange, bit hard into the skin with her shining white teeth, and sucked the juice. "Why it's bitter! Delicious bitter." She licked her lips.

"Fourth lesson." Ronya smiled affectionately. "First you peel an orange, then slice it. The rind is used as flavoring or glacéed in sugar to make candy. One does not eat the outside."

"Peeled? Like a common potato? What a waste!"

"You're as refreshing as an orange," Ronya said. "I confess I sometimes eat the peel."

Lydia came in to announce, "Lisette is here, my mistress."

"Good. Show her to the sewing room. We'll be right along."

It was a cheery place, filled with sunlight from the back courtyard, and today was a sea of color. Bolts of fabrics were unrolled on every chair and table and stacked in the corners.

Ronya introduced the dressmaker and Julie smiled but, lost in pleasure, did not speak, only reached out to stroke fine silks and muslins.

As soon as the girl had taken off her blouse and homespun skirt, Lisette measured her slim figure, adjusting a dressmaker's form to her measurements. Pins in mouth, shears in hand, she pronounced in a markedly French accent, "For thees one, fewer ruffles and less buckram than are the fashion." Ronya studied Julie and concurred. "Nothing extreme for our Julie. Give her what is becoming."

There would be dresses, but first came underthings—panties of Swiss muslin and thin cotton trimmed with lace. Some of the petticoats were to be long, some short, some flannel, others lined with taffeta.

Ronya called a halt when she saw that Julie was tiring.

"Will they be finished before Igor gets home?" Julie asked.

"Of course, young mistress," Lisette said. "As soon as I cut the materials, my seamstresses will get to work. Then I take a tuck here, make a dart there—and *voilà*—Miss Julie has a wardrobe. Does tomorrow at the same time suit you for a fitting?"

"If it suits Ronya, my mother," Julie said. "Thank you so much, Lisette."

During tea in Katya's upstairs sitting room, Ronya said, "We must visit the stables. What has Igor told you about the Blond One?"

Julie blushed and Ronya was not certain why.

"The Blond One is Igor's and Georgi's half brother," she explained, "though Boris, his father, has never granted him the right to use the name of Pirov, and rarely speaks to him directly. We are, however, extremely fond of him and his father is the first to be offended if anyone fails to treat him with respect."

What reaction Ronya had expected from Julie when the time came for this inescapable revelation, she was not sure, but it was certainly not such a stricken stare. But now that she had launched into family relationships she was determined to finish.

"The Blond One's mother is named Tamara and she is queen of our gypsies. When Igor returns he will take you to make a formal call on her, and she will smile on you and you will probably love her. She will make you a royal gift. Accept it. When all of us are forgotten, people will remember that she was a queen."

"I—I don't think I understand," Julie stammered.

"Someday you will. In the meantime, remember only this. Because Boris, his father, does not welcome the Blond One to his table, Igor and Georgi often eat with him in the kitchen or the stables. You are free to join them whenever you wish."

Julie seemed not to wish to hear any more about this disturbing subject.

"What does *voilà* mean?" she asked.

Ronya had no sooner explained than Georgi charged into the room and pulled Julie unceremoniously to her feet. "I've been looking for you everywhere," he complained. "Come on. We've got a surprise."

Georgi's surprise started with showing Julie the stables. Legs planted apart, hands jammed into his pockets, he looked up at her triumphantly. "Aren't they great?" he demanded. To his horror Julie ran out into the sunshine, her nose pinched as though she felt cold. He followed and found her leaning limply against the wall.

92

"What's the matter with *you?* You feel sick?" he asked anxiously.

Julie brushed a lock of hair back from her forehead. "Can you keep a secret?"

"Sure thing," said Georgi.

"I'm afraid of horses," confessed Julie and, though he looked appalled, she continued doggedly, "and that's not all. I'm afraid of the river. I can't swim."

Georgi saw that telling him had been a struggle and, manfully, decided to look after her.

"Did you tell Igor?"

Julie shook her head.

"That's good. There's nothing to swimming. Tomorrow I'll throw you into the river. As soon as you start drowning, I'll save you. I'll keep on throwing you in until you learn to float. Then I'll teach you how to swim."

Georgi's plan sounded desperate to Julie. "I'll be terrified."

"We Pirovs aren't scared of *any*thing," Georgi bragged.

Julie slipped her hand into Georgi's and said, more to herself than him, "But what about horses?"

Georgi swallowed. "Too late," he whispered for Boris had just come around a corner. "Be careful or he'll find out you're scared."

They watched Boris dismount from the white stallion, light a cigarette and stop to speak to the groom. Georgi tried to warn Julie what was in store for her. "She's only a filly, Julie," he said.

Julie looked at him helplessly, then saw the groom lead a small black mare to Boris. "Let her stand." He smiled with pleasure. "She's a champion, Julie," he said, "and she's yours."

At his words Julie went white and Boris understood. Before she had time to think, he was up on the stallion again with her in his arms. "Go—boy!"

The great horse pounded around the ring and Julie's panic gradually subsided. When she opened her eyes, Boris put the horse to a walk. "Your filly has a sweet nature, Julie," he said. "She'll be easy to ride."

She looked up at him, snuggling closer.

"Still afraid?"

93

"With you, Boris, my father, a regiment of horses wouldn't frighten me. Without you I am still afraid of a horse."

Boris threw back his head and roared with laughter.

X

RUSSIA was changing. Under the placid surface of the summer of 1901, new currents began to run. The peasants, on whom the vast, cumbersome economy depended, were finding tongues, after centuries, to voice discontent at their lot. By September factory workers were openly rebellious. Meeting in poor squares at night, crowds formulated their grievances and shouted, "A shorter day! Freedom!" The Tsar's own Cossacks rode them down.

For the most part the powerful and aristocratic ignored the rising ferment, and when they could not, shrugged their shoulders and deplored the weakness of a regime that was unable to control its subjects. A few liberals in St. Petersburg, like Alexis Brusilov, were sensitive to the seriousness of the situation. They cautioned the Emperor and advised concessions—free hospitals and elementary schools, a free press, free enterprise, religious tolerance. Among the most energetic of these men was Sergius Witte, then minister of finance. At the beginning of his career he had been a protégé of David von Glasman and had learned from that realistic politician to read the signs of a crisis in the making. Now he stood on the side of the enlightened few to press for reform but even he was no match for the palace clique. Nicholas no longer heeded his mother, the Dowager Empress. It was to his ambitious, tyrannical wife, the German Alix, that he turned, and she urged him to play the autocrat God had decreed he was.

The Ukraine was far away from the center of the rising tide

but it felt the ripples of unrest. Yet the von Glasman lands and tenants remained peaceful, as they had through all past disturbances. Everyone believed that their private golden age would continue to the end of time.

Ronya, in close correspondence with Alexis, left nothing to chance. To her peasants she gave land to plow and seed to sow. Moreover, the church was theirs and the school. Their aged were pensioned, their sick doctored. They had ample food and vodka and, most glittering of all, they had Boris and his white stallion to keep alive their dreams. They ate, drank, coupled and enjoyed themselves.

The men in the stables had no complaints. Igor would retain the championship, they agreed proudly, and wagered their savings on him. In their hearts they knew that Georgi would soon outride his brother but of this they did not speak.

The gypsies, too, were satisfied. If they had not been, Tamara would have given the signal and led them to a new camp. Of all the people on the estate, they lived on the land without being tied to it. The tribe had lingered for generations beyond their ability to count, but on their own terms. No one would ever own them and they felt free to break whatever compact they had made with the von Glasmans. The sun would rise, the sun would set and Tamara would guard them.

Such a homebody had Boris now become that he even refused invitations to travel and judge horse shows, and the chore of cavalry deliveries was the Blond One's. However, on a certain morning while he and Ronya sat over breakfast in the sunny kitchen, he asked her playfully, "Will you grant me leave to spend an evening with my friends at cards or must I steal out of the house, like Georgi, by way of a window?"

"I can hardly bear it," Ronya teased, "but of course. What time will you be leaving?"

"About six," he said. "I'll come back from the stables to change and say goodbye." He laid down his napkin and started for the door, then turned and said, almost wistfully, "I *could* ride to the barracks and invite the men here."

For years Ronya had refused to tolerate his hard-drinking friends, and he had frankly looked forward to his nights away from home. It was only recently that he had come to hate spending so much as a single evening away from his wife.

Ronya's response was warm and immediate. "I'll cook dinner myself and it will be glorious!"

Not only was it a memorable meal but the hostess was utterly delightful during dinner, then retired early to leave the men to their own diversions. Touched and appreciative, Boris volunteered to go with her the next night to what he privately thought of as one of her damned, interminable meetings. He had never been to one and obstinately steered clear of any involvement.

Ronya accepted his offer and said, "I think perhaps you'd better come upstairs with me while I dress so I can tell you what we're up to."

At her dressing table, her hands busy piling her long hair into a knot, she regarded her husband, sprawled across the foot of their bed, in the mirror. "You've been ducking the meetings for years. I suppose you thought they'd be a bore?"

Boris stretched his arms above his head. "I'll bet I wasn't far wrong at that," he said. "Fat landowners, fat wives, fat talk." He yawned.

Ronya made a face at him. "You won't see your cronies there, I grant you, except for one particular one." (That would be Tromokov, he assumed.) "It's a serious group and an influential one but I wouldn't say they're stuffy. Ostensibly they meet to explore the possibilities of land reform but actually—"

He had gotten up and was standing behind her. "Ronya, my dove," he said, "you talk too much."

They arrived late to find that the main business had been deferred for Ronya. Boris was astonished at the greeting she got. It had never crossed his mind that she would be the only woman in the assemblage or that she carried so much weight in its deliberations. He solemnly shook hands with the men, all leaders in Kiev, feeling rather like a prince consort. Father Tromokov was, as he supposed, his one close friend there—Tromokov with whom he had ridden and drunk and brawled for so many years, he thought he knew everything about him. He would have summed the man up as loving horses, peasants, vodka and God—

96

in that order. What he soon learned on this evening was that Tromokov was the society's only radical. While the others advocated a *strong* Ukraine, he alone demanded a *sovereign* Ukraine in which there would be absolute separation of church and state. Moreover, he made no secret of the fact that his preferred church was Roman. Boris was dumbfounded—and admiring.

As the meeting went on, he was more and more impressed by the quality of devoted statesmanship that was being matter-of-factly evinced on a subject that lay close to his heart: the health and maintenance of the Ukraine.

So he was proud when Father Tromokov, toward the close of the proceedings, rose and proposed that he be admitted to membership. The movement was carried unanimously. Without hesitation Boris responded in deep sincerity, "Thank you, gentlemen. I am honored to accept."

Ronya was on her feet instantly. "And I, gentlemen, resign."

No one objected.

Father Tromokov rode part way home with them. Said Boris, "You, my old and dear, hard-drinking comrade, are a two-faced bastard."

The priest roared with laughter. "And you, I calculate, are still a good judge of horses—only!"

"Now what the hell does that mean?"

"It means," said Ronya sweetly, "that the next time I try to tell you something, you'd better listen."

A week before Rosh Hashanah, a letter arrived for Ronya. Rabbi Levinsky explained that he had had to leave Kiev for a time on urgent matters and continued, "Matchmaking is dealt with in the Talmudic treatises, and designated a distinctive calling. 'He is among the brave souls who devotes himself to the vital task—the sacred union of youth. It is a labor of devotion involving risk to life and limb.'

"Ronya, my dear, I found a letter from the village rabbi waiting for me on my return. You and Sara Baker are a remarkable pair of matchmakers. *Mazel tov!*

"Please bring Julie to see me.

97

"May the Jewish New Year bring health, peace and happiness to your house. Your devoted Joseph."

Late in the afternoon of the day before Rosh Hashanah, when Katya and Igor were hourly expected, Julie lingered in the kitchen with Lydia after the others had gone to their rooms to get ready for dinner. "Go pretty yourself," Lydia said. "Wear the dress with the lace yoke and puffed sleeves, the blue one."

Instead of obeying, Julie lazily watched Lydia sprinkle ground nuts cooked in buttered sugar and cinnamon over a cake, while she ate a dill pickle. Chewing thoughtfully, she asked, "Will the Countess Katya like a girl with no education?"

"You'll be educated soon enough," Lydia told her. "Your lessons start right after the holidays." She wiped her hands on her apron and gave Julie a smack on her bottom. "Now get along with you. Igor will be here any minute."

"I *am* here." Igor was standing in the doorway.

Julie clutched her pickle tightly and squeaked, "Igor! You came too soon. I'm not ready yet."

He took her in his arms. "Never mind about that, Julie. I like you tousled." He proceeded to tousle her still more.

Julie, who kissed his photograph dutifully each evening, had quite forgotten how very big and how very masculine her beloved was. She retreated into a prim shyness, struggling free to tuck in the ends of her hair and pull the bodice of her dress down. Igor's hands fell to his sides.

"Shoo, you two!" said Lydia beaming. "How do you expect me to get my work done if you hang around?"

They took refuge in the herb garden beside the back door. "I'm glad you're here, Julie," Igor said formally.

"I'm glad, too." Julie sounded like a little girl reciting polite phrases she had been taught by a nurse.

They sat down on a stone bench, stiff and unfamiliar.

"Has everyone been good to you?"

"Oh, yes, Igor! Very, very good."

"What have you been up to?"

"Last Tuesday, Ronya, my mother, took me to call on Rabbi Levinsky. He showed me the synagogue. It's the oldest synagogue in Russia and I never in my life saw such a huge court. With a fountain in the middle. You should see the houses on the Jewish street—so handsome and all built of stone.

"Did you know that Rabbi Levinsky was educated in Vienna and Jerusalem? He told me about grapes as large as small plums and olives and oil made from seeds and the fearful desert and caravans of camels and Arabs and Mount Zion—"

"Help! Julie." Igor was laughing. "I never heard you say so much so fast before."

"I never knew so much before. Now, what did you do in Moscow?"

"I read a lot. Practiced my jumps. Mostly just thought of you and counted the days." If this was only a fragment of the truth, it sufficed.

A little silence fell. Igor leaned forward, picked up a stick and sketched a funny face in the warm earth at his feet.

"Mother wrote that you and the Blond One go for long walks," he said.

Julie did not answer, and he added a halo of ringlets to his sketch, waiting hopefully. When she remained silent, he snapped the stick between his fingers and scuffed out the face. Next to his mother, the Blond One and Julie were the two people he loved most on earth and Igor longed for them to become friends. But Julie, even in her silence, seemed hostile to the idea.

Igor fished a small box out of his pocket and Julie sighed with relief. How could she explain her reservations about the Blond One? With her mind she knew them to be unfair; yet her heart was not persuaded.

The box held an emerald of great beauty, brilliant against the white velvet lining, mounted in a simple gold ring. Igor took it and slipped it onto Julie's third finger.

"Aunt Katya sent it to you for an engagement ring." Igor sealed their betrothal with a kiss, on Julie's part an altogether childish kiss. Ah, well, that was the way Igor preferred her for the time being.

At midnight the Day of Judgment began, the day when God reviews the deeds of the previous year and man's fate is decreed in heaven. *"Be Rosh Hashanah Yikusayvin"*—on the New Year it will be inscribed.

Outside her bedroom door Ronya stopped and took Boris' hand. "I chose well when I chose you, my beloved," she said.

He took her in his arms. "Good night, my darling."

To review the deeds . . . not alone of the past year but of a lifetime, Ronya thought, staring out into the darkness beyond her windows and listening to the murmur of the trees. If only David von Glasman had known what Boris would become. Through patience and love and, she confessed to herself, guile, she was leading him to champion her people, as Jews and as Ukrainians.

They had had an extraordinary life together, she and her father. David von Glasman took her everywhere with him—to Rome, Paris, Vienna and he planned that they would go to the East, to Manchuria, where he had many interests. But for her, David explained, the objective was to meet a man in Harbin. He talked often of Hsuan Hui Tsung, speaking in a tone he never used about anyone else. "He is old and frail, complex, mystical and addicted to opium," he said. "Behind walls he lives shielded from the world. Withdrawn though he is, his knowledge of men and affairs is universal, his wisdom expressed in symbols of dragons and bulls, lotus and peach. You must meet him. Or, if he dies, you must meet his son."

And so she would have, if she had not beheld Boris on horseback in the great square. After that, nothing could drag her from St. Petersburg while David negotiated with the Empress.

"She is shrewder than an Armenian merchant," he told Ronya. "First she praises me for my financial genius, calls me a wizard. 'From every deal you pick a meaty plum,' she says, 'but no matter, you are worth it to us. The young man, Sergius Witte, whom you have recommended to us, will be valuable. He has ability. We are pleased with him. How cleverly you pull the strings—like a puppeteer, unseen but making men dance, and blameless if things go wrong.' "

David had answered, "There will be no difficulties, Majesty. The Chinese have granted the concession. Sergius Witte can proceed with the plans to build a railroad across Siberia. Russia will have a foothold in Manchuria and access to her ports."

"Good." The Empress nodded. "Manchuria is reputed to have raw materials which will in time make us rich. And what other plans have you to make your sovereign prosperous?"

It was a challenge for which he was ready. Russia had for decades lagged, despite all her resources, while the mercantilism of Europe was making burghers and businessmen fat. It was high time to put Russia on the gold standard and collect revenue from sales of vodka by making it a government monopoly. Both of the schemes he outlined to the Empress and, as so often in the past, she was delighted by his shrewdness and devotion.

David von Glasman put a price on his services, a fact that had long been understood between them, for she was as astute about men as she was about commerce. For a reward she gave him her word that the von Glasmans might continue to live under the protection of the hereditary rulers of Russia. "You may," she concluded, "bring your daughter Katya to court. We shall receive her and are prepared to make special arrangements for her marriage. She will become a duchess." With a dutiful daughter so close to the throne, David's position would be immeasurably strengthened.

But when the Empress demanded Ronya as well, David was frankly troubled. Ronya was his and he intended her to live on his lands.

So all that winter he temporized while his daughters danced through the nights at royal balls and were courted by ambitious men who saw which way the wind blew. To David's delight, Count Alexis Brusilov singled out Katya and asked for her hand. It was not the match the Empress would have made for her. Alexis was too rich, too powerful, so powerful that she had no choice but to give her consent. His blood was bluer than Romanov blood.

And then Ronya saw Boris, and again David von Glasman sought an audience with his monarch. "Ronya is beautiful," she said, "full of charm and mischief. She is, as we have said, welcome at court. Why do you ask us to permit her to marry the Pirov boy? You know, of course, that he is penniless. He did not even buy his own horse—it was a gift." David's expression did

101

not change but he had a fair idea whose gift. "True, the women of the court fight over him. Even," she admitted, "his Empress smiles on him."

David countered, "I will pay exorbitantly for him—but only if he and Ronya have your leave to live in Kiev."

What Katya had told Ronya was true. The Empress said, "I see. A tooth for a tooth. A Christian for a Jewess."

David sheathed the sword between them. "Let us say rather, my liege, a son for a daughter."

"And does his father consent?"

"I shall have no difficulty with him."

She had promised then to bestow the decoration of the Ring of the Royal Crown on Boris as a wedding present.

He wore it when he married Ronya, a Ronya clad from neck to toes in tiers of white, trailing a long Venetian lace veil. Around her neck was her father's gift, twin strands of perfectly matched pearls. The ceremonial cup that Boris smashed, as ritual commanded, was white jade and the ring he put on her finger plain gold. She would not have traded it for all the Tsar's jewels.

After the last toast was drunk and the last guest had departed through the wide double doors, Ronya went to her room and prepared for her bridegroom. Her long hair fell in a dark cloud over the sheerest of white nightgowns; her eyes were wide and radiant as she lay on the bed listening for his step.

When at last he came, he stood towering before her, silent, his jaw jutting. He leaned down, ripped the fragile nightgown off and dropped it on the floor as if it was a rag. Then, with no word of love Boris took Ronya, brutally, vengefully.

After he had done, Ronya said bitterly, "I hate you," and her husband laughed.

The next morning she was sunny, he surly. She spoke amiably and he mistrusted her. But her smile was irresistible. He went off to the stables with nothing in mind but the coming night.

The evening began with a family dinner, Ronya contriving to be all—devoted daughter and sister and flirtatious bride. It was Alexis who suggested bed. Ronya cuddled against Boris' shoulder and said, "Give me a few minutes," dropping a light kiss on top of his head before going upstairs. He nodded, laughing to himself.

When he reached Ronya's door, he found it locked. Boris grinned. He had been tricked, but he liked her spirit. When he knocked, there was no reply. Then he braced his body and put a muscular shoulder against the upper panel. The door was stout and well made and did not give when he heaved. Going to his room, he hunted out a pocketknife and returned to the attack. One twist of the blade snapped the lock.

What he saw when the door flew open was glorious—Ronya stark naked, her delicious pink buttocks firmly braced, a whip in her hand.

Laughing hugely, Boris started to strip. It was when he leaned down to pull off his shoes that he realized the bedroom door stood open as he had left it. In the hall stood David von Glasman, pale with shock, staring in. Boris kicked the door shut.

As naked as she, Boris took a step toward Ronya. She lifted her arm. He took another step, and Boris suddenly realized that she was a virtuoso with her whip. Advancing toward her, he felt the leather bite into his fair skin, but he did not pause until he could reach her wrist. He pulled her to him; she dropped her whip.

Boris lifted Ronya and carried her to the bed. She relaxed utterly in his arms, heart to heart, so that it was impossible to say if one or two were beating.

"Do you still hate me?" he whispered.

"Will you ever love anybody else?"

"Never."

"Will you be faithful to me?"

"No, Ronya."

"In that case, I'll find ways to pay you back."

Boris held her shoulders so hard the color drained from her skin. "If you ever look at another man—"

"Hold me," she murmured.

One morning after Boris had slammed out of the house the night before and not returned until dawn, David von Glasman did not appear for breakfast. Lydia brought the message that he wished to see Ronya in the library. Ruth von Glasman looked up apprehensively.

"I'll go with you, Ronya," Boris said.

Ruth stopped him. "Let it be a private conversation," she advised. "Ronya is David's madness."

When Ronya entered the room, her father looked up sharply but his voice was controlled, even courtly. "Sit down, Ronya."

"I prefer to stand."

"Very well. What I have to say won't take long. I am taking your mother to Vienna to visit her people. You will accompany us. By the time we return to Kiev your marriage will be annulled."

Ronya stepped forward, searching her father's face. "Despite what happened last night, I love Boris. Our lives are *our* lives; don't interfere. I would like to remain here. You know how I love this place. But even that doesn't matter to me. Only Boris."

David said evenly, "I shall take Ruth to Vienna, as I said. And wait there for you. I can be patient. When you need me, send word and I will come."

For two and a half years he had waited in exile and no word came from Ronya. Then he died.

She had not had her fill of Boris. Nearly twenty years later she had not had her fill of him. But finally she was at peace.

XI

ON his way to his top-floor room and a bath, Igor could hear Georgi and Julie laughing. He looked in at her half-open door and saw that she was braiding her hair, looking ridiculously young and pretty. Georgi had draped himself on her bed—bare feet hanging over the end of it. In one hand he clutched a blue ribbon.

"Give it back, Georgi!"

"Come and get it."

"No, you'll muss me up."

Igor went in, partly amused, but not altogether. A subtle irritation nagged at him. Here were these two children playing while he sweated out his days in the ring and was made to mind his manners at night under the watchful eyes of his parents. Igor felt trapped. He must get a woman, soon. And he was going to insist that Julie outgrow her shyness and either go dancing with him in Kiev evenings or stay home. Alone.

At dinner he vaguely heard his mother say to Katya, who had arrived for the holiday and harvest, "What a pity Alexis was delayed and couldn't come with you, Katya. If we're all to meet the train tomorrow, we shall need two carriages." Igor had no intention of meeting his uncle. Boris said something, Ronya said something, then Georgi poked him.

"Wake up!"

"Why? Anything on your mind?"

It was Julie who answered.

"Igor and I will not be with you tomorrow."

If she had slapped him, Igor could not have been more astonished. It was all very well for him not to go to the station if he didn't feel like it, but this would be Julie's first opportunity to meet Alexis. Not to be at the station was out of the question.

"What in blazes do you mean?" he thundered.

Julie was not in the least disconcerted. "On the eve of Yom Kippur you will not ride in a carriage to the railroad station. You will walk with me to the synagogue."

Georgi chortled. "Walk! You should have started yesterday."

"Shut up, smarty," Igor said to his brother and, reproachfully, to Julie, "Don't speak for me and *don't* give orders. When you want me to do something, ask me. Nicely."

"What is there to ask?" Julie said with a touch of righteousness. "You knew how I feel about my religion when you asked me to marry you."

"Yes, Julie, of course. But that was in the village. You're here now. Don't ram your religion down my throat."

Julie persisted. "Why not? A little religion won't hurt you. I'm not asking you to become orthodox. I'm simply asking you to take me to the synagogue on high holy days."

Igor was suddenly achingly aware of the silence around the table, his mother speechless, Boris lost in contemplation, Katya perplexed. Somehow Julie had put him in the wrong.

He said, "You don't like horses. I don't like religion. That makes us even. Fair enough?"

Julie looked at Ronya. "I don't understand. Why did Igor go to the synagogue in the village?"

"Igor must answer that for himself, child," Ronya said.

And when he did not, Boris said sternly, "Answer!"

Igor protested, "Oh, for God's sake, let's drop it. I just did. That's all."

"Answer!" said Boris again.

Igor's mouth tightened in fury. At the same time he realized that Julie was frightened and trying to remain calm. He blurted out, "I went to protect Julie's reputation."

Julie blushed. "That was a nice reason." There was no hint of irony in her tone.

Georgi gave Igor a contemptuous look and plunged in. "I'll stay home with you tomorrow, Julie. You can fast and pray here."

"That won't do, I'm afraid, Georgi." She hesitated. "I did want to hear Kol Nidre and Rabbi Levinsky said the greatest cantor in Russia was right here and would sing it." She sighed. "I have such pretty clothes to wear this year."

"It's too far to walk, Julie child," Boris said. "A coachman will drive us. May I have the honor of escorting you to the synagogue to hear Kol Nidre?"

"I'm going, too," Georgi announced.

Igor slapped his thigh hard. "Why the hell didn't you tell me in the first place you wanted to hear Kol Nidre and show off your new clothes?" He said to Boris, "I'll take her."

Boris grinned. "Katya, with your permission, all the Pirovs will go to the synagogue. We'll see Alexis later back here."

"I," said Ronya, "shall go with you to meet Alexis." She got up, pushed back her chair and ran from the room.

"What's the matter with her?" Georgi asked.

"Get out," said his father sternly, then gave his arm to Katya and together they left the room.

"Is Ronya, our mother, ill?" Julie asked Igor.

"Never had a sick day in her life."

It was too baffling for Julie. Smiling, she said, "I've decided to like horses."

Igor shook his head. "No, Julie. I don't want you hanging around the stables. You stay here, in the house, where you belong. Now get your coat."

"Where are we going?" she asked.

"The Blond One is outside waiting to drive us to the camp. The gypsies are dancing tonight."

When they reached the clearing, the first thing they saw was Georgi dancing with Tamara.

Alexis greeted his wife and sister-in-law on the station platform affectionately. However puzzled he felt at the absence of the rest of the family, and especially of Julie, he withheld his questions until they were in the carriage. "My dear sister," he said with his customary diplomacy, "I am overjoyed that you are here but I must confess I had hoped to see more Pirovs. Tell me, what became of them?"

"There's nothing to tell, Alexis." She leaned back against the cushions and crossed one pretty leg over the other, looking so overamiable it was easy to see that she was controlling other emotions. "I chose to meet you. Boris, the boys and Julie chose to go to the synagogue to hear Kol Nidre. You'll meet Julie at dinner."

"I fear," said Alexis resignedly, "that to suppose Boris has suddenly embraced Judaism requires a greater degree of faith in miracles than I possess. Furthermore, when you, who have tried to make a Jew out of Boris ever since the day you married him, decline to go to the synagogue with him, I am utterly mystified."

Ronya was suddenly cross. "Oh, shut up, Alexis," she said.

He turned to Katya.

"I can only tell you what happened last night at dinner," she said and recounted the conversation. "Later Boris and I found ourselves in the library alone and he said, 'I'd like to go to her but her door will be locked and I'm in no humor to force it. With your indulgence, Katya, I'll drown my remorse in vodka. I may even get remorsefully drunk. Will you play for me?'"

107

"Boris said 'remorsefully'?" Ronya's eyes were round as saucers. "Are you certain?"

"Of course I am."

"Did he get drunk?"

"No. I played. We talked a little. That was all."

"What really happened, Ronya?"

"When Julie said, 'On the eve of Yom Kippur you will not ride in a carriage to the railroad station. You will walk with me to the synagogue,' I thought my senses were playing tricks on me. It was me, speaking years ago, only I put it differently. 'Boris,' I said, 'on the eve of Yom Kippur you will not join the thin-lipped reptilian horse thief Vladimir for a night of whores and vodka. You will order our handsomest carriage and most dashing horses and drive me to the synagogue.' Like Igor last night, he told me not to order him but to ask him nicely. I did, almost exactly the way Julie did—the new cantor, said to be the greatest in Russia, and how much I longed to hear him sing Kol Nidre.

"All he said was, 'Don't you shove your damned religion down my throat.'"

Alexis leaned forward and signaled the coachman to stop. "Take us to Rabbi Levinsky's synagogue," he said. "You drive Pirov horses, not oxen. Hurry or we shall be late."

A little before sunset on that Day of Atonement, the congregation was gathered in the courtyard, according to custom, so that Jew might greet Jew, "*Gut Yom Tov,*" and wish, "Well with the fast." Bearded elders, wise old men in white prayer shawls, swayed to and fro. Merchants, doctors, master craftsmen, scientists, traders, their heads covered, huddled together in groups. Youths in pairs talked gravely with one another in hope of impressing gentle-faced girls. Boys, students of the Torah, played a little, chafing at the solemnity.

The women kept apart. Young mothers hushed their children, and girls, gay feathers in their hats, laughter in their eyes, measured likely suitors for quality. Until the sun set, chatter, talk and bustle were allowed.

If the congregation found the arrival of the romantic Pirovs and the noble Brusilovs a stupefying surprise, they gave no visible sign. The von Glasman sisters were related to almost every man and woman there. The treasure of Katya's classic beauty and Ronya's extravagant beauty was Jewish, a heritage from Leah and Rachel, Deborah and Esther. And from Mary.

With entire correctness the congregation was friendly to the extent of smiles and nods of greeting; yet they drew an invisible line. Boris, the Tartar, was a symbol of fire and dagger; Alexis, the Christian, represented the Tsar and the Cross. Under the circumstances it seemed advisable to leave it to their rabbi to tender formal greetings. However, being human, everyone watched and weighed each movement the newcomers made.

With an unerring instinct for doing the right thing, Boris undertook to present Alexis to the rabbi. The Jews saw and approved.

The last faint rays of sunlight faded and a pale moon proclaimed it time. The Jews followed their rabbi, who led their guests, from the chill of the courtyard into the warmth of the synagogue. Julie waited with Ronya and Katya until the men were seated on wooden benches; then they climbed with the other women and small children to the gallery.

That sophisticated Muscovite, Count Alexis Brusilov, found grandeur in the austere dignity and simplicity of the interior, the display of the scrolls, the spectacle of the devout swaying in flickering candlelight. Beside him, Boris was unmoved. He rejected graven images and words inscribed on parchment. And he marveled at the childishness of man, who tried to imprison God within walls. The rhythms of love, the wild beat of dancing feet under an open sky had for him a grandeur worthy of worship. His mind wandered until the two elders recited from the scrolls, "In the tribunal of heaven and the tribunal of earth, by the permission of God—blessed be He—and by permission of this holy congregation, we hold it lawful to pray with the transgressors." Then his attention was caught.

And so it was that his ears were opened to the transfixing beauty of the cantor's extraordinary voice. Three times, twice in Hebrew and once in Russian, the cantor sang Kol Nidre, the saddest, most inspiring of Jewish prayers, the plaintive supplication to God for forgiveness, the story that echoes the martyrdom of a grief-stricken nation.

Julie was faced by a troublesome choice: whether to fast in atonement or feast for the harvest. She decided, "I have thought and thought. Were God unwilling for me to celebrate the harvest, he would not have sent Igor to my aunt's door." At that, Alexis raised his glass and they drank to Julie's indisputable logic, then applauded and laughed and sat down to Ronya's wonderful supper, which ended in toasts all around—to Igor, to Georgi, to horses, to good riding weather and, glasses brimming, to victory.

XII

ALL human history, or so it seemed then, had been merely a preparation for this golden time in the Ukraine. Any disturbing news came from afar off and failed to touch the lives of its people. On the Pirovs' rolling lands, the struggle between the British and the Japanese was more than counterbalanced by the running war between Georgi and his tutor; the plotting of the minister of the interior, Plehve, by the emergent leadership of Boris in the province; the increasing influence of France on Russia, by the increasing influence of Father Tromokov and Rabbi Levinsky on one another.

Boris, laboring in the pine forest in late autumn, read the signs of the season in flaming leaves and the nagging pain in his leg which in the last year had become a nuisance in cold weather; he realized that he had little time left in which to finish his task. Hands concentrated on sawing and nailing, his heart was free to rejoice over the house that he was building for Ronya. It was good—solid and spare—a house that would serve all weathers: hot days of summer, the flaming hours of autumn, white winter and spring, when the nearby stream was swollen.

He knew the house was as much for him as for Ronya. He was tired of never having her to himself, and he dreamed that it would blot out the memory of another house, the one on the hill in Kiev.

One afternoon some weeks before, intolerably lonely without her, he returned home from the stables and was greeted by a burst of laughter from Ronya's kitchen. At the door he met Igor leading Julie by the hand. "I'm taking her to Lydia," he said, his dimple showing. "She's had two glasses of kvass and she's drunk."

Julie giggled, her blue eyes hazy. "Igor is pulling a long bow because he just lost ten games of whist. He owes me a hundred rubles. That proves I'm judge sober . . . I mean—sober—as—a—"

Boris shook his head. "You, Julie, have a good head for cards. A bad one for hard cider. Igor's right. What you need is a nap."

Ronya, at the stove, plopped a peeled onion into a pan. "Hungry? I made piroshki and the soup is hot."

"Thanks, no. But I'll have some kvass—unless Julie drank it all."

The Blond One filled a glass and handed it to Boris, then spread caviar and sour cream on black bread for him. Boris accepted without looking up.

From the far end of the big deal table, Georgi, his cheek stuffed like a squirrel's, regarded his parents appraisingly. His mother was in a good mood. She had let Julie get tipsy. His father did not look stern. Still, he had doubts. What hell it was to be young! Consent for this, permission for that, tutors, Hebrew teachers— He'd better just jump in.

Georgi made his request: Tamara wanted him to go with her and the Blond One to Budapest to dance in the international conclave of gypsies. Ears deaf to the quality of the silence that greeted his words, he rushed on hopefully. "Tamara, my aunt, won't take me unless you both agree."

Ronya looked stunned as she tried to choke down her anger in order not to hurt the Blond One. She picked up a spoon so tensely Boris thought she would break it in half. Boris was equally furious; the way that gypsy tried repeatedly to get at him through his sons! With one hand he grabbed Georgi by the seat

111

of the pants, with the other the scruff of his neck, and lifted the boy off the floor. "You'll stay away from gypsies and you'll save your dancing for your own kind," he said. "May I remind you, my fine cock"—he gave his son a far from gentle shake—"that you'll be in the cavalry the day after your thirteenth birthday. Go get measured for your uniforms tomorrow." Boris released Georgi. "Tell your mother," he said acidly to the Blond One, "I'll break her neck if I ever catch her dancing with Georgi again."

Ronya's anger instantly transferred from Tamara to Boris for his unkindness to the Blond One. Wielding the spoon, coated with hot dissolved sugar, she hit Boris in the face. So violent was Boris' reflex that Georgi thought he was going to strike Ronya and flung forward. Boris, off balance, nearly fell.

The Blond One had been forgotten. He shared Boris' opinion of his mother, if Ronya had only known it. Now, with utmost dignity, he moved between Boris and Georgi. At full height his eyes were almost level with his father's. They exchanged a narrow gaze in which there was more understanding than they ever committed to words. The Blond One brushed back a lock of hair, clicked his tongue against the roof of his mouth and said, "Come on, Georgi. Let's go."

Boris was prouder of his bastard than he cared to admit, even to himself, and he was kindly disposed toward Georgi—the brat had backbone. "Teach that fresh limb of Satan how to drop a man on the first try," he said.

"Just what I had in mind." The Blond One herded Georgi out the door.

Ronya sighed. "Sit down, Boris." She went to the cold box and took out the butter, warmed some in her hands and spread it over Boris' burned face. "The skin's red but not broken. You won't blister."

He pulled her onto his lap, disregarding her buttery hands, and her head came to rest on his shoulder. "The old wound doesn't heal, Boris," she said. And then, as though speaking to herself, "Do I love Tamara? How raveled our lives are, hers and mine!"

That was the afternoon Boris had ridden several miles southward to the pine grove, had chosen a site and begun to clear the land for Ronya's house.

The rabbi met Ronya as she stepped down from her carriage and led her to his study. "It was good of you," she said, "to cancel an appointment and receive me on such short notice."

He regarded her affectionately. "As always, Ronya, it's a pleasure to see you."

In view of their previous talk and her bond concerning Georgi, Ronya had felt she must tell the rabbi of Katya's and Alexis' hope for the boy.

"Does Boris agree?"

"He isn't averse to the idea. In any case, Georgi leaves for the cavalry academy and St. Petersburg shortly. My heart would be greatly relieved if he were bar-mitzvahed before that, as we planned. I realize the ceremony in itself can't prevent anything, but who knows? The real implications might be planted and stay in Georgi's mind. One day he may remember and choose to throw in his lot with his people."

Rabbi Levinsky said soberly, "I shall prepare Georgi. In the presence of his father and witnessed by the required quorum of ten adult males, I shall confirm Georgi to Judaism."

Ronya thanked him, deeply moved.

They talked of Julie. "Watching her is like witnessing a rebirth," Ronya said. "My impression is that Julie is persuaded her life started the night she came to Kiev and that Boris and I are truly her biological parents.

"Perhaps that's partly why she's so—*right*—in her life with us. She and Georgi are dear together, romping along the trails to the river, he skipping stones, she sucking an orange. The peasants adore her for her frugal ways, gathering seeds for next year's garden on her hands and knees. The children swarm around Julie whooping, 'Sing, young mistress, sing!' Even more remarkable is her thirst for knowledge. She's forever asking questions and her comprehension is nothing short of brilliant."

"And yet you're troubled, Ronya. Why?"

She paused, frowning. "Igor—and Julie. Igor, my tarnished child, lives so feverishly. He has sudden, hot-blooded rages and

113

then his face breaks into that disarming grin. All totally without sense or discipline. And Julie doesn't help.

"Darling though she is with us, and composed and good-mannered with strangers, she still shies away from intimacy. With Igor she's all virgin, perfectly content just to hold hands. Julie *invents* excuses to stay at home, which doesn't displease Igor. He needs no encouragement to waste his energies."

Rabbi Levinsky leaned forward in his chair. "Forgive me for interrupting, Ronya, but I think you're unduly concerned. In two years Igor will be back from his military service, older and considerably wiser. He'll settle down and Julie will grow up. As long as she's happy, don't rush her. Let her grow at her own pace."

"That's what Boris says but I find it difficult to accept. Still, I haven't much choice, have I? And it's good to know that you agree with him. What a comfort you are, Joseph!" Her eyes were tender.

As the days shortened into winter, Boris rose before sunup and left the house at the first pale light of day. Darkness had long since fallen when he got home, just in time to bathe before dinner, and shortly thereafter he retired to his own room. Undeterred by the cold rain or punishing gales of autumn, he labored in a pine grove a half hour's ride from the house. If Ronya went out in the evening, she went alone and if she entertained at home he withdrew with a polite, unenlightening apology immediately after coffee. The only exception he made was to attend the bimonthly meetings of the Ukrainian Society.

Ronya was aware that something was afoot but its remoteness and the tall trees that sheltered the little house he was building kept Boris' secret well. For once Lydia was a sphinx. Igor, when questioned, answered, "He's in and out of the stables every day. What he does when I'm not around—" He grinned and shrugged.

In the past Ronya had had access to clues which he strewed around for her to unravel by the sense of smell. She could readily tell if he drank too much, and the clothes which he let fall when he changed might carry the heavy perfume of whores. Now he was in all ways secretive.

114

Entering the house by a side door, he used the back stairs and did not venture to cross the hall till sharp-eyed Lydia gave him a signal. The moment he stepped into his room, he emptied his pockets and gave his work clothes to the maid, who stood waiting, back modestly turned, eyes peeping.

The day he finished the house, Boris availed himself of the last bit of light to check that everything was in readiness. Tomorrow, wagons would deliver furniture which he had chosen with great care, and Lydia would bring a clock for the mantel, lamps, dishes and utensils, linens and provisions.

Satisfied that all was in order, he rode his stallion to the stables and walked home from there. When he swung open his door, he saw Ronya. With a toss of her head and a swish of her skirts, she took one sniff while he watched her delightedly. "Well?" he asked after this inspection.

"Delicious! You smell of pine and sweat and stars in a dim winter sky." One moment they were looking deep into each other's eyes, the next she was gone.

Dressed in a crimson robe, she was back before he was out of the tub.

"Would you like me to rub your back and bring you supper in bed?" she asked.

"Oh, Ronya—" he said.

A week later Boris and Ronya were dining in a corner of Kiev's most fashionable restaurant. It was the start of what Boris called a little vacation, but he had had to wheedle Ronya into agreeing to take it with him. Only his promise that they would not go far or for long, and that it would include a surprise, had persuaded her; surprises had a powerful fascination for the child in Ronya. Moreover, Boris had looked so eager when he mentioned it that she was consumed with curiosity. Ronya, having parted with Georgi only the day before, chattered on about him and how much she missed his mischief. Boris made no comment, concentrating on the excellent dinner. "You're not even listening," Ronya accused him.

He put down his spoon and fork, motioned for the waiter to clear the table while the wine steward poured brandy for them. "Leave the bottle," Boris said.

Ronya fixed her wonderful eyes appealingly on Boris. "Do you mind if I break your rule and smoke in public?"

Boris lit two cigarettes and passed one to her. It should have been a moment of mutual contentment, but he gave the impression of a man in pain, racked by unwelcome thoughts.

"Is your leg bothering you?"

"No. Why?"

She sipped her brandy and regarded Boris from under raised, questioning eyebrows. "What *is* the matter, darling? You look as if you were having an argument with yourself."

He poured himself another drink. "Your gloom doesn't promise well for our holiday," she spoke tartly. "Let's go home."

Boris put his elbow on the table and thrust his head forward so he could speak close to her ear. "Lower your voice, Ronya."

"Go to the devil!" Ronya said at the top of her lungs; then realizing that she, too, was endangering their first vacation away from home in several years, she restrained her impulse to indulge in a full-fledged quarrel and said amiably, "Where are we going? Lydia's probably packed all the wrong clothes."

Boris ignored her question, being deeply involved in one he himself had been considering asking all evening. Looking into the lovely face across from him, he yearned not to hurt her, yet felt he must know before he carried her across the threshold of the house in the grove. He reached across the table and took her hand. "Little dove," he said tenderly, "I hate to ask you but I must know one thing. Is Tamara your half sister?"

"Good God, no! Who told you such a lie?"

"I know it shocks you, but are you sure?"

"Of course, I'm sure. My father was *not* that kind of man," she declared fiercely.

"Ronya, my sweet, every man is that kind of man—even David von Glasman."

"No! Not my father. Not Alexis."

"Alexis is different," he agreed. "But I've heard stories about your father and Tamara's mother."

"Lies. All lies. My father never had a mistress—except Russia."

"Bless you, Ronya, for letting me talk about it."

"May we go now?" she asked, suddenly weary.

"In a few minutes, but there are a couple of things I'd like to clear up." Boris poured coffee for her, then told her that he had accepted the chairmanship of the Ukrainian Society. He was going to have to travel to every corner of the province in order to rally leaders and landowners to the cause. "There will be times when I'll need you," he explained. "Also, I've made certain commitments to Levinsky you can help with." Ronya's eyes lit up.

"Igor will be gone in a few months, so I'm putting the Blond One in charge of the stables. Breaking wild horses no longer excites me.

"Would you mind having him live in the house whenever we're away? I don't like the idea of Julie being alone there with no one but Lydia and the servants."

Ronya's delicate nostrils flared. "I want him in the house, too. I want him there all the time. Not just as a convenience, to take Igor's place. Why can't you love him? Why don't you appreciate all he does?"

"Because he's not yours," Boris said flatly.

"That's damn cold-blooded."

"Maybe so."

They had reached the end of that road; Ronya knew she could not bend her implacable man to her will.

However, being altogether feminine, she could not forgo probing to learn why he had asked about her father and Tamara's mother. "Supposing," she said, swiveling the stem of her brandy glass between her fingers, "Tamara really *was* my half sister?"

His chin set stubbornly. "I'd have to send him away, little dove."

Ronya smiled. "Boris dear, I think you must be part von Glasman, too."

Ronya was privately dismayed when she saw that Lydia had packed only two bags for her trip, but she contained her curiosity outwardly as she settled into the carriage and set off. She was even more dismayed when the coachman turned, at the first branch of the main road, onto a small road that led deep into their own property. Under a starry sky he drew up a half hour later, and through the trees she had her first glimpse of an enchanting house that had not been there the last time she rode this way.

A moment later, as Boris carried Ronya across the threshold of the house beneath the pines, she felt that at last he was not Boris the Arghun—the half Tartar. Ronya had the genius of her race to survive; Boris was prey to the superstitions and myths of his. But in that hour, the past forgotten, the future unknown, Ronya was young with excitement, Boris royally proud.

It was an entrancing house, ceilings high, fireplace huge, stone floors smooth as still water. On one side was a kitchen, its counters set at exactly the right height for its small mistress, on the other a bedroom, and beyond a separate porch shaded by a glorious old tree was reached by three steps of uncut rock.

The furniture made an amusing pattern of small and large for the two of them—Ronya's dressing table, under kerosene lamps, delicate and dainty; the chair beside her bed scaled to her measure; Boris' armchair and writing desk properly large for him. The cushioned sofa before the fire and the sturdy bed were heroic.

"It's *good*," Ronya breathed. "I can't wait to see it by daylight."

"Patience," Boris gentled his ardent wife. "Tomorrow I'll show you the cold cellar, built under the ground. We could fight a war from there, store thousands of rounds of ammunition— and feed an army."

Ronya shuddered. "Boris," she said, "are you thinking of the grotesque Rasputin and German Alix?"

He tried to dispel the worry in her voice. "Sorry, little dove. It happens with me now. I begin to think of our Ukraine as a separate country."

She let it go at that, went into the bedroom and kicked off her slippers. Not until she was sitting in her robe at the dressing table, a ribbon in her long hair, did he join her. "How beautiful it all is," she said, turning at his entrance.

"Your father gave you everything," he said without bitterness. "I wanted to give you a little something, too, my Ronya."

For three days they rose early. They rode over hills carpeted with clean pine needles. Evenings they sat before the fire talking and laughing. And at night, passionate and virile, Boris was a worthy mate to Ronya. They slept the sweet sleep of contentment.

The morning Boris and Ronya drove home, winter began. A slight snow was falling.

In the dim light of the stable, the men stood around Boris, hands in pockets, uncomfortable at the enforced idleness, caps pushed back from foreheads, straws between teeth, unnaturally quiet except for the sound of shuffling feet. Igor stood with his father; the Blond One, the boy who was not called son by his sire, behind him, waiting.

The big man straightened and turned to his eldest son. "The stables are yours, Igor," he announced authoritatively. Grooms, trainers, drivers and stable hands flashed quick, questioning glances one to another. "Now that you have them, forget them. You'll be in my regiment in a few weeks. I'm satisfied that you will do your duty. Meanwhile, enjoy yourself with Julie. The Blond One will be your deputy in charge."

The arrangement suited the two young men so well that they spontaneously hugged and pounded each other. The men caught the infectious outburst and milled around Boris' sons. The life and fame of the stables was guaranteed; their work would go on and new ribbons would be hung up in the tack room. They danced and kicked up their heels. Even the horses threw back their heads. Boris raised a restraining hand.

"Igor," he instructed his son, "hold our lady, the Empress Marie, in reverence when she is pleased to receive you into her guard of honor." There was a special vibrance in his voice.

"Fetch vodka, Sad Eyes," Boris ordered. He had a couple of drinks, then left the men to get drunk by way of celebrating Igor's and the Blond One's new authority. As Boris walked slowly toward the house, the Blond One, standing in the open doorway, again noticed his slight limp.

XIII

IGOR did not need to be told to enjoy himself. Where he disregarded his father's injunction was in not taking his pleasures with Julie. She proceeded with her lessons and household tasks, unperturbed and happy.

Only when his departure was imminent did Igor begin to haunt the house, following her from room to room, pestering her to promise she would miss him terribly and think of no one else once he was gone. Dutifully, her blue eyes wide and unblinking, she promised, and he vowed to love only her. "From morning to night," he said, "I'll be a soldier. From night to morning I'll think of you."

"When will you sleep?" she asked.

About a week before his twenty-first birthday Igor made so bold as to interrupt Julie in the middle of her lessons. Father Tromokov, who was tutoring her, pretended to take no notice, but when the boy lingered, he put down his book and asked sternly, "What is the meaning of this intrusion, Igor?"

"I have to talk to Julie."

"You may go now," said the priest. "And the next time you come in here, knock before you open the door."

Unabashed, Igor winked at Julie. "I think I liked your first tutor better. At least he minded his own business when I came to kiss my girl goodbye."

"Oh, no!" Julie protested. "You promised to take me——" She laid down her book. "Please, Father, may Igor and I talk a minute?"

The older man's eyes softened. "Just five minutes," he said gruffly and went to the corner table at the far end of the room to pour himself a drink.

For a moment there was silence while Igor bent his dark head and nuzzled Julie's cheek. "What are you reading?" he asked, self-consciously.

"A lovely book! All about France and Russia and how Napoleon Bonaparte invaded . . ." she rambled on cheerfully.

Tromokov's glass was empty. He looked at his watch. "In exactly two minutes, Igor," he said severely, "out!"

"I'm sorry about tonight. I'll take you tomorrow instead. *Swan Lake.* You'll love it. I'd forgotten our date and promised Anton Yurieff I'd go with him to the swearing-in of conscripts. Afterwards, he wants me to have dinner at the officers' club."

"All right," she said. "Have a good time," and returned to her reading before Igor was out of the room.

Igor Pirov, civilian, and Anton Yurieff, career captain in the Imperial cavalry, trudged doggedly through the gathering dusk, a raw wind lashing and buffeting them. Their destination, when they came in sight of it, was a wooden shack so dilapidated that Igor, his chin dug into his collar against the cold, lost all enthusiasm for the caper ahead, though Anton had promised him a rare bit of sport.

"The hell with this, Anton," he said. "I'm going back to the club where it's warm and I can recoup my losses. See you later."

Yurieff scoffed, "It'll be cold in hell the day *you* win at cards. But your old man wins twice what you lose, so what's the odds?"

"You won't believe me," Igor laughed, "but so help me, Julie beats him!"

"He lets her," Anton said. "Or she cheats."

Igor turned his back to the wind to catch his breath.

"Come on, Igor," the captain grumbled. "This filthy wind is getting stronger."

"So what's the great show I'm going to see?"

Yurieff warmed at the prospect. "I have a bastard of a sergeant, a genius at hazing. I leave the torture to him and watch the fun."

"It'd better be good."

"It will," Anton said. "It's their physical."

He assumed that Igor knew the barracks customs as well as he did—how on these occasions Jewish recruits were singled out

121

for special attention. It never occurred to Anton, however, that Igor might have reason to find the goings-on less than entertaining; that, as a Jew, he might be offended by the abuse of his race. Everyone from Kiev to St. Petersburg was familiar with the fact that his mother was a von Glasman, but the family could not possibly be identified with the anonymous rabble swept up in the net of army conscription. Igor was important in the same terms that, elsewhere in Europe, the scion of the house of Rothschild was important.

In a makeshift building at the center of a stony square, the young men climbed two flights of stairs, glad to be out of the cold. At the top they found themselves in an ugly box of a room, barren of furnishings except for a rickety straight chair and a dusty wooden table overlaid with induction forms. Behind it a sergeant, a short, stocky brute of a man with powerful shoulders, stood beside a large window. Around the walls were clownish louts, many of whom looked imbecilic. A few soldier servants idled on the outskirts of the crowd.

Though no command was given, the conscripts gradually drifted together at one end of the room in a forlorn crowd whose only bond was that they were all Jews. Among them was Igor's dear friend, Duvid Bulatski. Igor tried to catch his eye and speak but Duvid deliberately looked over his head.

From the sorry group rose the stink of nervous sweat and Igor sensed another smell—the odor of ancient hatreds. He had taken a step in Duvid's direction, at which the other Jews roused briefly from their resigned apathy to glance at him curiously. Fleetingly, he sensed their disgust.

Yurieff, oblivious of the undercurrents of feeling about him, made his way jauntily to Igor's side, issued an order for a soldier to open the big window and said gaily, "We're all set."

Thereupon the sergeant barked, "Strip, Jews!"

Fingers cold and clumsy, each man struggled with buttons and shoelaces, removed layer after layer of clothes and piled them in a neat bundle at his feet, until he stood naked.

Anton, apparently stirred by the sight of so much bare masculinity, put an arm across Igor's shoulders. So quickly did Igor shake it off and start across the room that Captain Yurieff was startled but decided his friend probably was seeking a better vantage point from which to see what was happening. He nodded to the sergeant to proceed.

"Get going!" the man boomed.

At that a soldier picked up one of the heaps of clothing and flung it out the open window.

"Four minutes, Christ killer," the sergeant howled, "to retrieve your putrid rags." There was no mistaking his amusement at the man's plight.

Igor's voice cut through the sudden stillness like a sliver of steel. "Refuse!"

The Jew, who was already scurrying toward the door, paused at the sound and turned for an instant toward that authoritative voice, loathing on his face at what he could only suppose was additional baiting. Then, quickly, he lurched through the door and was gone. Like his victim, Yurieff presumed that Igor had chosen to heighten the comedy. From window to icy slush below went pile after pile of pathetic clothes, each pursued by a naked man, running in unwavering obedience. Laughter rose among the soldiery at every ludicrous departure and breathless return.

When Duvid's turn came, he refused.

The laughter died and the sergeant shoved past the soldiers to confront Duvid. He found Igor looming in his path.

"Dismiss!" bawled Captain Anton Yurieff.

Igor's face darkened, his shoulders straightened. "Not so fast —friend!" he said.

"Cut it out, Igor. Don't be a fool."

Igor did not answer. He glanced at the captain venomously and began to take off his clothes. When he was quite naked, he arranged his clothes in an orderly bundle, impervious to the all-but-audible wave of shock that ran around the room.

The champion of the Ukraine, the hero and aristocrat, heir of the greatest house on the Dnieper, stood before them stripped. Like the other Jews he was circumcised.

"Throw my clothes out," he commanded the goggling sergeant.

Anton, desperate and frightened now, tried to intervene. "Igor! A lion doesn't go with a goat."

123

It was as though he had not spoken. "Throw my clothes out!" Igor reiterated. "Then fetch them back with those of my friend. Four minutes, pig!"

Veins thickening in his throat, the sergeant snarled, "You don't give orders around here, Jew boy!"

The blow that Igor landed on the man's face smashed his mouth to a bloody pulp.

What followed was inevitable and short. Against Igor's skill as a boxer the sergeant could not land a single blow. However, in a momentary lull, he scooped up Igor's clothes and sent them flying through the window, and found breath to taunt, "At least your old man's blond bastard isn't clipped, is he?"

Igor moved slowly, catlike, Boris-like, his hands seeming to have a separate vitality of their own. Strong as a vise they closed around the sergeant, lifted that chunky man and heaved him through the window.

There was no sound until Igor addressed the captain. "The fun is over," he said and, to one of the soldiers, "Get my clothes. I want them brushed and pressed."

"Yes, sir, Gospodin Pirov, my pleasure."

Anton shook himself out of his daze. "Man, that was beautiful," he said. Duvid handed Igor someone's coat.

In an instant the mood changed and Yurieff ordered beer to be brought. It had not yet arrived when the young soldier who had been detailed to retrieve Igor's and Duvid's clothes, burst into the room carrying them any which way. Deathly pale, he dropped them in front of Igor, went and whispered to the captain.

"You're certain?"

"Yes, sir."

"Igor," said Anton, "he's dead. His neck is broken. I'm sorry, I have to place you under arrest."

Igor paled.

The captain put on his greatcoat and turned up the collar. "Remain here," he said to the room at large from the doorway. "You are all witnesses. There was no fight. I was engaged in paperwork at the time and saw nothing of the accident."

On the way down the stairs Igor asked a favor.

"I will, of course, report myself to the commandant. Would

124

you do me the great kindness of going to my mother and telling her the whole truth, in detail? But be sure Julie doesn't over-hear you."

Already running, Yurieff called over his shoulder, "Of course. I'm on my way."

Twenty minutes later Igor was standing before Colonel Greg-ory Simmovich, a hard-eyed man, by repute addicted to violence but known to be devoted to Igor.

"Sit down, son," the colonel said.

Standing, Igor spoke formally. "This is official, sir. I had a run-in with a bastard of a sergeant and he got hurt."

The colonel chuckled. "Did you beat him up?"

"Yes, sir."

"Badly hurt?"

"Dead hurt, sir."

"You killed the sergeant with your bare hands?"

"No, sir."

"Sit down, Igor." This time Igor obeyed.

"Now talk!" the officer said, and talk Igor did.

When the whole story had been told, the colonel frowned. "Most irregular," he said.

"He's here to talk to you privately. About Master Igor." Lydia sucked in her breath noisily. "I always said that Captain Yurieff was a bad influence."

"Where's Julie?" Ronya cut her off.

"She's upstairs writing to Georgi. Don't fret about *her*. By the time she's looked up every little word in that dictionary, she'll be hours."

"Show the captain into the library, Lydia. Give him a drink and say I'll be right down."

He had not had time to pour it before Ronya, with a haste born of anxiety, was in the room. By an immense effort of will she made herself walk slowly, and look composed. "How good of you to come, Anton!" He might have dropped in for tea. "Let's sit here by the fire. You must be freezing after your ride."

But she was already at the end of her tether and abandoned make-believe.

"Is Igor hurt?"

"No, Mistress Ronya, he's fine."

"What is it then?"

He told her the whole story then, and Ronya listened with every part of her being. When there was nothing to add, she rose and said, "Excuse me while I send for my husband," and rang for Lydia.

"I want Boris at once," she said. "If he's not in the stables, every man there is to turn out and hunt for him." She came back to Anton and resumed her sociable manner. "May I pour you another drink? Something to eat, perhaps?"

"Thank you, no," he stammered. "Got to get back to the post. Shall I take a message to Igor?"

"Yes," said Ronya. "Tell him whatever he does to keep his mouth shut."

Christ, what a woman! Anton marveled. No wonder Igor worships her.

He had gone and Ronya was standing on the front porch when Boris emerged from the trees and came across the lawn, running. Even so she called, "Hurry!"

"What's happened?" he panted.

She took both his hands in hers and shook her head dolefully. Upstairs in her own room, she kicked the door shut and sobbed out the whole ghastly episode. "I'm frightened, Boris!" And that admission cut him more deeply than her tears.

Two hours later the adjutant reported to his colonel, "He just rode in, sir."

"On his white stallion?"

"Yes, sir. Wearing full uniform. Very imposing."

In a private sitting room, smelling of well-polished wood and fine leather, where food and vodka were set out, the two old acquaintances met and drew armchairs up before a blazing fire.

"Why so late getting here?" asked Colonel Simmovich.

"There was a hurry?" Boris' eyebrows rose a trifle theatrically.

"I waited supper for you."

"Good of you. I'm starving."

The commandant poured vodka, raised his glass and toasted, "To Igor!" Then they filled their plates and, true to his word, Boris ate hugely and with evident enjoyment. After the table

126

had been cleared and they had lit cigars, the colonel asked, "Ready to talk?"

"Any time."

"Want to play a few hands? I feel lucky," said Simmovich.

"I've got all night."

His vis-à-vis laughed. "I like your nerve. Let's talk. Things look hopeful. When Igor stands trial there will be no trouble—no evidence, no witnesses. The men, like blind deaf-mutes, will have seen nothing, heard nothing."

"There'll be no trial."

The officer stiffened. "Be reasonable, Boris. I've got a corpse on my hands."

"Bury it."

"And if someone cleans house—and digs it up?"

"Ronya and I leave for St. Petersburg tomorrow. The whole matter will be taken care of from there."

"Boris, I have got to notify—"

"Gregory, I've just lost two stallions and a thousand rubles."

The corner of Simmovich's mouth curled under his military moustache. "Your deal," he said.

Boris went to the table and began shuffling the pack. "Do not, under any circumstances, turn Igor over to the civil authorities while we're gone. If the sergeant left a family, see that they're taken care of. Add your expenses to my gambling lesson."

"Anything else?"

"Yes. Those fifty recruits. All unfit for military service. Give them a month's pay and send them home."

"Forty-nine, Boris, faceless and nameless. But not the Bulatski lad."

"You're right," Boris acknowledged. "Hold Duvid for the time being but treat him well."

They played a token hand or two, listlessly, the business of the evening being concluded. Boris glanced at his watch. "I'm spending the night in town. Where's Igor? May I see him?"

"Down the corridor. First door to your left. He's got a double room."

"Thank you, Gregory. Good night."

The next morning father and son breakfasted together. "Your

127

mother and I will be back in about a week," Boris said. "Don't try to see Julie and above all else, don't talk. Father Tromokov will visit you. Rely on him."

From the post Boris rode to the center of town to call on the chief of police for Kiev. Nikita Orloff was an excellent official, and like his province's police chief, Mischuk, incorruptible. He and Boris, in the course of dealings over the years, had developed genuine respect for each other's characters and integrity. Quite recently the bonds between them had been further strengthened. Orloff was an active advocate of the Ukrainian movement.

To have a call from Boris was usual enough, but to have him arrive early in the morning in full dress uniform with all his medals shining on his chest reduced Orloff to silence. Taking advantage of the attention granted him, Boris told the whole tale, evading none of its implications.

"You are quite right, Boris," Orloff concurred at the end. "The incident must be wound up in St. Petersburg."

"Am I to understand from that, Nikita, that you will make no official investigation?"

"Officially the affair is entirely out of my jurisdiction, a matter of concern only to the military."

"Good! I'm glad you see it that way." Boris rose.

"One thing more, Boris. I don't like seeing you exposed like this. Your friend Colonel Simmovich is a dangerous man and an accomplished blackmailer. He can bleed you for a lifetime."

"You have proof of that?"

"I have data a mile long. He is also a small-time secret agent and befriender of the Black Hundreds. In May 1900 he did nothing to stop them from staging a pogrom—against my orders—on a Jewish village that lay in his command area. My file on his graft could send him to Siberia. Would you like to read it?"

"Only if I have to, which I doubt I shall. He won't cross me. As for my gambling losses," Boris grinned, "there'll be other games." He pointed at the filing cabinets. "Got anything on Captain Anton Yurieff?"

"Never heard of him. Do you know anything against the man?"

Boris shrugged. "An ordinary officer."

"A change of scene might be in order?"

Boris flicked the ash from his cigarette and rose. "Good idea. See you when I get back," he said.

Ronya took a great deal of trouble over the story she told Julie, but there was no evading the fact that Igor was in trouble and that she and Boris must go to St. Petersburg. The child sat, hands limp in her lap, hair touched with sun from the breakfast-room window, looking very doleful and puzzled.

"It's no use, Ronya, my mother, I'll never understand him."

With that she began to cry slow tears that rolled down her fair cheeks unchecked. She was still crying when Boris got home. He carried her upstairs and Ronya put her to bed. Lydia brought hot tea, fortified with brandy and lemon, which, to please Boris, she drank.

"Julie, my dear, you have Lydia," Ronya comforted. "The Blond One will take good care of you, too. But we have to leave. The sooner this bothersome matter is settled, the sooner Igor will come home to you."

"Don't leave me," Julie moaned. "I feel dizzy and there's a terrible pressure on my chest."

Lydia was too down to earth for any such nonsense. "I'll soon fix that. A hot garlic and onion plaster is the best medicine. Don't be afraid, little mistress, you won't blister badly."

The mere mention of the treatment was a cure. Julie at once admitted, in a frail voice, to feeling better.

When the hour for parting came, she clung to Ronya and charged her to tell Georgi how much she missed him, then threw herself into Boris' arms.

"Give me a little smile, Julie," he cajoled her, and, childlike, she tried.

A team of three black horses drew the carriage, emblazoned with the Pirov colors, through mud and slush and rain and the biting wind from the Gulf of Finland. A few miles outside St. Petersburg the Pirovs transferred to a sleigh with thin runners for the snow.

The city was already dazzling white and snow whirled and

eddied along the broad avenues. Through the cruel cold, Boris drove at a fearsome pace along the quays, past fashionable shops and restaurants and along the street of embassies, churches and the opera house. Doormen in black caracul coats, Cossacks on horses, droshky drivers with frozen beards, looked up and were transfixed. They recognized the driver before they saw his colors and shouted gleefully to each other: "Boris Pirov rides!"

In their palatial house, Count and Countess Alexis Brusilov, together with Ronya and Boris Pirov, received their guests in a vast hall, the crystal of chandeliers tinkling each time the door opened, conversation dropping a little each time the majordomo announced another regal name. The last of all was Her Majesty's.

She kissed Katya, admiring again the flawless bearing of the woman and the inspired way she wore clothes. She kissed Ronya, held her off and said, "Let me look at you, child." In that moment her heart, rather than her eyes, saw, and the old queen was lonely for the father of these remarkable daughters.

Balls were commonplace at the beginning of the twentieth century in the capital of Russia, but this, one of the last great ones, was long remembered. As the hours passed, protocol gave way to adventure—gentlemen chose partners without taking thought of consequences. The Empress claimed Boris for her escort and he, having consumed enormous quantities of vodka, told stories which would otherwise scarcely have passed muster, danced wild Russian dances, and waltzed his sovereign to the banquet table.

On that night, the Empress Maria, Queen Mother of Russia, was again faithful to David von Glasman. And Count Alexis Brusilov collected a political debt. She promised to sanction the arrangements he planned to make.

For a few hours the "incident" was discussed in ornate corridors of the Admiralty and in the office of the Chief of Staff.

The decision, in essence, was summed up in four parts:

I. That Captain Igor von Glasman Pirov be fined a quarter of four months' pay for being out of uniform while on duty.

II. That the same Captain Pirov proceed to Manchuria to take command of the military post at Harbin and to assist in guarding the harbor of Port Arthur under the command of Piotr Yarsolov.

III. Said duty to continue for not less than six months or more than one year. At which time he return to his regiment for further orders.

IV. That Igor von Glasman Pirov, a captain in the service of his Imperial Highness at the time of the accident, was within his military rights in taking action against an insolent sergeant.

The incident was closed.

Boris and Ronya did not get back to Kiev in time to say goodbye to Igor. At the invitation of the commandant, Father Tromokov and Julie had a day with him, however. He was delighted with his assignment, delighted, too, that Duvid would be traveling with him.

XIV

ONE month to the day after he waved goodbye to Father Tromokov and Julie, Igor, weather-beaten and bearded, rode into Port Arthur on the narrow saddle of a Mongolian pony and made his way to the naval base. A sentry, alerted to his arrival, saluted and said, "The captain is expected at the residence of the admiral. Full dress, sir. Eight o'clock sharp. I am to escort the captain to his apartment in the officers' quarters."

The naval barracks, Igor sensed at once, was much like the cavalry barracks in Kiev, where the main activities were drinking, gaming and the exchange of soldierly banter. Wanting,

131

above everything else, to shave, bathe and amuse himself with his fellow officers, he dutifully resisted temptation.

An hour and fifty minutes later Igor was the recipient of a garlic-tinctured kiss on either cheek. Admiral Piotr Yarsolov bestowed these benevolences, he made it clear, as suitable toward the son of an old friend.

"True, I'm an admiral," the bearded worthy declaimed, "and you are only a captain. However, between us, my boy, there'll be no social distinctions. I want you to think of me as a father." Igor hoped he did not show his embarrassment at this effusion. "Now that I contemplate your face I know why, from the moment you walked in the door, I felt so well disposed toward you. You're the spittin' image of Ronya, your mother. It makes me feel young just to look at you."

The admiral had barely begun. He babbled on and on, commanding Igor to drink with him while he unburdened himself of dull confidences, punctuated with such disclaimers as, "Wouldn't dream of sharing my secrets with an ordinary officer, y'know." Poor Igor was reduced to chanting, "Yes, sir," at the expected intervals and swallowing rising yawns as best he might.

At the words "My very special dinner guests will be here soon," Igor was cheered at the prospect of relief from this tedious old bore. "We'll kiss 'em—just the way the fox kissed the hen right down to her tail feathers." The admiral laughed at his borrowed wit. "You'll be here for several days of instruction and indoctrination before going on to your service in Harbin. Consider this evening your first lesson. If you think of us (you and me) as fellow guardians of our Little Father, all will be well. I'll rephrase that. Consider yourself the soldier who pulls the trigger, and me the leader who directs your fire. That way, when the time comes, we both go before God with clean hearts.

"Now to the plain facts. Adam ate the apple. Russia eats Manchuria, all Siberia and Korea. Very sustaining fare. But Nippon is the snake in the grass. Aims to stop us. To extend her own sphere of influence. Greedy! Greedy! This we cannot allow, clearly we cannot. The Little Father desires us to annex. Understand?"

"Annex what, sir?"

"Everything." The admiral made a vague and sweeping gesture. "All the vastness between the Urals and the Pacific Ocean. Does that please you?"

Igor closed his mind, forced open his eyes, and said, "Yes, sir."

"Good. This evening should be valuable to you. I have included several prominent Nipponese citizens and two of their high-ranking naval officers among my guests. It is good to know your enemy, advisable to understand him. Take notice. Be on your toes."

"Yes, sir."

"Damned inferior people." The admiral drew himself up and spread his shoulders. "Shorter than we are. No feelings. No feelings at all. Nonentities, that's what they are, with the gall to intrude on what properly belongs to Russia. Keep all this in mind for your special assignment."

It was a miserable evening. Igor, trusting by nature and an innocent when it came to intrigue, took no part in the conversation, not from prudence but because the liquor, heavy meal and heat of the rooms made him unbearably sleepy. All his energy was concentrated on staying awake.

Piotr Yarsolov, admiral of the naval base of Port Arthur through no merit of his own but because his mother was a Romanov connection, decided that the son of Ronya was very clever. He plays the fool to deceive our rivals! What an excellent decision of the high command to send him here!

Only a profoundly stupid man would have tried to make a spy out of Igor Pirov; but a spy, Igor, no man to question orders, became—a part-time spy on horseback. In Harbin, where he went to take up his duties, the Chinese were attracted by his naïve boyishness and his dimpled smile and soon came to love him. However, Igor was not so guileless as to take his spying very earnestly. His command occupied most of his time and called out his real talents; Igor shaped up a well-disciplined fighting unit. Never had Harbin been so well policed, its citizenry so protected against robber bands.

From the beginning he was drawn to the Chinese and, despite a total ignorance of their language, Igor believed he understood them. His spying took him down to Pristan, the congested dock area, a part of the city he loved. The Sungari brothels and gaming houses and dives were gathering places for buyers and sellers of rumors and gossip.

The handsome Russian cavalry officer was soon known as a man who could easily be parted from his money—a fat pigeon. Deckhands, sailors, poor owners of sampans and rich masters of sailing vessels that carried harvests to market from the fertile hinterland, captains of barges that loaded timber, all shaped a course for Igor. From everyone he bought misinformation.

Only one person spoke unvarnished truth to him and that was Anna Marie, who ran a famous house and was regarded as first Madam of Manchuria. She scolded him for being a gullible novice. "The Nipponese are clever, industrious, cunning, and brave," ran her briefing. She also provided him with girls, though she was chary of what foreigners she admitted to her bordello.

It was many weeks before Igor received the one summons that he wanted. Huang Hui Tsung, of whose father he had heard so much from Ronya, was lord and ruler of the Manchurian Chinese. On the day he was bidden to tea, Igor found he was nervous. He dressed with minute attention, discarding three clean handkerchiefs before he found one in his drawer which he considered satisfactorily folded. "I'll be back when I'm back," he told his lieutenant. "You know where to find me if you need to."

Igor was no stranger to elegance but he was staggered by the Huang compound. Across the threshold a maze of buildings confronted him: an observatory, pagodas, temples, dwelling houses, pavilions, storehouses, galleries, terraces of white marble—constituting a walled city. Within the massive outer fortifications and overlooked by periodic observation towers, were secondary walls dividing compounds and courtyards, penetrated by ornamental gates.

Huang Hui Tsung received Igor in the study of the main house, a room rich with books and manuscripts and paintings, opening onto its own garden of flowers and foliage, bronze and stone statuary. Igor bowed low and found it impossible to disentangle the man before him from the image of his father Ronya

134

had painted. That he was old was certain, but what age it was impossible to guess, so fine-drawn was the ivory skin. He was frail insofar as he moved with the slow, deliberate tempo of age; yet hands as well as face were unlined. Only the withdrawn eyes gave the impression of endless expanses of time lived and stored away.

Igor was immeasurably relieved when Huang greeted him in flawless, unaccented Russian, thanked him for coming and motioned him to sit down. If his own Tsar had told him to be seated in the imperial presence, Igor could not have been more conscious that he was being honored by an absolute monarch.

He took his place on a low ottoman beside a lacquered table, and servants poured tea into spinach-hued jade cups and passed little cakes, thin as parchment. As Huang Hui Tsung spoke of David von Glasman, he studied his grandson to discover physical resemblances.

"He was," Huang concluded, "a man so fiercely loyal to his sovereign that my father, whose interests were seldom his, came to cherish him above all men for his incorruptibility."

He paused, considering the nature of loyalty, and, following his scholar's bent, launched into a disquisition on the nature of faith and truth and goodness—pure goodness in and of itself good. Igor, who thought of himself as an intellectual when he was with his Russian admiral, felt like a barbarian before this subtle, wonderfully cultivated Chinese.

Without warning he was brought up short. Huang seemed to take on added physical stature and dynamism as he said, "Igor von Glasman Pirov, you bear a proud name. You wear the honorable dress of a cavalry officer. Why, then, are you a spy? A very bad one, I might add."

So this was the reason for the words on truth and goodness! Igor was so caught off balance that he responded with the plain facts of his situation. "I'm a good soldier, sir, though I can't deny being a bad spy. I obey orders. My superiors command me to gather information. Appraisal and amplification of what I find out is not demanded of me."

Huang slowly brought the fingertips of his left hand to touch the fingertips of his right and there was a faint suggestion of a pleased smile on his face. "Your assignment, captain," he said sternly, "is ill-judged and tasteless. It amuses and gives comfort to the—intruder. *And* it offends me and every other Chinese dignitary here."

"Yes, sir. I'm sorry, sir," Igor gulped.

"You will make this known to your superiors in your next report."

"Yes, sir." Igor sat waiting. The reprimand was surely the end of the interview, but he had no idea of the social conventions proper to making his farewells. Huang would, he assumed, dismiss him.

His host noted his uneasiness with approval, then said what he had known, for over an hour, he would say. "My own interest in you, Igor, transcends by far my distaste for the present ruler of your country. I shall, therefore, help you. Do not send that report. Carry on in your usual manner. Continue to be defrauded. Let confusion reign; it is of no importance. No earthshaking decision will be reached here in Manchuria. Look to Berlin, to Tokyo, to London and St. Petersburg for war and peace.

"If and when you seriously need aid, come to me. It may even comfort you to know that both for the welfare of my people and from choice I am aligned with Russia against the Japanese."

"Thank you, sir," said Igor, now thoroughly convinced that the time had come to leave.

"And Igor—don't call me 'sir.' "

"Yes, sir."

Their laughter brought down the barriers between them. Together they dined that night and Igor, like Huang, wore a Chinese robe. Later he slept in what was known as the room of Jerusalem, from whose walls frescoed patriarchs looked down. Its splendid Western furnishings and exquisite art objects had been the gift of David von Glasman.

The intimacy established that night deepened with the passing weeks. To no other living man except the Blond One had Igor talked so frankly of what was closest to his heart, of his mother and Julie and, boastfully, of Boris, of Georgi and Katya and Alexis. He even described Lydia, mimicking her rolling gait. But he never mentioned Tamara.

Alexis had tried unsuccessfully to teach Igor to play chess with

136

his grandfather's white jade chessmen. Now, with Huang, he enjoyed the game, though he never could, at the last, win. And gradually he began to master Chinese; he had an excellent ear and a sympathetic teacher.

Huang, too, learned from Igor the meaning of the word 'son.' Watching Igor ride and win cavalry races, he felt a father's pride.

Igor received long accounts from his mother of the estate and its people, short fond letters from the Blond One reporting progress of the stables, unwilling scrawls from Georgi, bragging about his run-ins with authority, and meticulous, conventional letters from Julie. Even Boris, never happy with pen in hand, wrote occasional notes about the horses, the weather, the crops and how Julie was growing more adorable every day.

Igor's replies were stilted and infrequent, many of them written in Huang's study or the room of Jerusalem. From the first he sent more gifts than letters to Julie, chests, lacquered boxes, brocades, jade bowls and lapis lazuli; to the Blond One a splendid saddle; Ronya a remarkable whip; Boris a T'ang horse and Georgi a scroll painting of Chinese dragons.

"In Port Arthur," Igor wrote, pausing often to chew the end of his pen, "my duties keep me on the go. Here in Harbin I am free as a bird most of the time. A first-rate lieutenant sees to routine chores for me—policing and all that, now that I have it running—which leaves me more time to concentrate on learning Chinese. It's an infuriating language, but important to my job, so I sweat it out every day. The monosyllabic words are easy enough but the different tones are pure hell. Huang laughs at me, says it's not at all hard (not for him!) and I have a gift for making a witty language ridiculous."

His letters were all addressed to the family except one which was intended for his mother's eyes alone.

"I know of no words," he wrote, "to describe the walled city within the city of Harbin, or Huang's palace, or him. He is tall, almost as tall as I and far thinner. Often he is a westerner, a fastidious gentleman whose bearing puts me in mind of Uncle Alexis. At other times he is the great one, a sort of prince. Sometimes I find him damned inscrutable. He sits, a figure of tranquillity, mysterious and bloodless, his lids drooping, turning prayer beads between his fingers. The shift from the hard-headed realist whom I recognize and understand, to the Oriental mystic, is very confusing.

"You would love to hear him talk about Grandfather. He tells wonderful stories of those days. Except that he has no real interest in horses and sports, I think Huang Hui Tsung is the most remarkable person I have ever known."

Another letter came for Ronya, delivered by private courier at a time when Boris was away from Kiev.

Ronya, my lady,

China has taken a deep hold on your son Igor. His days and nights are filled with adventure, not all to my liking. However, 'Light and sun rise from darkness.' At his age I, too, fancied myself the conqueror of a dream. The delicate contours, the preference for gentler notes, emerge later.

In the twilight, Igor and I walk in my walled garden. From a distance we hear the eternal chanting of monks, the ringing of silver bells.

If I have had my pipe, I indulge in the pleasing delusion that Igor is my son. I shall preserve this fancy. I want Igor to go back to the blue-eyed Julie who waits for him. Igor rides a tiger.

Your devoted servant,
Huang Hui Tsung

It was a good month after the last packing case of gifts had arrived from Manchuria before anyone noticed that no letters had been received.

At last even Julie realized that Igor's silence was overlong and began to feel apprehensive. One morning she found Ronya at her writing table composing a letter to Huang, in which she was expressing her own anxiety. Folding the paper quickly, she inquired gently, "What is it, Julie? You look pale."

"I'm worried about Igor."

"That's silly," Ronya said with a joviality she was far from feeling. "Igor loves to send presents and hates to write letters. He's probably on spring maneuvers, anyway. It may be weeks and weeks before we hear again."

Julie sat down close to her adopted mother. "I'm a little scared."

"But darling," Ronya reached out and took the girl's hand, "if Igor were sick or in some sort of trouble, we'd have been notified. Don't fret."

As though she had not heard, Julie looked up broodingly. "Do you believe in dreams, Ronya, my mother?"

Ronya smiled. "For you I believe in raw prunes and a good cathartic. Tell me your dream and then forget it."

"It was awful." Julie shivered. "Igor was falling from a high tower. I tried to catch him but I couldn't. In my dream I knew that only you had hands strong enough to hold him. I called to you to save Igor but you were trying on a new red dress in front of Boris and you didn't hear me."

Ronya got up. "Come along, child. Let's go for a walk."

They did not go far, just strolled along the path to the apple orchard. "Don't go reading meanings into your dream, dear," Ronya advised. "Dreams aren't a bit reliable, whatever the gypsies say. I wouldn't take yours seriously."

But that night Ronya's sleep was restless. When Lydia trundled in with her tea the next morning, she said, "If any letter comes from Harbin or Port Arthur, bring it directly to me. Don't leave it lying around on the hall table with the rest of the post."

The one that Lydia carried to her in her apron pocket a few days later had been mailed May 1, 1903. It bore an official seal: The Office of the Commander of the Naval Base of Port Arthur. Ronya locked her door before she tore away the seal and ripped open the envelope.

My dear Ronya,

When we were children you once said something I am sure you have forgotten but which I cannot. You called me a self-made coward. Perhaps you were right. I should be writing this to Igor's father, not to his mother. However, like most of your friends, I met Boris at your wedding. In all the years since I have had only an occasional encounter and so I cannot bring myself to write to him.

Enough beating about the bush! Here are the facts. Igor saved the life of a Mandarin girl in a boating accident; became involved with her—now, she is with child. Nothing unusual so far. What is serious about the affair is that the girl is Lotus, only child of Huang Hui Tsung, who wears silks of yellow, the color of an emperor. He is secular ruler of all Chinese Manchuria. He is the emblem of China. I cannot impress you deeply enough with his prestige and power.

Ronya, there are many puzzles, many unanswerable questions here. As you must know, in the East, gossip does not touch the disgrace of an aristocratic girl. Why, then, was I sent an unsigned letter written by a female hand in perfect Russian? Why does Igor remain unharmed, unthreatened, unpunished? Are the Chinese saving him for some unmentionable torture? According to custom, unless Igor marries her, Lotus must kill herself. It's beyond me.

Officially I cannot question him since there has been no complaint. But unofficially I have pleaded with him. "Marry the girl, Igor. I'll arrange an immediate transfer for you. A quiet divorce and no one the wiser."

This he refuses, says, "No, sir. Never! Julie, my wife-to-be, is waiting for me." And he will not fill in the forms necessary to get a transfer. I hesitate to ask for orders from St. Petersburg.

After debating a long time, Ronya, it seems to me that you should come at once. Maybe you can talk some sense into him.

Igor is a fine soldier, the best. He is popular with the Chinese and his men worship him.

Give my love to Tamara. Tell her I miss her spicy gypsy gossip as much as I miss Ronya's whip.

Your devoted friend and admirer,
Piotr Yarsolov

XV

ALL that day Ronya stayed locked in her room. When Lydia knocked loudly and Julie timidly, she sent them away, refusing both company and food, insisting that she had a terrible headache. Again and again she succumbed to crying spells, flinging herself dejectedly on her bed. She would splash water on her face then and, smoking incessantly, prowl up and down the room, trying to find a solution to the problem, some way to dispel the nightmare that encompassed her.

Toward evening she began to feel a return of her usual vitality and with it a course of action took shape in her mind. She opened the windows to clear the air of smoke, and unlocked her door. Just as she was finishing dressing, Boris came in, kissed her lightly on the lips and remarked agreeably, "Julie's already downstairs. I'll wash up and join you at dinner."

Ronya gave him a black look. "Where have you been all day?"

Irritated at her tone, Boris did not answer.

"Did you see Tamara?"

He said, "Yes," unselfconsciously.

"She makes herself useful, doesn't she?" Ronya's voice and her color were high. "I suppose her men brought in more wild horses so that she could summon you to come over and take your pick."

Boris grabbed Ronya roughly by the shoulders. "The minute Tamara's name is spoken you go out of your mind. I'm damn sick of it, Ronya. It's done. It's over. I will not let you cut yourself to pieces like this. Or cut me to pieces."

Far from appeased, Ronya jerked herself free. "Oh! Pour yourself a drink," she sneered. "You need it."

Then, in a small, very serious voice, she said, "Sit down,

141

please. I have to talk to you about Igor." She sank onto her chaise, with difficulty fighting down a desire to weep once more.

Boris looked down at the lovely, heart-shaped face and sorrowed for her. It was all so clear now that he knew she was disturbed about Igor. Ronya waited, silent, until he sat down.

"Nothing changes," she said. "Nothing at all. In Manchuria a Pirov child will be born to a Mandarin girl—to Huang's daughter."

She gave Boris the letter. He read it hastily. Black Tartar fury mounted in him but, not wanting to add to Ronya's misery, he kept his eyes lowered as he crushed the paper in his hand and flung it into the fireplace.

"Wordy bastard, isn't he? A fool like that commander of the Pacific fleet! Incredible!"

"Is that all you have to say?"

"No! Your friend Piotr is a raving idiot. Any mackerel could have pirated that flower."

"Do you really believe that, Boris?"

"What else is there to believe? Let's assume that Huang really has a daughter, though neither he nor Igor have ever mentioned her. Let's further assume, on meager evidence—an alleged letter written anonymously—that she's pregnant. Why Igor? And if he did fill that Chinese belly it must have been easy. With all his faults Igor is not the sort of fellow to betray a friend or seduce his daughter. Why hasn't Huang taken action? Either because Igor is innocent or no blame attaches to what he's done. It's the only possible answer."

With all her heart Ronya wanted to dismiss Piotr's letter as the folly of a fool. She could not. In her mind's eye she kept seeing the man she had never seen. She could not forget Julie's dream. And, strongest deterrent of all, she had learned long ago to trust her own heart.

Laying cold hands on his warm ones, Ronya said, "I'm going to Harbin, Boris."

As if he were a coiled spring suddenly released, Boris leaped to his feet. "Like hell you are!" he raged.

She gave him time to recover from his angry amazement, before speaking very gently. "Yes, my love, I am. I have to."

"Why?—Ronya—why?"

The anguish of his outcry shocked Ronya. Boris sat down on the floor beside her and tried to reach her heart through her mind. "What can you do in this improbable situation?" he asked slowly. "Marriage is out of the question. Huang is well able to take care of his daughter. *She* doesn't need you. As for Igor, you can't go on wiping his nose forever. He's a man, darling."

It was as though he had not spoken. Ronya only repeated, "I'm going. I have to go. Nothing can stop me. No one can stop me."

Silent at her feet, Boris admitted to himself that he did not care about Igor—he was fighting for himself. And he was losing the battle. Her mind was closed to argument. There was no use in trying to dissuade her. He capitulated. "All right, little dove. I can't hold you back. I'll go with you."

"No. I have to go alone."

The moment's silence between them was painful.

"Why?"

"Julie is one reason." Ronya was looking at him now. "She must never know. The rest? If it's necessary to explain, then you can't understand."

Boris knew and it frightened him. He felt shame that he was part of the cause, despair that the past would not die. All he wanted on earth was to keep Ronya physically at home. Suddenly he pulled her into his arms and kissed her passionately. "You know how much I need you," he pleaded, "how I love you. How can you think of leaving me?"

She pulled herself free. "I'm not leaving you," she said, as if she were speaking to a fractious child. "I'm just going away for a few weeks—that's all." And in a less gentle voice, "Knowing what fidelity meant to me. . . . Knowing how much I needed you—all of you—how could you be repeatedly unfaithful to me? How could you rob me for Tamara?"

The bitterness in his voice matched her own. "That's a fair comparison, Ronya," he said, and left the room.

Before he slept that night, Boris wrote a letter to Alexis and Katya which ended:

> It will serve no useful purpose to argue further. Ronya iden-
> tifies the accusation against Igor with my own past lapses. She

143

sees Lotus as Tamara (whom she still hates and yet can't help loving).

I feel sure that you will feel the way I do about Ronya's setting out on this journey. Thank heaven you are in Moscow. Perhaps by the time you meet her train she will be amenable to reason. Stop her if you can, I beg of you.

Boris

Ronya woke with a start in the middle of the night. Boris, by her side, asked, "What's the matter, little one?"

"The letter, Boris. I forgot to burn it."

"Go back to sleep. I've taken care of it." His arm tightened around her, and she touched his lips with her fingertips. "I do love you, Boris," she murmured sleepily. "I'll never know why. But when I'm angry or frightened I have to hurt you.' He held her still tighter and in a moment she slept.

When Lydia appeared with the tea tray the next morning, Ronya said, "Sit down, my friend. We have some planning to do." As always, she confided everything to Lydia. At the end of her recital, the old woman nodded. "You are right to go, my mistress, and God go with you."

"It may be that I will not be welcome in the walled house," Ronya speculated. "Pack a large supply of bed linen and whatever I may need to stop at primitive inns. I shall count on you to see that everything here runs as usual but if there should be any difficulty, send for Katya."

The day passed in a flurry of preparations. After Boris returned from booking her railroad accommodations and getting a large supply of currency, Ronya finally had a moment with him.

"Write often to Georgi," she fussed. "If he gets home for a few days, do, please, keep an eye on him. Don't let him run wild."

Julie was told only that Ronya had to go to Moscow while Alexis and Katya were still there. "I'd like to take you with me, but—"

"Excuse me, Ronya, my mother," Julie interrupted. "But I honestly don't want to go. Boris, my father, would be lonesome with us both away. Besides, I want to be here if Georgi comes home."

When she parted from Julie next day, Ronya saw that she need have no misgivings. The girl was already consumed with pleasure at the prospect of playing young mistress. She gave Ronya a sunny smile, an affectionate hug and a warm kiss. "My love to my aunt and uncle."

Boris filled her arms with a great bunch of spring flowers, lifted her tenderly up the steep step and followed her into the compartment. "Good luck on your ridiculous journey, my pet. Come back to me soon." He kissed her and swung down onto the platform.

The train rolled through the flat lands, beige with young wheat, and the motion quieted Ronya's inner turmoil. Now she could put aside dark forebodings. She would soon know the truth. Her spirits rose.

Lying comfortably on the long red plush seat, she dreamed of her journey's end—of a man she imagined as majestic, wise and serene who would talk to her of her father and clear her son, to live in honor. All day she drowsed periodically and her delight increased. This would be a glorious adventure. It was a rested, restored Ronya who stepped off the train in Moscow.

There was no doubt in her mind, as soon as she laid eyes on Alexis and Katya, that they had been forewarned by Boris. Only Alexis opened his arms at her impetuous advance and embraced her warmly. Katya waited, withdrawn and stiff, her eyes blank. Her kiss was perfunctory.

"What in heaven's name did Boris manage to cram into his telegram besides the hour of my arrival?"

"Nothing!" Katya said. "The details of your mad undertaking and his plea, 'Stop her if you can,' came by mail yesterday."

"Oh, I'm sorry. I wanted to tell you everything myself."

"I expect you will." Katya's voice was hard with anger. "Somehow you'll doubtless succeed in justifying this stupid trip to Manchuria. It's an old story, your willfulness. What is it, Ronya? Has life become too tranquil for you? Does the new, adoring Boris bore you?"

Ronya's laugh broke in on this inquisition. "Boris bore me! Really, Katya, you are a silly."

Alexis took up for Katya. "Give us at least one good reason for your impetuous and, if I may be forgiven for saying so, rather theatrical behavior. Why must you do what we, who love you, feel is a mistake?"

Ronya's voice was warm, her expression soft. "A long time ago I saw a man and my heart said, 'You were born for him and he for you.' Now my heart says, 'Run to Manchuria, Ronya. Igor needs you.'"

"Remarkable!" Alexis said. Katya, who had known the ways of Ronya's heart all her life, smiled. She touched Ronya's hand. "Go, little sister," she said. "You have the perfect reason."

While porters passed the luggage in through the open window, Ronya, at the end of the car, waved once more and threw one more kiss to Alexis and Katya. Then the train started and the conductor, a man called Lev, who had been liberally tipped by Alexis, bowed and escorted her to a compartment. There, while they traveled through the marshaling yards, he informed her, "Most ladies choose the lower bunk. That's a big mistake, Mistress Pirov. The upper one—that's the one. It's away from the vibration of the wheels." Ronya gave him an encouraging smile. "Tea with lemon and sugar is free for the first class. Ring anytime, day or night." Ronya nodded. "The next car is the diner. We serve good food. Good plain food. The steward purchases fresh butter, black bread, long white radishes, green onions, sour cream, caviar, fresh fish and fowl at each station. But no fruit, no fruit of any kind. I buy that from the peasant women. Right now wild berries are the best thing available. Shall I get you some?"

"Thank you, Lev," Ronya said softly. "That would be nice."

Entranced, Lev said earnestly, "In a train it is wise to be careful. Keep your door locked and be sure to fasten the safety catch before you go to sleep."

Again she thanked him. "I'll have dinner while the porter makes up the compartment," she said. "My linens and blankets are in the large trunk. I shall need only the suitcase on the seat. The rest of my luggage can be put away."

When Ronya entered the dining car, merchants, timber barons and naval officers looked up and fell silent as the steward led her through the smoke-filled carriage to an unoccupied table. Several men rose to pull out her chair and her thanks included them all and dismissed them all. A fleeting smile lighted the steward's face. "May I select a menu for Madame?"

Meal followed meal with a monotony matching the regularity of the stations on what came to seem an endless journey. Lev devotedly created small diversions for her, including a tour of the train. In the second class there were soldiers, sailors and workmen, and a few women traveling in search of husbands, preferably rich Orientals. Meanwhile, competing cheerfully among themselves, they plied their trade behind drawn curtains and, presumably, filled their stockings with rubles.

The stench of the lice-infested third-class car, the passive endurance of the women and children there, brought tears to Ronya's eyes. It was the poorest and dirtiest sight she had ever seen, some sixty humans crowded together, not counting swarming cats, dogs and goats. She had not dreamed, traveling only a few cars away in cleanliness and comfort, that poverty-stricken people were huddled on hard benches while their putty-faced children shared the aisle with animals in a morass of onion peels, skeletons of salt fish and droppings, human and animal.

Lev slammed the door.

"Why don't they use the toilet?" Ronya gasped.

"They get tired. The first day or two they stand in line for hours to reach the washroom. Then they just give up."

"But why isn't the car kept clean?"

"The dirt is older than they are. They don't mind. You'd be surprised how quickly such people get used to such things." Lev tried to comfort Ronya, whose concern was still manifest. "You are too soft-hearted, Mistress Pirov. 'The tears of peasants are only water.'"

How tragic, Ronya thought. In a few sentences this simple man has expressed the philosophy of a nation.

During the second week, for no apparent reason, since the train was in the middle of a field, it came to an abrupt halt in response to a red flag. Civilian and military officials swarmed aboard and ordered the first-class passengers into the dining car. There they waited while armed soldiers went through the second and third class. After a seemingly endless delay, an officer

147

announced: "All traffic in and out of Harbin is forbidden. There is an epidemic of Asiatic cholera and the city is under quarantine. It's spreading through the whole province."

Everyone started babbling hysterically. There were demands to return the train to Russia at once, threats, curses and something akin to panic.

"Silence!" shouted an official.

Only Ronya was not to be silenced. She declared, "My son is in Harbin. I must go on." She cajoled, "I'm not afraid of cholera. You'll need good nurses and I'm a good nurse." She threatened, "I am Ronya von Glasman Pirov. Not one of you has the authority to stop me."

There was no answer to that.

Then, for the first time, Ronya noticed a thin man, lips framed by a beard and pursed in concentration. He was watching her and, she sensed, reaching a decision. He moved to her side. "Ronya von Glasman Pirov," he said, "you are a formidable woman." She turned the full charm of her smile on this stranger. When he returned her smile, she felt that she had won. Together they made their way to a corner of the dining car where he spoke in a whisper. "My employer, Huang Hui Tsung, awaits you. Have you the strength and courage to continue?"

"Has a bird the strength to sing?"

"Very well," he regarded her levelly. "I am instructed to escort you to Harbin."

"Who are you?" Ronya asked and, receiving no answer, "How is Igor?"

"Two days ago he was well, though tired from his self-imposed duties."

He worked his way through the crowd to the front of the carriage, where he raised a hand for silence. "Your attention, please. The Trans-Siberian Railway has acceded to Madame Pirov's request. This train, stripped and emptied of all passengers except Madame and myself and of all employees except the engineer and his crew, will proceed to Harbin. You will all remain under military protection. Another train is already on the way from Moscow to pick you up. I earnestly request that you debark in an orderly fashion. The second- and third-class passengers have already left their cars."

It took nearly two hours to empty the first class of frantic, furious passengers. Two men plotted to bribe the engineer and steal the train to return them to European Russia. Others schemed to prevent its leaving for Harbin, and everybody succeeded in confounding the general confusion by pushing and shouting. A sharp command to "heave your belongings onto the track and get off" was met by a unanimous "No!"

A warning shot, fired into the air, had the desired effect. The passengers, aware that words were no match for guns, began to obey. Standing beside Ronya on the observation platform, the thin man spoke to the mass of upraised faces. "Anyone caught stealing will be shot. Look," he pointed southward, "about half a mile away you can see smoke. There is an encampment there where women are cooking soup, men are skinning game and drinking milk vodka. Knock on the door of any yurt and you'll be welcome. Hospitality is natural in this country."

The whistle shrilled through the thin air; officials jumped onto their Mongolian ponies; the train jerked and the cluster of angry passengers began to recede into the distance.

Ronya and her mysterious escort went to her compartment. Her curiosity about the man was almost past bearing, but she knew she would have to use every trick at her command to learn anything about him. Considering her first move, she opened her bag and took out a cigarette, which he lit for her. "Will you have one?" she asked.

"No, thank you," he said. "I see you carry a pistol."

"Loaded," said Ronya, "and I know how to use it, though frankly I feel safer with a whip in my hand."

"That's what I imagined."

"Excuse me," she countered quickly, "you said 'imagined.' Don't you mean that you knew?"

"Yes."

"Won't you please tell me your name?"

Without inflection he replied, "I go by many names."

"One will do."

"Give me a name and I'll answer to it."

"What did my father call you?"

"You really want to know?"

Ronya nodded.

149

"By birth I am a Pole. My father was accused of high treason and killed himself. I was nineteen at the time and a civilian but I was arrested and tried in his place. David von Glasman was my Zola. At the court-martial he defended me and won my acquittal. Since then my profession has been learning government secrets."

Ronya stared at this proud, lacerated man. "Would you tell me one more thing?" she asked. He nodded.

"Are you the mysterious secretary?"

"I served your father," he answered. "When he retired from public life, he sent me to Huang."

Knowing that she would get no more out of him, Ronya stood up, stretched and said, "I'm hungry. Now I'm going to the galley to get dinner for us and the crew. Come whenever you're ready, Ladislaus."

Nearly a quarter of a century had passed since he had heard his name spoken. "Is that the name you give me?"

"Ah, no," she said. "It is the name your father gave you. I shall call you Reuben. And you may call me Ronya."

He smiled then. "Why Reuben?"

She went out the door and down the corridor, leaving the question hanging in air.

A few hours before the train was due to pull into Harbin, Reuben said, to Ronya's horror, "I've decided to order the train back."

Aware that he had the power to do so, she said, "Calculate the risk, Reuben, my friend. I shall, in all probability, break a leg when I jump. It's a long crawl to the camp."

Curiously enough, he seemed to believe her. "Promise me at least," he said, "that you'll go directly to the safety of the hills. I shall bring Igor to you."

"No," she said, "I will not go to the hills. I won't even go to the walled house. I shall go straight to my son."

The tall man got up and stood looking down at Ronya. "It will be as you wish. Get ready. We're almost there."

Three hours later he said goodbye to her. "We may never meet again, Ronya." She gave him her gloved hand and he carried it to his lips.

"Goodbye, Reuben. God bless you."

In a dormitory of rotting timbers, filth and musk, she found Igor, and many others. Thirteen of them were dead.

XVI

SO steel-cold had been the winter of 1902-1903 that when at last it melted into spring, the trees remained naked and bore no fruit. Nor was there a rainy season that year and in parched fields corn and wheat, tea and soy beans blackened and produced no crops. Famine walked hand in hand with disease that killed domestic animals. When mulberry trees died, rich silk mer-merchants ceased paying wages, and workers were left without money to buy imported rice.

Empty-bellied, the populace groveled for roots and swilled contaminated water. Babies sucked dry breasts, wizened and dying. The rats of Harbin crawled over their swollen, lice-infested bodies. Inevitably, plague broke out.

From the new city, the rich—merchants, bankers, even teachers and civil servants—ignoring the plight of the destitute they were powerless to save, fled to the hills.

Igor and his men remained. He put away private life, forgot the Nipponese, the saboteurs and espionage. He even forgot horses. He had only one luxury—when he stretched out, usually fully clothed, on his bed for a few hours' rest, he allowed himself dreams of Julie, of her sweet cleanness and gentle songs.

In this crisis he turned Harbin into a police city, enforcing law implacably. The patrols Igor ordered out to protect property guarded the walled city discreetly. He himself did duty in the old Chinese quarter, taking only volunteers on his rounds. To every filthy building, large or small, they put the torch and

151

into the flames heaved the bodies piled up in festering alleyways.

Wherever he could find it, Igor stole food and tried to get it to the children, but the need was bottomless, supplies small. Attempts to purify the drinking water were utterly unsuccessful. The people, dirty, heedless and thirsty, did not understand what he was trying to do.

It was inevitable that cholera felled his men, one by one. Igor himself, thin and weak, was forced at last to return to the barracks, where he did everything he could for them, except ask aid from Huang, the one human being who could and would have helped him.

When Igor began to vomit and knew that he was burning with fever, he weakly pushed a dead man off a cot and lay down.

Until Ronya knelt by his side, whispering motherly words, he swam in the world of semiconsciousness. When he opened his eyes and saw her, he was not at all surprised. He needed her and she was there.

Igor spoke clearly for the first time in days. "Have you a ricksha, Mother?"

"Yes, my son."

"Go at once to the house behind the great wall. Tell Huang we need food and pure water. But speak to Duvid first. If he's still alive."

Ronya found Duvid on a sweat-soaked mat on the floor, but he was almost beyond recognition—exuding the stench of vomit and excrement, his breathing labored and stertorous, his skin so contracted that his bones stood out sharply. Yet she sat in the dirt and stroked his cold forehead. His eyelids flickered, his lips moved and he whimpered "Mama," and died.

With complete outward calm, Ronya opened the trunk which she had had set in the middle of the dormitory and took out a bottle of vodka, opened it with an expert twist and splashed it over her hands and arms. She lifted out two white sheets, with one of which she covered Duvid's body, laying the other over the corpse beside Igor's bed.

Every man in the room who could see watched her avidly. Inspired by the hope she saw in their faces, Ronya unfastened her soiled skirt, let it fall to the floor, and stepped into a clean one. Then, holding a small hand mirror, she tied her hair with a rib-

152

bon. At that moment the men stopped thinking about themselves.

Ronya turned to a young soldier whose eyes were clouded and huge with fear.

"How many men have we lost?" the mother of their captain asked.

Private Yurily Zybine mustered his strength and said, "Don't know."

"We'll lose no more," Ronya announced positively.

And every man there believed her, even the terrified eighteen-year-old who, in a stronger tone, said, "The rest of the command is out with the lieutenant on orders from the captain."

"Who's in charge here now, son?"

"You are, Madame Captain." The whisper came from a man with the face of a sick fox.

Ronya managed a smile. "In that case, you will pass on my orders to the lieutenant. I am going for help. Should he return before I do, tell him not to burn the bodies of Duvid and the other lad. They will be given burial in accordance with their faith."

As Madame Captain departed for the walled house, the men on cots, on mats, on the bare floor, feebly raised their hands in salute.

The extraordinary circumstances of their meeting threw their characters into bold contrast. Ronya suppressed her desire to speak of Lotus, instead accepting as her first obligation the saving of Igor and his men. Huang had no interest beyond her and Igor.

To Huang, student of humanity at large, of history and legend, authority on the game of politics and the art of government as they contributed to social evolution, the individual, save for those close to him, was trivial. To Ronya, a woman with scant patience for theory, what counted was the here and now of survival, and her heart belonged to all sufferers.

Huang was confronted not with a pale princess but with a determined, earthy woman, too intent on her mission to waste time over niceties. When he offered her tea and delicate cakes, she said, "I need a large, hot meal."

Hearing that Igor was stricken, he grieved. "Only a few days ago he was well and still in the Chinese quarter. This need never have happened if he had heeded my letter asking that the old city be declared out of bounds for all Russian personnel. I shall send a litter to him. At once."

To his amazement, Ronya said, "Rubbish, Huang, my friend. You know as well as I do that Igor must remain and take his chances with his men. May I eat now and talk later?"

Huang had not known that such a woman as Ronya existed and so he concluded there *was* no other woman like her. Sensitive to her forthrightness, he abandoned the stylized manners of a Chinese host and began to speak an idiom not unlike her own.

Ronya laughed at his quick appreciation of what was called for in this hour and said, "Bear with me. I shall be decorous and seemly when time allows. Then, too, I shall enjoy the beautiful apartment you have offered me."

Huang, a man of delicate appetite, turned his eyes to his folded hands as servants in long robes passed Ronya platters of food. Not having eaten since the night before, she helped herself generously and with obvious pleasure.

With amused eyes he watched Ronya devour iced soup, fresh crabmeat, bean sprouts mixed with water chestnuts, steamed dumplings served with shredded chicken and chopped vegetables, ripe figs and almond tea.

It was fortunate that he possessed the wealth of an emperor and that in his Eastern mind there was an admixture of Westernism, for by the time Ronya had finished cataloging her needs, she had enlarged her campaign area to include the entire old quarter. "We cannot limit ourselves to saving the lives of a few soldiers," she said. "We must wipe out the epidemic."

He promised everything she asked, fresh food, pure water, medical supplies, building materials, coolie labor. But when she said, "Two bodies remain in the barracks, one Jewish, one Greek Catholic, and I have promised the soldiers that each will be buried in the rites of his religion. Please arrange it," Huang said, "No."

"Ronya, my lady, though I wish to do whatever you ask me, I am not omnipotent. What you would have me undertake is

154

against the law. Those who died of the plague must be cremated."

"You are the law in Harbin," she said stubbornly. "If we seal the bodies in coffins filled with lye, there will be no danger. And if there is no rabbi in Harbin, any priest may officiate."

He smiled. "Ronya, my lady, do you know of any place on earth where there is no Jewish rabbi?"

"Certainly," she said. "In a Christian cemetery."

Huang raised his hands in surrender. "When the epidemic is over, the dead soldiers will be given appropriate funerals."

With these matters settled, Ronya felt she could speak of her reason for coming to Harbin. "Though I tremble to hear, I must know. Tell me about Lotus, your daughter, and my son Igor. Do not give me a sugarcoated account."

"What has Igor told you?"

"Nothing. Not once, in any letter, has he mentioned her or any other girl. Our information came from a childhood friend of mine, Admiral Yarsolov, who received an anonymous letter from Harbin."

Ronya stopped, appalled at the look on Huang's face. It disappeared in an instant and he said gently, "There are many things we have to tell each other. The time will come. For the present, know that no blame, no guilt or dishonor reflects on Igor."

Ronya's eyes filled with tears of relief. She asked for nothing more. Now she was eager to get to work, but in deference to his kindness, she went with Huang into his innermost garden, where they drank tea together. Only the fact that she needed something else kept her from leaving. Ronya had hoped Huang himself would offer what she must have. Nurses. That he did not was no oversight. Ronya could accomplish little without them but Huang did not wish to bring his Chinese women back from the hills to nurse Russian soldiers. She set her cup down, got up and looked around. "When all else vanishes, Huang, my friend, may this garden with its peace, its cool shade and beauty remain. Thank you for everything and now I must go."

They strolled to the outer gate, where he handed her into her waiting ricksha and said, "Convey my love to Igor." Ronya gave him her hand and, looking down into his face, said, "Please in-

struct the boy to take me to Harbin's most exclusive brothel."
With an impish smile, she added, "I need nurses."

"My lady! I am prepared to send—"

She waved him silent. "No, thank you, Huang."

"Take Madame Pirov to the establishment of Madame Anna Marie," Huang commanded.

XVII

LIFE had taught Anna Marie that protected women like Ronya Pirov despised females like her. Only a very pressing need could have brought this great lady to her house, and Anna Marie stood in her ornate entranceway, surveying the great lady with an unwinking stare. I'll be damned if I make it easy for her, she decided.

Her rudeness was calculated. "I am Anna Marie from Berdichev, my own mistress, beholden to no one. You are Ronya von Glasman Pirov from Kiev. I am a very direct woman; that's all you need know about me. If you have come to the wrong place at the wrong time of day, that takes care of you."

Ronya was not disconcerted, even when it seemed the door would be shut in her face. "Anna Marie from Berdichev. What a nice name!"

Anna Marie smiled without meaning to. "The hell with playing games and jockeying for position," she said and led the way through beaded portieres into a tidy parlor. "Sit down." She clapped her hands and a maid's head appeared through the beadwork. "Tea," she commanded, and the head disappeared. "I'm sorry I can't offer you sweets or fruits. That captain-son of yours has run off with my supplies."

"Thank you," Ronya said. "I've eaten but I would like a cigarette."

Anna Marie produced a box of Russian cigarettes from a pocket in her skirt.

After the women were smoking, Ronya suppressing waves of impatience to get down to business, Anna Marie asked, "What have you come here for?"

"I need your help, Anna Marie."

"So that fancy Chinaman turned you down! The bastard."

"You knew I went to the walled house?"

"I know everything that happens in this town," Anna Marie said. "Often before it happens."

Ronya was too tired for diplomacy. "Anna Marie," she said. "The day is nearly over. You say that you are a direct woman. Good. I, too, am partial to directness. The honorable Huang Hui Tsung gave beyond counting, everything except the thing sick men need most—nurses. For them I have come to you."

"Hmmm," said Anna Marie. "That's a sizable order."

"Yes it is," Ronya admitted. "Nursing cholera involves the danger of death."

The stocky Russian woman was mortally offended. "Don't think that *I'm* afraid of it! It's just that during an epidemic— and I've survived more than my share of them—I use good common sense to save my life. I've only got one. And to protect this business. I have a lifetime invested in it.

"So I close up shop, send my girls to the hills, where they make a fortune. They're good girls," her eyes were almost soft. "They do their work and they don't cheat me of my share. I remain here to look after our—home. Boil water. Boil everything. *And* I survive!"

"Bring the girls back. Russian men need nurses."

"That's easy for you to say."

Fearing she might lose her temper and destroy whatever chances she had, Ronya said, "I'm going back to the barracks to look after my son. I shall do what I can for the other men. Tomorrow, I will notify Huang Hui Tsung that I must have Chinese women."

Anna Marie was vexed. "You just can't understand, can you?

157

My girls are precious to me, as precious as your son is to you. No pimp whips or robs a girl of mine. I see to that. *I* choose their clients. After working here most of them find good husbands, and when they do, each one gets a lovely wedding—my treat—and brings her man a handsome dowry. Now do you understand?"

"The only thing I understand is that Russian soldiers will die if I cannot get nurses for them."

Anna Marie clapped her hands and two pretty, young Chinese girls came demurely through the portieres. She spoke to them rapidly in Chinese and they ran nimbly toward the front door.

"My girls will be here tomorrow evening. When you know them, Ronya Pirov, you will understand what I have been trying to tell you."

Exhausted, in this moment of victory Ronya could only say, "Thank you," as she rose to follow the girls out the door.

"Where do you think you're going?" Anna Marie's voice was harsh with emotion. "You're not leaving without me. Wait where you are." Even while she was speaking, the careful housekeeper was straightening chairs, plumping up pillows, turning down lamps. "The devil take this weather! This damnable heat! Pestilence thrives on high temperatures and humidity." She saw Ronya frowning with impatience. "I'm ready. We'll just take shawls. It may cool off."

In the ricksha Anna Marie remarked smugly, "It can never be said that Anna Marie from Berdichev let her Tsar down."

"You'll be a heroine," Ronya said.

The other woman laughed raucously. "No, my friend. You'll be the heroine. I'll still be an old whore."

Their ricksha halted in front of the dingy barracks. Ronya did not move.

"Your house is very close to the barracks," she said.

"I have the best location in Harbin."

Ronya put her hand on Anna Marie's knee. "May I ask you a favor? Until the men are well, may I live with you? The walled house is too far. I'd waste so much time running back and forth."

It was many years since anything had shocked Anna Marie,

158

but she stared at Ronya, profoundly shocked now. "No!" she said. "It is not fitting. What's the matter with ladies these days? The sister of a countess living with—"

Ronya was touched. She said gravely, "Why not, my friend? Your house is a nice house. I like it."

The tough little woman who dropped a tear at christenings and weddings—though not at funerals—wiped her eyes with the back of one hand.

That night, at Igor's side, Ronya strove fiercely to stay awake and only knew when she woke with a jerk that she had dozed in her chair. Each time she looked around, there was Anna Marie, her usually ruddy face drained of color by fatigue, moving from man to man, talking with one, washing another, bringing a bedpan to a third. Hour after hour the men called and Anna Marie gave them what they needed.

Toward daybreak Ronya got stiffly out of her chair and went to the other woman. "Get some rest," she whispered. "I'll take over."

"I'm all right."

"We won't make it," Ronya cautioned, "unless we spell each other."

"Maybe so. Wake me around ten. I'll be outside in the ricksha."

When Ronya stepped into the street, Anna Marie was lost to the world, huddled in the ricksha seat, sun blazing into her face. "What is it?" she asked thickly.

Ronya pointed down the dusty road to the camp and Anna Marie was instantly on her feet. Along it came a caravan of wagons, loaded with supplies and edged with long lines of coolies. She sat down abruptly and Ronya handed her tea and a slice of white bread. "Where did you get it?"

"The lieutenant brought it."

While Anna Marie ate, Ronya talked. "I've selected a new campsite, on a flat field about a mile from here and closer to the river. The lieutenant is a very obliging fellow—able, too. He's put every healthy man he's got to work. By the time your girls arrive we should have a makeshift hospital ready, at least four walls and a roof over our heads, and a floor raised above the dampness and clean cots draped with cheesecloth."

"That's good," Anna Marie approved. "Go on."

"We'll have to divide responsibility. I'm a good cook but I'd rather take charge of nursing."

It did not occur to Anna Marie to question the arrangement. "I'll take on the kitchen and help you, too." She looked at the sky. "With this weather there's no reason we can't set the cook-stoves up outside and our supply station, too. The girls can take turns sleeping in tents, like the men. That pleasant lieutenant had better station a guard with a rifle." Her smile was knowing. "Cholera or no cholera, I don't trust men."

By the time the girls arrived, looking prim and subdued at what lay before them, every sick man had been bathed, shaved, his hair washed, and was wearing clean nightclothes. Then began the transfer by stretcher to the rough shelter in the field. Igor, the captain, was the last man the orderlies carried out of the barracks and down the road to the new quarters. Anna Marie walked by his side.

With a detail of men, Ronya remained behind, infinitely relieved to be free to light an oily rag and set fire to the building and all it contained. The rotting wood caught quickly and flared up against the twilight sky. As the flames leaped into the night she could heard the racing feet of trapped rats.

For the next few days the weather remained hot and moist all day, hot and depressing all night. The men had not improved in spite of their clean new surroundings and the constant care of the women. Tormented by vomiting, diarrhea and inability to urinate, they complained incessantly of nagging thirst. Yet they could not keep down so much as a sip of water.

With sorrowing eyes, Anna Marie and Ronya watched them shrink to skeletons and knew that somehow a different treatment must be found. Nothing they did was of any avail. Desperate, Ronya suggested, "Let's try irrigations. We've got to replenish their body fluids. We have plenty of kettles so all we need is rubber tubing to put together enemas."

"Where the devil will we get rubber tubing?" Anna Marie asked.

"From Huang, of course. Where else?"

Ronya wrote:

160

Dear friend,

The men are dying. They cannot last much longer and only their amazing will and the girls' indescribable devotion and care have brought them this far.

Igor is in better condition than the rest, being less dehydrated and blessed with the ability to sleep in spite of discomfort. I believe he alone is defeating the infection. However, if we are to save the others I again need help, this time rubber tubing for enemas and more salt.

In answer to your inquiry: I get a fair share of rest. Don't worry about me. When I close my eyes I see your garden and feel refreshed.

Since there are no words to express my gratitude, I shall not try.

Ronya

P.S. I almost forgot. There is no urgency about the burials. However, one more favor. May they have carved headstones of white marble, since in your country white is the color of death? The inscriptions:

Private Leo Pirodsky
Born 1882   Smolensk, Russia
Died 1903   Harbin, Manchuria
In the service of his Tsar

Private Duvid Bulatski
Born 1882   Warsaw, Poland
Died 1903   Harbin, Manchuria
He died only because he lived

Some hours later, she looked up when she heard Anna Marie squeal, "My God!"

Framed in the doorway was a very elegant figure, Huang unmistakably Western, tailored by Savile Row and looking as if Buckingham Palace would make a better setting for him than a field hospital. Happy though Ronya was to see him, she could not resist scolding. "You shouldn't have come! It's much too dangerous."

Huang bowed with a trace of irony. "I do not suppose the danger is greater for me than for you admirable ladies," he said, and held out a package. "I have brought what you asked and also a gift of sleep for your men—dried poppyheads. Boil them to

161

make a concentrated solution, then feed your charges a spoonful every few hours. They will rest. We Chinese are wise in ways of dealing with cholera."

Ronya's voice was husky as she took the package. "I shall never forget this, Huang." Then, remembering that she had not introduced Anna Marie, Ronya looked around for her. That tactful woman had gone. "I may as well start boiling this," Ronya said. "Come show me how much water to use."

"Take me first to Igor. Then give the poppyheads to Miss Anna Marie. She will know how to fix them."

Igor managed a weak smile when his foster father appeared at the foot of his bed and murmured, "I'm thankful to see you."

"Don't try to talk. Rest, my son." Huang sat down in Ronya's chair, his face tender and melancholy. Shaken by the intensity of his love for her son, Ronya left them together.

She could not know that Huang was repelled by the bleak room, the desolate, half-dead men, the buxom, lively girls. All this he shut out of his physical vision, fixing his gaze on Igor. He was so lost in contemplation of the beloved boy it was several seconds before he responded to the touch on his shoulder. Ronya looked down at her sleeping son, put a finger to her lips and beckoned Huang to follow her.

Outside he apologized. "I must have been dreaming."

"With your eyes wide open. We've given the men their first dose of the broth. Now, please, come eat with us. Anna Marie has cooked a wonderful dinner in your honor."

Ronya, the great Russian lady; Huang, secular leader and true ruler of Manchuria; Anna Marie, bawdy-house madam; her girls and Lieutenant Simon Petipa dined together in warm friendship and high spirits while the sick soldiers slept.

The sun disappeared behind clouds two days later and a high, cool wind sprang up. Ronya immediately called her staff together. "Secure the tents," she said to Anna Marie and the lieutenant, "and tell the men that at last our prayers are answered. We shall have rain."

There was peace in the infirmary. The men lay content as a result of the bitter broth they had been given. They drank and retained moisture. They ate and their ashy skins took on a human glow.

162

The hard, clean rain washed away the cholera. At the end of the third day, when the sun came out again, the epidemic was over. And in a shining world Ronya prepared to keep her promise to bury Privates Bulatski and Pirodsky. It was not an easy task.

The rabbi, no Joseph Levinsky, the priest, no Father Tromokov, flatly refused what she asked of them. "I shall bury my own," said the priest, said the rabbi.

But Ronya, whose own sons had roots in both Testaments, the Old and the New, stood firm. "Let them sleep through eternity as they lived and died—together. No one grave is more holy than another."

She could suggest no settlement that suited them. However, a leisurely visit from a man with a beard made them cooperative. The thin man had his methods and his orders. It pleased Huang Hiu Tsung to please Madame Pirov.

Leo Pirodsky and Duvid Bulatski were buried side by side in a Buddhist shrine. Over the grave of one was a Byzantine cross; over the other the Star of David. The rabbi, supported by the required *minyan* of ten adult Jews, and the priest, with acolytes, officiated at the rites. Ronya and her friends Huang and Anna Marie were the only mourners.

The farewell party the girls gave Ronya was over. Unexpectedly it simply stopped. The exhausted girls had fallen asleep.

Ronya and Anna Marie, older but far more durable, were wide awake. Seated on the couch, her bare feet stretched out on a cushion. Ronya listened to the faint ticking of the clock on the mantel. She thought, It is ticking away my last night in the brothel, and she wondered how soon after she left Anna Marie would reopen its door. Watching her collect glasses, empty ashtrays and flick invisible dust off tabletops, Ronya said softly, "Stop fussing and sit down. I want to talk to you."

"There's no point in talking, Ronya. I'm going into the kitchen and make another glass of tea. While the water's heating I'll put away the leftovers."

Ronya's look stopped her. "I'm not going back to Kiev yet and I won't be far away. We'll see each other," she said.

"No, we won't," Anna Marie snapped. "I don't want you coming here ever again. The cholera is over. You go home. Go back to Kiev where you belong."

"I have unfinished business in Harbin," said Ronya.

"Go home, Ronya. Done is done."

"I can't. . . . That's funny. My husband says, 'Done is done.' "

"He's right. I'll fix the tea."

Returning from the kitchen, she found Ronya smoking and was startled to hear her ask, "Are you rich?"

Without resentment or evasion, she replied like a real Russian, "What kind of rich is that?"

"You tell me."

"If you lie, you die," said Anna Marie. "If you don't lie, you die. So it's better to tell the truth. Besides, counting my money won't make me richer or you poorer—maybe it's the other way round—make me poorer or you richer. Anyway, a financial leviathan I am not. You might say that to the rich I'm poor, and to the poor I'm rich. Starve I won't. Now, are you satisfied?"

Ronya smiled. "Any family in Russia?"

"Of course! Do you think I sprouted from a shrub?" Anna Marie sighed. "The money I've sent to Berdichev! Married off all my nieces, two to doctors, and doctors *cost*, Ronya, my friend."

"Do they know how you got the money?"

"You know the old saying: 'There's a cover for every pot.' Years ago I wrote that I'd married a rich lumber man. As long as the money runs from here to there, no one asks questions."

"Listen, Anna Marie. Retire. You have just lost your husband. He died of cholera. I, Ronya Pirov, shall attest to that." Ronya was delighted with her own ingenuity. "Rich widow, go back to Berdichev. Find yourself a widower, one with plenty of pepper left and a few rambunctious children to keep you busy. Boris and I will dance at your wedding."

Anna Marie sighed. "I won't use fancy words." Again she quoted a Russian proverb, " 'A man's sin stays outside on his doorstep; a woman's sin enters the house.' "

And suddenly, sitting up straight, she said what was deep in

164

her mind. "Why should I go back to Berdichev? Here in Harbin, I'm *some*body!"

Ronya kissed her friend. "Good night and goodbye till tomorrow," she said, "Anna Marie of Harbin."

XVIII

"YOU are thinner than when first I saw you, my lady Ronya," Huang said, as he helped her out of her ricksha early the next morning. It did not occur to her to wonder that the great gate swung open and her host came out to meet her the instant the wheels of her small vehicle stopped turning. The household and its master had been waiting for her arrival since daybreak.

She turned a white, exhausted face up to him. "For the first time in years I'm really tired, though I didn't discover it until this morning when I was faced, all of a sudden, with nothing to do."

Huang knew this was only a half-truth. Her face could not conceal the recollection that her primary reason for coming lay between them, unresolved. He was about to suggest that any serious discussion be put off when she herself proposed it.

"Would you consider me rude if I asked leave to retire to the lovely apartment you showed me the other night—heavens! what a long time ago that was—and rest there for a few days? Right now I need to blot out everything and everybody. After lots of sleep I'll wake up ravenously hungry, and as good as new."

Huang's smile relieved Ronya of any possible sense of guilt. He summoned a Chinese woman who spoke Russian and instructed her, "I leave Lady Ronya's comfort and well-being in your capable hands."

As she rose, Huang handed Ronya a note from home:

Little Dove,
    I am lonely. I eat. I work. I talk. And I am lonely. I lie in your bed, my arms empty. Come back to me.

All of my love now and always,

Boris

She fell asleep with the letter in her hand.

Saturday, Sunday and most of Monday Ronya slept, stirring only occasionally to put out her hands for the glass of fruit juice or bowl of soup which her guardian brought her. After fifty-seven hours of rest, she awoke, as she had predicted she would, fresh and vigorous.

To Boris she then wrote, "I miss you, too, darling. There is, however, reason for me to stay on. I shall return to Kiev when the time is right. If you are so foolish as to carry out your threat to follow me here, I shall refuse to see you."

Huang's garden became a refuge for Ronya, as blessedly isolated as a cloister. One day, alone there, Ronya kicked off her slippers and plunged her feet into the cool lake where golden streaks of sunlight raced across the surface. This was a particular place she had not seen before and when she found it, her heart had given a sudden leap. On a little island stood a small marble edifice, half buried in vines and flowering shrubs, their colors intensified by the whiteness of the stone. Shadows were moving across the grass before Huang found her.

"You have missed tea, Lady Ronya."

"I'm in love with this peaceful place," she said. "Stay a while. It's a mellow time of day, filled with mystery. Igor promised me you would tell me about my father. If you're in the mood, I'd love that."

Sitting in the grass beside her, Huang began, "He shaped history and my life by ending our dynasty.

"When I was still young, David von Glasman brought to this house a man just my age, Sergius Witte. They wanted to build a railroad—the Trans-Siberian Railroad. And between them they managed to steal Manchuria from us so cleverly that my father believed he had made a wise decision in granting Russia a foothold in Manchuria—that his bargain was a triumph." Ronya felt a slight shiver run through her.

"Father was innocent of ambition. For centuries our house had had no call for ambition. So he lived in Buddhist orthodoxy, an alien to the world of conquest and intrigue. His sole duty in life was to his ancestors, who had conquered all China: it was to produce an heir. That he accomplished with my birth.

"Thereafter he became, if possible, even more detached from the rough and tumble of politics and people, drifting into frail old age addicted to opium and passing his days painting in the classical style of T'ang.

"In his defense I must say that he was not altogether lost to reality and responsibility. Robber bands were growing bolder; outbreaks of hostilities between rival family associations more violent and frequent. Against a background of such disturbances, he listened to the recommendations of David von Glasman, not only as a man he personally trusted but also as envoy of Her Majesty Empress Marie of Russia."

Huang paused and stared at the water.

"You know how powerful David von Glasman's personality was, and even a more worldly man than Father might have believed the promises he extended in the name of his sovereign. All he asked was that Russia be allowed to come into Manchuria on a limited basis. Between them they would shorten the distance between Irkutsk and Vladivostok, link Russian power and Chinese greatness—for surely they had nothing to fear from each other and everything to fear from the Nipponese. Russia, professed proponent of world peace, wished the privilege of establishing a military post in Harbin, whose specific purpose would be to police and protect China against her internal enemies, against the possibility of brutal aggression by Germany, and from the Chinese Emperor himself, that enigmatic figure who was discontented and bellicose. The price? No price. Only a small gift. The right to build a railway."

Ronya had never before heard bitterness in Huang's voice. She breathed, "Oh, Huang!"

167

He shrugged. "The rest you know as well as I do. Russia got her railroad, a spear whose head probed farther into Manchuria and Korea. Sergius got power and wealth. And I, my father's only descendant, got—" He faltered. "Ronya, my lady, it is impossible for me to conceal anything from you. I developed a taste for Westernism and my great pretension—" He stopped and held out his hand to Ronya. "The day has run away from us."

Heedless of her wet feet, Ronya started across the velvety softness of the lawn toward the house, leaving Huang to gather up her slippers. When they were well away from the lake, she spoke broodingly.

"I think I never understood my father. Ruth, my mother, did, and my sister Katya. But not I. I saw him only as I wanted to see him. After I married Boris, he left us and later I chose to remember him as I had idiolized him. . . . You will tell me the rest of your story?"

"Tomorrow," he said, "in our garden."

Preceding him through the door, she turned. "I shall meet you here. Tonight I want to write to Boris. Suddenly he, and home, seem very far away."

A fat envelope was on her morning tea tray. It held a sheaf of clippings which she read cursorily, then stuffed back into the envelope. Later, after she had learned what she had come to find out, would be time enough for news from Russia.

In the garden Ronya found Huang, seemingly cheerful.

"Shall I go on with my tale?" he asked.

"Please do."

The death of his mother had changed his life. There was no one left with whom he could communicate, no one to love, so he turned to books. Although the people in the palace were kind enough, he felt set apart from them and no human being had meant anything to him until David von Glasman and Sergius Witte arrived. Falling under the spell of David, he became passionately jealous of Sergius.

"I made myself useful to your father in every way I could, set on having him take me with him when he left Harbin. He seemed touched by my devotion and began calling me 'son,' and telling me about you, Ronya—young, wild, the most beautiful girl in Russia. I fell in love with you." He smiled wistfully. "Day after day I badgered him with questions and he added to the portrait he had painted." Ronya made a comic gesture of dismay.

"Ah, yes," Huang persisted, "you had a fancy for all wild things—gypsy music, untamed horses, swimming in the river under a summer moon, sleeping in the fields, running through the forest keeping pace with the fawn.

" 'Tell me of her face,' I implored him.

"And he spoke like a poet of your chin—a bit too determined, your mouth—a bit too wide, cheekbones—a bit too high, far-spaced eyes and the glorious harmony of your skin.

"I dreamed and dared not confide my hopes to him. Then, one day, drinking tea not in our fashion from a porcelain cup, but like the Westerner he was and I aspired to be, from tall, thin glasses, he said to my father, 'Let me take your son for a time. I want to show him Europe, my Europe, and I want him to attend Harvard University in the United States.'

"And my father gave his permission. On that day, for the first time, I ceased calling your father Gospodin von Glasman and addressed him as David, my father."

All had gone well for a while. David von Glasman set about teaching his adopted son his ways and the German language. Together they traveled in unimaginable luxury and news of their journey traveled before them, so they were received everywhere like diplomats. Only one thing marred the pleasure of their companionship. In his jealousy Huang became convinced that David intended Ronya for Sergius. On the day of his departure for the United States, he could bear the uncertainty no longer and, reverting to his position as a Mandarin prince, asked for her hand in marriage. The suit was rejected instantly and firmly. Ronya was destined, David said, not for Huang nor for Sergius, but seeing the boy's stricken face, he added softly, "Forgive me, Huang, my son."

So wounded was Huang's pride that he determined to remove himself, physically, from David von Glasman's presence. They met only once again. That was on the same afternoon in the stateroom of a ship bound for Boston. "Huang, my son," said

169

David, "your destiny and Ronya's lie worlds apart but last night I dreamed of calamities befalling her. If ever my Ronya needs you, serve her well."

Huang promised. They embraced and parted.

Yet the link between them was never broken. For the rest of David's life they wrote and David gave Huang two precious gifts: a trusted servant, the man Ronya had called Reuben, and a miniature of Ronya.

The story was finished. A king had laid his devotion at her feet, but Ronya could not rejoice. In the mirror of her mind she would never again be able to see the image of her father as it had long ago become reality to her, and which she preserved so jealously. It was irredeemably tarnished.

Huang entreated, "Do not be sad. He gave me a gift beyond compare."

"How can you be so philosophic! You *are* a confusing man, Huang. Now playing the European, now the very symbol of Chinese nobility. Which one are you really?"

"Does it matter, Ronya, my lady? Need either exclude the other?"

"Tell me to whom I am talking."

"A friend. Speak frankly."

"Not once have you mentioned Lotus or the private hell the poor girl must be suffering," Ronya said indignantly. "Neither has Igor. I'm through with guarding my tongue. Lotus carries my grandchild. She needs me. Why have I not met her? And furthermore, how dare you suggest that your dynasty is finished? Isn't the seed of Igor, whom you love and call son, worthy of your lineage? Will you repeat the arrogance of David von Glasman?"

Huang turned his eyes away.

"Look at me, Huang."

He looked and she was appalled at the suffering she saw. "There was never," he said, speaking with agonized slowness, "the slightest possibility of a child, Ronya. Lotus was a nymphomaniac. She was aborted and sterilized in Vienna two years before she forced herself on Igor."

A cry caught in Ronya's throat. Her eyes filled with tears.

170

"You keep saying 'was.' Where is Lotus? What have you done with her?"

"I put her to sleep."

Instinctively Ronya looked at Huang's hands. The color drained from his face and he rubbed his fingers on his silk robe. "She rests now, Ronya, free of torment, by the side of her mother." He raised his right hand, pointing to the white marble tomb. Ronya pressed her hands to her face and fled.

XIX

RONYA'S first impulse was to flee Huang's house as she had fled his presence. But, lying on the bed in her sumptuous room, her convulsion of sobbing soon passed and with it her terror. She had no right either to condemn or condone a tragedy governed by a code she, as a European, could not possibly comprehend. David von Glasman's behavior might well seem as monstrous to Chinese Huang as his did to her.

She slept that night and dreamed and arose untroubled. After her bath it seemed the most natural thing in the world to return to the garden and sit, as she had done so often before, looking at the white mausoleum reflected in the lake. When Huang joined her, she smiled at him and he managed to return her smile. It was all the bridge they could now build between them but it was enough.

Gradually their dialogue was resumed. Ronya spoke openly of Boris, of how they had met and loved and battled. Huang listened, expressionless. Out of the past she moved into the future and posed the question which, now that she knew the workings of his mind, she felt Huang alone might be able to answer for her. How could she insure the continuation of the house of von Glasman? Katya was the only representative of the family at court—there had been one since the von Glasmans first came to Russia. Should Georgi be yielded up to the Brusilovs and the house of Romanov to preserve the family—Igor and Georgi himself and the Blond One? She stopped. "Igor has told you about the Blond One?"

"No," said Huang gravely, "but I know of him."

Reuben, Ronya thought, that astonishing man.

"The garden is distracting," Huang said. "My brain functions better in my study. There, with the help of Isaiah, Plato, Aristotle and Sophocles, with the grim record of the decline of Rome and the inspiration of Locke and Voltaire and Thomas Jefferson, with maps, documents, reference books, I should like to reeducate you to find your own answer to that question."

For the rest of that week, Huang was teacher, brilliant, hard and practical. He spoke of the misfortunes of the Russian masses, the perverted appetites of their rulers, of the innate decay that threatened destruction and an end of the security she was seeking.

Nicholas II he characterized as a frog who leaps backward, the Empress Alix as a madwoman. "Alas, her influence on her husband is complete, and Rasputin's influence on her is such that she has forced Sergius out of office. Before she is done she will arrange for the dismissal of every devoted friend you have in government. The peasant monk will be the true ruler of Russia.

"You can seal no contract with a government dedicated to the divine right of kings and supporting its position with violence and the prison camps of Siberia."

He set Ronya the Jewess, with a tough instinct for survival, at war with Ronya the autocrat, who longed to hold onto her world. Could not the Ukraine outlast the Romanovs? Could not liberalism and compromise found a new state?

Huang explained that Armageddon allowed neither liberalism nor compromise to survive. Passionately, Ronya argued for a delaying action that might save them all. Huang warned her that with Vyacheslav Plehve as minister of the interior she was in grave danger. This she pooh-poohed. "However much he countenances pogroms, he won't touch me," she said. "He knows that every man in the gubernya of Kiev, Jew or gypsy, peasant

172

or landowner, every Tartar in Odessa would take up arms with Boris to protect me."

Perhaps, Huang conceded, but with no friends at court the weight of the Imperial power might be turned against her. "Alexis is working on the Tsar," she said. "You'll see. We'll get Witte back in, and our good friend Peter Stolypin must move into the central government." And, she reminded Huang, "The peasants are happy—so—far."

"They are not the real issue." Huang was relentless. "Granted that your peasants have enough to eat and wear shoes. That does not solve the problem of Russia's economy."

When it seemed to Huang that he had driven Ronya to the verge of mental exhaustion, he sent her and Igor to his lodge in the mountains for the weekend. Monday morning the inexorable analysis began again.

Nicholas II's downfall was already approaching, and demonstrations and uprisings could no longer be stemmed by brute repression. The Kaiser was watching from the sidelines for the moment when the Tsar would need a diversion, and he was ready to provide one in the form of a full-scale war.

Here in the East, Japan felt menaced by Russia's lust for conquest and was prepared to turn back further expansion in Korea. When the Nipponese fought, as they would, they would win because England and the United States wanted them to and because the Russian government was in the grip of a giant lethargy, its leaders divided, the Tsar installing his stupid relatives as admirals and generals and failing to supply his army in Manchuria.

A defeated Russia could no longer put down disturbances. Huang predicted a time not far off when peasants' voices would grow louder, shouting more and more subversive slogans, the Black Hundreds wax in strength, blood flow, and the Jews, always the Jews, the first target of hatred.

"Run! Lady Ronya, run!" Huang urged.

"Must I? It will break my heart. I love my land and the cabin Boris built me, my people, my life."

"I am not a prophet," Huang said compassionately, "only a student of history and philosophy. My agent visits the world's capitals and gathers secrets, which he brings to me. We combine his information with my knowledge and play a game of intrigue, plot and counterplot, form imaginary alliances and counter-alliances. We spy, expand, divide. My objective—Manchuria.

"My enemy mistrusts France but mistrusts Germany more. He shakes hands with Emperor Meiji Mutsuhito, on paper, and makes an unholy alliance.

"I abolish the old order, shout 'Long live science!' And envy the West. It is my model and I imitate it, claws sharpened. I want all Asia.

"My antagonist has a withered left arm. He is inferior, the variant offspring of Queen Victoria. 'I am superman!' he rants. 'Beware!' He wants Alsace and Lorraine and Morocco and he kisses Edward VII, his cousin, and spits on the portrait of his grandmother, Victoria."

Huang broke off from his weird fantasy.

"Europe is sick," he said simply. "It is time for you to go back to your family. You have begun to understand. Find your own answers—Tsarism and death or the United States and life."

"Boris and Alexis and Katya will be indignant," Ronya said. "They will regard what I have learned from you as pitiful defeatism. What I shall do I do not know, except that my grandchildren will not be murdered. That I promise.

"You are right, Huang, I must go home. I have learned all that I need to know."

"Not all," he smiled. "You will not decide in a day or a year. But prepare. Begin to liquidate your holdings in Kiev and transfer them out of Russia, to San Francisco. If you wish, I shall arrange it. I have dealings with the Wells Fargo Bank there."

"San Francisco?" Her face was puzzled. "Not New York?"

"A hill waits for you in San Francisco," he said.

"I shall do as you say."

"You are booked on tomorrow's train," Huang said gravely. "I will notify Boris of the time of your arrival."

The next morning for the first time Huang came to Ronya's apartment and held out parting gifts, jade and emerald jewelry, a gold rosary, each bead carved in the image of Buddha. At last he spoke.

"In the words of our ancestors I say, 'You have nursed your

174

sick, you have buried your dead, you have earned your place in heaven.' Go home. With one swift stroke cut Russia from your life. You can, because you must."

Ronya said only, "Goodbye, my friend." They did not embrace. It would not have been fitting.

Igor drove her to the station alone. As the two horses pulled them down the street, Igor said with a violence that surprised her, "You stayed too long, Ronya, my mother."

"In that case, don't you make the same mistake," Ronya replied tartly.

Wondering how to get past her son's defenses, Ronya pulled out a cigarette and, in the breeze that stirred through the carriage as it rumbled over the cobblestones, he lit it for her.

"How I wish you had requested a transfer back to Russia," she said. "Manchuria is exile."

"I like it here." His chin was set.

"You like having unchecked freedom."

Igor's eyes narrowed and an instant later he pulled up the team.

"It's not yet eleven," Ronya said, looking at the small watch that dangled from a pin on her suit. "How did we get here so soon?"

"I'm a good driver." Igor lifted her down. "We beat your trunks and suitcases."

Since the train was not scheduled to leave until noon, Ronya suggested that they walk a while. "I'll be cooped up for nearly two weeks."

Ronya put her arm in Igor's and smiled up at him and he grinned back. They always had taken pleasure in each other's company when they were not feuding. Looking even taller than his six feet one, he swaggered, for he had a very pretty, elegant woman at his side. Lost in thoughts of one another, they were surprised when two soldiers saluted Igor. He said, returning their salute, "You are charged with the care of my mother, here and on the train."

"Yes, sir," they answered in unison.

Sensing that something was amiss, Igor ordered, "If you have anything to say, say it. You, Corporal Leonsky."

The corporal looked at a man who seemed to be watching the

175

group. "He's a stranger in Harbin, sir. He's been asking questions. We think he's a journalist."

Ronya and Igor regarded the man with interest. He was stocky, short and hard-bitten. Seeing their attention on him, the fellow lifted his hat.

"Let's get on the train, Igor. If he follows us—"

"I do not believe in being followed." Directing his soldiers to take Ronya to her compartment, he said, "I'll make this brief."

"Poor reasoning," Ronya demurred. "You're playing right into his hands. He wants you to make a scene. It will be worth a lot to him."

"First he'll have to get out of the hospital," Igor said.

"Pay no attention to him, son! He doesn't disturb me in the least."

"He disturbs me!"

Ronya snuggled her hand into Igor's. "Please let's turn our backs on him and board the train. If you believe in my good character, you have no need to defend it."

He wanted to please Ronya but hoped the stranger would follow them and give him an excuse to settle the affair. Ronya took care of this neatly. She smiled at the soldiers. "Perhaps," she said, "since we've been through so much together, you would convince the gentleman that Captain Pirov represents the Tsar here in Harbin and that a civilian has no recourse against him." They touched their caps and went off to do as she asked.

In her compartment, Ronya pointed to the door. "Close it."

"Don't leave Harbin angry with me, Mother," Igor said.

"Come home," she urged. "Marry Julie now."

"I can't, Ronya, my mother."

Desperately, Ronya asked, "What holds you in Manchuria? Good or evil?"

His face was hard and he was silent, but she tried once more.

"China is quicksand for you, my darling. Tear yourself out of it. Bury your disquiet here and leave it. Sign the papers and come back to people like yourself, to your own land and your Julie."

All he said was, "No."

There were at least five minutes left before the train would

176

pull out but Igor, looking Ronya directly in the eyes, said
sweetly, "Tell Julie that I love her and that I'll come back to
her." He kissed her and left.

XX

THE day they were due in Moscow, Ronya went through the
newspaper clippings Boris had sent her in Harbin and later papers Lev had added. She arranged the cuttings and pamphlets
on the table in three piles, then propping up a pillow to form a
backrest, lay down on her bunk and began to read the lot. It was
an extraordinary mixture of adulation and attack, the former
largely concentrated in the government-controlled press, which
was extravagant in its praise of her heroism. However, she was
grimly aware that no reader of these panegyrics could possibly
conclude from them that she was a Jewess.

Next came headlines so sickening she was seldom able to read
beyond them: EXPOSÉ! RUSSIAN BEAUTY AND CHINESE POTEN-
TATE. . . . BORIS PIROV EXPRESSES HIMSELF BLUNTLY. . . .
DOCTORS SAY EDITOR MAY NOT SURVIVE BEATING. . . . SOLDIERS
HOLD THEIR BENEFACTRESS SACRED. . . . VON GLASMAN'S
DAUGHTER RECRUITS PROSTITUTES, FIGHTS CHOLERA.

The final collection was from the underground revolutionary
press. Thoughtfully, Ronya read every word and under the pepper and salt of sensationalism, discovered boiling hatred. Her
motives were assessed as "Not valor but personal glory, not compassion but self-interest—a desire for excitement more important than the life of a citizen-soldier."

Sick at heart, she locked the clippings in her trunk and was
trying to regain her composure when there was a knock at her

door. It was Lev with, he assured her grimly, news. Ronya gripped the door handle. The train was slowing down.

"What's the matter, Lev?"

"We have orders to pick up a very important passenger in about twenty minutes." Ronya saw a flicker of excitement in his eyes. "He must be a reporter from an influential paper, Mistress Pirov."

"I fancy you're right, Lev, and I depend on you not to fail me. Just repeat what you've been saying for me all along: 'Mistress Pirov refuses to give an interview.' If you're threatened or promised bribes, give in. The soldiers will keep him out."

"If you need protection," Lev protested, "I'll not be left out. The Russian conductor is a tough fellow and this one has some skill with guns. I, and not the soldiers, am responsible to your host, the Trans-Siberian Railway, for your safe conduct. "Besides," he spoke confidentially, "every male passenger in the first class, including those in short pants, has sworn to tear any stranger who dares approach you limb from limb."

Ronya's smile was sparkling. "I have no doubt, my good Lev, that you will thwart the intruder, no matter what his tricks."

Very proud, he asked, "Are you hungry, Mistress Pirov? Shall I bring you dinner here?"

"No, thank you," she answered. "Look our passenger over carefully, then bring me tea and report on him."

Ronya locked and bolted the door and pulled down the blind. Shut off from sunlight and air, she undressed, cooled herself with a sponge bath and put on a loose robe. Time dragged in the stuffy cubicle. Every nerve and every muscle clamored for action so, after switching from bunk to chair and back again without making herself comfortable, Ronya stood up and raised her arms above her head, then touched her toes. By the time she had counted a hundred bends and a hundred stretches, the train had stopped. She stared at the window, resisting a desire to peek out, cursing the delay that kept her from Boris.

There was a knock on the door and Ronya knew it could be no one but Lev, returning with tea. She unlatched it and called, "Come in." There was no time to step forward. Boris leaped through the door and caught her around the waist. Since her face was raised to his, he paused only long enough to slam the door.

The men who lingered in the corridor drifted away, any possible doubts of the Pirovs' feelings for one another, which might have been roused by newspaper gossip, stilled forever.

After Boris indulged in that first, honeyed kiss, he tilted his head, looked at her quizzically, and kissed her again. On the tip of her nose. With so much to say to each other, Ronya and Boris were silent. In the confines of the compartment, as the wheels of the train began to turn again, their bodies spoke directly, above the rhythmic drumming of passing railroad ties, until at last, filled with blissful contentment, they lay still.

Now he asked for reassurances in words which were altogether unnecessary, and Ronya told Boris she loved him and Boris told Ronya he loved her, and neither one found the protestations less than glorious.

For weeks Boris had tormented himself; now he emerged from his descent into the inferno of jealousy and the nights he had spent alone, made more agonizing when his mother, blond braids flying in a cold sea wind, pursued him through nightmare dreams over the hills. Ronya brought him release. She was still his, joined to him by a divine chemistry.

"Rest a little longer," he said, disentangling himself and getting up.

She burst out laughing. "I'm not tired. What I am is starved."

For days, even an hour ago, she had felt like a hunted animal, avoiding men. Now she wanted to flaunt her wonderful Boris and walked proudly by his side in public. From a trunk she had had no occasion to open since she left Kiev, she pulled out a suit Boris particularly liked. When he came out of the lavatory, his brow darkened. "Don't wear anything you wore for him. Not now. Not ever, Ronya."

She was aghast at his ferocity but would not say anything that might becloud this happy hour. "Done." She explained, "What I wore at the camp I burned. Almost everything else I gave to the wonderful Chinese women who served me."

He was not put off lightly. "Get rid of everything to do with the walled garden," he persisted. Ronya, remembering Huang,

179

his loyalty, his counsel, his princely gifts, remembered also—
only a foolish tongue speaks too soon. She held hers.

"Make yourself dazzling," Boris said.

"I'll try. Dig for my boots."

Was there something joyous in the air? The train crew was in-
fected by a holiday spirit and made no attempt to reach Moscow
on time. The Pirovs had plenty of leisure for dinner.

They entered the dining car to heart-warming acceptance.
Boris heard in it a confirmation of what he knew, that Ronya, in
her high-heeled, knee-length boots and form-fitting suit, the top
cut like a riding jacket and trimmed with sable, her small sable
hat framing her exquisite face, was the most beautiful woman in
Russia. Ronya considered Boris the most beautiful man on
earth.

Boris' pride in Ronya boiled over. "Drinks for everyone," he
said to the wine steward.

To the last man they rose; glasses were filled and toasts exchanged, spoken and unspoken. No words passed between
Ronya and Boris while they clicked glasses, looked into each
other's eyes, and drank.

The man who invented sleeping cars did not have giants in
mind. After struggling to compress his long body into the strait-
jacket of his berth on the train to Kiev, cursing under
his breath, Boris dragged pillows, sheets and blanket off it and
spread them on the floor. The floor was predictably hard and
he slept fitfully, so near Ronya and yet so divided from her.
Unable to bear the situation any longer, he got to his feet and
picked up his sleeping wife, who said, half dreaming, "In the
garden with Huang I found understanding." Hot fury stung
Boris and he took her, there on the floor, savagely.

"I'm sorry, dear love," he mumbled later, in shame.

Ronya, remembering what had roused his anger, said softly
once more, "Huang is in no way your rival, Boris."

His rage returned. "For Christ's sake, Ronya, don't reassure
me. Let's not refer to him again—*ever!*"

"That isn't possible, Boris. Huang is our friend and he has
taken nothing from you. He opened up a whole new world of

ideas to me and I mean to take his advice. Also, he probably saved your son's life." She told him about Lotus. At the end she said, "The blame falls on no one. Least of all Igor."

Contrite, Boris asked, "Did I hurt you, little dove?"

"I liked the echo of my wild Boris," she said.

"There was a time when you took a whip to me for less."

The rest of the night he held her in his arms as though she might run away.

Georgi and the Blond One showed off shamelessly. Riding like madmen along the side of the train, they leaped from their horses to the back platform as it began slowing up, laughing and yelling in their jubilation, then invaded compartment after compartment until they found Boris and Ronya. Georgi swung his mother off her feet and implanted a smacking great kiss on her lips. After he set her down, she went to the Blond One and embraced him as fervently as she had Georgi. Unmindful of Boris, the young man clung to her for a moment.

The half brothers made a seat with their hands and carried Ronya out for the waiting crowd to see. Cossacks began to sing and for a few happy minutes, the Pirovs lingered. Beside the carriage that waited for them were Julie and Alexis and Katya, all with arms outstretched to the homecomer. Seeing tears in Julie's eyes, Ronya hugged her first. "Igor sent you a message," she murmured into the girl's ear. "He talks about you endlessly and tells everyone, 'I belong to Julie, who waits for me in Kiev in the house of my parents.' "

At the gate to the Pirov estate, the gypsies, led by Tamara, and the peasants, led by Father Tromokov, came running and shouting. On the steps were neighbors and friends, among them the Ukrainian poet, Ivan Franko, who recited verses celebrating Ronya's heroism to the strumming of a bandore.

Ronya was the star of that evening's surprise party. Called upon to dance, she danced with spirit. Called upon to make a speech, she chose the perfect words. At the same time she was keenly aware of what went on—Julie slightly tipsy, displaying something like Pirovian abandon; Tamara vital and alluring, Boris avoiding so much as looking at her. Ronya realized with something like dismay that Georgi was now taller than Igor and that he danced not with the daughters of their distinguished guests but almost exclusively with Olga. Olga, Tamara's niece, was not the little Olga of a year ago but a voluptuous vixen, beautiful like her aunt. Ronya decided that Georgi must return to St. Petersburg the next day.

That night Boris and Ronya slept in the cabin beside the stream, returning to the big house in midafternoon for breakfast. After they had finished eating, Georgi, more from habit than any impelling sense of hurry, asked, "May I be excused?"

"Yes," said Boris. "Go upstairs and pack. The train for St. Petersburg leaves in just two hours. You're going to be on it."

Georgi looked to his mother for help.

"I know," said Ronya. "The gypsies will be inconsolable without you."

"You were invited for a party, not a vacation," Katya said.

Hope gone, Georgi winked at Julie. "Come help me pack."

Alexis waited for the door to close. "You know, Ronya, we haven't yet heard about Igor."

Boris was in no mood for the story of Harbin so soon again. "I'm going to the stables," he said. "Tell Georgi to meet me there and I'll drive him to the station."

"Come," Ronya said after he had left, "Let's say goodbye to Georgi and send Julie to see him off. Then we'll talk in my room. At least that way if Boris comes back he won't have to hear the whole thing twice."

An hour later, Alexis said, "My dear, Ronya, it's incredible."

Ronya turned to her sister. "You say nothing but your eyes are full of horror. Don't judge Huang harshly, either of you. I made the same mistake myself. Let's leave judgment to God."

The logs in the fireplace were crackling. Ronya sat on a settee, Boris, drink in hand, on a stool beside her. Katya and Alexis had chosen easy chairs and were comfortably relaxed.

Though Boris threw in an occasional disparaging epithet at mention of Huang, Ronya was conveying the gist of her new-found knowledge. Stung, at last, by Boris's interruptions, she began to defend Huang.

"And I say he's an alarmist," Boris snorted, "a depraved alarmist."

"Look here, Boris," Alexis said, "lashing out like that gets us nowhere. Let's hear it all."

Boris poured himself another drink and sat down on the stool again. "After tonight," he said, "if you must carry on about Harbin, limit yourself to your whores. I like to hear about whores. What a blasted lunatic I was to give them up!"

"You amaze me." Ronya wrinkled her forehead. "I thought Anna Marie's girls were so dull."

Boris controlled an impulse to grin. "At least they don't talk."

"But darling, they do! All the time. Chatter, chatter, chatter. And giggle day and night."

Alexis was not amused. "Suppose you save your enlightening discussion of trollops for later," he said. "As it happens, I am not deeply impressed with Huang's conclusions about the world situation and yet, oddly enough, I agree with him on some points. He's right that we are not prepared for war, neither the army, nor the navy, nor the people. The Tsar has no inkling what he is plunging Russia into."

Boris' eyes narrowed. "If war is inevitable, why are diplomats —theirs and ours—conferring right now in St. Petersburg to find a peaceful solution to our differences on Manchuria and Korea?"

"I don't know, Boris." Alexis spoke somberly. "I only know that Sergius Witte doesn't trust the Nipponese, and no more do I."

"All right," Boris sneered, "what do you propose to do? Bend and kiss the ass of your enemy or fight and beat the yellow bastards?"

It was Ronya who answered. "If Huang is right and we are attacked without warning, we are in no condition to win. We can't move an army or supply one over the single-track railroad to Manchuria."

"Wait a minute," Boris said. "The Nips are a nuisance. But beat us? Never! Give me Tartars and Cossacks and, without guns, with horses and our bare hands we'll tear the livers out of them."

The intensity of his faith and his childlike trust in the fighting heart of Russia silenced Ronya. She got up and moved to the hearth and stood facing them all.

183

"What I really want to concentrate on," she said, "is our family's future. God knows we've had warnings before and pulled through by means of bribes and alliances. Mind you, I happen to think at times we've paid too dearly for safety and favor and power. . . ."

Katya read into Ronya's words a threat to her own plans for Georgi and thought she might hear next that they could not have him. "Please, Ronya," she said. "Not now. You're overwrought from worrying about Igor. We do feel for you but there's no danger yet. I suggest—"

Ronya raised her head in a curt gesture. "Huang translated Thomas Jefferson's first inaugural address for me. I tried to memorize it so he copied it for me." She brought a sheet of paper out of her bag. " '. . . possessing a chosen country, with room enough for our descendants to the thousandth and thousandth generation, entertaining in due sense our equal rights to the use of our own faculties, to the acquisition of our own industry, to honor and confidence of our own citizens, resulting not from birth but from our actions and their sense of them; enlightened by a benign religion, professed, indeed, and practiced in various forms, yet all of them inculcating honesty, truth, temperance, gratitude and the love of men.' "

So moved were they, they hardly dared look at each other. Boris recovered first. "We all want that, little dove, but we want it here in the Ukraine. We don't subscribe to running away. Neither do you, really. Katya's right. You've been through too much and you're not so much frightened as exhausted."

"That's not true, Boris," Ronya said. "I live in dread and fear when I think of the Tsar and Rasputin. I despair when I think of my people. At best, darling, we're just marking time."

"You're not surrounded by enemies," Alexis said. "My dear, we're your devoted friends. Between us we'll work things out, somehow, here in our own country. We'll get rid of Rasputin, and the Empress will die without him—or go completely mad. You and yours are safe. I give you my word."

Ronya felt utterly alone. Julie was an obedient child. When told to go to bed, she murmured, "I love this house." Alexis and Katya were die-hard Tsarists, hopelessly conservative. And

Boris, her husband, with a Tartar's contempt for the Romanovs, why!—he owned everything—her, the Ukraine, even the Jews. Tsar Boris. Yet who else had the intestinal fortitude to defend them? And what if she were wrong and they right?

Boris abandoned argument, melted by the sight of Ronya's drawn face. He poured a brandy. "Drink that, my sweet, then come to bed. I'll rub your feet."

She drank and suddenly announced, "Except for this estate and our dacha and lands in Odessa, I want to liquidate all my holdings and deposit the proceeds, in dollars, in the United States. For this I need your consent, Katya."

The effect of her proposal on Alexis was electric. This financially and politically sapient man saw in the von Glasman money the lever he needed to manipulate his Tsar. Diplomat that he was, he said only, "Ronya, my pet, I'm bursting to talk. May I?"

And she, knowing that she had a potential ally in Alexis and wishing to sidestep any argument, drew on her feminine guile. "I don't dare to, Alexis. I can't face your indignation. You're such an incorrigible royalist."

Much to Boris' amusement, Alexis thought she was speaking frankly. "Two-thirds wrong, Ronya," he corrected her. "But what a remarkable woman you are! You leave on a family errand and build a military hospital for our Tsar with Huang's money. And now you propose exchanging sick rubles for healthy dollars, fat, important dollars that will flood back into Russia, year after year, generation after generation! Superb! Pure champagne! Worthy the brilliant mind of David von Glasman. In the name of our beloved Dowager Empress, I salute you."

Boris exploded into loud guffaws. Ronya didn't know whether to laugh or cry. "You've missed the point completely," she protested.

"Not at all, you marvel. I shall engineer matters so we'll put to rest your gloomy fears and still be able to leave a comfortable margin of safety in the United States."

Ronya saw Katya sneak a surreptitious look at the clock and said, "Let's go to bed."

They paused outside Katya's door and Katya, though she was dragging with weariness, said, "You see, Ronya, it's as I said. You were bewitched in that Chinese garden. At home things look different. Isn't that so?"

"Yes, it is," Ronya lied calmly.

Ronya lay in the darkness listening to the rain. She seemed to hear the faint, silvery notes of temple bells and a voice that said, "Save yourself. Save yourself. There is a raging current. If you ignore it you will drown."

XXI

IT was fantastically cold that night of February 6, 1904. An Arctic wind lashed clouds across the sky and tore at the long skirts of St. Petersburg's most aristocratic women as they descended from carriages mounted on runners and driven by top-hatted coachmen with icicles in their beards. Under glittering chandeliers in the theater foyer the ladies opened their sable and ermine wraps to display magnificent gowns and flashing parures.

St. Petersburg was *en fête,* for on that night the divine Pavlova danced, and the elite filled the theater and would later celebrate at suppers and receptions.

"Please follow me, Count Brusilov," an usher said and eyes turned to watch Alexis and Katya and Ronya proceed down the aisle to their seats. Heads, gleaming with jewels, drew together and thin lips whispered, "Have you heard?" It was all over the city that the Dowager Empress had told her ladies, "The von Glasman sisters could melt the heart of the devil himself and make him fall in love. I am afraid for them."

The house lights dimmed; the conductor took his place and was recognized with a perfunctory patter of applause from hands in white kid gloves. Whispering continued through the overture until the moment when a nineteen-year-old girl, eyes demurely downcast under soft hair, floated onto the stage. She seemed barely to touch the boards, to soar and fly, never earthbound, immortal and incandescently pure in a stupid, avaricious and sinful world. Rich old women with handsome young protégés, lecherous men with entree to the green room and designs on the coryphées, forgot, for an hour, that they were not simple, beautiful and young.

At last it was over and hands were torn from gloves to clap, well-bred voices raised to shout "Brava!" and "Encore!" as the snow maiden, hands crossed on her bosom, dropped a curtsy so deep that it left only the nape of her long neck and the knot of her dark hair to be seen in a froth of white tutu.

When the curtain had been lowered with finality, the crowd finally began gathering up their wraps and gloves and programs. Eyes, turned away from the stage, were recalled momentarily by a voice which asked for attention. It was almost sacrilege that where Pavlova had bowed so short a time before, a foppish man now stood, dressed in an altogether too theatrical black velvet dinner jacket.

"Ladies and gentlemen of Russia," he pleaded, "your attention please!" The audience waved and said good nights and started slowly up the aisles, chattering. Desperate, the man on the stage gave the orchestra a signal, and an ear-splitting shriek from the trumpet impelled silence.

"Ladies and gentlemen," he began again, "Russia has been attacked." Silence was instant and absolute. "With plans for a diplomatic settlement of our differences under discussion, Nippon struck at Port Arthur without declaring war. Most of our ships are sunk and those that survive are bottled up. We are at war."

Men and women, faces distorted with anger and dread, as though they could hear the booming of guns, fled up the aisles, stampeding and shoving like a herd of terrified animals.

The throng swept Ronya away from the Brusilovs but she showed no flicker of fear as she allowed herself to be carried out onto the pavement. The anxious coachman handed her into the carriage a quarter of an hour before Alexis and Katya succeeded in reaching it. They found her, eyes closed, lips moving in a silent prayer to Huang to take care of Igor.

The carriage edged through traffic and Alexis and Katya stared fixedly out of the window while Ronya's eyes remained hooded. At the house, Alexis took their sable wraps and Ronya, heedless of her long gloves, threw a fallen log back on the fire of the downstairs drawing room while Katya, looking pale and shaken, lit the samovar.

Ronya was the first to speak, with an irritation directed solely at herself. "If only I hadn't agreed so cheerfully, Boris wouldn't have rushed home to keep Julie from being lonely! He can't have reached Kiev."

"He'll hear on the way, Ronya, and come back," Katya said.

"That would be silly in this wretched weather. I'll take the train tomorrow."

"It's highly unlikely that any civilian will leave St. Petersburg tomorrow," Alexis said sadly, "or in the next few weeks."

"In that case I'll borrow a sleigh and driver from you, Alexis. I must get home."

"Dear Ronya," he said, "I can't let you. The roads won't be safe. We must wait until we hear from Boris. He can't be more than halfway to Kiev and he'll surely turn back at once when he knows, for both of you."

"Do I have to go, too?" Katya sounded hurt.

"Yes, why does she, Alexis?" Ronya asked.

"I would have spared you this if I could, my dear one," Alexis said to Katya. "The bitter truth is that your presence upsets the Tsarina, which makes the Tsar nervous—and me vulnerable. And there is no time now. I must, I must convince His Majesty to appoint Peter Stolypin to the premiership. I have to persuade him to call Sergius Witte back to St. Petersburg. Once our friends are in a position to shape government policy, I can walk boldly. Until then I'll tread softly."

For minutes that seemed like eternity the only sound in the room was the crackling of the fire. "Your Jewish family puts you in a bad bargaining position, doesn't it, Alexis?" Ronya asked tonelessly.

He answered "Yes" before he could stop himself; then, appalled, he said, "Katya dearest, for a little time I must go my own way—alone. When the tide turns we'll be together once more and never part again, not even for a single day."

Russia, Katya thought bitterly, had been her father's mistress. Now it was her husband's. It would always be so. Too miserable for words, she simply motioned Alexis to pour brandy and they sat quietly, sipping it, and looking into the fire. At last Katya spoke, brokenly. "Alexis is right, Ronya. Your participation in Jewish affairs is well known and the court shrugs its shoulders and prefers to remember only that you are the wife of Boris Pirov. On the other hand, most people consider my conversion pure farce. Igor walks into a Jewish village, falls in love with one of its daughters, and the Cossacks no longer inflict pogroms on it. All this is perfectly familiar yet suddenly our Jewishness overshadows everything else about us. Why?"

Ronya said, "Someone is back of this. Who is it, Alexis?"

Alexis bowed his head. "Rasputin!"

Katya's head reeled. Ronya might be right after all. Perhaps Russia was no longer fit to live in when a dirty, wild-eyed *moujik* like that could separate her from Alexis. "What has Rasputin to do with me or I with him?" she demanded.

Alexis hesitated. He was enormously tempted to lie and he debated with himself for as long as it took to light a cigarette for Ronya and put a cushion under Katya's small feet. When he could no longer evade the issue, he spoke—the whole truth. "Rasputin's spies are everywhere, and Rasputin wants nothing more than to blackmail me. Since he cannot, he attacks through you, Katya, sowing seeds of dislike and distrust. To our pious Empress he says, 'The Countess Brusilov is stirred by guilt for what she does. She locks her door and lights Sabbath eve candles and mutters unending curses against good Catholics.' He howls, 'Saturday, not Sunday, is God's day for the Jewess.' He tells the Tsarina, 'The beautiful Jewess holds her head higher than the head that wears the crown. She rules the traitorous count and through him the Tsar.' He reminds her that the mother of the Emperor sings your praises. He says, 'Alix, my Empress, my angel, my saint, my goddess, utter no word against the von Glasman sisters lest the Tsarevitch be seized and murdered, his dear naked body found circumcised.' And he attacks your husbands. 'Count Brusilov is rich, richer than the Tsar,' he says. 'Boris Pirov is a Tartar with a lust for power, strong, stronger than the Tsar.' "

Ronya and Katya listened, sickened. "In her icon-lined sitting room Rasputin poisoned the Tsarina's mind deliberately," Alexis went on, "and watched as her breathing became difficult and blotches began to break out on her skin. Then he would reverse his tactics. His expression softened; his eyes filled with an eerie, seductive light. It was at this moment that he laid his peasant hands on the Imperial skin and began caressing it. The Empress did nothing to stop him, while she moaned, 'Everywhere, Rasputin. Leave no part of me uncured by your divine touch.'

"In the ecstasy of consummation she promised, 'My beloved husband, the Tsar, will destroy your enemies,' and as he lulled her to sleep, 'My lord, I am yours.' "

"How did you find this out, Alexis?" Ronya was shivering.

"A girl who was one of Alix's maids for a short time fell victim to Rasputin's degeneracy and her life was completely ruined. He dressed her in his long black vestments, hung his cross around her neck, then offered her the ultimate in abuse. Out of that horror, she is trying to atone by serving us. For months we friends of the Tsar and enemies of Rasputin have hoped that we could open his eyes and that he would order Rasputin's arrest." He shook his head. "The uproar of war ends that hope."

"And that is why Katya must leave St. Petersburg?"

Alexis bowed his head. "Victory and peace first. The destruction of Rasputin, God willing, with the Empress, second."

"Is Boris your ally in your plans against the Empress and Rasputin?" Ronya asked.

He smiled and shrugged. "You know Boris! He says, 'Assassinate the bastard and the German, too, if necessary. It's the best thing you can do for the Tsar.' However, it's not in my nature to condone murder."

Alexis looked at his watch. "I suggest that we use what few quiet hours remain to get some rest."

Not two minutes after they reached their rooms, they heard a roar that woke the sleeping servants and all but shook the house.

190

Watching from their windows they saw riders spreading the alarm. "War!" they shouted and thundered on.

The day which, for the Brusilovs and Ronya, began well past noon, was stormy and no word came from Boris to relieve the gloom that settled over the family while they lounged or wandered restlessly about the house. Incapable of concentrating on reading or letter-writing and unwilling to go out lest a message arrive in their absence, they spoke idly of why they had no word from Boris.

"He knows," said Alexis for the dozenth time, "that *we* know he'll come at once when he finds out and sees no need to tell us so by telegraphing."

Ronya brightened. "Of course! That's the way his mind works."

Katya was not convinced. "I still think it's odd—not hearing. But really, Alexis, why don't you go about your business? Ronya and I will be here."

Just then the doorbell shrilled. Alexis cried, "Ah! A message."

They were totally unprepared for the caller who was announced. It was a lieutenant, an instructor from Georgi's academy. He was flustered to find Georgi's mother at the house of his uncle but had no choice but to deliver his bad news, which he did with blunt embarrassment.

Georgi had disappeared! A search of his quarters, the grounds and the stables indicated that he had run away and none of his teachers or classmates had an inkling where he could be found.

Nervously expecting Madame Pirov to have hysterics, the lieutenant was charmed and puzzled to see that she seemed, if anything, amused.

"I fancy there's no great mystery," Ronya said. "Have you a list of recruiting stations in this area?"

The lieutenant nodded and Alexis said, "If you'll be good enough to wait, I'll order my carriage and we'll go and find him."

"I think I'd better stay here in case he's in trouble and comes for help," Katya volunteered.

In the carriage, before any order was given to the coachman, Ronya asked the officer if he knew of any crack cavalry unit, trained and ready to be transported to the Manchurian front. When he said there was one, Alexis directed the driver to take them to its barracks. Less than two hours later they were talking to a sergeant who remembered having seen a tall, blond and extremely handsome Cossack lad.

"Did the boy sign up?" Ronya asked the captain who had been called in.

The officer nodded.

"Would you tell us precisely what happened?" Alexis asked. "You must have had some suspicion that he was under age."

"Well sir," the captain replied, "I did, of course, until he mounted a horse, laughed, said, 'Watch me!' and began riding. That young Cossack gave a performance that left us blinking. He did impossible stunts—plain impossible they were—and out on the range he was just as incredible with a gun. I sent for our commanding officer and after the lad had gone through his whole bag of tricks again, *he* said, 'You're another Boris Pirov, my boy,' and instructed me to induct him immediately."

"That's our Georgi!" Alexis beamed.

The captain leaned back in his chair. "I don't know, Count Brusilov. The Cossack answers your description of the missing cadet but he can hardly communicate in Russian, he's so uneducated. What he said was colorful, all right, but definitely Cossack dialect. Why, he can't even write. Had to sign his name, Peder Zedorov, with a cross."

The enlistment papers were sent for and revealed additional data: age—21; place of birth—unknown; family—orphan, no near kin, unmarried; occupation—circus rider, currently unemployed.

Ronya and Alexis both laughed. The officers did not. The captain ground out his cigarette, pressed a button and said to the sergeant who answered, "Bring Private Peter Zedorov here."

The young man who slumped into the office a minute or two later saluted with the gravity and unfamiliarity of a civilian. Even his stance lacked military coordination, as if the army were still alien to him. His eyes showed no sign of recognizing anyone there except the captain, on whom he bestowed a shy smile.

192

"Do you know any of these people, Private Zedorov?" the captain waved at Ronya and Alexis and the officer from the academy.

With a singular lack of interest, the recruit answered, "No, Captain."

"Think before you answer, private. Have you ever heard of Georgi von Glasman Pirov?"

"Don't know nothing about no Pirov," the lad said. "But the Georgi part . . . Couple of weeks back I ride past some gypsy wagons and the folks yell, 'Heigh, Georgi.' I tie up nothin' with that name so I don't even look back. They rush after me, shouting, 'Heigh, Georgi, wait!' Never heard the name Georgi since until now."

"What do you think?" the captain asked the lieutenant.

To Ronya's and Alexis' amazement, the lieutenant said uncertainly, "The voice bothers me. Except for that I'd swear he's Cadet Pirov. Still—"

The captain lit a cigarette. He looked unhappy. "Are you sure, private, you never saw these people before?"

The boy stared at each in turn. "Yes, sir, I'm sure."

"And you, Madame Pirov, and you, Count Brusilov, do you know this young man to be Georgi von Glasman Pirov?"

"Of course," Ronya said. "Certainly," Alexis confirmed.

The captain looked out the window, shook his head and turned his attention back to his guests. "I see no way of releasing this soldier into your custody. It is my responsibility to turn the whole matter over to my superior who, I am certain, will order a complete investigation. Unless we're moved out of here, we should have the answer in a few days. I regret that your son is missing, Madame."

If it had not been for the words, "Unless we're moved out of here," Ronya would have left Georgi to be dealt with by Boris. "Stop your play-acting," she scolded. "Not quite fifteen and you want to be a soldier. Have you any idea what it's like? And do you think Igor hasn't enough to worry about? Does he need you to look after, too?"

The volunteer rolled his eyes to the ceiling. "You sure do go on, lady," he said.

Alexis said, "Make out your report, Captain. I am going to

193

the admiralty to get an order permitting me to take my nephew away. That will give him approximately two hours to change his clothes and get ready. Thank you for your courtesy and good afternoon."

The bone of contention eyed his captain and asked, "May I go, sir?"

"Not so fast, Cossack lad," Ronya said. She left the room and returned in a minute with the coachman's whip in her hands. As they all watched her, she took off her fur coat and dropped it onto a chair, then circled the young man. Having judged the appropriate distance she took her place. Alexis and the officers stepped back out of range.

Ronya did not whip him—but she put him through a series of acrobatic leaps, high and low, showy and fast. As he bounded, he pressed his hands together prayerfully. There were about six men in the outer room and Alexis invited them in to enjoy the performance. By now Georgi had abandoned pretext and was throwing himself into the act. He winked at his mother and danced to her whip. She laughed back at him and made music with its crack, crack, crack.

By the time Ronya said, "Enough," everyone was roaring and clapping and stamping their feet. The soldiers cried out for more and as an encore Ronya threw her whip four times toward the four corners of the room and each time, as Georgi turned, it flew past his eyebrows.

What a pair! thought the captain, joining in the applause. From the top of his desk he picked the papers of Private Peter Zedorov, tore them across and tossed the scraps into his wastebasket.

"Is that all, sir?" the lieutenant from the academy asked quickly.

"That's all," the captain said. "No one by the name of Georgi von Glasman Pirov was ever inducted."

"Yes, sir. Thank you, sir. We appreciate it, sir."

"May I add my thanks, Captain?" Ronya said.

Smiling to himself, he answered, "I wouldn't have missed today's circus for anything. It is I who thank you, Madame Pirov." He looked at Georgi. "Sorry to lose you, cadet."

"I'll hurry and graduate, sir," Georgi grinned. "Then I'll be back."

The second morning of the war, Alexis left home early and returned late. The Tsar, he told Katya and Ronya that evening, was "numb" with fear. He was haunted by the memory that the Kaiser (whom Queen Victoria always seated on her right) promised him an empire in Asia and called him Admiral of the Pacific. And now he thought his cousin George of England was going to make that dream impossible. The Tsarina, Alexis said, was adding to the general muddle by telling the poor fellow to rely on Rasputin and to punish the Jews. Of that he was sure. And that she advised that the peasants, who were always clamoring for more bread, be sent to war. That would put fear and respect into their wretched souls.

"The court, of course, is a hornet's nest. You never heard such angry buzzing. They want to sting the Jews to death, to censor the press, to hang Sergius Witte!"

Alexis sighed. "Poor, childish Nicholas. Today, at the audience, he wore white trousers, a nautical jacket and his yachting cap. When I addressed him as 'Admiral,' he beamed."

Katya wanted to know if he had also listened to and approved Alexis' suggestions.

"I won a point, I lost a point." He shrugged. "Argument makes him petulant. The only thing that works at all is patience."

"Marvelous!" Ronya sneered. "I can hardly wait for Boris to come and take us away from this damned city."

He came but not until after Ronya had spent hours at a front window watching every carriage and sleigh that raced past across the ice and snow, her worry over Igor mounting. Boris was a long time coming because first he had dashed to Julie with reassurances. "Igor was born to fight. We'll win. You'll see." She believed him implicitly. Next he fetched Sara from the village to be with Julie and instructed the Blond One to guard her with his life.

When at last Ronya saw her man he was in the first of two carriages built specially for the icy roads and driven by Cossacks armed to the teeth. He limped into the house and the boot had to be cut from his swollen foot. While it was soaking, Ronya returned to her arguments. "Why won't you all face the future?" she asked her family. "The court is dissolute and greedy. The army wants power. The navy wants power. The church wants gold. The secret police is corrupt. The peasants want bread and we all want the Manchurian timber and minerals. But no one, absolutely no one, wants to fight. Let's get out before it's too late."

Boris pooh-poohed her. "The Ukraine," he said, "is a rock. We won't be crushed by a pebble."

Alexis reminded Boris that Russia was one country and the Ukraine did not fly a separate flag.

Katya, close to collapse, turned on Ronya. "You're more of a gypsy than Tamara. Even as a child it was useless to double-bolt your door—you got out. I'll tell you what to do about your incurable restlessness. It takes only a week to cross the ocean. Go see. Have a look at the red Indians. Make headlines. This time you can be an international scandal. But do me one favor, spare us the 'My heart tells me to go to America' cant."

In the face of Katya's denunciation and the hard Tartar light in Boris' eyes, Ronya took a deep breath, reached for Boris' hand and said tenderly to Katya, "Darling, my heart and my head go in opposite directions. Have patience with me until I have news from Manchuria." A storm of sobbing seized Katya and she threw herself into Ronya's arms.

There were more tears, terrible, silent tears, at the hour of parting. Even in the carriage, where the air was so cold it stung her face, great tears ran slowly down Katya's cheeks. On her lap Alexis had set her jewel box and now Boris took it from her and locked it away, then got in, sat between the sisters, and put his arms around Katya, who sobbed aloud.

Alexis had turned back toward the house after his farewell kiss, and so Boris cradled his weeping sister-in-law in his arms until the convulsive sobs abated.

He hugged her, dropped a kiss on the end of Ronya's nose, and shouted, "Time to go home!" then leaped out of the carriage, mounted the coachman's box and gathered up the reins. Back went the laughing, golden head. "Home," he said to his team. "Some fool started a war. It'll be a hard trip."

XXII

IGOR heard of the surprise attack on Port Arthur. Messages and orders began to reach him within the hour, so hysterical, contradictory and bewildering that he crumpled them up and tried to evaluate the situation independently. Thousands of miles separated the garrison from the high command, where everything was apparently at sixes and sevens. It was up to him to decide on a course of action and he began to see it in terms of a private war between himself and the people he called the "Nips."

It was going to be a lonely war, he realized, in which his men killed alone and were killed alone, quite out of touch with the main Russian army. The price would undoubtedly be inestimable, and so it proved. The Japanese were not the only enemies of Igor's men—they were sick of, and sick from, the maggots that crawled over putrid food, and when ammunition ran out they faced guns with knives. Enemy fire, a few suicides, the swollen horror of the frost deprived him of manpower, and Igor lacked nearly everything that makes it possible for men to fight. More bitter than all the rest was the utter indifference of the high command when Igor reported his forces' position and needs.

One night during a few hours of peace, Igor woke sweating with fury. He sat up, swung his feet onto the cold, bare floor, rolled a cigarette, and began to take inventory. Lacks. Lacks. Lacks. Men so discouraged they could not endure much more. What could he enter on the credit side of the ledger? Only one thing—he knew the terrain.

197

In the coldest of all Manchurian winters, more severe even than the preceding one, without warm clothing, bullets, medicine or vodka, he had no choice but to switch strategy and take to the hills. Street fighting was too costly. As a guerilla he could strike fast and hard, then disappear into a hideout. Yet even this kind of operation called for supplies. Possibly Igor might have got them without robbing and plundering. The truth was he didn't want to.

Since, in all the loathsome business, no one seemed to him more detestable than the war profiteers who dealt with his enemies, he sent his men out three times marauding. Once he himself went, alone. Then he presented himself at Huang's great gate.

"Empty the pockets of the profiteers," he rasped angrily after he was admitted. "I need gold."

And Huang, his heart sore at Igor's suffering and distress, found him the gold. With it Igor bought an army, paying well for the sons of poor and hungry Chinese—and they were many. These peasant boys seemed rough and tough, and so they proved to be when it came to carrying out his commands.

Food was still desperately short. "Steal," said Igor and they stole. Horses, too. And paint. Against the trackless snow his men would move like wraiths—their equipment, saddles, clothes white.

They wanted women but Igor said, "No," and, vicious though they were, not one had the temerity to challenge his ruling.

Again he went to Huang and caught himself asking for what he needed before he even said hello. "I need arms, ammunition, sharp swords for silent attacks, skin tents, Siberian clothing, snow boots, sleds. . . ." And Huang recalled another voice which had said, "I need fresh food, pure water, medical supplies, laborers, rubber tubing, and white marble. . . ."

For Ronya's sake he acceded to all Igor's demands; then he said, "I am glad you came, Igor. I have been considering coming to you. I want to ask *you* a favor."

Without hesitation, Igor said, "Anything. Anything at all, Huang, my father."

"Leave this war."

198

Impatiently, Igor said, "Let me have a bath. Give me clean clothes. I'm too tired to play games."

Huang knew it was useless, but he persisted. "There is no honor in this war. The Tsar is not worth your life and from death there is no return. Let me get you out of Manchuria and to the United States. I have made you my heir. Take your inheritance now and your mother will bring Julie to you."

Igor pulled up a chair and sat down. "May I bring my wounded here?" he asked.

"Yes, Igor." Huang smiled in resignation. "Spend the night here with me, my son." There was anguish in his voice.

"I plan to," Igor said. "I want to do my buying and be on hand for the loading-up."

Two nights later Igor rode out of Huang's walled palace at the head of a caravan. A rendezvous had been set in the foothills with his men and he led the pack train to it. Toward morning the united band found their camp. By some astounding instinct, Igor had been able to ferret out a stronghold that he had never seen before, a natural garrison cleft in the rocks. Here smoke could rise unseen from cooking fires. They made camp with speed, ate, and for the day which followed they slept. Night was their time for fighting.

As the last light faded from the sky, the men gathered around Igor. He it was who selected the route by which they dropped down to the edge of the plain. There they separated into small teams. While soldiers were to work together, every man was his own master. They fanned out and attacked smoothly, silently, invisibly and with terrible boldness.

With surprise and luck favoring them, the men made successful strikes every night for weeks. In the darkness of May 18, Igor planned to attack and burn a supply depot with three companions, one Russian, two Chinese. Their mission was almost routine by then and went precisely according to plan. However, Igor was in a flamboyant, Tartar mood. A few minutes' ride away was a building the Nipponese cherished and he resented, a temporary wooden structure that contained such amenities as ceremonial rooms and even a theater. It was not properly a military target but Igor knew that destroying it would taunt and infuriate the Nips. Moreover, a price had been set on his head, which aroused in him not fear but a wild desire to clown.

Savagely excited, he dismounted and led his men at a crouching lope up to a barbed-wire fence around the building. After scouting the best place to jump it, he whispered to Leo, the Russian, to go back, untether the horses and bring them up close for a split-second getaway. Leo crossed himself. "Not me, Captain," he whispered. "I'm waiting for you back there." Leo pointed toward the ponies. The Chinese, their faces blank, melted into the darkness.

He would go it alone, then. Over the fence he vaulted and ran at top speed and in absolute silence to the building where, sheltered under overhanging eaves, he lit a bundle of kerosene-soaked rags he had brought for the purpose and tossed it through a half-open window. He had barely turned to race for safety when the whole flimsy building blazed. Men tumbled out of adjoining barracks, snatching up guns. Most of the shellfire went wild, but Igor's left leg and thigh were hit three times.

Leo reached the barbed-wire fence at a gallop with Igor's horse in tow. He quickly hoisted the wounded man over the fence and into the saddle. The sky began to lighten.

"Get going," Igor moaned. "I can make it on my own."

Leo gave one look at the pursuing Nipponese and spurred his nag off toward the hills. Igor was alone, strength ebbing, blood pouring onto his saddle leather and the horse's flank. At its smell, the beast fled with his half-conscious rider, for home and safety. Home to him was the stables of the walled house in Harbin.

At Huang's gate, Huang's people lifted Igor down, staining their hands and robes with blood, and caught him as he swayed and fainted.

It was ten hours before he swam up out of the refuge of unconsciousness to see Huang and his doctor standing at the foot of the bed. "How soon can I go back?" Igor asked.

"Soon," the doctor said and slipped an opiate into a cup of broth.

Even in the delirium of fever Igor was obsessed by the war, which was being so expensively lost. "Bitch!" he cried, starting up, and "Coward! Traitor! Maggot!" All these epithets were for

Stësel, the commandant of Port Arthur, who had surrendered on January 2, 1905, with two million rounds of ammunition left. Igor screamed, "That coward!" and the doctor reached for another bowl of opium broth while Huang took up the spoon.

Drugged, Igor's body mended and, mending, his rebellion grew. By evening of the seventh day, when he threw his medicines at the doctor and tore off his bandages, Huang knew that he was well. Despite warnings, he got out of bed and began exercising his leg. Huang went out of the room and bolted the door behind him.

They dined, Huang and Igor, outwardly polite, inwardly tense. Huang kept a sharp eye on his guest who, furtively, let his eyes stray frequently to a clock on a golden wall bracket. They both knew that he wanted to be with his men that very night, as soon as common courtesy had been observed and he was free to ride up into the hills. Huang was unusually silent and across the table Igor began to feel nervously that he was about to be bullied again about his course of action. They drank their tea and Huang rose and led the way to the library, where candles were lit and the air was sweet with flowers. "Sit down, Igor," he said.

Now Igor's uneasiness mounted to something darker. Huang was frowning and it crossed Igor's mind that he had, perhaps, had bad news from Russia. At the thought, he was so close to panic he dared not ask what had happened.

For his part, Huang was searching for some way to spare Igor and it took every ounce of his will power to say what he knew must be said.

Words came harshly out of his distress. "It is all over, Igor. Russia has surrendered to Nippon."

It was as if a sword hung between them.

"What in hell do you mean!" Igor was beyond manners.

Huang leaned forward in his chair. Deliberately he pounded home the dreadful news. "Russia has given up. Yielded. Formally withdrawn from the war. . . . I am ashamed."

Waves of emotion swept across Igor's face—incredulity succeeded by fury and sick humiliation. Young, healthy Igor started to shake.

"Cry," Huang pleaded. "Man was born with tears in his soul."

201

And looking into the white face before him, "Think of your mother. Think of Julie."

Huang had never seen Boris, had no idea how Boris looked in a rage. Igor was suddenly transformed into a stranger, a Tartar capable of madness. The voice in which he spoke was steel cold. "I've been out of touch. What happened?"

"Germany pulled strings. France paid. Nicholas II danced to their tunes. Count Bursilov, your uncle, warned him; Sergius Witte warned him; I warned him; the United States and Great Britain warned him. But your Tsar, blunderer of blunderers, was pleased to delude himself. His little war with Nippon was diverting, a golden opportunity to be 'Lord and Admiral of the Pacific.' Like an idiot child he sent the Baltic fleet around the world, manned by land sailors and without provision for refueling. His asinine order was simply, 'Sink and destroy the Nipponese fleet in the Yellow Sea.'

"Why break our hearts over that ghastly voyage? What matters is the end. Admiral Togo intercepted his enemy in the Tsushima Strait. It took less than an hour to annihilate the Russians. They were massacred, though it is rumored three vessels escaped. In any case, the war is over."

Igor, who had become a man within the last hour, could not free himself from his boy's declaration of a personal war. "No. It isn't. I haven't surrendered. We haven't even begun to fight."

This, Huang saw, was a boy trained to win and wretched because his side had lost. Just the same he was a brave and lovable boy, trying all by himself to save his country's honor.

He said sternly, "You no longer have my permission to use Chinese soldiers nor will I supply you with horses and matériel in order for you to become a bandit. Accept your country's reverses. What you contemplate is treason."

Igor, already dreaming of Boris and the Blond One joining him at the head of an army of Tartars and Cossacks—real soldiers—was astonished when Huang dashed his hopes.

"How can you let the Nips take over? Are you so fond of them? Will they respect your rank and honor you the way we do? How can you carry on about freedom and be willing at the same time to hand Harbin over to the blighters?"

Huang remained dignified and reasonable. "These are considerations that need not concern you. History teaches that China always conquers her conquerors. Nippon will not find Manchuria hospitable."

Igor looked longingly at the door, with difficulty restraining his impulse to bolt back to his men. Huang was the sharper of the two. He not only saw, he had foreseen. "Don't try it, Igor. You are my prisoner."

The reaction was pure admiration. "I'll be Goddamned! I'd have thought only Boris would have pulled a trick like that."

Huang smiled wanly. "I have learned from you and my lady Ronya."

Hours before, he had sent runners to the mountains carrying orders issued in Igor's name. The men were to disband and ride into Harbin, there to be paid. As Russia had no plan for repatriating her soldiers, and since he knew how much their welfare meant to Igor, he had arranged for them to have safe conduct out of Manchuria. Now he explained all this to Igor.

"You," he concluded, "will be ordered to St. Petersburg to receive, like your mother, an honorable medal. Nicholas will kiss you on both cheeks. Not, I warn you, because he wishes to, but because he now needs men like Witte and Stolypin and your uncle to negotiate peace. You, my dear son, are already a major. The Tsar is on his throne. Yellow mustard and tiny bluets reveal that spring is here, and I have one more message for you, Major. You are to wait here until your orders arrive. Are you content to be my guest, or must I—"

"I'd rather be your prisoner," Igor said petulantly.

Huang accepted his rudeness. "You are at liberty to move freely within the walls. Do not try to leave. It will be impossible." Then, softening, he said, "It is the climate of our times, not I, that holds you prisoner."

"Tell that to my men! I promised them victory and they believed me."

Huang said, "Good night, my son," and left him.

On May 13, while Huang and Igor were still at breakfast, a servant brought in a telegram for Major Igor Pirov. It was laid beside Huang's place and he passed it over to Igor, saying, "This is perhaps the last meal we shall have together."

"No," said Igor. "I'll be back."

On a shining morning toward the end of June, Igor jumped off the train in Kiev to find all the Pirov clan, save his mother, his aunt and his girl, assembled to welcome him home. Julie, Boris told him, was safe at home, but Ronya had popped her into bed when she seemed overwrought from the excitement of his return. His mother and aunt preferred to welcome him far from the crowd. The curious throng included the Pirov gypsies and Tamara, as well as a cavalry escort. Igor himself was in such a state that he could never recall his journey to the white house. But from the moment he came into the room where Julie lay, every smallest detail was etched on his mind. He scarcely dared believe that the nymph he saw was flesh and blood, so long had he dreamed of her.

"I feel perfectly awful!" a very human little voice said, and when he sought to gather her in his arms she held him off for a moment and studied his face. There was something changed in it, but the magic of his dimple was the same and the sweetness of his laugh. Julie flushed healthily with joy.

Igor sat down on the bed beside her and pulled off the covers. She wore a white nightdress that made her look little and lost. He put his arms around her and felt her quiver. Then he did an astonishing thing—for Igor. He talked gently, fondly, until, fear dispelled, Julie gave him a happy little kiss. It neither tormented Igor, made his heart race, nor satisfied him, but it was what he wanted from Julie.

He drew up the covers and settled himself comfortably beside her. "Sing to me, little Julie," he said and when she did, he knew he was home at last.

The door opened and Ronya appeared. "I'm lonesome," she said, joining them.

"I'm glad you came," Igor said. "Now I won't have to walk downstairs to tell you to get ready for a wedding."

Ronya laughed her wonderful laugh. "Oh, Igor, that's the first sensible thing I've heard you say since you got here."

They both turned to Julie. She breathed blissfully. "Igor, let's never leave this house. Not even for a wedding trip."

The wedding was almost superfluous. In four years under the Pirov roof Julie had become a Pirov, the name of Brodsky forgotten by the peasants, who accepted her as daughter to Ronya, precious to Boris and therefore young mistress. The gypsies had adopted her for her music and for being Igor's. The house servants pampered her as a member of the family; Father Tromokov loved her for her rare sweetness and inquiring mind; Rabbi Levinsky worried lest she be getting too much education and too little religion. Except that it gave her the right to sleep with Igor, marriage could in no way affect her status.

A grand wedding would have involved the dilemma of how to combine Abraham and Rhea and all their children, Sara and the baker, and Julie's friend the peasant, with the society of Kiev. Nor was it conceivable to ask Rabbi Levinsky to perform the Jewish ceremony in the presence of guests some of whom were undoubtedly members of the Black Hundreds, that ominous organization which had sponsored and engineered orgies of rape and murder in the pogroms of Kishinev and Odessa.

There was another reason—unspoken but menacingly real. On a Sunday when, ironically, Igor in Manchuria, fighting the enemies of the Tsar, had no bullets, the guards at the Winter Palace, from which the Imperial family was absent, were well armed. A mighty mob of people led by a young priest and bearing icons and pictures of their Tsar converged on the palace. The priest, Father Gapon, held in his hands a petition to the Little Father for an eight-hour day, a wage of a ruble a day. "We are seeking here," it said, "the last salvation." Through the wide avenues which Peter the Great had laid out rolled the strains of "God Save the Tsar." Workers, their wives and children were singing.

The soldiers answered the petition with bullets, fired point-blank at a range of ten feet. Five hundred people died on Bloody Sunday, the old quietly, the children screaming. Blood ran in the snow-covered streets and could not be staunched. It flowed to Moscow, in a red ribbon, and there the tide of revolution swelled.

A modest home wedding for a time of trouble.

The Tsar sent a present to Julie. He needed, as Huang knew, Witte and Stolypin and Brusilov, now that horror was added to the humiliation of defeat. He needed the crops in Ronya's granaries and he owed Boris money for horses. More, he needed Boris, who said that Little Russia—the Ukraine—did not need him, Nicholas II.

Rabbi Levinsky sighed and Father Tromokov muttered, "I'd rather take a curse from a demon," but Julie liked it. Julie always liked presents and she set the photograph of the royal family with Nicholas in the center, framed in silver, next to her silver candlesticks, though Levinsky disapproved. "The Tsar," he said, "is mighty, but God is mightier. You can't be a Jew without being a Jew, Julie."

Julie answered, "Igor is."

At twilight on September 5, 1905, the Blond One walked with Georgi from the library, through the central hall and into the large reception room. Behind the bride and her attendants, Tamara strode, head high, her bright dress striking a bizarre note against the pastel shades worn by the other women. By her side was Katya, almost as tall as she, but infinitely more aristocratic. Count Alexis Brusilov had Sara, truly elegant in flowered chiffon which had come from Paris and was a gift from Ronya, on his arm. Father Tromokov walked alone, the last of the party.

Lydia, who had pressed the wedding dress herself and supervised getting Julie into it, appeared, at Ronya's insistence, and was ushered into the front row to sit with the family, moist-eyed and at the same time worried at being out of the kitchen where her helpers were putting the final touches on a sumptuous supper.

In hushed voices Julie and Igor exchanged their vows before the small congregation of relations and friends. Then he lifted her veil and her lips clung to his.

Hand in hand they walked out onto the wide veranda where peasants and gypsies waited quietly. It had been a day of waiting, not alone for them but for all Russians, a somber day on which news raced by cable over the ocean floor from Portsmouth, New

Hampshire, in the United States of America. A courier now brought a message to Boris: PEACE TREATY SIGNED.

For most of the world those three words signaled the end of a foolish war. For Igor they were anguish, and that night he forgot to be gentle with Julie.

XXIII

ANY hope or dream that life would be more placid in the Pirov family once Julie and Igor were married was roughly shaken a few months later. On a moment's notice Boris carried Ronya off to their house in the woods, his face so stiff with misery that she did not question him until he slammed the door behind them.

"Tamara's niece, Olga, is going to have a child by Georgi," he said in a half-choked voice.

"Oh my God!" She pulled away from him. "Another Pirov bastard."

Boris would have comforted her but she flung away furiously. With shaking hands she tore open a pack of cigarettes, took one, fumbled in lighting it and inhaled so recklessly she was convulsed with coughing. Boris took the cigarette and flipped it into the fireplace.

"Calm down, my love," he said, suddenly calmer himself.

She mimicked him bitterly. "Calm down, my love!" It was years since he had seen her so angry. "Are you proud of Georgi for living up to your reputation? Is Olga the reason why you got him extra leave after the wedding?"

Boris responded by stamping into the bathroom and setting the bathtub faucets running. "Get the hell in there and cool off or, so help me, I'll give you a rough idea of my cooperation," he said, glaring. Ronya glared back and, for good measure, stuck out her tongue, but she obeyed.

Left alone, Boris grinned at her small-girl defiance, lit a lamp and poured himself a drink. When she returned, wearing a warm robe, her expression was wistful. The battle was over.

Ronya settled herself on the sofa and said, with a little shiver, "It's cold in here."

"I'll fix a fire." As soon as the flames were licking up over the logs, Boris sat down next to Ronya and put his right leg on a footstool. He waited for her to ask the questions he knew he must answer.

"How did you find out?" she said at last.

"Tamara."

Ronya was instantly jealous. "Why didn't she tell me?"

"How could she, when you won't talk to her?"

It was true, Ronya admitted. For years she had taken a perverse pleasure in acknowledging Tamara queen of the gypsies, publicly, and shutting her out as a person, privately.

"What's Tamara's price?"

Boris did not try to evade that crucial point. "For Georgi to inherit Alexis' title."

"The hell you say!" What a woman, Ronya thought, with grudging admiration. Like Katya she understood the value of having a friend close to the throne. She felt trapped. "And what does the little baggage want?"

"She'd like to be queen."

It was too much for Ronya. "Doubtless Tamara promised her just that for seducing Georgi," she said scathingly.

Boris burst out laughing. "If it makes you any happier to think Georgi was seduced, then—"

Eyebrows arched in reproach, Ronya said, "And you don't think that was how it was?"

"I damn well don't."

"Perhaps I'm wrong," said Ronya, "but one thing I do know. Tamara could have broken the affair up before it became serious."

Boris shrugged. "Possibly."

Suddenly Ronya realized that Boris was profoundly tired and that whenever he moved, it was with difficulty, as if his leg were

208

causing him pain. "I don't know, Boris," she said. "I suppose I try to blame Tamara because everything is contradictory and confused." She dropped her head on his shoulder.

"You're all right, Ronya?" he asked anxiously.

She snuggled her head against him. "Yes. . . . Father used to say that under the big man, the man of preeminent breeding, is the little man and he's mean. Under the courageous me is a very scared me. But I have to know the story, the whole story!"

He stroked her hair while he told of the events which had begun to unfold during a trip the previous week to St. Petersburg. He had gone at the insistence of Alexis, who believed that his committee might have some ace up its sleeve to force the Tsar to appoint Stolypin minister of the interior at once instead of the following July. Unfortunately there were divisions of opinion within the committee, so Boris had nothing to propose to his brother-in-law but delaying actions.

Alexis met him at the station saying, "Our Georgi is an indiscriminate democrat. He rides with the cavalry to police the mobs one day and destroys government property the next."

They had driven straight to the academy, where Boris had a session with the commandant and another with Georgi. Boris then promised Georgi's superior that the boy would henceforth behave.

That evening, before dinner, Alexis took his brother-in-law to the rooms which Georgi called his own. Set on platforms were five models, two of churches, one of a town house and two of country houses, painstakingly and beautifully built from bits of wood and colored stones. Boris whistled. They were magnificent. Being something of a carpenter himself, he saw not only the sureness of technique but the promise of genius.

"How wonderful!" Ronya sighed. "Our daring son is capable of something more than chasing girls, turning cartwheels and standing on his head on horseback."

"Well," Boris resumed, "I began to get an inkling of what Georgi's future might be, that he ought to abandon his military training and begin to study architecture. When you came back from Manchuria, Alexis told me, he and Huang began to correspond and out of their letters a friendship has developed. Huang suggested to Alexis that Georgi be sent to the United

209

States, not to Harvard, but to a smaller college in California called Stanford, to follow his bent. My immediate inclination is to overrule that but I'm not sure."

Boris had ridden back to the academy and had a second talk with his son. When he asked, "Do you want to be an architect?" Georgi replied, "Yes, sir. But not yet. I want to win the national championship. I want to graduate and get my commission before I become a student." Boris puffed with pride at that and took him to supper.

"Why didn't you tell me before, Boris?" Ronya asked.

"He made me promise. He knows *you* and how you dote on managing things."

"And does Tamara's claim on Georgi ruin your dream of his being the national champion?"

"Let's eat," was his answer.

"Are you hungry?"

"No, but you are."

Over the supper table Boris told of his meeting with Tamara. The upshot of their hour together was that she had offered a deal. If the Pirovs would agree to making Georgi Alexis' heir, she was prepared to take care of Olga. After her confinement the girl would be sent away, to be queen of a minor tribe, where Georgi would never find her. The child would become Tamara's.

Boris, fearing tricks, pressed to find out why Tamara was so willing to part with her niece. She merely pointed at a photograph of Ronya and said, "Ask her."

"It's an act of friendship," Ronya explained later. "She needs the child, but she doesn't want Georgi to have to pay for the rest of his life by being saddled with Olga."

"I offered her a compromise," Boris went on. "Everything she demands but when Georgi comes of age, he will be free to decide whether or not he wants to become Count Georgi Brusilov. Nobody, not you or Katya or Alexis or I, is to try to influence him." He paused. "We agreed to that deal, Ronya."

For a long time she sat, chin in hand, deep in thought. Boris to get his champion, Georgi his championship, Tamara sharing political protection and the Brusilovs a fair hope that Georgi would be theirs. But still there was a chance that she, Ronya, would send one son to America.

"You made a fair bargain," she said at last, and Boris kissed her.

Not two days later Boris asked, as he and Ronya breakfasted in her room, "Are you positive that Julie's vomiting proves she's pregnant?"

"Absolutely. The doctor examined her again yesterday morning. She's seven or eight weeks gone."

"Good," he said. "Now I can deal with Igor."

"What in the world are you talking about?" Ronya protested.

"Christ! my dear love, I wish I could spare you and Julie and Katya this."

"Oh, Boris," Ronya groaned. "I've been afraid of more trouble. There's a kind of mad excitement about Igor these days."

Boris gave her a sharp look. "You're observant. I didn't think he'd been around enough for anyone to notice anything about him."

"Poor little Julie!" she mourned. "She won't know how to cope with a rival, and bastards shame her."

"I wish to God Igor's trouble was a woman," Boris said. "That would be easy."

For weeks Boris had suspected Igor was up to something. Julie had been in bed and asleep for hours by the time he came home, if, indeed, he came home at all. In his saddlebags Boris had found four loaded pistols, and the grooms admitted that his stallion often looked as if it had been traveling hard for a week. The Blond One was, as always, Igor's shadow and the Blond One, the stablemen reported to Boris, was armed. Boris, proud of the job Igor had done in the war, ignored the clues until he got a message from a man named Krasmikov, chief of the secret police. "Hide Igor," it warned. "He's on the road to Siberia, and it's wide. The lane back is narrow."

Boris went directly to Mischuk.

"What do you know about Igor?" he asked.

"Not a damn thing."

He questioned Mischuk about the villages. Had there been

sudden violences? Again, the answer was no. His third question
—what breeze was blowing from the Kazak strongholds—lit a
spark.

"There are strange rumors," Mischuk said. "Two thousand
Cossacks under arms, a mysterious rider who supplies them with
funds and rides in and out of the villages. The rank and file
never see him. He's said to meet only the chiefs."

He had gathered from Boris' questions who the man might be
and suggested, "Let's make sure. Tell Tamara to send along her
gypsy spies . . . they beat the Tsar's by a mile. They'll give us
the picture."

Boris declined, but by the time they finished making plans it
was past three in the morning. Late the next afternoon Mischuk
paid an unofficial visit to Krasmikov. With him he took a man
he described to Boris as an "honest burglar." Together they entered the headquarters, and parted. Mischuk's business with
Krasmikov stretched out till long after working hours. Then
Mischuk said, as if on the spur of the minute, "My good friend,
thank you for your excellent advice. Won't you have dinner
with me?" Krasmikov was flattered but wary. "Delighted," he
said, "but don't think you can take advantage of my absence
from this building. The Tsar's secrets are safe in my keeping."

Without bothering to reply, Mischuk led the way down the
street to one of the best restaurants in town. Everyone saw them
there—the honest chief of the Kiev police, dining with the
Tsar's butcher. At about ten, while they were having a last
vodka, Mischuk clapped his hand to his head in horror.

"Christ!" he gulped. "I forgot all about Boris. He's waiting
for me at the barracks."

Krasmikov, slightly the worse for liquor, roared, "Let's go!
The giant is in my debt. I'll collect over cards."

As to that he was quite correct. Boris played badly and was in
a vile temper, complaining that he'd waited hours for Mischuk
and his reward was to lose a fortune to Krasmikov. When he
judged he'd paid enough for the warning of Igor's danger, he
began to win and Krasmikov was delighted to quit.

The moment he was out of sight, Boris and Mischuk drove
straight to Mischuk's house. The burglar had deposited a secret

file on Igor in the study. Attached to it was a letter from the chief in St. Petersburg. All that Boris had feared was borne out. Igor, backed by a fantastic amount of gold, plotting to reopen hostilities in Manchuria, was up to his ears in an extraordinary piece of double-dealing. The Germans, from whom he was buying arms, thought they were to be used against the Tsar. The French, who were selling him rifles, thought they were to be used against the Germans. Mischuk and Boris sorted through the evidence and removed a couple of incriminating papers which they burned. The file would be returned as if it had not been removed and it was unlikely that the theft would be soon discovered.

If Boris thought Ronya would be distracted by Igor's danger, her response was a distinct shock. Clearly the fantastic story of her son's behavior distressed her less than if he had been unfaithful to Julie.

What buoyed Ronya up was that this provided a prelude to removing them all from Russia. A weapon had come to hand in her ideological battle with Boris and Katya, but she wisely said nothing except, "How do you plan to stop Igor? With the key evidence destroyed, you have a breathing spell, but—"

"Listen, my sweet, the top-echelon people in the secret police are in no hurry to lay hands on him. Their instructions to Krasmikov make that clear. Some even see merit in Igor's scheme. Others are more concerned to discover the source of his financing. Besides, it's a bit thick to arrest a man as a traitor just after making a hero out of him. Sentiment is with the brave boys who tried to win the war and against the Tsar who lost it.

"We're safe until they find out who Igor's backers are, and I mean to beat them to it. I'll have to move cautiously. War has taught Igor to operate too smartly for my comfort.

"The first thing is to disarm the Cossacks. That'll be easy if we can get Igor out of the way. We've got to get him out of Russia. Julie will stay here, of course."

"Suppose Igor refuses?"

"I don't know," Boris confessed. "Can you think of a way to make him go?"

"Go out," she said, "and let me think about it."

He was back in an hour.

"What's the answer, Ronya?" he asked, confident that she would solve everything.

"Have a good ride?" Ronya did not like to be rushed.

"Fine."

"If Julie were more like us," Ronya began slowly, "Igor would be less restless."

"Why blame Julie?" Boris snapped.

Ronya sighed. "Some other time, darling. Right now I—"

"No, Ronya. You can't open a door like that, then slam it in my face. What about Julie?"

"Perhaps I should have left the door shut. Double-locked."

"Too late."

"Very well, Boris," Ronya acceded, "since you can't see it yourself, Julie is a rope hobbling Igor. It's all very well for you to say Igor goes, Julie stays. But, damn it, she's *his* wife, not yours! She belongs wherever he is. Don't you see that?"

"Julie isn't well enough to travel. Igor'll be back in a couple of months. She's better off here," Boris said.

"She's plenty well enough."

"That's enough, Ronya." He was growing angry. "If Igor wants to wreck her health dragging her all over hell and gone, who's stopping him? But you stay out of it!"

Ronya shook her head dispiritedly. "If God himself were to say to Julie, 'Follow your husband,' she wouldn't go. Her reasons are not simple. Nothing about Julie is simple. She's a very complex human being.

"Julie has a steel-hard, steel-strong instinct for self-preservation, and thank God for that! She'd never have survived her childhood without it. Now it centers on us and the land. Not that she counts the money Igor will inherit someday. But she looks around at the house, the orchards, the wheat fields, the stables and to her it's the Garden of Eden. To hold onto it, from the very start, she's given Igor all the rein he asks, whether it takes him away from her or not. Julie's key to what she sees as heaven will be her son.

"Believe me, I've seen her inspecting the outline of her breasts, stroking them in anticipation of the milk that will flow.

She's still as slim as a faun but she thrusts her belly out experimentally. All day long she does nothing but graze, intent on making the life within her big and strong. She doesn't mind Igor's absences. In fact, she dreads his love-making. I know, because she asked me the other day how to fend off Igor. 'He'll hurt the baby, Ronya, my mother,' she said.

"When I told her it's glorious for a baby's parents to take and give pleasure together, she blushed and acted ashamed."

For an awful moment Boris remembered Ronya's face when she had looked, breathless with wonder, at the small dark creature who was Igor and he, Boris, drank the bitter cup of rejection. Yet Julie, with her timid smile, all of her fused into inaccessible virginity, was the perfect daughter.

Ronya led the conversation away from Julie. "About Igor's money, Boris," she said, "it must come from Huang."

"Of course, little dove, that was my first thought but I put it away as idiocy. Consider the man. I've read his letters to Alexis and they reveal him as a philosopher and pacifist. No, my sweet, he loves Igor too much to put a noose around his neck."

"There's one thing you're not taking into account," Ronya said. "Left alone, Huang cuts himself off from reality through his opium dreams. Suppose, in his loneliness, he decided to force Igor to return to Manchuria where he thinks he can protect him."

"I can't believe that will happen."

Ronya sighed. "No more can I, really! But the gold must come from China. We'll have to get in touch with Reuben."

"How, Ronya? With the secret police on Igor's tail, any message you send is sure to be opened, no matter who carries it."

"Simple!" she laughed. "We'll talk to Reuben in a place where everyone looks and no one sees."

"Ronya," Boris applauded. "It's a masterstroke and gives me a way to get Igor to America."

It was Ronya's turn to clap her hands. "And so, when you then suggest that he and Georgi go to America to try and find land for us to buy, like a sensible conspirator, he'll agree. Oh, Boris, Boris, it's sheer genius." She hugged him.

Suddenly she looked stricken. "What are we to tell Julie?"

215

"The truth, Ronya."

Ronya sat looking out into the rain-dark grove and wondered
—whose truth? Theirs? Igor's? But she only said, "Not now,
Boris. Let Julie be happy."

XXIV

"JULIE! Come out! Come sit with me in the library!"

"I can't." It was a small wail, sounding faintly through the
heavy door of the bathroom. Igor opened it a crack and leaned
against the jamb.

"Come *on!*"

"You don't understand." Indignation lent power to her voice.
"I'm too sick. I think I'm going to throw up."

"Goodbye, then, Julie. Give that damned tadpole of yours
my regards."

"Wait! Wait! You can't go like that. I'll be ready in a minute."

He closed the door and waited until she came out and
climbed into bed, her hair brushed back from her forehead,
which was shiny from the dousing of cold water she had given
her face. In a high-necked, long-sleeved nightgown she looked
about fourteen, a proper little boarding school miss. Igor felt
masculine and protective.

"I want an orange, Igor."

He snorted. "Lydia told me you'd eaten everything on your
supper tray and I know how she stuffs you. I'll get some dry toast
or matzo later. That'll keep you from feeling queasy."

Julie made a naughty face, screwing up her pretty mouth and
pantomiming revulsion. "Dry matzo! I'd sooner eat straw. . . .
Igor?"

She was such a baby he couldn't be cross with her.

"I've been thinking and thinking—I believe I'd rather have hot chocolate and a sour pickle than an orange."

A baby. A pregnant baby. So silly and precious. He lay down beside her but did not attempt to touch his snow-maiden wife.

"Igor?" He stirred to indicate he was awake and listening. "What new craziness is this? Your running off to America? I think you're being just plain selfish—"

"You've got it wrong, Julie," Igor said. "I'm not running. I'm going. As to being selfish—"

Julie put her hand across his mouth. "Please don't start that again." Her voice quavered. "How can I travel now?"

He kissed her hand.

"For heaven's sake, Julie, what a silly you are. Travel won't hurt you. Everyone has babies and you're perfectly healthy. What is all this namby-pamby talk anyway?"

"I'm delicate," Julie said with a trace of pride. "I have to be looked after. I can't go skittering around just because you want me to."

He had known it would end like this. It always did. He was a fool to keep on trying. He sat up and lit a cigarette. Looking panicky, Julie clapped her hand to her mouth. Igor ground out the cigarette, his hand unsteady. "All right," he said. "But darling, can't you see? It's all right for you but what about me? I'm no midwife. I can't just sit around waiting for the tadpole to turn into a frog and the frog turn into a fairy prince. There are things to be done, places to see, and it would be so wonderful to have you with me."

Julie's eyes filled with tears. "Be nice," she said.

"Come with me, please." Love and urgency were in his voice. "You'll come? My dearest."

His wife lay very quiet and when at last she spoke it was in a still voice, remote and alien. "I can't," she said. "I'm sorry, Igor. I can't. Our son has to be born in this house. In this bed." She stopped. "Never in your life have you had any idea what it's like to grow up poor and alone. How could you? Until you and Boris, my father, found me I belonged to no one and nowhere. The only thing that kept me alive was my dream. You can't believe that but it's true.

"Oh, Igor!" Suddenly she clung to him, eyes filled with tears.

"What's to become of us? How can I ever understand you? Sometimes you seem like two people, the Igor I love, who took me away from the village, and this you—the man who has to be charging around the world and can't appreciate his home. Your mother tells me it's perfectly natural for you to be contradictory, that all men are restless, but I never knew one who acted that way before. She says I should come to terms with you as you are, that I wanted you and I've got you and now all I have to do is accept you. I try, darling, but I'm not brave like Ronya and when you're wild and your face is stony and frozen, you frighten me. You're like a stranger—"

She lay back on the pillow and Igor put his arms around her tenderly. Her tears were falling like rain.

"I'm a coward," Julie said, self-pityingly. "I can't ride a horse. I can't swing a whip or fight cholera. But in one thing I'm iron. You can go to America. You can go anywhere on earth but our son will be born here."

Igor stroked her hair. When at length she quieted down, he said, "Julie, unbraid your hair." She looked desperately away, and he said, "No, I don't want to make love to you. I want to tell you everything."

The story which Boris and Ronya had spent hours trying to piece together came then. Huang, he said, had given him gold and sent him home a rich man to marry Julie and found a dynasty. And Igor had betrayed his trust and gotten himself so deeply into trouble that now he had to go away. Huang had forgiven him and sent his agent to prevent Igor's daring from becoming madness.

Julie looked bewildered as Igor tried desperately to explain. Like his mother he wanted the world to be free, a place where Jew and Christian, Moslem and Buddhist, could live in peace, where no man plundered another with impunity and respect replaced prejudice. Something was stirring here in Russia. The war had made him come alive and come to care. When he promised his men victory, it was as an idealist to whom his word was his bond. In victory Russia would set all men free. His life seemed charmed after he found his mission. He, Igor, would free Manchuria, leaving Boris and the Blond One to free the

Ukraine. With the Ukraine's wealth—wheat and apples, and its all-weather seaport—and with the minerals, the timber and the furs of Manchuria, an empire would be born with no court and no ruling family but a constitution and a tribunal modeled on the United States, its leaders elected by the people.

Then, after his war in Manchuria collapsed with the defeat of Russia, Igor still dreamed his shining dreams. He decided to raise his own army. But somehow everything had misfired and now he was branded a rebel, and he was being shipped off until the dream had faded and been forgotten. Now he doubted if he wanted to return to Russia, ever.

Julie's face was pale against the white pillows, and it struck Igor that perhaps he had been mad to confide all this in her. She stumbled to her feet and tottered to the bathroom, where he could hear her strangled, reflexive retching. He went and picked her up and carried her back to bed, where she sank back exhausted.

"What came over you, dear heart?"

"You, Igor," she said faintly. "With all your fancy talk. All that about governments and rebellions and wars. You sound as complicated as Uncle Alexis."

Lord, Lord, why do we try to talk? Igor wondered. She can't see that though my education came late, it came. It came in all the hours Huang devoted to me and I then thought tedious. Yet, Julie, my sweet baby, still no older than the fourteen she was the day we met, thinks I'm still eighteen.

From under her long lashes Julie stared up at Igor, at the face she loved, how gentle and good—even noble—the face he had worn when they played together like children at the edge of the forest. Since he could still look like that, like the old Igor she had fallen in love with, she was content to let him go. Igor would come back.

"I forgive you," she said.

Igor suddenly boiled with anger and disappointment. He was not Tartar Boris' son for nothing and it was all he could do to keep his hands off her. Every desire left him except to hurt Julie and if not physically, there were other ways.

"Forgive me this, Julie!" He spat it out. "There was a girl, a Mandarin girl. Let me tell you what happened between her and

219

me. It'll make your skin crawl!" He stopped, stricken. "Don't look at me like that, Julie!"

Julie was beyond looking at Igor or anything else. She had fainted. When she opened her eyes, a contrite Igor was sponging her face with a towel soaked in cologne. Humbly he said, looking awkward and shamed, "She had nothing to do with us, darling. I love you."

A surprising girl, Julie, though only Ronya had fathomed just how surprising. Sensing that her house was firm on its rock once more, she said complacently, "I don't ever want to hear about your girls, Igor Pirov. Now you get me an orange and a fresh nightdress."

Wearily, he laid down the towel and fetched a delightful gown, a special occasions thing, white and beribboned, helped her brush out her hair, put on a dressing gown and went to find the orange.

His mother's door was ajar and he went in and threw himself across her bed. She held out her hand and with all his heart Igor wanted to creep into her arms, to draw on her strength the way he had as a child. "She won't go," he said.

"I didn't think she would, Igor," Ronya said reasonably. "And in a way I'm glad. I'm just sentimental enough to want our first grandchild to be born here. There's a sort of fragrance out of the past that laces the generations together."

He shook his head impatiently. "What is the answer, Mother?"

"Time, Igor," Ronya said. "Now go back to Julie."

"I have to go downstairs first and get her an orange."

Ronya chuckled. "Now don't you go peeling it or cutting it up," she said. "Julie likes to suck oranges."

"I know. Good night, Mother."

"Good night, son." Her eyes followed him to the door.

Julie held the orange in her small white hands, gaily sucking away. When it was flat, the last drop of juice drained, she put it down and licked her lips. Igor, calmed equally by his mother's good sense and Julie's pleasure in small things, wished he could capture the scene and hold it forever in his memory, the way

Julie held an orange. He undressed, got into bed, gave Julie a brotherly kiss and said, "Sing to me."

"Sing? In the middle of the night?"

"Please, Julie."

She drew his head down till it lay alongside her firm young breast and sang, softly, every song he loved. Usually her songs brought him release, but for once he found no peace in them. "Come to America, Julie," he said when she stopped. She turned away from him and Igor wept.

XXV

"LORD, how I've missed you," Ronya said to Katya as they sat down at tea. "It seems as if you've been away four years instead of four months. How's Alexis?"

Katya edged her chair close to Ronya's. "He's fine. Let's talk about him and Moscow some other time. Now what has happened to Julie? Why have you let her get so monstrous? The girl's deformed! All her beauty gone—her eyes, her hair—I don't recognize her. Just a purple face and a ballooning belly. She's one massive lump."

Ronya irritated her by seeming thoroughly composed. "What can I do? With Igor for her lover, she is carrying Boris."

"My god, Ronya! Tell me what you mean."

"Oh, willingly. I've had to hold my tongue for months and I never felt lonelier. If I say one word to Julie, Boris stands instantly between us, accusing me of frustrating her. I think he's as insanely proud of her belly as she is. I have a feeling, vague I must own, that he uses Julie in some way to bolster his hope that nothing sinister can enter this house. And gentle and compliant though Julie is, she's a bit of a fanatic. I think she believes destiny saved her so that she could save this house."

"It's utterly crazy."

"I know. I caution her to set no value on sticks and stones and remind her that Igor is worth ten times all this. She says confidently that her first duty is toward Boris, who found her, and that Igor will come home. She sees them starting all over again and promises that the house will have many sons."

Katya pressed her hands against her forehead. "Listen," she said. "I think Julie makes more sense than you do, and Igor's behavior is nothing less than outrageous. If I were his wife, I'd sit in bed munching chocolates all day, too."

"Rubbish," said Ronya.

Katya was growing really cross. "Ronya," she said, "sometimes I wish Igor had been banished to Siberia for a month or two. Then he'd be home by now—and mighty glad to be here."

Her sister looked into Katya's eyes unflinchingly. "I write to Igor almost every day and beg him to stay where he is. In every letter I lie about Julie and tell him she's never been prettier, that she glows. And I promise him, in God's name, to bring Julie and the baby to him."

"Why?" Katya's voice rose shrilly.

"My dear sister," Ronya said, "you don't know Igor as well as I do, but can you honestly see him sitting around Kiev waiting for his father to die so he can inherit this place? Igor has no sentiment about family possessions. What he cares about is virgin land and he's found it, some hundred and fifty miles south of the city of San Francisco. It's Igor's mountain—no giant, he writes, but wreathed in wild flowers and set with tall trees. There's nothing much there, not even abundant water, but it looks down over the ocean and Igor is in love with its beauty and its moods. Georgi will design a house for him that will spread out like a lake in the cypress forest.

"*That's* Igor's dream, Katya, to ride over his own land with Julie and his child beside him and it fits in perfectly with my plan to leave Russia."

Katya's anger had risen. "Boris is still an eagle and you try to clip his wings! You've been afraid ever since you were bewitched by Huang in that damned garden. I give you fair warning. Bring Igor home or I will."

"Very well," Ronya said amiably. "Go ahead. And take the consequences. Do you want Igor to see Julie now? Would you say she's the girl he loves? How will he disguise his horror at sight of her? Even Boris, for several reasons, doesn't want him back yet." Katya was staring at Ronya, astounded. "You hadn't thought of that?"

"It hadn't entered my mind."

"After the baby is born," Ronya said, her chin resolute, "I'll starve and exercise Julie into shape, if I have to slash the fat off her, layer by layer, with my whip!"

"Then you'll bring Igor home?"

"I'm going out now." Ronya rose. "I really feel the need of fresh air."

"No." Katya put her hand on Ronya's arm. "You *must* have the doctor see Julie every day from now on. He should be in charge of her—not you or Boris."

"I'll send for him right away."

The doctor came that evening. Ronya left Boris and Katya sitting out on the terrace and took him to Julie's room. As they climbed the stairs she said, "You know Gospodin Pirov and I are good practical midwives, having delivered many a mare together. Since this noon we've been worried. We think the baby's movements are fading."

The doctor paused and squinted over his spectacles at her. "Mistress Julie hasn't become despondent, has she? Have you followed my instructions and indulged her whims?"

Ronya said, "My husband certainly has. To the letter. I, however, am bound to admit there are times when I wonder whether a bit of melancholy wouldn't be less damaging than sweet cream and quantities of almonds soaked in butter."

"Mistress Pirov, I ask your pardon, but food is good for the baby."

"I hope you're right, doctor." Ronya knocked on Julie's door and they went in. Lydia pushed herself out of the rocker beside the bed and smiled protectively at Julie. "I'll be back, pretty one," she said.

223

Covered with only a silk sheet, Julie had been listening to the evening song of birds outside her open window. She lifted herself with great effort. "I feel so tired, doctor."

He set down his small black bag, drew up a straight chair and fell to examining his ungainly patient. Julie raised blue, shadowed eyes to him.

"Is everything all right?"

"Marvelous—simply marvelous."

Ronya, listening from the doorway, knew that finally the doctor was worried about Julie, too. He was overdoing his geniality. Paradoxically, the fact comforted her. She went over to Julie and pulled down her nightdress. "You're doing fine, dear," she said, stroking Julie's hair. "I'll see you later, doctor, at dinner. Until then I'll sit with Julie."

The next two days dragged for them all. Julie refused even water and, head buried in her pillows, wept almost continuously. From time to time she dozed. The night of the second day, after supper, the doctor confessed, "We should not have allowed the girl to become so bloated. And the position of the foetus is too low—there's an abnormal accumulation of fluid in the birth sac. All her tissues are waterlogged. But with your help, Mistress Pirov," he stroked his gray beard, "we may pull her through."

Boris leaped from his chair and stretched out his arm as if to grab the man. "You damn well better pull her through!" He stormed out of the room. Neither Ronya nor Katya apologized, and the doctor merely said, "Gospodin Pirov remembers that I dissuaded him from discouraging Mistress Julie's appetite."

Just then the first hard screams of labor sent fear shivering through all of them. Ronya ran, the doctor following her. Katya flung her hands up to cover her ears and rushed to Boris. As the screams continued, she clung to him and in panic they both stared helplessly up the stairs. Tears rained down Katya's cheeks. "Ronya won't let her die," she said, and they sat down together in a misery of helplessness. Time passed with unbearable slowness and the level in Boris' vodka bottle dropped.

"It's hot in here," he said, tugging at his collar.

"Should you be drinking quite so much?"

"Yes."

"The bottle's empty."

"I'll open another." His face was twisted in pain. "Here!" he said, and poured a drink for Katya, who drank it and began to weep again. "Why don't they *give* her something?"

"They need her help, Katya."

Hour after hour Julie moaned and cried out, her voice rasping until it sounded like an animal's. The night was almost over when the door flew open. It was Lydia. "Come, master!" she cried and fled, her skirts whipping around her sturdy legs. Boris dashed after her.

He and dawn entered Julie's room together. Ronya greeted Boris with a frightened look, pulling back her tired shoulders.

Bending over Julie, she repeated her refrain, "Push, Julie, push. Bear down. Help us! Push, Julie—"

The thing on the bed, the immense agony which no longer resembled a human being, screamed, thrashed and fought, her breathing coming in irregular gasps. Though she was panting, she kept on howling and Boris realized she could not last much longer. They all knew it, he and Ronya, Lydia and the doctor.

Perfect wordless communication established itself between husband and wife. She went to the foot of the bed, he leaned over Julie, put his lips close to her ear and said, very quietly, "Look at me, Julie." She obeyed and he looked into her staring, wild eyes and smiled. The miracle of Boris, his vibrant strength and assurance reached her and Julie became quieter.

"Julie, baby, I'm going to help you." He spaced the words so each one broke through to her wavering consciousness. "Be brave and do exactly as I say."

A spasm of pain ran through her and Julie sank her nails into Boris' hand.

"That's fine," he said. "Now push strongly." The desperate outcries ceased and were replaced by grunting groans.

"Pull on me, Julie, and push."

It was no use. Julie's contractions had stopped.

"Julie, honey, I want you to drink this." Like an automaton she did as she was told and swallowed the vodka, choked and coughed. "You're going to feel as if you were splitting in half. Don't be afraid. Hang on to me and make all the noise you want."

As the doctor dragged her dead grandson, enormous and perfectly formed, out of Julie's womb, Ronya marveled at the wonder of Boris.

Late that afternoon they buried Julie's and Igor's firstborn, and before she went to bed, Katya wrote in her diary: "Twice dead! Unable to escape from his mother's body and with the umbilical cord wrapped around his neck.

"Julie lies in a daze, breasts gorged with milk. Boris has sent for Igor to come. We are in mourning."

The next entry she made eight days later: "Ronya, with her inborn wisdom, has sent for Rabbi Levinsky. Neither Boris nor I have found a way to break into Julie's spasmodic hysteria. Until today she has eaten nothing, though she willingly submits to being bathed and groomed.

"On this eight day after his birth, Julie's boy would have been circumcised and given his name. Poor Julie! No songs will be sung in the name of God and Elijah, the prophet, and the Angel of the Covenant will not come down from heaven. Poor Julie! No ornaments of gold and silver, no threads of pearl, no cushions of silk."

Ronya, with stoic imperturbability, nursed Julie and gradually, almost imperceptibly, the girl began to mend. Then Ronya sat down with Boris and Katya in Katya's sitting room and told them her plans. "The first thing I've got to concentrate on is restoring Julie's looks. To do it I'm going to have to ask you two to give me a free hand. If I'm right, you pay too much attention to her and unconsciously encourage her self-pity. Moreover, I don't believe it's a good idea to argue with her. Tomorrow I mean to bring her downstairs."

Ronya became the general and Julie, perforce, the slogging foot soldier. She obeyed orders but remained withdrawn into her private misery. Days passed and with her strength assured, Ronya began butchering off the pounds. A Swedish masseuse helped, tautening the slack muscles and strengthening the delicate bone structure until Julie's body was firmer than it had ever been. For her hard work she was rewarded with one slice of lean meat, a raw apple, a lettuce leaf, a radish or two and sugarless tea. Three weeks passed on this meager diet.

One morning, as Ronya was shaking Julie awake, the girl sat up in bed and glanced across the room to her dressing-table mirror. "My hair looks awful," she muttered, dismayed. Ronya, seeing her so small and unhappy, had compunctions. "Sieep a little longer," she said, pulling the covers up over the slight form. "I'll call you later."

Back in her own room she sat down at her desk and drew out a sheet of notepaper. "Tamara," she wrote, "busy yourself with your herbs and make me a potion to restore the gloss to Julie's hair." She sat chewing the end of her pen, then continued, "Julie sets great store by prophecy. The Blond One will bring her to see you secretly. Foretell Igor's return (he should be here any day now) and tell her to charm him utterly so that he will give her another child." She sent the letter by the hand of the Blond One.

Ronya proved as good a magic-maker as Tamara. Igor arrived, as if in answer to her summons, the very day that Julie visited Tamara. He came in through the kitchen door and found himself alone except for the hissing samovar. The table was laid for three. Mother, Father, Aunt Katya— Terrified, he galloped up the stairs. My God! he thought, where is everybody?

By a supreme effort he stopped himself from bursting into Julie's room and instead opened the door softly. Julie, seated at her dressing table, and humming, saw him mirrored behind her, cried out, "Igor!" and ran into his arms.

Igor buried his face in her hair and she, feeling the pounding of his heart, began to weep quietly. They were her first true tears of mourning. Before her lament could flower into a mother's wail, Igor stifled the sound by stopping her mouth with his. Then he carried her to their bed and they lay, fully clothed, bodies pressed close, her head on his hard, broad shoulder.

"My God, how beautiful you are, Julie," he said.

"And how thin you are, darling."

He hooted with mirth. "Not thin," he said. "Just in need of a shave."

"Igor," Julie said sadly, apprehensively.

"Don't talk about it, Julie. You had a bad dream."

A troubled look came into her eyes. "You mustn't say that,

darling. It might be bad luck. Our son has got to be real because Tamara saw in her crystal ball that he would be born again, twice born since he was twice dead. It's true. She looked in my hand and read the tea leaves to make sure. *And* she invoked a— voice. It always came out the same."

Content to give Julie her peace, Igor maintained a sober expression. Awed by her own daring, Julie confessed, "I got to Tamara in the strangest way. Ronya, my mother, left me alone in the meadow and told me to rest and soak up the sunlight for at least an hour before coming home. As soon as she was gone, I began picking daisies to braid into a chain and the Blond One came, running."

Igor's dimple was bewitching. "And you haven't breathed to a living soul till now that you went to see Tamara?"

"That's right, Igor."

He pulled her closer. "Your secret is safe, I promise," he said.

Julie stirred. She had to confess before she could allow herself to enjoy the feelings his nearness roused in her. "I have to tell you, Igor," she said.

"What, little Julie?"

"You gave me a fine son, Igor dearest, and I killed him. I didn't mean to. I was so eager to have him big he got too big to be born. . . . I am sorry."

All his love for Julie was gathered together in a great surge. "I don't care about him," he whispered, "only about you."

"Is that true?"

"True, Julie."

She smiled. "We have to wait, my love. I'm still torn inside."

"I know." His voice was low. The room was silent except for Igor's breathing, which was so hard it frightened him. He swung himself off the bed, and Julie, reaching for his hand, said, "I'll get up, too."

"By the way," said Igor, "who taught you to kiss that way?"

Julie blushed. "Did you bring me a present?"

Her husband roared with pleasure. "No, infant. I came too fast."

She led him to the closet. "Choose which dress you like me to wear; then go find your mother and tell her that, beginning to-night, I'll be eating downstairs."

Igor pressed her hand to his lips. "I'll bathe and change," he said. "Then we'll tell her together."

XXVI

IT was September, 1907, and Russia was economically healthy. Peter Stolypin, now in office as minister-president, was bringing in foreign firms such as International Harvester and Singer Sewing Machine, erecting factories, raising the living conditions of the peasants and even building a few schools for their children. The hot surge of revolution was cooling—even Ukrainian separatists were quiescent.

Again the harvest was rich and landowners along the Dnieper bought furs and caviar and vodka, as did Moscovites and the wealthy in St. Petersburg. What remained, Stolypin exported. In this Indian summer, this golden and peaceable hour, Ronya's warnings fell on deaf ears and Boris would not read Huang's letters. In one, Huang reminded Ronya, "It is still a grave and complicated time. Below the surface sickness and evil germinate. Your Tsar's belief in the divine right of kings burgeons and he will revoke the slight concessions forced upon him by the revolution of 1905. He worships false gods—he is a false god. Run!"

With Igor at home Boris was less than ever susceptible to being budged. He was even conferring with his committee about entering Georgi in the national championship for the following year.

Only Igor in all the house of Pirov was restless. Julie had laid by her role of adoring wife and turned away from him, reproachfully asking once more if he wanted to hurt the baby she would bear in the spring. When the first snows began to turn the valley white, it was obvious that he was again amusing himself as he pleased. Ronya sent for him.

"Why do you tread everything decent under foot?" she asked.

"I'm suffocating," he said, sullenly.

"You'll regret it bitterly one day, Igor."

Boris opened the door and said, "I thought I gave you a job to do, Igor." Igor looked at him stonily, turned on the high heels of his boots, and walked out.

He went not to the stables but to the library, and not for a book but to write a letter, to Prince Yusupov. In it, by implication that would be understood by the prince, he committed himself to a terrible deed. As soon as he had mailed it, he would willingly have recalled his rash offer. He was repelled and frightened. Miserable, he returned to Julie, hoping that she at least could ease his pain. That possibility he himself shattered by bringing up the subject which always widened the gap between them.

"Let's leave all this and go to what is truly yours," he said for the hundredth time.

"Wait, Igor," she said. "I am with child. I cannot travel."

So Igor went to bed—with Tolstoy.

One night his male frustration took Igor to a gypsy fire, but Tamara came and slapped the girl hard across the mouth. And to Igor she said, "Out! Go home to Julie, your wife."

He wiped the sweat from his brow. "Go to hell, Tamara."

Tamara rolled a cigarette and lit it. "Would you like to see your niece?" she asked sweetly. "She looks like you, Igor, a shade or two darker." Handing him his sable-lined parka, she commanded, "Walk!"

Someone was following him. He heard steps crunching in the snow and allowed the Blond One to overtake him. "I'm sorry," Igor said, as the two men fell into step. "That was stupid."

"Everything you do these days is stupid," the Blond One said gravely. "Why? You're not a stupid fellow."

"Because I'm near the end of my patience with Julie."

"And that means you have to imitate Boris when he's angry with Ronya?"

Igor conceded the analogy. "We both imitate him."

"I know, and neither of us is big enough to get away with it."
The Blond One slipped his arm through Igor's and they walked
along looking like identical snowmen. "Don't pick your way
from brothel to brothel, Igor. Don't think you can find a girl
who will make you contented. And stop believing that fate has
chosen you to eliminate Rasputin."

"I've promised to try, if I'm called." He had no secrets from
the Blond One.

"If you're called, I'll honor your pledge. What you've got to
do is atone to Julie. Her screams that night she bore your dead
son will fill my ears if I live a hundred years."

"You were there?" Igor turned and faced his half brother.

"On her balcony, the whole time."

"Did she call for me?" Igor asked shyly.

"With every breath." Knowing that the Blond One never
lied, Igor felt joyously that he was needed, wanted. "There's a
lot to understand about Julie," he mused. "The meanness of her
village made her afraid." They reached the house. "Sleeping
here?" he asked.

"Every night since you've been on the prowl," the Blond One
said.

"I'll see you at the stables tomorrow morning," Igor said.
"Early." They smiled. "In the war, when I was somebody, and in
America, where I was free, I was more like you than like me."

He climbed the stairs two at a time. In her room Julie stood at
the window watching the snowflakes whirl and dance in gusts of
wind. Indisputably her figure had altered, her belly rounded but
her body slender still, and she looked, in her long flannel nightgown, absurdly young. Watchful, she noted that Igor was relaxed and friendly and thanked heaven. Ronya had warned her
not to provoke scenes while she was denying Igor his husband's
rights.

"I'm glad you've come," she said. "I was lonesome, very lonesome, here by myself sleeping in this big bed alone."

In an ecstasy of relief, Igor caught her to him and embraced
her gently. "You should have told me sooner," he said. "I
thought you were glad to be by yourself." He bent down and
kissed the top of her head.

Before they slept, in the sweet communion of the shared bed,

Igor spoke drowsily of his hopes and dreams. "Little Julie," he said, "I'm going to take very good care of you. As soon after your confinement as it's safe for you to travel, I'm taking you and our baby to San Francisco. We'll live there part of the time, because I want to work the rest of the time on my mountain. I don't want our children to know only paved streets and the incessant noise of the city."

Julie was silent and she breathed softly, but she vowed to herself, "I'd rather die than leave this house and live in a strange country."

One day in April when the leaves were just beginning to take on color, the meadows to fill with buds, Father Tromokov's church, under its small onion dome, was crowded with flat-faced peasant women and red-cheeked girls decorating every corner with white flowers. The Jews, gay in the absence of accusations against them, burned their candles and chanted their prayers while sacramental wine, like drops of holy red rain, graced the hour. It was the eve of Easter Sunday and Passover—the evening of the first Seder.

But Igor was in Julie's room when her labor began and somehow forced his legs to bear him, running, to Ronya. He charged in like a bull, then raced back to Julie, who was soon screaming, "My back! I can't stand the pain in my back!" She caught hold of Igor's hand and groaned, "Get—" Before she could finish they were all there, Ronya and Boris and Igor. He kept his eyes on his mother who ordered, "Keep her on her feet. Keep her moving." Ronya was utterly composed. Crying out in pain and fear, Julie clung to the bedpost, wailing, "No. I can't. I can't bear it."

Ronya's voice was stern. "Keep quiet, Julie. Take a deep breath and hold it. Don't exhaust yourself yelling."

Instead Julie clawed at Igor. He looked at Ronya. Ronya looked at Boris, who said, "Put her to bed." Just then the door opened and Lydia poked her head in. "The Blond One has gone for the doctor," she said and Boris frowned. He could not arrive in time.

The next three hours taxed Igor more than they did Julie. "For Christ's sake, don't faint," he said to himself and, aloud, wept, "Oh, God, spare Julie please." Between contractions Julie sleepily relaxed. Not so Igor. He felt terror, even rage, as he watched Julie refuse to assist his mother and father. This baby, however, was so ready to be born it needed no help from her. Against tense resistance it shoved its head through the floor of Julie's pelvis. Inch by inch it moved forward. As it struggled free, Boris hooked a large finger under the tiny chin, then dangled the small body upside down. There was one explosive cry as the infant filled its lungs and opened its eyes.

Boris held up his grandchild for Julie to see, to marvel at the beauty of the perfect head, crowned with golden fuzz. But Julie, body slack, had slipped off into snoring sleep. To Igor his baby represented nothing except the cause of Julie's monstrous torture.

It was after the doctor had come and gone that Julie opened her eyes and said, "Give me my son."

Igor stroked her damp hair. "We have a daughter, Julie," he said.

"She's beautiful." Boris picked the baby up from her cradle but Julie could not see her; she was blinded with tears. "Have her named Rachel," she said and turned her head away. On his knees at her side, Igor said, "She doesn't matter."

Ronya did not trust herself to speak. Boris put an arm around her, saying, "Come, little dove." At the door he stopped and spoke to Lydia: "Have the cradle moved to the old nursery." So the little procession, Boris carrying Rachel, with Ronya on his other arm, walked down the hall. Rachel was so small cuddled against his body that Boris, looking down at her, lost his heart.

That was a night—a pinnacle of a night—for Boris and Ronya. They put their grandchild down in her cradle in the nursery, had an early supper, and immediately went blissfully to bed, where they talked of the wonder that had befallen them and their house. There was no bitterness in them at Julie's rejection of her enchanting daughter—she had so desperately wanted a son.

Before Ronya was awake, Boris left the house and returned carrying a puppy. He tiptoed into Ronya's room. The door into the adjoining nursery stood ajar and for a moment he contemplated putting the animal in there, next to the cradle. Sight of the wet nurse, legs spraddled, dozing in her rocker, deterred him. Lord, he thought, contemplating his sleeping wife, what a fortunate man you are!—I remember that cow when she was something to enjoy. Ronya, one cheek in a cupped hand, dark hair fanning out over the pillow, was so lovely she made his heart ache. She had thrown the covers off during the night and the lines of her body, seen through pale crepe de chine, were beautiful.

Stroking the wriggling bundle in his arms, he laid it down beside Ronya. On her dressing table he left a note: His name is Beljik. He's pure Siberian husky and I've been training him for weeks. He practically speaks and he knows he belongs to Rachel. Tell him you're Ronya.

In the instant it took Boris to get out of the room, his soothing effect on the little dog wore off. Ronya was wakened by a warm, moist tongue exploring her face.

"Well, good morning!" she laughed. "Perhaps you'll tell me where you came from?" In reply the puppy bounced off her bed, trotted across the room and through the open door. From where she lay, Ronya could see him stretch out under the cradle as if it were the one place on earth where he meant to stay forever. Rachel, asleep, gave a little, contented gurgling sigh.

Now that the Pirovs had a new princess everyone in the house began bustling. For seven days they all, the Blond One, too, honored an ancient von Glasman custom by giving alms to the poor, donations to hospitals, churches, synagogues. Baskets of choice delicacies were sent to the gentry and even newcomers and visitors to Kiev had only to present themselves at the door to be welcomed with gifts. No more would have been done for a son. Birth in itself was the occasion for joy, thanks for joy expressed in giving.

Julie spent the week recuperating in bed but managed to get up long enough to be measured for a splendid new dress. Aside from this and sending an offering to her village, she did not acknowledge the existence of Rachel. Ronya sent a note to Tamara, inviting her to the celebration that would be held at he end of the week and asking her for a prophecy that would make

Rachel glow in her mother's eyes. "Her imagination," she wrote, "is peopled only by sons."

Tamara replied:

Ronya,
When the sun sets tomorrow, I will read Rachel's future. I will read it true.

But you, goddess to a god, remember this. You have two granddaughters, my unnamed one and Rachel. One cousin cannot escape the fate of the other.

Tamara

Ronya answered at once:

Tamara:
My prophecy is different: For yours the gypsy camp. For mine —America.

Ronya

"I warn you," Tamara replied, "give up this madness. Conversant as I am with the affairs of heaven and hell, I know and repeat, Boris tastes death here."

"I passionately resent your nonsense," wrote Ronya. "Therefore make your gift of prophecy to Rachel acceptable. I do not petition. I command."

On the eighth day of Rachel's life, the estate was looking its most festive. Lanterns hung in the trees, cooking fires were ready to be lit, and a wooden platform where acrobats and tumblers would perform had been erected on the lawn in front of the house. Boris had discovered that a clown who was the rage of all Europe was currently in Kiev and engaged him for the party. And no Pirov celebration was thinkable without some form of horsemanship. Ponies were to trot back and forth from house to stables, stables to house, children on their backs.

Katya and Alexis, with a fine sense of showmanship, asked the gypsies to drive their bright wagons, red-wheeled, green-wheeled, yellow-wheeled, to form a semicircle under the trees and serve as an informal amphitheater for spectators. Indoors, the Brusilovs filled the rooms with flowers and garlands and cleared the great central hall and living room to make ready for the banquet and ball with prizes heaped on tables for the best waltzers, the steadiest drinkers. Everywhere guests, without distinction between men in evening jackets and men in no jackets at all, women in ball gowns or peasant shawls, would be free to come and go, participate or watch.

Normally, on a day which would be so busy from noon on, she gave up her morning to rest and relaxation, but Ronya found herself wide awake shortly after dawn on this great day. She got up, drew the curtains and saw that the sky was cloudless, the garden bright in the early light. There was no sound except for the heavy step of the wet nurse in the next room. She picked up her dressing gown and went to the bathroom to take a sensuously scented bath, brush her teeth and arrange her hair. Then she walked across the hall. "It's seven o'clock," she said softly, "so don't pretend you're still asleep."

Boris opened one eye. "I'm not pretending. I'm looking at what belongs to me and do you know what that is? It's a huntress! I am seeing—" but what it was he never said. Ronya had climbed into his bed.

She tucked her feet under her robe. "I came to talk."

Boris grinned indulgently, thinking, like hell you did!

"Are you listening?"

"No."

It was a blow to his pride and his desire when she went right on to chatter, "Tamara and I threw a few stones at each other yesterday. Her and her damn predictions! There was a game we used to play when we were little—who could out-omen the other. We'd get some poor innocent and swear our messages came from Tamara's mother. That scared them half to death. Yesterday she tried to—"

Boris growled. "*You* listen! There is no room for Tamara in our bed. Nor for Huang. Get that blasted gypsy bitch out of your mind—or off your land. I won't have her snaking in and out of our lives. That's final, Ronya." She lay back, hair dark on the pillow, amused at his flare-up, looking slim and deliciously wanton. "Let's forget it," Boris said, shamefaced.

"You're quite right, Boris," Ronya said charmingly, "I did come here to be loved and found you, my darling, ready the in-

236

stant I opened the door. But when you looked at me you made me feel too naked, too fast. And I remembered my dream. Since Igor came back you've been using your beautiful self to bind me here, making love so gloriously it's as if you were asking how I could bear to leave you. Of course, the answer you expect is that I can't. Dear one, I know what you're up to and I *can*."

She had hit the mark uncannily.

"My own darling," she went on, speaking what was in both their hearts, "always before we've made up our rows in bed. But now I'm frightened. Boris, when our lovemaking gives way to age, how will we settle our differences? I had a dream . . ."

"What did you dream, Ronya?"

"I dreamt that instead of 'little dove' you called me 'little grandmother.' "

Boris roared with laughter but was stilled by the sight of her, chin propped on her hand, looking down at him in a way that made him catch his breath. She put her mouth on his full lips and closed her eyes to the glint of his hair. Boris restored her confidence in her youth.

A little later Ronya said, "Boris, I can't ever put Tamara out of my heart. Neither can I put her off my land. But we could leave."

He shook his head. "You talk too much, little grandmother. Be still and listen." Outside the peasants were singing to gypsy guitars.

Igor carried Julie outside when the sun was high. From a chaise covered with a satin quilt, she watched the party assembling, carriages driving up in a steady stream. Suddenly she half stood up and cried out over the noise of the company, pointing way down the drive. "Ronya, my mother—look!" Ronya jumped up and was so startled by what she saw, she in turn called out, "Boris!" The three of them watched in astonishment as Rabbi Levinsky marched toward the house, followed by every Jew in Kiev. Boris descended the steps to meet them, thinking Ronya was behind him, but as the Jews exchanged singsong greetings of *"Mazel tov, Mazel tov,* Gospodin Pirov," he realized that she had disappeared.

He found her later, stretched across her bed, weeping. For the first time in their married life, Boris was uncertain. He had not seen Ronya cry when David, her father, died, or when they buried David, their son, or when they took the body of Julie's baby to his little grave. Not even, though she was numb with grief, the day the Blond One was born.

Lifting her from the bed, he carried her to his favorite chair and gazed over her head out at the gentle green of the leaves, just holding her, saying nothing. When at length she quieted, he said, "Wash your face, little dove, or our absence will cause more notice than Rachel's presence."

Through the mist of her last tears, Ronya smiled. "Aren't you going to ask me why?"

"I know why. For the first time since you became my wife, your people will dance in your house. And why should they not have come? Julie is theirs, not even one generation removed from the pale. And Igor earned their gratitude the day he stepped in front of his friend Duvid and killed his tormentor."

"No, love, you're wrong," Ronya said. "Julie and Igor, except for providing Rachel, have nothing to do with their being here. The Jews have come to say, 'We are no longer ashamed of you, Ronya von Glasman, for having married a Tartar. Therefore we come to say *Mazel tov*, Ronya Pirov, *Mazel tov*, Boris Pirov.' "

"And that makes you so happy you weep. Why?"

"Because the Jews are God's chosen people," Ronya said.

The sun was setting, the caldrons, ready for boiling the shochet-butchered chickens the women had brought, hung beside spits where pigs were roasting. It was the time and the crowd knew it. They left their cooking and their drinking and merrymaking to join hands, Gentile with Jew, along every path, every rose walk, on the green lawn by each bush and tree. A chant went up: "We want Rachel!"

Lydia emerged from the house carrying the small creature who was altogether engulfed in festooning, trailing lace, and put Julie's daughter in Julie's arms. From the vast throng no sound went up and Julie thought they must all hear the pounding of her heart.

Tamara stepped forward and mounted the steps. This was what they had been waiting for and they emitted a little sigh,

238

like a spring breeze. Boris, standing at Julie's left, stepped forward to meet her and place a chair for the gypsy, who made no acknowledgment but sank into it, immersed in her role as prophetess. Tamara contemplated Rachel and Rachel, a born first lady, contemplated Tamara steadily, her golden eyebrows arching. What seemed like minutes passed; then, like a goddess in gypsy dress, Tamara rose and said three times, "Blessed."

The crowd stirred in anticipation. "Appointed by fate," she declaimed, "watched over by an eagle, lulled by a mother's song, from destiny Rachel's legend is begotten. This day is Rachel's."

All who had glasses raised them, Christians toasting, "Long live Rachel," Jews, "Long live life," and everyone "May we dance at her wedding."

Tamara took the baby from Julie and held her up for all to see. She gave her back to her mother and spoke again. "I, Tamara, queen of the gypsies, give you, Rachel, daughter of the house: Laughter!" A roar went up.

To Julie, when it was once more still, she said, "You may ask the queen three questions."

Shining with delight at Tamara's magnificent present, Julie asked, "Queen, who will Rachel be like?"

"She will be a little like each of us. Therefore uniquely different."

Imploringly Julie posed her second question, "Queen, will her eyes be as dark as Igor's?"

"As black as Igor's. As seeing as Ronya's."

Having asked two fond and foolish questions, Julie searched her mind frantically for something that might reveal the future. Igor, at her right, said, "Let me ask the third question."

"Is that allowed?" she asked Tamara.

Tamara caught Ronya's eye. "Ask the third question," she directed Igor.

"Who is the eagle who will watch over Rachel?"

Tamara's face darkened. "Repeat your question. Properly!"

"Queen—Tamara—who is the eagle who will watch over Rachel?"

"A lusty eagle, a public eagle, a superb eagle. An eagle with no tarnish on his glory."

The magic and the mystery were over and voices rose again.

239

People shifted into different patterns. Boris, thoroughly amused, whispered to Ronya, "Threw a few stones at each other! You hurled a boulder, my sweet. And she hurled a bigger one."

The byplay and the questioning of the crowd were lost on Julie, who was delighted with the prophecy. In her limited vocabulary there was only one eagle—Boris.

XXVII

"RACHEL is *not* a princess. She is my daughter and I'm taking her to America. Get ready to travel, Julie." Igor's black eyes were blazing.

"I have no milk." Julie's blue eyes were frightened. "You can't take your daughter anywhere."

"Let me be a man, Julie! Believe in me. Trust me. Take a chance on me."

She begged, "Please, Igor, be satisfied. Such a house! Such a family! Such land! Boris, our father, is making the Ukraine safe and strong. Stolypin has promised equal rights to the Jews. The Cossacks stay peacefully in their own villages. Can't you see that the reasons for staying outweigh your excuses for leaving? There's so much work for you here. And Georgi will be coming home. And you admit that when you're away from him you're always lonesome for the Blond One."

"It's hopeless, Julie," Igor insisted. "Nothing really changes. Nothing ever will. Everything is *his*—the horses are his, my mother is his, you and Rachel are his. The right to take a blind chance and cut us off from escape is his, too."

"Why, Igor Pirov," Julie pouted, "that's a horrible thing to say. I've seen how he looks at you when he calls you Igor, my son, and you turn away."

Julie was glad they were on a back road near the river bank

where no one could hear him when Igor bellowed, "That's too damn bad! What a hero! You didn't see his face the first time I caught him in the stables with a wench. Or the Blond One's when he hurled the name bastard in his face. Or how Tamara makes herself dirt in front of him when she's drunk."

"Oh, Igor, have you no pity for your father? He wasn't blessed with a Jewish mother. If he's committed sins"—she could not really believe this—"you can atone for them. Come to *shul* with me and pray."

Igor groaned. "For Christ's sake, Julie, let's go home."

"Don't swear," she said primly.

Julie forgot. Igor did not. The yellow grain danced in the late summer breeze and he begged her again. Again she did not hear. There was no more shared laughter between them and Igor, black with anger, returned to the whores. At length Ronya judged the time ripe and sent for Igor.

"My son," she said, "you're paying too high a price for Julie's stubbornness. Go to America and stay there."

"What about Julie?"

"She'll be obliged to give in."

"And Boris?"

"I'll find a way."

"When, Ronya, my mother?"

She drummed on the arm of her chair. "When the Tsar does what his Empress and Rasputin want him to." She raised mocking eyes. "Yes, Igor, I have confidence in our Tsar. He's a great man, a clever man, a tremendous help to the revolutionaries— worth a million Lenins. Our Tsar belongs on the stage, playing high comedy."

"Supposing," Igor said, "Father refuses to go. On account of the curse."

"I am not afraid, Igor." Ronya spoke proudly. "Once before I told him to choose. When the time comes I shall make him choose again."

Ronya spoke confidently, but she was secretly torn, knowing how much Igor adored Julie and Rachel, yet fearing to do anything except save her son. In his hands lay the future and she began to sketch it for him. "Don't make a life of being a dilettante horse-breeder in California. Become a useful citizen. Build a treasure of a house for Julie with gardens and a fine stable. Select friends Julie will be happy to live among.

"After you have done these things, send me word and I will bring you Julie and Rachel. And, Igor, if you need help, my money is yours."

On his last night at home, Igor stood before his wife in their bedroom and said, "I am leaving, Julie, and I am not coming back. Ever. Do you understand?"

"I understand that no matter what you have you will always want something else," she said.

He shook his head wearily. "Thanks, Julie. That's quite a tribute."

"It's my duty to tell you the truth."

It was also, Igor thought bitterly, her duty to share his life but he had told her that so often and with so little effect, he held his tongue. Perhaps his body could persuade her. Yet in the morning Julie said stonily, "I will never leave this house."

To his own surprise, Igor found himself hunting for his father. On this final day at home, he longed to talk to him. Boris, discovered finishing breakfast, led the way toward the library.

"I'd rather talk in the stables," Igor demurred.

"Too many interruptions," his father said. "Let's ride out into the forest. It's a wonderful day."

An hour later they chose a spot on a high bluff overlooking the Dnieper and dismounted. After tethering their horses, they half sat, half lay with backs against the trunk of a magnificent tree.

Boris said, "If it's restlessness, take your trip, Igor, and come back."

"It's restlessness," Igor granted, "and it's more than that. I've come to hate Russia and like the United States. And it's more than *that*. I think it's mostly you."

"Is that an accusation?"

"Not exactly. It's more an admission of failure."

"Yours or mine?"

"Damned if I know."

No anger stirred in either of them, only an immense sadness.

"Igor," Boris said, "fathers and sons have been in conflict before. That's no reason for you to go. I'm sorry that we've been antagonists and rivals sometimes. Remember, son, we are more often comrades and friends. As for sin, I guess we're about even."

It was an extraordinarily temperate speech for Boris. But it was very much in character that he got to his feet, went to his horse and pulled a vodka bottle out of the saddlebag.

"Want a drink?" he asked, offering far more.

Igor shook his head. "Got a match?" he asked. It was a small thing but it was something.

As he smoked, it was all he could do to keep from saying the old, placating words to which he had been so rigorously trained —I'm sorry, Father. He found that, much as he longed to, he could not utter them and sweat broke out in the palms of his hands. To part as strangers. . . He struggled to recapture his poise, tried to find a safe middle ground.

"If I were alone," he said, "I'd rather go to Manchuria. But I can't ask Julie to share that kind of life."

The door had opened a crack between them.

"How much do you love Julie?" Boris flung it wide.

"How much do you love my mother?" Igor said.

"That much?"

"Yes, that much."

In a flash of intuition Boris asked, "Is there anyone else?"

Igor found himself shaking. He looked at the man at his side, a man of granite. "She's dead," Boris said. "Cast her out. She's a disease." There was silence and Igor's face was so seamed with pain that he appeared suddenly to have aged. "Until you do," Boris said, "I will not release Julie and Rachel to you."

There were tears in Igor's eyes His father had understood and now he willingly gave his secret into the large man's hands. "I can't. She's a rope around—my soul. I'll see her as long as I live."

Compassionately, Boris said, "You punish yourself needlessly, Igor. Only your imagination and the ugly circumstance of her death keep Lotus alive in you, just as Ronya's fierce sense of outrage kept Tamara a torment to me for so long."

Almost as though Igor had some inkling of the dark memories that had overtaken Boris, he asked, "Why is it, Father, that the Blond One, Tamara's son, is a saint, while I am—what I am?"

Boris' head sank forward. "What gall more bitter," he said as if to himself, "could either of you have found with which to re-

243

proach me?" For the first time in his life Igor felt pity for his father.

"I'll stay if you wish," he said.

"What do *you* want, Igor?"

"I want to go."

"Then go, my son. And when you can smell nothing but the earth of your mother's land, come home." Boris dropped his cigarette and crushed it out with the heel of his boot, waiting. Igor gave a short, dry laugh. "I told you that I hate Russia."

"Why?"

"Because she betrayed herself and lost the war. Because I am ashamed. In Manchuria I thought myself a man. In America I think myself a man. Here I am forced to think of myself as a Jew. A Cossack sneezes and a Jew trembles. That makes me a Jew. A Jewish virgin is raped. That makes me a Jew. A Jew is beaten. The idiot goes to the synagogue and thanks God that he is still alive. And that damned coward makes me a Jew."

"And you agree with your mother and Huang that Russia is doomed?"

Igor shrugged. "I don't know, but she is smeared with blood."

"May I put a proposition to you? First, I want us to stay together, as a family. I can't leave. Neither Julie nor Katya nor Alexis wants to leave. To keep you and your mother with us, Alexis and I must right the wrongs and make you want to give Russia another chance. I ask that for the present you not say goodbye forever. Give me time to work on this. Either I succeed in making the Ukraine safe and you and Georgi come home, or I fulfill my mother's curse and die alone. Do you agree to that?"

"You pick a pretty uncomfortable way to pay for failure," Igor said. "Wouldn't it be more sensible to bury that old Tartar nonsense?"

Boris grinned at him. "It's remarkable," he said conversationally, "how easy it is to give good advice. I say, 'Forget Lotus'; you say, 'Forsake your destiny,' and we end up going our own ways."

He untied the horses. "When are you leaving?" He swung easily into the saddle.

"As soon as we reach the stables. The Blond One is picking up my gear."

"Warsaw?"

244

"No," Igor said absently, "I changed my mind. To Moscow."

They halted once before they reached the stable, just long enough for Igor to say, "Tell Julie and Mother about our agreement."

Boris nodded. "Anything else?" They had come into the stable yard.

"Take care of your leg, Boris, my father."

Boris walked away as the Blond One came through the door.

"How long will you be gone this time?" the younger man asked.

Igor said, "I don't know. I have confidence in Father, if not in his being able to save Russia. But Ronya is aware of how things stand and my going fits into her plans."

"How about Julie? It's shameful the way you keep leaving her."

Igor suddenly felt deeply fatigued. If only he had resolved his conflict with Boris and struck to the heart of his feelings before last night's struggle with Julie! He would be staying home now, but it was too late. If he turned back he could never, for the rest of his life, forgive Julie.

"Why are you going to Moscow?" the Blond One asked.

Igor did not answer this question, either.

"You are your own enemy," his half brother said. "Neither Manchuria nor America will cure anything. Come back to the house. Please." Igor flung his arms around the Blond One, jumped into the waiting carriage and drove off without looking back.

Winter enclosed the manor house in a white blanket and life continued like a bright tapestry, seemingly unchanged. Rachel, emerging from the cocoon of babyhood, was half pixie, half angel, pure delight. Boris, golden and romantic still, was mellower and more effective than ever in the affairs of the province. He had become the voice of the Ukraine. Ronya still enchanted him, while Julie awakened his tenderness by her fears, her confused loyalties and her unshakable honesty. Katya, who visited them often, roused his protectiveness. Boris very much enjoyed being the one strutting male in a houseful of women.

During the day Julie was the loving mother and daughter and

245

sat in the center of the close family circle. But at night she was often alone at her wide window singing sad songs. In the darkness of her room, lying in her lonesome bed, she wept.

There was no word from Igor.

XXVIII

IN the spring of 1910, twelve hundred Jewish families were told to leave Kiev and Russia. No particular animosity lay behind the order. For the Tsar it was a matter of honor—the Tsarina and Rasputin demanded more. Stolypin's hands were tied until Rasputin could be shorn of power. Alexis could not but agree. It seemed dangerous to rouse hatred against Nicholas, who was feeble but not evil. To extinguish the flame that was Rasputin was what mattered. Only after that would the Tsar be able to put an end to the oppression and ill-treatment of all his people, not alone the Jews.

But while Stolypin might hold himself personally aloof from the sufferings of the Jews, Alexis could not. Katya, from Kiev, wrote bitterly, "It does seem to me Peter is a lukewarm friend. How can he ask Boris to support his government and still persecute our people? For years relations between Christians and Jews in Kiev have been good. Why now annul the privileges granted so long ago? It humiliates and frightens the neo-Christians—the Russified Jews—too, and they feel resentment toward the Tsar. Do what you can for the Jews, Alexis, my love."

He went to see Stolypin, who greeted him warmly. "An unexpected honor, Alexis! Come in. Come right in. I'm working on an address to deliver to the Duma, advocating new reforms. Sit down, do. I'll lock the door. This is indeed a fortunate surprise! I need your advice on certain phrases."

"I've come to quarrel with you, Peter," Alexis said agreeably to the black-bearded premier. "Your intentions are not good enough. My Katya is distracted over the injustice to innocent people, good Russians, who have been given an ultimatum to leave Kiev. You aren't going to effect a reconciliation between St. Petersburg and the Ukraine that way."

Peter put a finger to his lips. "Lower your voice, Alexis," he begged. "You know Rasputin's spies are everywhere."

Alexis sat in grim silence, waiting. The stoniness of his gaze nudged the minister to say, "There's been no violence, Alexis, no looting. The edict certainly contravenes my policy but the game for freedom and justice takes time to play. I must keep the Tsar happy by letting him take a trick or two."

"While the world shouts—'Shame'?" Alexis said scornfully. "Foreign opinion does not distinguish between Nicholas and Rasputin. Furthermore, my Katya hints that Boris leans toward shifting his weight to the fire-eaters in the Ukrainian party. Father Tromokov will be quick to seize the offensive. . . . Civil war would be a disaster, Peter."

Loyal though he is to the Tsar, Stolypin thought, von Glasman's daughters are a heavy drain on him, and he's lonely. If Katya were in St. Petersburg, he'd take no such gloomy view. With the boom in international trade and the expansion of our railways, he'd stop tormenting himself about the Jews. "Alexis," he said, his voice less friendly than it had been, "I want to ask you a question."

Peter's question surprised him.

"How is the enchanting Katya? Why don't you bring her home? We need her. She is our closest link to the Dowager Empress." So that was the way he meant to maneuver!

His face a polite mask, Alexis answered, "Of course Katya will return to St. Petersburg as soon as we rid the palace of Rasputin. Meanwhile Katya and Ronya keep each other company. I am occupied with government responsibilities. And Boris rides in all directions." The mask dropped and the seasoned diplomatist spoke with a directness he seldom invoked.

"The situation in the Ukraine is precarious, Peter, and Boris alone holds the liberal forces from joining with the Socialists.

He has also proclaimed that there shall be no disputes between Cossacks and Tartars. So they are pouring their united energies into working for the Ukraine's future, instead of feuding.

"Meet Boris *now*, Peter. End the danger of a Ukrainian revolt."

Brilliant though he was, Peter Stolypin was an obstinate as a *moujik*. How could Boris turn so swiftly from horses and vodka to holding the reins of the Ukraine in his hands? He remembered Pirov dancing with Tamara at his wedding reception—and the disgust on David von Glasman's face. No, he wanted nothing to do with that blond giant—he would almost as soon sit down at the conference table with Rasputin. And, Boris was Alexis' brother-in-law. That made it more difficult, but perhaps he could dispose of Boris without antagonizing Alexis, which would give him time. Stolypin was a master of stalling and compromise—his career built on those tactics.

Peter turned his attractive smile on his visitor. "I'm sorry, Alexis. My schedule has me absolutely pinned down for the present. I fear Boris will have to wait. Tell him how much I admire him. Tell him not to press for a separate Ukraine and no more Jews will be compelled to quit Russia."

"Boris will not be easy to handle," Alexis said. "Ronya holds him responsible for the Jews. Talk to him yourself. Summon him to St. Petersburg. Make your position perfectly clear. It's vitally important."

"The Jews are irrelevant at this time. I leave Boris to you," Stolypin said with a touch of levity.

Alexis was not amused. "I expected something better from you, Peter."

Like Alexis, Peter was nettled. "The divine Katya is one of us," he returned to the attack. "She belongs here. As for Ronya, she's perfectly safe, definitely safe. They live under the personal protection of the Empress Mother, and the Tsar, knowing Boris for a fighter, has no desire to provoke him.

"You ask me to make my position clear, Alexis. Let me do so. Tell the Pirovs I dislike persecution. However, I cannot afford to act hastily nor can I perform miracles. As soon as Rasputin is in Siberia, I shall end this awkward situation. Toward the end of the year I'll send Boris papers documenting my reform program, and ask him, as head of the Ukrainian party, to evaluate them. Then we'll meet and arrange matters between us. Is that satisfactory?"

"Not entirely, Peter. It's a postponement, not a solution. There's more on Boris' mind than the Ukrainian party. His sons' rooms are empty and I can take him no real assurance that your program makes it ridiculous for Igor and Georgi to seek freedom abroad. Remember, Ronya's sons are Jews."

What a pity, Stolypin thought, offering Alexis his hand. Alexis had no alternative but to take it. "Peter, no one who lives with evil escapes contamination. Bargain with Boris honestly, especially over what pertains to the Ukraine and our wives' people. Unlike you, I cannot take the plight of the Jews philosophically."

Stolypin unlocked the door and peered out. Sure that no aide or servant was within earshot, he said softly, "You're having an audience with the Tsar. Be careful, Alexis. Take no risks. His heart is big but his head is empty. If you must refer to Jews as 'my wife's people,' come here to do it—and even here quietly. The house has ears. Don't mention them at Tsarskoye Selo. As yet no one suspects you of any interest above your Tsar."

Alexis left Stolypin thinking, I'd better make plans for Katya.

At the audience, Nicholas II announced that all was well. "We have weathered the financial crisis," he said complacently, "and need not return to the Winter Palace. St. Petersburg has really grown too trying, what with the commoner Stolypin charging the Duma to make itself effective." He turned his vacuous stare on Brusilov. "Stolypin was your choice, Alexis; consequently he's your responsibility. It lies within our prerogative to dismiss whom we choose, whenever we feel it our duty to do so. Caution him."

Alexis drove to the heart of the city in a thoughtful mood. At the door of a house, he descended from his carriage, and was admitted at once. A few steps down the hall he let himself into a room where a marble-topped table stood beside a brass bed on which newspaper editorials and proofs were strewn ostentatiously. Alexis went through the door into the adjoining sitting room to find a maid bringing a tray with breakfast to Reuben.

249

"*Guten Tag,* Graf Brusilov," said Reuben, and Alexis remembered that he posed as editor of a small-town German newspaper when he came to St. Petersburg. "Be so good as to take a chair." The maid put the tray on a round table with a lace cover, and he instructed her, "We are not to be disturbed."

As soon as the door closed behind her, Reuben put an arm around Alexis' shoulder. "Hello, my friend." He pulled his watch out of his pocket. "You're fifteen minutes late. I was beginning to worry, having traveled a long way to meet you. You don't mind if I breakfast? I've had nothing to eat today." He and Alexis both spoke in German.

"While I," Alexis replied, waving him to proceed with his meal, "had no idea you could possibly be so prompt. I was prepared to wait a week if necessary. It's good to see you."

"Before we get down to business, give me news of my Lady Ronya," Reuben said, pouring coffee.

"My beautiful sister-in-law is beautiful. My healthy sister-in-law is well. My determined sister-in-law is a mule. Now, what's the news of Igor?"

"He's dubious about coming home and every time I get back from Russia he asks me how near his father is to reaching a decision. Huang thinks it would be disastrous for him to go to the United States and have to wait too long. He wonders whether you can possibly persuade Julie to join him in California and stay there until the present situation resolves itself."

Alexis took a sip of coffee. "Julie is not yet strong enough to manage Igor without Ronya. She has been deeply disturbed by the months with no word from him, and has become more dependent than ever on Boris. Although she and Ronya—all of us, in fact—have known that he didn't sail for California this time, Julie has no idea he is in Manchuria. I haven't dared tell even Katya all that Huang has written me."

"Just what sort of girl *is* Julie? What one gets from Igor, of course, is descriptions of a goddess. Is his Julie an illusion too?"

Of all the family Alexis was best qualified to assess Julie dispassionately. "She's a quiet girl but I would say has a better mind than Igor. And she's pretty, unusually pretty. But it's neither her intelligence nor her looks that make her so appealing. Part of it is in her voice—she sings like an angel, quite irresistible. More than that, she's unpredictable, childlike with flashes of uncommon intuition, fiercely loyal, simple, kind and generous.

"If only she could get over being afraid!" He sketched in a little of her childhood. "That, coupled with her fanatical attachment to the house in Kiev and her hunger for a father, makes a situation that is complex, to say the least."

"*Gott in Himmel!*" Reuben threw up his hands. "More dreams and delusions. If I were Ronya, I'd try to take the crutch of Boris away from her and force her to walk alone to Igor. However, I'm no authority on young lovers or how to deal with them. . . . What am I to tell Igor when I get back to Harbin?"

"Tell him," Alexis ticked off the points on his fingers, "that there will be a decision soon. He's to stay on with Huang or go to California, whichever he prefers. Tell him that Julie is well and that I believe there is no advantage, for him or for the family, to his coming home at this time. He is to trust Boris—it will work out. And, tell him for God's sake to *write!*"

Reuben was astounded. "What in the devil's name has happened to you?" he asked. "The last time we talked you were hell-bent on his coming back to Kiev, to the ancestral acres."

"Among other recent happenings," Alexis responded frankly, "it is the grim misfortune of the Jews of Kiev. Knowing our Igor, I can only suppose that if he were here he would resort to drastic and illegal reprisals. I want reform without revolution. No assassinations.

"Even more important, Igor is quite capable of ruining everything Boris has accomplished. As I see it, nothing will change much for the next six months or so. After Stolypin keeps his promises, Boris and I want Igor home because then he can use his energies constructively."

To Reuben, Alexis' optimism verged on political naïveté. The time to take steps to save the family was, he believed, now, before the world was turned upside down by war and escape became impossible.

"Listen, Alexis, Stolypin can't win. I'll be amazed if he even manages to stay alive. Your own Tsar is chiseling away at his headstone. But even if he escapes a martyr's grave, even if he succeeds in shipping Rasputin off to Siberia, he can't open any golden gates. If you're ignoring Lenin, you're blind. Furthermore, Russia's problems are not all internal. The Kaiser and Austria want war. Be sensible, Alexis. Make the Pirovs go. Arrange asylum for yourself and Katya immediately. Your world is going up in smoke."

Alexis was obviously troubled. "Today," he said, "I've already had two conversations that went a long way toward shaking my confidence. . . . However, in true Russian fashion, I vacillate.

"I know what the German high command wants and what vast sums the Kaiser has invested in the Bolsheviks. These dangers enabled me to dissuade Boris from provoking civil war. If he won independence in the Ukraine, he'd be handing Russia over to Germany. I urged him to negotiate with Stolypin rather than seize power he can't possibly hold. That much I have accomplished. But restrain the Pirovs?—no! A team of wild horses could neither move nor hold Ronya. For the moment she's quiescent on account of Boris, bound by her own uncertainty. But that won't last. A Tartar mother and Ronya's land are what tie Boris down."

They sat brooding for a little; then Reuben laughed, a grim laugh. "To defeat the Tartar woman, Ronya must get her man out of Russia. She knows that, Alexis. Don't try to change her mind. What a devilish joke! If Boris wins, he loses."

Taking up a glass of vodka Reuben had placed before him, Alexis said, his eyes sad, "I want to talk to you about Katya."

"Good." Reuben wondered why it had taken Alexis so long to come to the point. "Now you *are* being sensible."

Alexis smiled. "Just in case . . ."

"Go on." Reuben was not smiling.

"If I am betrayed or anything happens to me at a time when Katya is not with Boris and Ronya, go to the archbishop of Moscow. Katya will be with him and he will turn her over to you. Take her to Ronya."

Reuben's composure dissolved. "For God's sake, Alexis—not the archbishop of Moscow!"

"Calm, calm," said Alexis. "Very few people remember, but I assumed you were one of the few who might. David von Glasman's aunt was the archbishop's grandmother. Katya is named for her."

Reuben whistled. "I'll be damned!"

"A dull remark." Alexis laughed. "Has it never occurred to you to wonder why Father Tromokov wasn't defrocked?"

Reuben bowed. "Count Brusilov, I am your respectful servant. I believed I knew everything about the von Glasmans." Reuben settled back in his chair. "In my opinion, it's more than time for Igor to take his final farewell of Huang."

That was what Alexis had hoped to hear. "Tell Igor," he said, "in any words which seem appropriate, that the situation here is either-or, and that Boris will let him know which as soon as he can. You may, I think, say that Julie is no longer absolutely opposed to leaving Kiev. And about Rachel, she takes after him with a beauty all her own. A delightful child. An absolute charmer."

Dusk had overtaken them. Reuben got up, drew the curtains and lighted a lamp. When he turned back to Alexis, he found him putting on his coat, knowing that Reuben would have many things to do before he started east again. "What an unconscionable lot I do talk," he said. "But there's just one more thing. I *can* count on you? About Katya, I mean."

"I will not leave her side until she is in Ronya's arms," Reuben said.

XXIX

THERE were many to whom the deportation of the Jews was a signal victory. The Black Hundreds hailed it with joy as proof of how well they had done their work—Stolypin would repair nothing. The revolutionaries saw in it cause for the rising fever of their revolution.

Jews the length and breadth of Europe closed their shops and mourned. They had no appetite for business-as-usual. Now there was one dream left to them, America.

Ronya was passionately upset, but Boris avoided the subject. The day she asked him, "Rabbi Levinsky is on his way here; will you stay and talk to him?" Boris, despite his fondness for the rabbi, said, "No, Ronya." She would have argued but he put her off. "Joseph will come wearing his wide belt. Fill it for him, little dove. If Tromokov drops in, tell him I said, 'Good luck.'"

Her eyes widened. Boris, grinning with self-satisfaction, went to the door, tossing, "I'll be at the cabin later," over his shoulder. She watched him from the window as he rode off.

Ten minutes later Rabbi Levinsky found Ronya waiting, elbows on the tea table, head in her hands. She had been thinking, how can Boris divorce himself from the suffering of my people, he who can't do enough for a pregnant mare!

"Don't get up," the rabbi said and, when she offered him tea, "Not yet. Where is Boris? And where are Katya and Julie? The storm over Kiev concerns us all."

"Katya's managed to take Julie to Moscow and, as it happens, nothing could please me more. Every step out of this house is a step forward for Julie."

"And Boris?"

"He left his regrets, Joseph."

Ronya shared the disapproval she saw in his face but nonetheless resented it. "Why is it so desperately important for Boris to be here? Have you any idea how hard he works or how important what he's doing is?"

"Ronya, Ronya, if you're excusing Boris for your own sake—" He thrust out his lower lip. "If you're excusing him for mine, don't bother. I am not Julie. To me, Boris is no champion of Jewry. I have learned to put my faith in God, not in Boris, Tartar *or* Arghun. We must rebuild Jerusalem and recreate the Jewish nation if we are ever to reconstitute the kingdom of righteousness.

"Why am I telling you this? You know perfectly well it's because I need money. Jews all over the world, rich and poor, are contributing." Ronya needed no urging to pledge a donation for herself and Katya, so great was her relief. She had dreaded a more painful reason for his visit. Then it came.

"I have other things to talk about."

"If you don't mind, I'll fortify myself with a cigarette, Joseph."

"I do mind," he said. "I don't like to see a woman smoke." Her ready compliance pleased Levinsky and he went on less sternly. "Pour me a cup of tea, Ronya, and don't look so downcast. I didn't come here to demand that Boris take a whip to Stolypin. As a matter of fact, I'd rather he didn't. It would only lead to more bloodshed. And that is what I came to tell Boris."

Ronya drew a deep breath. "Thank you, Joseph," she said. "I got a letter from Alexis today. Boris hasn't seen it yet. Stolypin has put off meeting Boris again. That leaves us still neither here nor there. I don't know what effect this will have—Boris is gambling everything on Peter."

"Very foolish," Levinsky said gravely. "I don't trust Stolypin. Any crime can be committed against a Jew with impunity under his regime. We have no rights. No rights at all. The throne is in league with the Black Hundreds. Get out of Russia, Ronya."

"How can I? I can't leave Boris. I can't take Rachel away from her mother. I can't budge Julie. And there's so little time." Her voice had risen.

Joseph Levinsky's eyes narrowed. "What steps have you taken, Ronya?"

Looking deep into her eyes, he saw that she understood his meaning. "Take another step, Ronya."

At that precise moment the door flew open and, like a gust of wind, Father Tromokov rushed in, swearing. "Damn it, Ronya, pour me a drink! There is nothing left to do but ask you for money." Moderating his pace and tone at the sight of Levinsky, he continued, "I know—I know, Joseph. I promised I wouldn't. But if you have the crazy notion that my blasted word will stop me, you're wrong."

Ronya did not stir. "Pour your own vodka. I expect you're not altogether parched." She turned to Rabbi Levinsky. "You tell me about it, Joseph, since the two of you seem to be in whatever this is together."

Smiling widely, Father Tromokov opened the doors of a lacquered Chinese cabinet and took out a bottle he found there.

The rabbi began. "There are, among the families ordered out

of Kiev, some who are even less fortunate than others . . ."

"In a damned mess, that's what they are!" roared Tromokov from the table where he was filling a glass.

"Come sit near us and stop howling," Ronya said.

The priest's bright eyes twinkled. "I prefer to sit near the vodka," he said with sham dignity. "Carry on, Joseph."

"If you'll be quiet, I'll try." Levinsky gave Tromokov a fond look. "In order to obey the Tsar's edict, even the poorest need money and the barest necessities for travel. At first my violent friend here was all in favor of our disobeying. He offered asylum in his church, promising that his peasants would defend it and slaughter any soldier who laid hands on a Jew. However, under no circumstances could I accept, especially since his church is on your land, Ronya. Then he ordered his peasants to contribute to a fund to help the Jews get away and they did, but not enough. Even steerage for three hundred families comes to quite a sum."

"Why didn't you come to me, Joseph Levinsky?" Her question was a rebuke.

He smiled. "I hesitated to ask you for one kind of money when I wanted the other kind that you have just promised."

"Rabbi Levinsky is a modest man," Tromokov chanted, delighted. "He does one good deed at a time." He emptied his glass. "Go, Ronya, get the rubles."

"Goodness," said Ronya, "I haven't got that kind of money in the house. I'll send it along to you tomorrow, Joseph."

No thanks were spoken. It is in the Jewish tradition that to deserve paradise one must give alms, from the heart. The room was very still and Ronya sat wondering why they often called Rabbi Levinsky "Joseph" but the priest was always "Father Tromokov." That bear of a man lumbered to his feet, came to her tea table and began filling a plate with sandwiches and cakes. Glancing at the rabbi's empty tea glass, he shook his head. "You'll poison yourself with that stuff," he warned. "All that lemon— ugh! Bound to cause sour stomach. Join us vodka drinkers, Joseph. With vodka in its belly, a sheep becomes a wolf."

The rabbi shoved his chair back as if he feared that the Gargantuan padre might crush his frail frame. "With vodka a man, too, becomes a wolf," he said amiably.

Ronya looked at them both almost maternally. Like two children, she thought, forever baiting each other and both loving it. "Please stay," she said. "Lydia is making a delicious kosher dinner and the table is set. I'm sorry but neither Boris nor I will be here."

The priest eyed her owlishly. "Don't go yet," he said mildly, "and when you do go, take plenty of food. Boris will be late and he'll be ravenous."

Ronya's sculptured eyebrows lifted. "How do you know?"

"If you tell Boris," he said slowly, "so help me, Ronya, he'll kill me!"

"And *I* will if you don't," she said with charming candor.

He came to rest, sitting on the arm of the sofa. "It's simple justice, Ronya. Twelve hundred good Jewish families ordered out of Kiev. The property of twelve hundred troublemakers—a plague on them—burned to the ground."

Ronya had known, of course, in her heart of hearts, and hoped it was not true. Now that rare intruder, fear, engulfed her and the priest was heartbroken at the anguish in her eyes.

"No, Ronya, not Boris," he said. "A masked man who wears a black hood and rides a black stallion, a phantom, a revenge rider."

She knew that her friend was lying. "Give me proof positive that the rider is not Boris or I will tell on you," she said evenly.

"You wouldn't, Ronya!"

"Oh yes I would. Just like that!" Ronya snapped her fingers.

Rabbi Levinsky, unable to bear seeing the priest cornered, undertook to compound his falsehood. "How could Boris ride anywhere without being spotted?" he asked reasonably. "He's the most conspicuous man in Russia. Smoke a cigarette. I give you my permission."

"Your permission only adds to my alarm," she said. She turned to the priest. "Why, when I wanted to leave for the cabin, wouldn't you let me? Was it to give Boris time to cover his tracks?"

"In regard to time, yes, you're right, Ronya. By tomorrow, after two fires, Boris is bound to be suspected. He's played a gay tune all afternoon, slapping backs, exchanging jokes, buying drinks—being seen miles from the fire. Tonight, soon after midnight and long after he's back, open your cabin door. You'll see flames in the sky, even smell smoke. Does that convince you?"

"No!" said Ronya. "It only proves that the revenge rider, as you call him, is more than one man. You're the other. And if there is a third, it's the Blond One."

The priest shrieked with laughter and the rabbi looked so awestruck he blushed. "And the scripture commands us: Get thee at a distance from falsehood," he said.

Ronya looked at him mockingly. "So you don't want Boris to lead a war party. So the Jews always seek peace—do they? Or at least, of course, the armchair socialists, the intellectuals. Well, Joseph, how do our robust Jews fight? With shaking prayers or in fiery passion, like Boris? Still he is beneath your spiritual consideration, isn't he? The weak have a universal weakness. They let the strong fight for them. Don't drop your eyes. I'm talking to you," she stormed.

"Oh, Ronya, Ronya, from the start I disliked the whole idea. I told Boris his dream of a free Russia was a false dream and to take you and Julie and Rachel to America. Do you think he or Father Tromokov listened to me? They said if anything went wrong all I'd know was what I read in the papers. They made fun of me, asked me to ride with them and left me sitting right in this chair."

Her eyes like large stars, Ronya smiled at the rabbi. "Don't worry, Joseph," she said. "Nothing will go wrong. On the contrary, the revenge rider will force Stolypin's hand. And if anyone should try to make you bear witness against Boris you're to swear that Boris is the revenge rider and that Tamara hides him after his raids."

The priest almost fell off the sofa. "Beautiful! Beautiful!" he applauded. "I, myself, may start the rumor."

Rabbi Levinsky looked reproachfully at his friend. "Don't go around starting any rumors. There's nothing funny about making the sky glow red. And tell Boris that the next time he rides on a dangerous mission, he'd better do it at night. Today he behaved not like a brave man but like a reckless young fool."

The priest raised his right hand and shook his finger. "No, Joseph, you're wrong. It had to be done once by daylight to establish the myth of a phantom."

Such a wily stratagem would never have occurred to Levinsky. He laughed. "Go along now, Ronya. You've wasted enough time with us. When you see Boris, don't show your worries in your eyes. He's got enough of his own."

Father Tromokov was studying Ronya.

"What is it, Ivan?" she said and realized it was the first time she had used his given name since he, the son of peasants on the place, had returned from the seminary a priest.

He went to her and laid a large paw lightly on her shoulder. "Tell Boris I told you. Whatever he shares with you is easy for him to bear. Alone, he's a flickering light. With you he burns with a steady flame. I'll take you to the cabin. I promised not to let you go alone."

"I'm ready," Ronya said, "and there's enough food in the kitchen to feed a regiment." She sat a moment longer. "Sleep here tonight, Joseph."

"All right," he said. "And I give you my word that when Father Tromokov—when Ivan—returns, I'll be at the front door with a bottle of vodka in my hand."

The moment she arrived at the cabin, Ronya went to the kitchen and lighted the stove to heat soup.

"Is that you, Ronya?" Boris' voice, from the bedroom, sounded impatient. "What in God's name kept you so long?"

"Come and eat," she called.

"I've eaten. Found bread and butter and cold meat."

She disregarded him and went on fixing a substantial supper.

"Ronya! I'm *not* hungry, I tell you. Come in here."

"What?" she said mildly. From the cold box Ronya took cubed beef, stewed in onion, tomatoes and spices, put it in a heavy iron skillet on the stove and started stirring. When a heavenly aroma filled the kitchen, Boris appeared in a long robe and leaned lazily against the door. He looked, she noted, as if he'd had a little nap. Nothing about him suggested that he had been under any more of a strain than the aggravation of having been kept waiting. "I damn near broke my neck getting here," he

259

said. "Thought you'd be waiting. What, if it's no secret, kept you so late?"

Suspecting that Boris had reached the cabin just in time to bathe and shave and perhaps collapse into sleep for ten minutes, before she arrived, Ronya played up to him. "Can you manage to lay the table? I'd like to change."

Boris leaned down and kissed her. "Let down your hair. You look like an old maid governess with it done up tight like that." Ronya, an accomplished actress, made a proud exit, only to have her aplomb shattered by Boris' firm hand on her bottom, propelling her down the hall.

He took plates and bowls from a shelf and set flat silver and linen napkins on the table. Catching whiffs from a pot of cabbage soup, his appetite revived, and at her appearance he said, "I was about to eat by myself."

"How ungallant!" she said, serving their plates.

"Why didn't you take your hair down?"

"I thought we'd talk first," she said. "It occurred to me you might want to explain a couple of things."

He grinned and started eating the beef and vegetables.

"Just how long did you think you could fool me?" she asked sweetly.

"Finish," he said, pointing to her plate. "I'll build a fire." He pushed back his chair. "But don't be long. *And* take down your hair."

"Well, my aging giant," Ronya said after she had crawled over his recumbent form on the sofa and ensconced herself in the corner, "what did you do for my Jews today?" She reached up and touched the end of his nose. "Tartar!"

"The hell with Tartars," he said, and Ronya could not retort because his mouth was on hers. Their lovemaking, which started surgingly, ended slowly. Boris, feeling that Ronya, as she clung to him, was growing cold, spread his robe over her and built up the fire. From a cabinet he took two glasses and a bottle, filled them and put one in Ronya's hand. She took a sip of the cognac; Boris drank his in a single gulp. "I've wanted a drink all day," he said.

"How did you do it, darling?"

"By a vain display of horsemanship, little dove." He kissed

her lightly. "Most of the credit goes to my horses. They arrived where wanted, alone, and waited for me. Each one did his job, then vanished. My stallions managed to be everywhere. . . . A thousand people will swear they saw me in a hundred places."

"How many did you use?"

"Four," Boris said. "Three of them jet black."

"Where do you hide them?"

"We are indebted to Tamara for her hospitality," he said stiffly.

"Don't do it again, Boris. Not by daylight. Not even at night if there's a moon," Ronya begged.

He answered soberly, "I'm not at all anxious to ride again in the daytime. At one point I was nearly caught and I thought I heard my mother's voice." Ronya's hands flew to her mouth. "I know," he said. "It frightens me now, in retrospect, but it didn't then. At the time it gave me confidence the way it did when I was little and she rode at my side teaching me. Once, on a bitter winter day, I almost got myself killed trying to please her and she said, 'Well done,' and rode off leaving me to find my way back to Odessa through wild, rugged country. I managed simply because that Tartar woman said, 'Well done.' "

Boris' manner changed abruptly. "I'm going to St. Petersburg tomorrow," he said harshly. "I want to see Reuben if I can. If not I'll have to get a message to Igor some other way. It's time he cleared out of Harbin and went to San Francisco."

Ronya sat up. "We move from crisis to crisis," she snapped, "while Igor waits. How much longer have I got to go on telling Julie he loves her and is incapable of loving any other woman?

"You've no idea of the state she's in, Boris. You think she's contented as a cat. She's not. She's seething. Do you think she'll ever forgive Igor for robbing her of these years? You seem to believe the reason she sleeps so badly is because she's delicate—a bit anemic. Rubbish! When she does fall asleep she dreams of Igor, naked in the arms of a faceless Chinese girl.

"Julie wants her man, Boris. And she wants sons."

Boris was profoundly shocked; to him Julie was eternally virginal. Now, he had to admit to himself that he had chosen to think of Julie and Igor as brother and sister, and Rachel as his own child.

"How do you know all this?" he demanded.

"Julie tells Katya and Katya tells me. It's a conspiracy to make me bring Igor home. But I won't, Boris. I may go to him but I won't bring my firstborn back to his death or Siberia. If Julie wants sons, she'll have to go to him That's up to her—and you."

Boris frowned. "How me, Ronya?"

"Julie will never leave you, not even for Igor." Her voice was deep with conviction. "Oh, Boris, you will try to see Stolypin?"

"No," he said. "I mean to make him come to me. If I fail you and Julie and Rachel, go to Igor. Georgi decides for himself." His leg had been bothering him ever since he came in but now the pain subsided and he scooped Ronya up into his arms. On the way down the passage she said into his ear, "If you win, we all stay. If you lose we all go."

For the second time that day Boris heard his mother's voice. It was intoning a curse. The agony gripped him again and he just managed to let Ronya down on the bed safely. She put her arms around him. "Hold me tight," she said.

And Boris whispered, "As long as I can, little dove, as long as I can."

XXX

FOR six months after the night of the fires, the Revenge Rider was hunted. Accusations were hurled hysterically and Igor was named again and again. This one had seen him with his own eyes; that one had almost caught him. Julie was frantic and had to be told at last that Boris and Ronya and the Brusilovs knew of Igor's whereabouts—that he was in China and that their news of him came from Huang. Julie's weeping gave way to a frozen stoicism that troubled Boris more than her childish weeping and wailing. When she complained now, it was because she didn't hear often enough from Georgi and that when she did, he wrote so happily about California. He loved Stanford, he loved the United States, he apparently could not get very worked up about the turmoil at home. "He ought to *be* here," Julie would storm. "You have no *right* to let him be so far away from his family!"

A picture of Igor arrived one day from Harbin and they all studied it with passionate interest, especially Julie. Compared to the Blond One, though he was nine months older, he still looked younger, lithe and well, his hair as abundant and burnished as ever, his eyes astonishingly dark and aggressively bright. He was as beautiful as an angel in Julie's opinion and no one disagreed with her. There was a letter for Julie, too, which she held, unopened in her hand.

"Oh, Julie! Read your letter," implored Ronya.

"I can't," she said, getting out of her chair. "I've waited too long. "You read it."

"What a little goose you are!" Ronya said, but she took the letter and in a voice which, in that silent room, had the quality of a clear bell, read:

Harbin, Manchuria
July 4, 1911

My little Julie,

I have arranged for this letter to reach you on the date above because on that day I disembark at San Francisco.

Dearest, I'm so lonesome. I want to tie a ribbon around your lovely black hair, to see my mother's face, to watch Rachel and Beljik roll in the red clover. And I miss going to the stables with Father. I see him in my mind's eye negotiating with Stolypin and I keep hoping he'll make it possible for Georgi and me to come back to you. Tell Boris to deal the cards when he meets Stolypin, to see that he ties the Tsar up. That bastard sold us out of the war.

But if it should be America after all, don't be afraid. I'll build you a wonderful house and if you want, I'll come and get you.

Julie, Julie, I do love you. Only you. I want you. I want Ronya, my mother, and Boris, my father. I want us all to be together again and I want to give you sons.

Your
Igor

In the two women, months of pent-up emotion were un-dammed. Julie burst into tears and Ronya, at the window, eyes dry, pulled out a handkerchief and held it to her mouth to hide her trembling lips. When Julie's sobs subsided, a shyness lingered between them and neither one could speak. The room was too full of Igor.

It was a short-lived silence. Lydia flew through the door, looked sharply at them and ran to the oven scolding, "If I'd come five minutes later we'd all be dead of smoke." She grabbed a towel and hauled the pan out. The gingerbread man was burned black. "It's a scandal," she babbled. "Two grown women can't even keep watch. Now what'll I give Rachel when she gets back?"

"Give her good news," said Ronya. "Tell her she's got a man for a father." Lydia crossed herself.

Julie had gone, clutching her letter like a talisman, and Lydia, after making a great to-do about cleaning up the mess, hurried nimbly across the room and shut the door.

Ronya pulled out a cigarette, and Lydia lit it for her before she asked, "Did you hear the commotion at the door?"

Ronya shook her head. "When was it?"

"Less than half an hour ago. There was a great knocking and Father Tromokov yelling for me. I yelled back, 'I'm coming,' and ran to the door. He said, 'Keep this to yourself, Lydia, until you and Ronya are alone. I'm riding to get Rabbi Levinsky. Tell her she's got guests for dinner.' Without so much as a goodbye, he jumped up to the seat of his carriage and drove off whipping his horses like a crazy man."

Ronya threw away her half-smoked cigarette. "It's Saturday," she said, bewildered. That the good rabbi should break the Sabbath! "Sit down, Lydia." Then, like the two good friends they were, they talked until Ronya remembered she needed flowers for the table and went out to cut roses.

It was still light when she heard them arrive, and deliberately remained at the writing desk in her room, finishing letters to her sons. For once she hated going to her friends, alone. She wished Boris were home, and when he walked in it was like an answer to prayer.

"Oh, Boris! I *am* glad to see you!"

"Anything wrong?" His eyes went to the letter in her hands.

"Julie brought Igor's letter in for you to read." She handed it to him and he threw himself down on the bed. Watching his eyes skim the page, she could catch no flicker of reaction but she knew he was relieved when he put it down, saying, "Let's go to the cabin, Ronya."

There was nothing on earth Ronya wanted to do more than just that but she was forced to say, "We can't. I don't know why, but Joseph and Father Tromokov have invited themselves to dinner."

"Good," Boris said. "They'll keep Julie company. When they've got each other they don't need us. Frankly, my angel, I'm so mixed up by their theoretical theology I can't tell the Christian from the Jew and neither can they."

"Boris, this is Saturday."

"So?"

"So why should Rabbi Levinsky ride in a carriage?"

"Oh, he'll wait till sundown," Boris said lightly. "Change into something suitable for the cabin, pet, and come along."

Again she said, "No. They're already here, and it must be serious because Lydia says Tromokov rang and asked her to bring him a cup of tea."

"That proves nothing," Boris retaliated. "He's not so prejudiced against tea as you think. At least twice in the past twenty-five years I've caught him taking a gulp—by accident."

"That's not funny," said Ronya, "and not the point. Joseph is breaking the Sabbath. Don't you realize what that means?"

Boris sighed. "How gloomy you are, you and your foregone conclusions!"

The hour before dinner might have been like any other when the Pirovs were entertaining friends but a first sign of difference was given by Joseph Levinsky. To Boris' surprise, he made no objection when Boris poured him a drink and, at news of Igor's arrival in America, he proposed a toast. And to Julie, lovely in a floating, sea-green dress, with Alexis' magnificent emerald and Ronya's pearls, he said, "Tonight you are in the great von Glasman tradition of romantic women, my dear. You look like a forest sprite."

At dinner the talk was cheerful and trivial. Not until the clock struck nine did Father Tromokov come to the matter for which they were all waiting.

"Is there any reason why we should play cat-and-mouse about the purpose of this visit?" he asked.

Julie, assuming that politics was what was on his mind, rose and asked to be excused.

"I'm truly sorry to have to bother you and Boris again," Rabbi Levinsky apologized.

Boris and Ronya sat watching his face, but he said nothing until Father Tromokov wheeled on him. "Tell them what's happened. Or I will."

"This morning," Levinsky began slowly, "about a quarter of an hour after I'd said my last '*Guten Shabbes*' of the service, I found a man waiting in my office—a working man—someone I'd never seen before. He seemed terrified. The blind on the narrow window above the street was pulled down and his first words were, 'Are we alone?'

"I assured him we were and asked him to sit down. Instead, he went and locked the door and said, 'It won't take long to say my piece and then I'm getting out of Kiev.'

"You read about the murder in the factory district?" he asked Boris.

"They both know," Tromokov put in. "Mischuk told them."

"I heard something else about it a few nights ago," Boris said. "I arrived at the barracks just as Mischuk was leaving. He told me he'd had orders from the Tsar's secret police to release the boy they'd taken and he couldn't, for the life of him, figure out any connection between the washerwoman's son and His Imperial Highness."

At this Father Tromokov exploded his bomb.

"Ritual murder!" he thundered.

In wild panic, Ronya watched Boris. They all did. Everything gentle in his face drained out of it. "Talk!" he said to Levinsky, his jaw hard.

"A laborer by the name of Mendel Beilis, employed in the brick kiln, was dragged from his neighborhood *shul* this morning and arrested. He is accused not alone of killing the Christian boy but is also charged with ritual murder. The Black Hundreds

266

are behind it and they demand the death penalty and that every Jew in the area share the guilt. That means about fifty families. The only way they can escape punishment is to embrace Christianity. Notices are being distributed today that all debts owed Jews are null and void. Next Friday, while they are praying in their temple, there will be a raid."

Ronya was ice cold yet dripping with sweat at the same time.

"For the moment the target is the poor, but the Black Hundreds mean to wipe out the entire Jewish community of Kiev, the choice always being death or baptism. They have already petitioned the Tsar to prevent escape by closing the borders."

Ronya's voice was shaking. "No local group could possibly be committing such a vicious crime. It's the Tsarina's revenge for Rasputin's being sent to Siberia. I'm certain we can find a way to make the Tsar listen to Russia's responsible leaders. We've got to. Time is running out."

Boris' voice was steady and cold. "There will be no forced baptism—no murder—no death penalty for an innocent man." He rose. "Come along!"

"Boris, take care!" The rabbi's words rang out. "Irresponsible revenge will only widen the breach between Christian and Jew."

"Don't complicate things, Joseph," Ronya stormed. "Everything depends on the Revenge Rider now."

"Joseph, stop worrying," Tromokov crowed. "Our timing is always perfect. We'll fire wheat fields, haystacks, toolsheds but no houses or barns. Still, the bastards won't know where to expect the next outburst of flames."

Boris smiled down on Ronya and she raised her face for his kiss. "No moon, no stars," she said like a priestess and a loving wife. "I'll have hot food waiting for you when your work is done. And," she said to Tromokov, "you'll be back in time for early mass."

Boris straightened up. "Tomorrow, Joseph," he said, "we'll see Mischuk and hire lawyers."

Alone with Levinsky, Ronya remarked in her ordinary voice, "We live in a country not worth living in and yet I get hungry about this time of night. Meet me in the kitchen and we'll have hot tea and something light to eat."

When he joined her, the rabbi was frowning and though he sat down and tucked a napkin under his chin, he accepted only tea.

"Ronya von Glasman Pirov," he said, "tonight it was plain to me that you would have liked nothing better than to ride with the men. I don't like that. And I don't like Boris and Ivan coming too close to death too often. If I were less of a friend and more of a rabbi, I'd say—"

"Don't, Joseph, because I can guess and it's nonsense. You want results and don't approve of taking risks. Besides, I hadn't a ghost of a chance of stopping Boris. His leg is stiff tonight; that's handicap enough without my adding to his burdens, which are greater than even you know."

"Oh, no!"

"Yes, and not even Father Tromokov has heard and don't you go telling him. He loves Boris and he's a hothead. Joseph, Stolypin has ignored Alexis again. Peter's last letter to Boris was distinctly cool. He thinks that if he can capture the Revenge Rider he can deal with the Ukraine. Harshly. I suppose he's entitled to a last desperate effort to appease the Tsarina."

"Ronya, Ronya, wouldn't it be better if you took yourself out of Russia?"

"Certainly it would be better, and took Katya, too. Stolypin insists that, as a show of good faith on Alexis' part, she stay in St. Petersburg. For Igor and Julie it's a necessity. In staying I'm taking a calculated risk."

"But why, Ronya? You know and I know and I think Boris knows that nothing will come out of his meeting with Stolypin. The Tsar uses him now. Later he'll throw him out. Rasputin may be in Siberia but he's alive and that road can be traveled two ways. Nothing is changed."

"You and Huang and I, we three agree. However," Ronya's head went up, "I have made a bargain with Boris. Until he, himself, is convinced that it's hopeless, there'll be no separate lifeboats for us. If he fails and the whole of the Ukraine sinks, we'll swim for our lives."

Rabbi Levinsky leaned across the white cloth and patted her hand. "Ronya von Glasman Pirov, you hate the idea of leaving as much as Boris does, don't you?"

268

She looked tired. "Of course, Joseph. My ancestors were chosen people who chose to live in Russia. I was born in this house and so were my sons and my grandchild. I'm going, I leave part of myself behind . . ."

He wanted passionately to comfort her. "America is a country of Europeans."

"I know," her voice was small. "But for a time, for all of Boris' and my time, the Pirovs will be foreigners."

The rabbi became a rabbi once more. "You do understand, Ronya, that whatever happens to the meek and humble, whatever happens to Mendel Beilis, happens to Rachel von Glasman Pirov, don't you? Promise me that in America you'll live a Jew among Jews."

Something of the old fire lit her face. "In America, Joseph, I'll live an American among Americans, my religious and political beliefs my own. I'm not foolish enough to think that Boris or my sons or I, for that matter, will ever be content to live exclusively among Jews. In a country where—before the law—all men are equal, why isolate ourselves from our neighbors?"

"But," the rabbi spoke, "you will devote yourself to the service of Jews less fortunate than you—the Jews left in Poland and Roumania and here?"

"Of course, Joseph."

He bowed to her warmth and wisdom. "I think I'll go to my room. Good night, dearest Ronya."

XXXI

EVEN Krasmikov, his crafty and dishonest friend, warned Boris to leave the Beilis case alone. "If I embarrass you," Boris retorted sharply, "cut me dead at the barracks. I won't hold it against you."

A strange fellow, the rascally Krasmilov! He had a warm spot in his cold heart for Boris, nor could he have borne being excluded from parties at the officers' club. To convince Boris of his undying loyalty, he gave him free access to his secret files, including the dossiers of Peter Stolypin and Boris Pirov. The former revealed a curious fact, that the door to the royal sanctum, open to Katya and Alexis, was shut to the premier.

In his own file Boris found, to his horror, a command that, wherever Ronya went, to her dressmaker, her bootmaker, her glovemaker, to lunch or dinner with friends, she was to be followed by a man with an unsavory record—a criminal record—who had one talent making himself unseen.

Boris decided it would be madness to warn Ronya. He did not want her shooting the bounder or cutting him to ribbons with her whip. Ronya, unsuspecting, was charmed and flattered by the constancy with which the Blond One dogged her steps. However, she was finally driven to say, "I love you, I love being with you. We have fun together. But, please, in the name of good sense, go find yourself a girl to dance and hold hands with." The Blond One grinned like Boris and wherever Ronya went, he was at her side.

Not only the Blond One but the stable hands, Tamara's men and the most dependable of the peasants were armed. Boris had seen to that. A twenty-four-hour guard stood duty at all approaches to the estate. Having taken care for his own, Boris went out after distant game. In the files he had discovered the identities of a band of plundering *moujiks*, listed not as ex-convicts but as police aides. Boris called in a few relatives from Odessa. The Tartars were happy to oblige their Golden One, their cousin.

From time to time he still rode, above all if the mission was particularly dangerous, in the Blond One's place. What time he could snatch from the intricate and perilous web he had woven, he devoted to Rachel; and Ronya, seeing his need for relief from plots and counterplots, made no demands on him and did not even let Julie intrude. If the cramps in his leg reached unbearable proportions, he locked himself in his room and got quietly drunk and sometimes heard again the maddening voice of his mother, saying, "The Golden Ones never escape."

The letter from Alexis came as a reprieve. Ronya read it to Boris and Julie. Boris liked Ronya to read to him. Her emphasis and shadings penetrated the meaning and gave him valuable insights. Alexis' letters invariably posed problems, so indirect is the language of diplomacy.

Beloved family:

My letter goes to you. My person returns to Moscow so I must make haste. Katya is waiting tea. It grows cold—a tiresome thing —cold tea.

I suggest that our friend who travels soon to Kiev, the exact date yet inexact, be served hot tea. The big talk is agreed on; small talk goes well with tea. Perhaps thin cucumber sandwiches and the tea not too strong.

I had an hour with our friend in his upstairs sitting room and he inquired about Igor and Georgi. Right and proper, I thought. Some moments later he was off about the Revenge Rider. It seems his capture is much on the exalted mind. I assured him it is much on your minds, too.

Tamara's statement to the press created a great brouhaha here. Imagine her looking into her teacup (or was it saucer?) and seeing Peter the Great! Rather monstrous, the idea of a dead emperor burning all that wheat. Not that it matters now the wheat is gone.

Such a holocaust! Do be careful, Boris, when you light Ronya's cigarette. Fire in bed is dangerous.

It is an avuncular prerogative to reprove, and, though I pat Rachel on her adorable head, I find myself speculating on the document before me, and what happens to all the other little girls in Russia if she has a monopoly on sugar and spice. I recommend your teaching her a little humility, or perhaps a sense of responsibility. Our precious child is being greedy. For this I hold you, Boris, entirely to blame. Tell her I shall arrive with suitable gifts, within reason.

Mercy! I almost closed without telling you my dream. You, Boris, resplendent, rode a lion and your skillful hands directed him but you, too, were held by other hands that steer a middle course.

Soon Katya and I will be in Kiev. Let the tea be hot.

I remain a Pirov *aficionado,* in love with you all,

Alexis

271

Neither Boris, sitting behind the desk which he now used as an office, nor Ronya, nearby in a low chair, was paying any attention to Julie.

"I really don't understand my Uncle Alexis," she said. "He spoils Rachel ten times more than any of us."

"Julie," Ronya said, disregarding her comment, "it's been quiet in the house for hours. Beljik seems to have forgotten to bring Rachel home. Will you send someone out to look for them?"

The young woman did not stir from the window seat. "It's a waste of time, Ronya, my mother. They'll come back when they're ready to."

"You see?" Boris said. "Julie means to stay here."

"With your permission," Julie said.

"As you like. But Boris and I are going to talk politics and you often complain that politics makes your head ache. The letter is a riddle about politics, did you understand that?" Julie shook her head. "The document Alexis mentions is the Ukrainian Bill of Rights, which we want him to present to the Tsar. Obviously Alexis and Peter think it should ask less—sugar and spice—both being advocates of moderation and gradual change. The reference to Georgi and Igor is criticism of us for sending them out of Russia. Stolypin thinks, not without reason, that we speak and act more freely because no one can attack us through our sons, as long as they are beyond the Tsar's reach. The dream is simple. The lion is the Ukraine, with a lion's share of Russia's natural resources, especially wheat. Alexis reminds us that we exaggerate our power if we think we can hold onto more than our fair share. The question is where the power lies. Alexis says in the nation, ruled now by Stolypin for the Tsar.

"How much compromise the Ukraine will accept, we can't know until Stolypin's visit. You see that pile of papers on your father's desk? They are Stolypin's proposals for reform and his ideas about the administration of justice. We've got to study them. How much we support Stolypin will depend on what measures he suggests for limiting the monarchy and putting the government in the hands of the premier and an elected Duma. One real difference of opinion between us is that we believe the

272

premier, too, should be elected, and not appointed by the Tsar."

Boris, enchanted by the clarity of Ronya's recital and Julie's wide-eyed concentration, bellowed, "Atten-shun! To your stations, troops. You, Julie, wear your new blue dress and you, Ronya, the burgundy. I'm ordering the carriage and we're going into town for lunch."

"Whatever are you talking about, Boris Pirov?" Ronya asked. "You yourself told everybody to be here by four o'clock." Boris looked at her guiltily. He could have been Georgi caught with a cookie in his hand. Ronya laughed. "We've just got time for lunch. Then back to work."

"It seems," Boris said to Julie, "that I have a previous commitment." Julie pouted and Ronya soothed. "If things work out for us with Peter, your husband and brother will come home and there'll be no end of parties and trips to town."

Boris pushed back his chair. "How you do go on, my dove!"

Suddenly Julie screamed. Beljik stood in the doorway, between his teeth, by the seat of her panties, he held a soiled and limp Rachel. Boris had leaped before Julie's wild cry stopped echoing and now Ronya, unconscious of having left her chair, took the bedraggled child out of Boris' arms. Some part of her realized that Julie had fainted but not even Julie existed for her now.

"She's breathing, Boris, but she's on fire. Ride like the devil for the doctor." She never actually saw him leave.

Ronya carried Rachel into her kitchen, trailed by Julie. "Get Lydia," she said. "Then fetch flannel crib sheets and Rachel's blankets, and have one of the men move her crib down from the nursery. Hurry!"

Julie fled and when she returned Ronya was sponging the child with a cloth soaked in vodka diluted with warm water. She said only, "Close the door. There's a draught."

At sight of the child, Julie's panic returned and she splashed her mother-in-law's hand with tears. Beljik pressed his head against Julie's thigh, hoping for a reassuring pressure from her hand which she was beyond giving him.

Ronya lowered Rachel into the cradle and said, as she tucked her in, "Sit and sing to her, Julie. It'll put her to sleep."

273

The instant the doctor arrived, Boris brought him to the kitchen and they stood together looking down at the child. While the medical man opened his instrument case and washed his hands at the sink, Boris said quietly to his wife, "The Blond One is riding all over Kiev, telling the men not to come. By now several of our friends are at the station to meet the out-of-towners. And I've wired Stolypin that for the next week or two, I think it unlikely that I shall be able to see him."

Ronya looked up inquiringly.

"To hell with him!" said Rachel's grandfather, and thus a small girl shaped history.

Examination complete, the doctor wanted to know if anyone else on the place was sick. Ronya had already sent runners to the peasants' houses and the gypsy camp and had just learned that Rachel had shared lunch with a gypsy family, eating from the common pot, but none of them were unwell. "Strange," said the doctor and returned to the sink where he scrubbed and asked for a fresh towel.

"Talk," said Boris, "I'm not a patient man."

"Frankly, Gospodin Pirov, I am not familiar with your granddaughter's disease. Her symptoms are atypical of anything I know. Perhaps typhus, perhaps—"

Ronya finished his sentence for him. "Yes," the doctor said, "cholera is a possibility. In any case, her dysentery has reached dangerous proportions. The child's life is in the hands of God. Time will deliver the verdict."

Boris' impatience flared into rage. "Never mind about time! You cure her."

"Don't blame me for having no magic with which to save the child, Gospodin Pirov. I am being generous as it is. I could and should quarantine the whole property."

Ronya silenced Boris with a look. "Quarantine us," she said. "It's your duty, doctor. And I think we can manage this case ourselves."

The doctor hurriedly bowed himself out, thankful that the mad Pirovs had not set their monster of a dog on him.

Boris marveled at Ronya's efficiency and coolness as she took over, and then he saw Julie, who sat quietly weeping. He looked helplessly at Ronya, who went over to the girl and whispered,

"Come with me," and led her out to the stone bench in the herb garden.

"Listen to me, Julie." She took her hand firmly. "I don't want you paying any attention to the doctor. He doesn't know Rachel the way we do. She's a fighter and she's blessed with the greatest curative of all—sleep. All my life I've slept away pain and illness. What Rachel needs most from now on is her family around her and your songs. We'll take turns caring for her, all of us. We'll eat and sleep and enjoy the outdoors, laugh and talk of everyday things. Gloomy, worn-out people are exactly what Rachel does not need. Can you do it, Julie, my child?"

"I'll try," Julie said shakily and together they went back into the kitchen, Ronya wishing that in her heart she was as optimistic as she sounded.

She had learned in Harbin the vital importance of replenishing body fluids, but she knew that with a small child she would have to do it largely through the skin. When she plunged the small body into a spongy mass of flax seeds, though she did not know it, she was recapturing the intra-uterine heat and she saw that it made the baby more comfortable. Frequent applications of mild boric-acid dressings, followed by vegetable oil, ended an acid skin irritation caused by watery stools, and frequent spoonfuls of barley water provided nourishment.

In spite of everything, after forty-eight hours, Rachel's eyes were black pits over shrunken cheeks, her abdomen distended and tense. Even in sleep her mouth, drawn and stirring constantly, reflected pain. And Beljik, his great shoulder muscles hunched, his thick cream coat dingy yellow, was as sick as Rachel. Boris was still as a stone and Julie, almost beyond hope, was perilously near collapse.

Ronya sent for the Blond One. She gave him instructions, charging him to go directly to her room and wait for her there when he returned. An hour later, when the kitchen door opened, Ronya assumed that it was Julie. Had not Boris spoken, she would probably not have looked up. His "Get out!" made her jump.

"I came," said Tamara, "to help nurse Rachel."

"We don't need you."

"The dream foretells. I have much to say."

275

"Ronya! Tell her to get out or, so help me—"

Ronya said, "Shut up," and held out her hand for what Tamara had brought. "Stay," she said and without another word went to the stove to prepare an infusion of poppy heads. When she had done, she poured the liquid into a jar, capped it, and gave it to Boris. "A few drops every hour," she instructed him. "Tomorrow she'll be able to eat solid food."

"Where in hell are you off to?" Boris roared.

"Wherever I damn well please, and stop yelling. You've waked Rachel. Now give her the opium tea." On her way out of the room Ronya picked an apple up from a pewter platter and threw it at Tamara. The queen, delighted by this show of jealousy, kicked up one leg and jangled the coins that hung on a chain around her slender ankle. She was still laughing when the door closed behind Ronya.

By the time Ronya reached Julie's room she was herself again. The girl was looking dewy, if pale, after a short nap, and when Ronya confessed that she was drowsy, Julie suggested she lie down there. "I'll throw on something and go down," Julie said.

"No rush, dear. Tamara is with your father. She's cheerful company for him. Her lips are smeared with red and her petticoats, layers of them, swish musically when she dances around the room."

Never had Ronya seen Julie move so fast. However, when she lingered in the bathroom, Ronya opened the door and saw that she was arranging her long hair in a complicated and becoming chignon. She blushed guiltily.

"I thought I'd put on a pretty dress and look nice," she said.

"It really doesn't matter," Ronya said. "Your father is used to us. All we need is to be well-scrubbed and nurse Rachel. . . . Perhaps you should wear something cheerful at that. Rachel likes bright colors and she's getting better. . . . She'll be well in a couple of days."

"You don't mean—?" Julie's eyes widened.

"I do indeed," Ronya said, and explained the miracle of opium to her, how it eliminates pain and controls diarrhea.

"Oh, Ronya, my mother, I've been so frightened."

Ronya took Julie's most becoming dress off a hanger and helped her into it. At the head of the stairs she said, "If your father has to go out, don't be afraid to leave Tamara with Rachel. She's an excellent nurse."

The Blond One was standing at a French window in Ronya's room. Without a word he went to her night table, took out a cigarette and lit it for her.

"I suppose you know?" she said.

He nodded. "I'm sorry. Why can't she be more like you?"

Ronya blew a puff of smoke over her head. "Your mother and I aren't as unlike as you think." He dropped onto the stool at her dressing table. "We just happen to love the same man, and a woman in love has no pride. On the other hand, a woman who is loved can afford to be a lady. Yes, under everything, we're very much alike, almost as alike as you and Igor, who both—do you mind my saying this—love the same girl. Maybe you fell in love with Julie before you ever laid eyes on her, just because Igor loved her. Heaven knows Tamara had decided to fall in love with your father before she saw him.

"Come to think of it, Tamara and I are one woman, sacred and profane. And you and Igor are one son to Boris." He reached out and took her hand in his large, warm grasp.

"Oh, young Boris, I wish you were mine!"

A shudder ran through him. "Is that my name—Boris?"

"It must be, dear. I always think of you as young Boris."

The Blond One bent down and kissed the hand he held. "You won't ever tell Julie? Igor knows."

Her eyes gave him her promise. "Go dress your handsome self up in your finest. On your way, stop and tell Father Tromokov I think your father is going to need a drinking companion tonight and you and I are lifting the quarantine—with soft lights and champagne."

He was on his feet. "I love you."

As he left the room he heard Ronya murmur, "I know."

But it was the Blond One who vetoed Ronya's plan. While she was still in her bath, Lydia waddled in with a note which read, "You can't do that, Ronya, my mother. Punish him privately and when Rachel doesn't need you."

Lydia asked, "Why are you grinning like a cat?"

"Because a beautiful young gentleman turned me down. Scrub my back. I've got to go down to Rachel."

"He's got more sense than you." Lydia attacked Ronya's firm skin severely. Ronya went right on smiling.

She chose a dress trimmed with sequins and originally bought for a masquerade. It was a costume Ronya put on only when she wanted to infuriate Boris. He hated her to bare so much of her breasts and disliked the way the tight skirt revealed the outline of her buttocks. Lydia, talking and picking up, did not realize what Ronya was up to until her mistress began making up her face. Then Lydia stood back, hands on hips, watching Ronya darken her eyelashes, shadow her eyelids with green crayon and daub rouge on her cheeks. Her lips she painted blood red.

"You've made yourself *her!*" Lydia gasped.

"That's right," Ronya said smugly. "I'm tired of being a grandmother and an authority on everything from soup to poultices. Damned tired of it!"

"Take your whip to her," Lydia exulted. "Serve her right."

Boris was standing in the doorway.

"I wasn't expecting you, but come in since you're here," Ronya said coolly. "Lydia's just going."

When she was gone, Boris stripped, pulled back the satin bedspread and lay down. Ronya, half suspecting a trick, saw his eyes close, his whole body relax, and decided that he was really spent. She tiptoed to her chaise, got her afghan and covered him, rather relieved to be spared the emotional scene she herself had set up, went to the bathroom, undressed and washed off the war paint. The afghan, she saw as she came back, had slipped off Boris' feet. She debated whether she would wake him if she pulled it down and in that moment was lost. Without warning he toppled her onto the bed and pinned her down.

"Beast!" shrieked Ronya.

"So," he said, "you wanted to play the siren. Maybe I can help?"

"You're very tired, Boris." Ronya was choking with laughter.

"Tired, yes," he said, not relaxing his grip on her. "Tired of being alone!"

She tried to raise her head. "I must go to Rachel."

"Rachel's fine and so drugged she won't stir till morning."

So Ronya pulled out her hairpins and sent them scattering

278

across the room. Under the dark curtain of her hair, Tamara was forgotten.

Two days later Ronya's kitchen was again her kitchen and Rachel was recuperating happily in the nursery. Beljik's angled wolf eyes no longer looked like an old man's and Julie sang. She asked Tamara to give her lessons in magic and whenever Ronya came into the kitchen they were at it. To avoid Tamara, Boris worked in his own room, the door ajar so he could catch glimpses of Ronya on her housekeeping rounds. Sometimes, when he looked up, she was reading over his shoulder. Then at times the whole house would resound with laughter when she played games with Rachel.

Only one thing seemed incongruous—almost incredible—to Boris, that Ronya and Tamara were plainly having a good time together. They smoked each other's cigarettes, Ronya making fun of the way Tamara rolled hers. They climbed into a two-wheeled buggy and took turns with the reins, vying to see who was the more dashing driver. They went for long walks. Almost, they seeemd to have reverted to their girlhood past.

Late one afternoon, while they were approaching the house, Ronya leaned forward impulsively and kissed Tamara. "Boris wants you to go home," she said. "Besides, Katya and Alexis arrive tomorrow."

Tamara nodded. "It's been a good time, Ronya."

They came to the big oak at the beginning of the formal garden. "Stop a moment," said Tamara.

Ronya kept on walking. "I know what you're going to ask and the answer has to be no. Boris refuses to receive you except on the occasions that justify your coming here in the person of a queen."

Tamara said, "Let's be frank."

"No, Tamara. There's nothing you can say. As for us, you and me, I know we still have unfinished business and I'll send for you when the time is right."

Julie met them at the door. "I've been waiting," she said. "You promised to read the future."

"Later, Julie, after dinner," Ronya spoke lightly.

279

"I'm sorry, Ronya. I forgot to tell you I can't stay for dinner. If you don't mind, I'll read for Julie now."

She and Julie and Ronya went into the kitchen and closed the door. At the sink Tamara half filled an iron pot with water and put it on the stove. While she waited for it to boil she strolled around the room and though Ronya watched her closely it was impossible to see from where she produced a handful of lumps of gray metal.

"You must do exactly as I say. Do you agree, both of you?"

"Oh, yes!" Julie breathed.

"All right," Ronya concurred and thought, what rubbish!

"Now shut your eyes. Don't turn your heads or try to watch. It might blind you. If there's an explosion, hang onto the arms of your chairs but don't move. If you smell something, don't try to avoid the fumes. In five minutes you can open your eyes."

Exasperation mingled with Ronya's amusement. When she judged the time to be nearer fifteen minutes than five, she began tapping her foot.

"Open," commanded Tamara.

Ronya smothered her laughter, Julie gaped. Tamara stood before them, shoulders bare, back stiff, black hair flowing to her waist. Her black lashes hung like curtains over purple eyes and she was smiling a mysterious smile. Tamara at that moment was undeniably beautiful.

In her outstretched hands she held the lumps of metal, molten now and twisted into strange shapes. Her husky voice fell to a plaintive whisper.

"I see death on a warm night. I see a ghostly chase, a voyage beset with danger, a great dance in the sky. . . .

"I see generations beyond counting and in each a few who soar and one who sails alone."

God, Ronya thought, suddenly serious, how can she? The same mumbo-jumbo her people have been dispensing for thousands of years. Is it possible she believes in it? Tamara's much too smart. But perhaps, with the world about to go up in flames, it's as good as anything.

XXXII

Boris, my esteemed friend,

At long last you are to meet Stolypin! Be prepared to be relentless. Peter Stolypin is no architect of democracy. No man can serve two masters and Stolypin serves Stolypin and, indirectly, Tsarism. In his luggage for the trip to Kiev he has packed a dagger for the Ukraine.

So far as it goes, his program is good. Or sounds good. Full citizenship for Jews, a stronger Duma, a free press, disbanding the Black Hundreds (how? when?). His agrarian reforms are a mirage. The peasants remain enslaved, the big landowners inviolate.

Let me remind you that Stolypin recommends not the elimination of the Tsar's secret police but lessening their power. What of his private police force, and of Rasputin's? Yes, Boris, even from Siberia, Rasputin pulls strings. And the state church has its own network.

His proposition is a sorry thing: Give the people a *limited* degree of representation. The man is no more than another instrument of appeasement and postponement.

I take the liberty, however, of urging you to know and then judge the man yourself. Consult with my Lady Ronya, to whom my greetings. She can paint his portrait.

In closing I send my respects to Julie and her little Rachel. My best wishes and deep concern go with this letter which Reuben brings you.

Your friend,
Huang

Boris put the letter down and stamped his right foot to get the circulation going. How easy it would be to fall in with Huang's

281

estimate of Stolypin, how hard to be sure of anything about the man. Was he loyal to Alexis? Did he use the issue of the peasants, like stirrups, to keep his feet in the saddle? Boris damned Stolypin, damned the peasants—lazy, ignorant bastards—damned the land grabbers. A pox on them all! Give me horses. He had an impulse to gather up Ronya and clear out of Russia, a state of mind that frightened him. If I want to give up now, he scolded himself, I'm either scared or going crazy.

A second letter lay on the desk, addressed in Alexis' flowing hand.

The letter was long and devious and Boris was puzzled. Why had Alexis thought his message so crucial and confidential that he had sent it by messenger? On the third page he found his answer.

"As a result of the Ukraine's passion for independence, the Tsar, quite hoarse from inveighing against you all, has broken his wife's lead chain and bolted back to his mama and his friends, Peter and me. He will make a goodwill tour of the Ukraine with Olga and Tatiana, first stop Kiev. Press your uniform. Shine your medals. We attend the opera the night of September 14. You, Boris, are to lead the honor guard. Official orders will reach you soon from the high command. From what I gather, after the Imperial party reaches the royal box, you are to join Peter, Ronya and Julie, Katya and me in the front row of the orchestra.

"Read me carefully, Boris. I have a terrifying suspicion that between them Ronya and Huang have shaken your faith in Stolypin. Why else would you defer Georgi's return to ride in the national championships for another year?

"Peter and I have reached an agreement: I bring Katya back to St. Petersburg; in return he talks absolutely openly with you. In exchange for Mendel Beilis' acquittal and a public apology to the Jews, he demands the Revenge Rider. A more likely candidate than the ghost of Peter the Great must be found."

He ended with a message from Katya, who wanted Ronya to know that three 'divine' creations were on their way from Paris so that the three ladies would outshine the other gentry at the

282

opera. Boris lit a match and the two letters were charred when he heard the door open.

Ronya knew at once that the day's mail had brought problems.

"Come upstairs for the political session. If it'll make it any easier for you, I shall sit in a straight chair, fully clothed." She laughed and his tense look relaxed.

Stretched out on the bed beside Ronya, Boris described in detail the conflict he was caught up in, and asked her to mediate.

"You know how I feel," she said. "I think what I've thought for years, and I never could see Peter as an ardent champion of democracy. What's worse, time is against him now."

"But do you trust him, Ronya?"

She considered. "Not entirely, Boris. And when you talk to him, remember he's just as smart as you are and politically a great deal shrewder."

"Alexis says he's mellowed, since his villa was bombed and his daughter crippled."

Ronya shrugged. "That may be. Personally I doubt it." She put out the cigarette she had barely begun. "I'm sorry to discourage you. I know you want the boys home. I do too." She brushed back her hair and saw that the frown on Boris' face was more pain than worry. Possibly a drink would ease his suffering. She got up and poured him one.

"Thanks, Ronya. But come back; I haven't finished."

She resettled herself on the pillows.

"I really have to get to know the man for myself, I suppose," he said. "I only saw him once. At our wedding. He seemed like a prig. But I expect he thought I wasn't much more than a boor." He smiled mirthlessly. "What I want from you is some idea of the young Stolypin. The boy is father of the man and all that."

"It's hard to know how far back to go, Boris. When I was very young, before he started courting Katya, I hated him. He was rude to Tamara and treated Lydia like dirt. Once I overheard him tell Katya it had been wrong of our mother to convert and that father's insistence on remaining a Jew was a reverse snobbery and were he Tsar he wouldn't stand for it."

Boris looked quizzical.

"I know. It must seem crazy that, summer after summer, his father sent him to visit a Jew's estate. Well, there was a practical reason for that. Peter's father was the largest landowner in Kovno province and his holdings on the Volga adjoined von Glasman properties. The old man wanted to combine the estates through marriage. He simply ignored our Jewishness and sent Peter to study finances and management under David von Glasman, 'the German.'"

Ronya paused. "I must be fair. With Peter it wasn't all land and money and influence at court. He was mad about Katya. For two summers they had a romance. I considered him dull, smelling of chickens and cows.

"A few months before Empress Maria sent for Katya, Peter was staying at our house in St. Petersburg, and when he and Katya came in from a ball, she stormed up to her room without saying good night. Peter went into Father's study and I ran after him, heaven knows why. They exchanged a few remarks; then Peter bowed and said he was worried about his mother and would have to leave for home. I was amazed. If his mother was sick he'd never have gone to a ball, but Father seemed glad to get him out of the house. 'I fully understand,' he said. 'My man will pack for you. He will have you ready to leave the first thing in the morning.'

"The minute Peter reached his room, Father and I made a dash for Katya. She blurted the whole thing out, poor darling, that Peter said he loved her but had decided to go into government. Working for the Tsar was the surest way to a title, so it just wasn't sensible to marry a Jewess.

"I'd never seen Father angry before. 'Peter Stolypin,' he said, 'will get no title as long as the Empress Maria or I live. I shall see to that.' Then he said, 'Katya, he's an expedient young man; he *belongs* in government. He may even be canny enough to preserve the monarchy.'

"For a while we didn't see Peter, but as soon as Katya's engagement to Alexis was announced, he paid us a surprise visit, to congratulate her. It was she who persuaded Alexis to sponsor him. You know Katya. She never stays angry long." Ronya smiled lovingly.

"The rest is an old story. But even now that he's premier of Russia, Peter has no title. Maria is still alive."

The next day started where the last one ended, with talk about the pressures they faced. Over an early breakfast, Ronya argued, "It's all very well asking for an apology to the Jews, but what good will it do? It will only make things worse, in fact. Look, the Tsarina is sick and arrogant and she loathes us. Don't push her too far. After all, being separated from Rasputin is punishment enough for the miserable woman. Just get Beilis off and the devil take sanctimonious apologies. Trade them for the Revenge Rider. It's the police's job to find him, not yours. Use the power you have, the power of the Ukraine, for something more solid."

Boris agreed in part but insisted that to back down on every issue would be political suicide. He left, telling her to go back to bed and stop worrying, that he had his own plans for Jew-haters, secret police, dishonest tax collectors and other Tsarist swine.

Ronya did not go back to bed. Instead she put on a riding habit and went to the stables for a horse. For hours she rode over her land, only avoiding the gypsy camp. Peasants smiled up at her, children waved, and though she responded with a warm smile, her heart was heavy. Soon she would not have any of this. She wondered what San Francisco was really like.

> Dear Tamara:
> It is time to settle things between us. Boris is out for the night. Come early.
>
> Ronya

As she sealed her note, Lydia came in. "Did you meet Boris, my master? He came back looking for you."

"No, what did he want?"

"Only to say the meeting is in the cabin instead of in town and you're to expect him around midnight."

It might be better to send for Tamara another time, but no— she'd waited long enough.

There was a clanging and clinking of gold. Ronya, stretched out on Katya's lounge, opened her eyes. "How can any one woman wear so much gold?" she asked.

"The rewards of generations of sin, Ronya." Tamara's eyes were mocking.

"Why so late? I was nearly asleep."

"Callers." Tamara strolled over to the serving table and picked up an olive. "Move your feet," she said, "so I can sit down."

Ronya pointed to a chair. "Sit there. Tonight I want to look at you."

"Very flattering. Before we warm up, I have news for you."

"Make it sweet. I'm sick of news."

"Come to think of it," Tamara bit into the olive, "it's sweet at that. Stolypin's police are looking for Igor."

"I guessed as much," said Ronya. "They've been trailing me. Let's eat before you tell me the details."

A half hour later they were both smoking, Ronya curled up on a sofa, Tamara, opposite her on the chaise longue. Tamara had been talking for some minutes. ". . . a big, good-looking bastard with plenty of excitement in him. Decked out in expensive clothes, behaved as though he were God's gift to women. I told him to sit down and cool off or get the hell out. He edged his hand toward the holster that held his revolver, so I said flirtatiously, 'I have to be alone or I can't. They're watching us through every window.' 'Pull down the shades,' says he. Then he turned mean. 'I've got enough to railroad you to Siberia for life.'

"I wanted to give him a lesson in manners but instead I went timid. 'Will my cooperation entitle me to clemency?' I asked, twisting my hands. He was grand then. 'My friends get off scot-free,' he boasted.

"Acting nervous, I said, 'Let's have a drink and talk first. There must be a mistake. The police get their share of my people's thieving.'

"I poured two drinks and gave him my attention. 'It's astonishing'—I was being sweet and wistful—'all this fuss because my gypsies help themselves to a few souvenirs at fairs and carnivals. Everyone expects them to steal. It's routine—like fortune-telling and tinkering and fiddling.'

" 'That may be. But you're accused not of stealing but of concealing a murderer.'

" 'Who?' I asked.

"He looked a bit put out at that. 'His file reads: A man who rides like the wind, charges furiously, then melts into the mist.'

"I said, 'The avenging angel, the black demon and the Revenge Rider fit.'

" 'A mighty fine answer,' he sneered. 'Now tell me who can outride Igor Pirov.'

" 'Boris Pirov,' I told him.

" 'No,' he said. 'We know that can't be. We have proof. Let's understand each other. We know Igor Pirov is the Revenge Rider. Admit it!'

" 'Well,' I said, very thoughtful, 'he has the courage, all right, and he sits his saddle like a true Russian.'

"He pushed his coarse face so close to mine our noses almost touched.

" 'Take me to him!'

" 'To America?'

"At that he hit the ceiling. 'I'm warning you! We have evidence. Young Pirov alleged that he was going to the United States, then sneaked back into Russia. He's hidden here in Kiev, in this very camp, most likely. And don't give me that American bilge. He was heading for Manchuria.'

" 'That's quite impossible.' I was firm about it. 'As long as you're here, why don't you look for yourself? That way you can make me a present of an apology.'

" 'Oh, we'll search all right, don't you fear!' He was a swaggering brute. 'After you look into your crystal ball and tell me what you see. For your sake it better not be Tsar Peter's ghost.'

"Ronya, I did, and gave it to him straight. 'Summer begins tomorrow,' I told him, 'and there is no fall. I see doom.'

"That did it, I can tell you! He made for the door and fired a shot into the air. They came from everywhere at the signal—tough men I'd never seen before—and searched every wagon, every tent, every house, every barn. After they'd rounded my men up, the fellow said, 'Anyone who talks about this will have his tongue cut out.'

287

"Lover man threw me a coin. 'For the reading. I'll be back.' I just smiled. 'I'll be waiting.' "

Ronya rubbed her bare arms. "It makes me shiver. How do you know they were Stolypin's boys—not the Tsar's?"

Tamara raised laughing eyes. "Krasmikov and I aren't exactly strangers."

"I've heard you were keeping company. Why don't you marry him, Tamara? You'll be lonely after we're gone. The more I hear about Stolypin the sooner I think it will be."

The blood rushed to Tamara's face. "Boris can't leave Russia."

"Oh, yes, he can."

Tamara protested, "Even if he could he wouldn't."

"He's promised," Ronya said flatly. "Short of absolute Ukrainian sovereignty, we go to set up a new home for ourselves."

"It's a lie."

"No, Tamara, it's too late for lies."

The gypsy groped for a cigarette. "For God's sake, Ronya, believe in his fate. He can't leave. Nor can Alexis. Nor can I. If Russia dies, we die."

"And Katya?"

"A full life and a peaceful death for von Glasman's daughters." Quivering, Tamara cried, "Go to America and you go alone."

Ronya was magnificently cool. "You see what you want to see, Tamara, and embroider what you see. You imagine Boris, abandoned by us, turning to you, your son and Georgi's daughter as a second family. You're wrong, my friend, because you don't understand Boris. You never have. If the Blond One had inherited your features and coloring, Boris would have denied siring him. Not because Boris is a liar but because you are. The sad thing is that your biggest lie is yourself."

Tamara's eyes were burning, her ripeness suddenly overripe and she was screaming. "Don't understand Boris! I understood well enough that my body was driving him out of his mind. When he couldn't stand it any longer, he trapped me in the stables and I had to yield. He tore at my skirt and cried out in anger against you, 'Even a dog mates with a bitch his own size.'

Then he plunged, begging, 'Faster, Tamara, faster,' and poured his great strength into me until daylight. There was enough gold in Boris that night for a hundred women."

Ronya slid off the sofa and poured brandy into a glass of tea, adding a slice of lemon and two lumps of sugar. Stirring this brew, she carried it to Tamara, saying, "Drink this, my dear."

Tamara stared, not believing, then swooped forward and clutched Ronya around the knees. "Don't take him away," she moaned.

"Drink your tea, Tamara, and I'll tell you why I sent for you."

The woman quieted but could not resist one last display of bluff. "If I'd been content to be his pastime, I'd certainly be his mistress today."

Ronya took her empty glass from her. "Look at me, Tamara, and try to go back to the times before Boris—the beautiful times we had together when we loved each other. Because of them I've made legal arrangements for the camp to go to you. If we leave, the rest of the estate, which is never to be sold, is deeded to the Blond One, a gift neither despite nor because he is your son and Boris' but because I love him. The rents paid to him are to accrue and be delivered to your adopted daughter when she becomes queen. If the Blond One continues, mistakenly, to consider himself unfit for marriage and therefore leaves no legitimate heirs, everything goes to her and her descendants."

Like a woman demented, Tamara said, "You're no Katya with perfect manners. I just tore your pride to shreds and demolished your dream that, in one moment of weakness, Boris seduced me. Get your whip! Make me pay!"

"You *have* paid, Tamara."

Tamara's pride was at stake. "Do you really want to settle accounts, Ronya?" she persisted.

Oh, you poor fool, Ronya thought, you're making me tell you. "I'll never admit that Boris wanted you or any other woman more than me. The night the Blond One was conceived turned his fondness for you to loathing. I know because I was there."

"Liar! You were in your confinement bed. Igor's *briss* was the next morning, an hour after Boris and I parted. We had to rush to get ready, he for the circumcision, I for the celebration. My mother took one look at me—a blind woman could have seen that I'd had a night of kisses—and asked, 'Is gypsy vase filled with gold bud?' I answered, 'Yes, my queen.' She said, 'You may absent yourself from the festivities. Take to your bed. You did well, my daughter.' "

"I started to tell you," Ronya went on as if Tamara had not spoken, "after Boris stormed out of the house, Lydia started to fetch him back but he came of his own accord. When Boris left the second time, after he'd come in while I was nursing Igor and I'd told him to get out, she told me she'd seen you and guessed you were planning some devilment.

"So she ran to her own barn, hitched her husband's mare up to a cart and came back for me. I was stronger than that old mare, I can tell you. While Lydia, bless her soul, fussed, I checked to make sure Boris' pistol was loaded. Lydia threw a long black cape over me and we ran to the cart together and drove it into the clump of pines just west of the stables. I stationed Lydia behind a tree to see that no one came near the place. Then I went on alone on bare feet, walking so lightly that even inside the stables I scarcely disturbed the straw. By the light of a lantern hanging on a nail, I took aim, making sure I'd hit only you.

"Before I could pull the trigger you said something, and Boris smashed you in the face. That's why you didn't come to Igor's party. Your beautiful face was a bloody mess."

At last Tamara was silenced. The two of them sat, curiously comfortable in the completeness of their understanding. When Tamara spoke again, it was in Romany, the language of their childhood. "If I'd been you," she said companionably, "I'd have shot Boris."

Ronya answered in Russian. "That's the difference between us."

"Me, you would have wounded, maybe killed, without a qualm?"

"That's right."

"You'll never give me a chance to talk about it again," Tamara said. "But, does Boris know?"

Ronya said simply, "Boris hears a single leaf fall in the forest."

Tamara rose, took two cigarettes from an ivory box and lit

one for herself, one for Ronya. "I never wanted to steal Boris from you—only to share him. As long as I live I'll keep on trying."

Ronya looked at the clock on the mantel. It was one. "I'll see you to the door, my dear." On the front verandah, Tamara paused to say, "It had to be that way, little Ronya. Spiritual twins. We had to love the same man. It's fate."

"No, Tamara, it's not fate at all. As a child you always wanted to eat from my plate."

She did not deny it. "But you do know, Ronya"—she started down the steps—"that in everything else I'm loyal to you?"

Ronya said softly, "I do know that."

Her bedroom was empty so Ronya went to his. Boris' voice from the bed was fractious. "You took your own good time getting rid of your visitor." She turned up the lamp and he rolled over to avoid the light. When she slipped into bed and cuddled up to the wall of his back, there was no response.

"Don't be cross. I'd asked her before I knew you'd be home. Then we got reminiscing and I forgot the time."

Boris turned over and took her in his arms. In the beating of his heart Ronya heard a knell tolling, a deeper sorrow than Tamara could evoke now. She unwound his arms, sat up, lit the lamp once more and looked at him.

"Lie down again, my love." He laid his arm across his eyes.

"Has something happened to Georgi or Igor?"

"No. My mother is dead."

Ronya moved back into his arms and said nothing. She knew that it was not her voice he needed but his own. At last it came. "The Blond One was standing guard when he heard the step of a Tartar boot. He gave the thrush call and I, who always listen, stepped outside and was waiting when the man came up to the house.

"He said, 'Your mother sleeps, Golden One. She is buried on her hill.'

"I asked him to stay but he pointed in the direction of Odessa and said, 'I'll be back when the weather is cold,' and vanished."

Boris asked cautiously, "What did he mean, darling?"

She was quiet so long he began to fear she did not know the answer. Ronya was considering. "Your mother lived in loneliness. She said and did queer things. Between you and me it's all different. Even death cannot separate us. We won't die—we live in our sons and Rachel. Give up your will to misfortune, Boris."

"Well," he said, "if my mother wants me, she's got a long way to come."

XXXIII

BORIS had to admit Ronya was right. She had just said, "What if an assassin follows Stolypin here? With three attempts on his life in the last few weeks, it looks to me as if the Tsarina would stop at nothing to get rid of him and I think it would suit her very well to have him murdered in our house. The accusation would be that we were determined not to lose our properties and would do anything to scotch his land reforms.

"Please, dear, take precautions. Alix is crazy and quite capable of pulling the country down in ruins in order to bring that devil, Rasputin, back from Siberia."

Boris drained the last of his brandy and put down his glass. "I've my work cut out for the next few hours," he said. "Don't wait up for me."

Ronya suddenly realized—I'm uncommonly afraid tonight.

"Boris!" There was a catch in her voice.

He looked at his watch. "I have to go now."

"Boris," Ronya repeated, "wouldn't Rachel be safer with Tamara than here? In gypsy clothes with little gold rings in her ears, her hair darkened, you can't tell her from the gypsy children."

"No, Ronya." Boris' arms tightened around her. "In a few days it will be over and done. Settled. All or nothing." He kissed her good night.

Before eight the next morning, Boris faced his men. "For the first time in years, Peter Stolypin is visiting this estate. And I am responsible for his safety. You all know that I have a strong distaste for treachery. Guard him well. His life has been threatened repeatedly of late. After he joins our Imperial Highness, you can relax. The military and police will take over.

"Tell your women to leave him in peace—not to hang around the house in hopes of getting a closer look at him. If any of the Tsar's officials who are staying in town request permission to call, stand firm on your right of search. If there's a fuss, hand the bastard over to Father Tromokov.

"That's all. Thank you and good luck!"

The men, carrying rifles, began to fan out to familiarize themselves with their posts. A few drew swords—these were the Cossacks. The whole band looked bizarre, like a company of actors, against the peaceful landscape. Boris turned back to the stables. Halfway to his stallion's stall he met the Blond One. Boris lifted his thumb and jerked it toward the tackroom. "I want to talk to you."

Inside, Boris commanded, "Close the door," and poured himself a drink. "Want one?"

"Too early for me."

"My breakfast," Boris grinned. Slumped in his big leather chair he thought—strange lad, now why in hell does he love me? He had quite forgotten what he had meant to say and silence lay heavy. "Anything on your mind?"

"You." The answer seemed to come from a long way off.

"Let's have it."

"You'll have plenty of time to drink after Stolypin is gone," the Blond One said. "Go back to the house. Pull down the shades and sleep. You've got an impression to make. The way you are now, you're dragging."

The brass of him! "I do not like being told what to do. Fetch me another drink."

The Blond One took a step closer. "Why?"

"Damn it! Because I'm thirsty—that's why."

"I don't think so," the Blond One said. "I think your leg is killing you. You've got all day to rest with your foot up. The train is sure to be late and Stolypin shouldn't get here until seven. Dinner isn't till nine."

293

Suddenly Boris wished this understanding son were Igor. He said, "It's too hot to sleep, but drive me home. Tell Sad Eyes to take charge here. I want you at the house. You'll be useful."

On the drive he outlined the Blond One's duties. "You won't be rubbing elbows with the Premier but I want him to see you around. Never mind about Julie. Your job is Rachel. Unless she's with me, don't let her out of your sight. If you take her away from the house, have Beljik along on a lead. And I don't need to tell you what to do—if you have to. Turn Beljik loose first."

The weather, living up to Tamara's prophecy, was uncommonly hot for September. The peasants left their fields and went to dress in their Sunday best. Father Tromokov had already mounted the pulpit when they arrived at the church.

"Ronya, your mistress," he addressed them, when the last one had shuffled in, "requests me to say that there will be no work tomorrow or the day after that. Tables are set in the south meadow. Take your pleasure on the grass and draw strength from the provisions supplied by the big house.

"You are not to gorge or drink yourselves sodden. It's too hot. You are to make it clear to His Excellency that, whatever problems other landowners have, they do not exist here. So relax and rest and *don't* get drunk.

"Stand a safe distance from the Premier—safe for you, or some guard crouched behind a tree may say to himself, 'That one looks ferocious,' and shoot.

"You have a great deal to be grateful for. Show your gratitude now or I may take disciplinary action, and hear your confessions afterwards."

Father Tromokov was not joking and his congregation were not laughing as they filed out of church.

The ball of fire which had parched the day was below the horizon but the sky was still streaked with copper. Ronya's people crowded the broad carriageway, listening for the galloping hooves that would herald Stolypin's approach. The older peasants, remembering when he had come to the house as a young man, remembered, too, that they hadn't much cared for him 'way back' and grumbled, "Crazy hot weather—a bad omen."

The younger ones, flushed and happy, waved banners inscribed, "Long live Stolypin," "Long live the People's Champion." Sunbrowned children, large-eyed with excitement, rehearsed a Ukrainian song Julie composed, which they were to sing in honor of the great man. The gypsy girls, in bright low-necked dresses, flirted freely, thereby making the sentries' duty less lonely. A smile on a girl's lips and a smile in a man's eyes exchanged promises for later, maybe for all the freezing winter, when no rifle kept a fellow from putting a strong arm around a gentle curve.

At the same hour, the Pirovs, on the station platform, were a sensation, as, accompanied by the Brusilovs, they led an escort prepared to do battle.

Peter Stolypin, descending from the train, rather regretted that his enemy, Rasputin, was not there to see the show. Thousands of people crowded behind the official party. There was no mistaking the popularity of the Pirovs. Stolypin's eyes adjusted themselves from the dusk of his compartment in the train to the sea of faces turned toward him under unfurled pennants in the paling daylight. They sought and found Katya. She might—he shut out the thought. With her were Alexis and a girl child with a face like the young Ronya's, a tall, blond young man with broad shoulders, and an easy stance, and a big dog.

He walked down the platform to meet them. The little girl curtsied and put into his hands a bunch of golden Ukrainian wheat. The gesture was not lost on the Premier. "You are Rachel?" "I am Rachel," the child said, "and I am wearing my best dress. Ronya, my grandmother, said, 'Peter Stolypin is a man who pays attention to details.' "

The Premier of Russia laughed. "Little Rachel, what else did your grandmother say?"

There was a gleam in Rachel's eye. "She said, 'Don't get dirty!' "

Alexis intervened. "Rachel is full of fascinating revelations. Greetings, Peter. You may kiss my wife's hand."

Stolypin walked out of the group that encircled Rachel, drew Katya to him gently and touched not her hand but her cheek with his lips.

"Katya, Katya," he breathed. "How lovely you are! Our Em-

295

press Mother will make a great occasion of your return to St. Petersburg."

"Thank you, Peter," Katya said without emotion.

Ronya gave him her hand. "You look tired, Peter. I'm glad I overrode all the ladies of Kiev and arranged a quiet evening for you."

"How good of you, Ronya! The hours drag and the years fly. I'm obliged to admit that I'm a tired old man. But you, Ronya, time is your lover. You are still the most beautiful girl in Kiev."

"Now there's a compliment I approve," she laughed. "May I present my daughter-in-law, Igor's wife?"

Stolypin bowed and asked, "Are you wearing your best dress, too?"

"Mercy no, Excellency! I'm saving it for the opera."

Now Boris and Stolypin were face-to-face. They looked at each other appraisingly. Big and burly though he was, the Premier was dwarfed by Boris. What a Tsar he would have made, Stolypin could not resist thinking. Boris mentally shrugged his shoulders, deciding here was no savior but an almost defeated politician carrying far too heavy a load. Arrayed in a tailcoat and holding Rachel's bouquet self-consciously, he looked the perfect provincial mayor. As if sensing Boris' evaluation, Peter handed the wheat to a guard, turned back to Boris and kissed him on both cheeks.

"A most handsome reception," he said, "and you have gone to all kinds of bother to protect me."

"No trouble—an honor, Peter." He took Stolypin's arm. "There are a few men I'd like you to meet and I fear the crowd expects a speech."

The crowd, almost entirely peasants and workers, looked peaceable enough but, frowning heavily, the Premier said through tight lips, "I must refuse all introductions and wait till later to meet the Ukrainian Party committee. I have no speech prepared and an injudicious word would be reported in the press and turned against me. The devil with our enemies, Boris. We're menaced from all sides."

Boris thought, Coward! "Let's go," he said abruptly.

Stolypin was well aware of the impression he was making. "You must make allowances for the situation with which we have to deal. The Tsar brings a royal gift to Kiev. You and I are not deceived but we must be careful not to offend him. Let us be circumspect and not herald my association with your party. We will arrive at an understanding now and sign an official document later."

"When?"

"Certainly before winter." A hot breeze had sprung up and the Premier looked uncomfortably warm. "May we go to the carriage now where I can take off my hat, which I shall wave at my public and thereby fan myself?"

Boris did not smile at his contrived pleasantry but commanded the guards to open a lane for the Premier. In the first carriage, with Ronya on his right, Boris on his left, Stolypin appeared self-confident as he leaned forward and bowed from side to side, acknowledging the cheers.

At the main gate to the Pirov property, the lead escort pulled aside and the coachman reined in his team, signaling for the second carriage and rearguard to stop. Accustomed to warm welcomes from the peasantry, Peter Stolypin was amazed by this dazzling display of flowers, and the shouts and laughter of Ronya's people. Boris jumped to the ground and lifted Ronya down, then gave his hand to Peter. Tamara was the first to greet him.

Over deafening shouts, Stolypin managed to make himself heard. "Tamara, you're as young as I remember you."

She threw back her head roguishly. "Liar!"

Father Tromokov came forward and the two big men gripped each other's hands and used Christian names—Peter and Ivan. Lydia had made her way to Ronya's side. "The samovar hisses, mistress."

The women started strolling toward the house, the men following while the gypsies followed their queen back to the camp.

"You must be starved and dinner is late. Won't you have tea?" Ronya asked.

"I'd like nothing better," Stolypin said, "in about half an hour. But first may I go to my room? It was a hot, dirty trip."

However, at Father Tromokov's insistence, he remained downstairs long enough for a vodka. The Premier raised his glass, "To the Tsar, long may he reign," and emptied it in a single swallow. Boris, lounging in the doorway, grinned. I've got him, Boris decided. No guts.

Startlingly, Alexis contradicted his unspoken words after Stolypin left the library. "You're wrong, Boris."

Ronya led the way upstairs. "I thought you'd like your old room, Peter."

There was something immensely reassuring to Stolypin at finding himself in a world where there was so little change. He remembered the yellow quilt, the Chinese teak table topped with honey-colored marble. On the bedside table was a garlanded porcelain bowl filled with the tawny apples he had so loved as a boy. An old crystal decanter of cognac stood on a chest beneath a shelf of books. Only one thing was different and at that his eyes widened.

"Father Tromokov put the Lady there to watch over you."

"Stop a while," Peter urged, "and talk to me."

"Only if you promise to relax," she said. His hands trembled as he poured himself a small glass of brandy. "Perhaps I had better go, Peter. The strain of your job is terrible and you must be exhausted after your trip."

"No, Ronya. I do want to talk to you—alone. Before the magnetism of Boris confuses me. Don't forget how little time I have in Kiev and how much depends on my sessions with your husband."

Ronya sat while he sipped his brandy and openly studied his face. "I remember a girl," Stolypin reminisced, "who danced with gypsies and performed all sorts of tricks with her whip and was incurably outspoken."

"I dance only with Boris now," Ronya said primly, "and it's a long time since I've used my whip."

"But you still think and speak for yourself?"

"Pretty much, Peter."

He peered at her disconcertingly and Ronya smiled.

"I remember that look," she said. "It never frightened me. If your intention is to be intimidating, you're wasting your time."

Stolypin continued to fix her with a piercing glance. "Where are your sons, Ronya?"

"I expect you, as well as the Tsar, know perfectly well that both Igor and Georgi are in San Francisco," she said easily.

"And why is Igor separated from his wife and that lovely child?"

"Boris wanted him out of Russia for a while. He feared for his safety. As you know, Igor got himself into a packet of trouble."

"*Boris* wanted! And what did you want, Ronya?"

"I wanted him out of the smothering complacency and wealth of this place for a time."

"Three years, is it? A very long time."

"Yes, Peter," she agreed, "too long."

"When is he coming home?" Stolypin made his question sound like a social inquiry.

"When Boris says to."

The suggestion of a smile on Ronya's lips recalled the young beauty he had known but Stolypin sternly put away sentimentality. Only Ronya, he was convinced, and consideration for Ronya's Jews, were making Boris intractable.

"Ronya, the time has come for plain speaking."

"I agree absolutely, Peter," she said.

Stolypin, collecting himself, picked up his glass and took two sips. "I don't like the rumor that you plan to emigrate to America. As your friend, I deny it but," he raised his hand, "indulge me. It is my business to know the truth. Can you leave this land, this kingly gift from Peter the Great, which your ancestor earned for his work in helping Peter create his city? Can you leave Katya and Alexis?"

Ronya sighed but her voice was firm. "I can if I must and I fear I must. I have waited this long to make sure. It's all up to you, Peter."

He choked, not from brandy but from anger. "Tell me if I'm wrong but my impression is that the von Glasmans have lived in Russia on a footing with royalty. Perhaps I am mistaken and the guarantees made by Tsar Peter to your German forebear have not been honored. If you have a just complaint, name the offense and the offender."

Peter had given her the opening she wanted. "I am delighted if you think I look like the girl you remember. But I am not. She was arrogant and overconfident. I am middle-aged and have a social conscience. I didn't get it all at once. It was a long process, not simple to explain and you need rest."

"I am prepared to hear it if it takes all night," Peter Stolypin said grimly. "I must know everything before I begin to bargain with Boris. In all honesty, though, I warn you that I sit in judgment as a representative of the Little Father and Mother Russia. I shall not rest and I shall use all the power of my office to teach the Ukraine that she is part of one great whole." Then, in a very different tone, "Nothing you say will go beyond these four walls. I am your friend, Ronya."

She got up and rang for a maid. "We shall not be down for tea. Tell Countess Katya that His Excellency the Premier wishes dinner delayed an hour." Peter's eyes followed the maid until she departed.

"Why in the world do you stare so at everyone?" Ronya asked.

It was his turn to sigh. "I don't know. I suppose it's a disease one contracts after being bombed and shot at. In the last few weeks I've begun thinking that every strange face may be the face of my assassin."

"That's part of what I mean," Ronya said thoughtfully.

Stolypin regarded her. "You were going to tell me—?"

Her education, she said, had begun in Manchuria and in the appalling realization of the conditions under which Russia's soldiers lived and died—died often when they need not, because the Tsar had failed to provide them with equipment. While Rasputin caroused at court, the Tsar chose to ignore the disaster on the Eastern front, made no move to send doctors, nurses, decent food for the troops, Russian and Chinese. That one company had been saved was due to Russian women, collectively prostitutes but individually more honorable than the pious Tsarina. And Ronya's reward for what she had done to help? Virulent attacks in the press, only possible with her monarch's consent.

"It was then I took my first step out of Russia," she said.

She told Stolypin how she had visited a Chinese—a man of great wisdom and deep knowledge of humanity, how he had clarified her thinking, and taught her many of the implications and lessons of history she had never known before. After the shameful surrender, and after Igor came home and looked into her face, she knew that she had no choice.

"Then I took a long step out of Russia."

The Premier seemed to shrink under the load of her accusations.

"Do you really want me to go on, Peter?"

"I particularly want to hear the rest."

The rest was the revolution of 1905, the bestial pogrom in Odessa and other atrocities against the Jews.

"Is any land worth shame and sorrow? My people are being murdered. Can I be loyal to a Tsar who allows that to happen? I feel guilty, Peter."

Stolypin straightened in his chair. "The tragic times for the Jews are almost over. I am a sworn enemy of anti-Semitism. A mass exodus of Jews would drain the country of skilled artisans and professional people. You can rely on me. I shall push through legislation both because it is humane and for Russia's own good. And, Ronya, it's no secret that the Dowager Empress prefers you and Katya to the Tsarina herself, poor soul."

"The Empress is an old woman, my dear. Who will prefer my granddaughter, Rachel? She is a Jewess."

"I, Ronya. I give you my word I will prefer and protect Rachel."

"And who will protect the Mendel Beilises of Russia?"

Stolypin got up and poured himself another brandy. "I want to discuss him with you. To get him off I shall have to have two names, one of a man, the other of his hiding place."

She had known what she was risking when she brought up Beilis' name and she was not ready to tackle that matter yet. She looked at the clock. "It is time for me to go now, Peter."

"We will talk again, Ronya." He rose.

"Talk to Boris, Peter. It's he, not I, who is the voice of the Ukraine." On the spur of the moment she made an appeal. "Please watch over Katya."

"Always, dear Ronya," his face relaxed. "However, you have no reason to worry. St. Petersburg isn't Sodom anymore."

As she started to the door, it swung open and Boris, grinning, appeared. "I've come to see if you need protection!"

"I took the liberty of an old friend," Stolypin returned his smile, "to detain my hostess."

Ronya put her hand on Boris' arm and looked back to say, "Have a leisurely bath, Peter. There's plenty of time." At the

301

door of her own room, she raised her eyes to Boris. "Come unhook my dress. The maids are busy downstairs."

As soon as they were alone, Ronya's expression changed. "I'm very angry with you," she said. Boris, struggling with the hooks in her flowered dress, did not ask why.

"You are overconfident and you undervalue Stolypin. He had a moment of panic but he is *not* a coward."

Boris laid his hands on her bare back. "How much do you want to bet?" he asked impudently.

"All right, you'll find out. It's just that he represents a side of the Russian character you don't understand. He doesn't thunder, so you're deaf to his ear-splitting subtlety. He's uncertain of you and under pressure to produce the Revenge Rider. His vanity is wounded because the Tsar listens to Rasputin and he's shaken by the attacks on his life. But even on the defensive, Peter Stolypin is a leader."

Boris' hands had been busy during her tirade.

"Stop!"

He knew that Ronya had barely twenty minutes to dress, so he merely bowed low. "No sacrifice is too great for the Ukraine."

XXXIV

PETER Stolypin bowed before Rachel in his most courtly manner. "Sweet child, may I have the honor of taking you in to dinner?"

Bursting with excitement, Rachel confided, "I had a long nap and I am to be very good and eat like a lady."

Her grandmother interrupted. "Rachel was allowed to stay up late because we hope she will remember this evening, and sitting beside the Premier of Russia, all her life."

Dinner provided the relaxation Peter Stolypin so badly needed, with nothing to do but enjoy superb cooking, the wit of Father Tromokov, and the warmth of the hospitality. Watching her across the table, Peter took a great shine to Julie who, despite her exquisite manners, eyed him shyly, an expression of awe in her face. Rachel was talkative and enchanting, admiring his fine beard, much nicer than the Tsar's, whose picture she had seen on her mother's dower chest. Accepting her first mouthful of dessert from the Premier's spoon, Rachel leaned close to him and asked, "Are you my uncle?"

"Blessed child," he replied, "I am your Uncle Peter."

Alexis threw up his hands in dismay. "It could not be more tragic. Our friend," he said to Katya, "has stolen our niece, and way past her bedtime at that. I weep into my finger bowl."

Rachel's eyes danced. One of her friends, she announced to the table at large, had nine uncles, none of them as funny as Uncle Alexis. Ronya rose and started toward the drawing room, stopping in the hall to say to Lydia, "His Excellency likes chicory in his coffee," while Boris turned Rachel over to Beljik who was waiting to take her to bed.

After his demitasse, Stolypin asked Katya to play for him. She reached back in her memory and played one of Mendelssohn's "Songs Without Words" with uncommon tenderness because she wanted to show Peter her gratitude for his coming to Kiev to put an end to trouble.

"That was lovely," he said.

With all the finesse of a bull in a china shop, Father Tromokov clumped to the door. "Ronya, your damned chicory coffee's made me dizzy. Is there a bed open for me to crawl into or do I have to go home?"

To have him in the house was precisely what Ronya wanted. "Take Igor's room. It's cool and it's always ready."

"I'll see you tomorrow, Ivan," Peter called out.

Katya, whose heart was always vulnerable, worried. Tromokov had waited in the sun at the station for hours, had consumed vast quantities of vodka and eaten a huge dinner. Boris, too, was conscious of some unspoken warning. He tried to catch the priest's eye but could not and simply added his own "Sleep well," to the others.

The door closed, the latch clicked and Stolypin was on his feet
—transformed. This was not the man who had shown and confessed fear to Boris, not the man who played uncle to Rachel
and cast admiring glances at Katya. It was the Tsar's minister
who turned, challengingly, on Alexis.

"Against staggering odds I persuaded His Majesty to believe
there were advantages to be gained from a heart-to-heart talk between Boris and me. Because *you* asked me to. Months ago I
warned you to prepare Boris to produce the Revenge Rider.
From the coziness of this evening, spent in a friendlier atmosphere than I dared hope for, I now emerge defeated. It has become obvious that none of you intends to mention the Revenge
Rider. In a very few days I must give my Tsar an explanation.
What am I to say?"

Alexis had anticipated this moment but he was rocked by its
violence.

"Peter," he said. "The Revenge Rider is a myth. The first fire
was an accident. A forgotten lantern hung too close to a dry
beam. A burning matchstick, tossed into a field, caused the second. Any small carelessness can start a fire. For reasons beyond
my ken, setting fires became popular. A whistling boy, a peasant
prodding his mule homeward, a courting couple bent on amusement—these are the Revenge Rider."

Damn clever, Stolypin thought. Damn revealing, too. I am reminded that von Glasman's daughters are above the Tsar's
ukase. Or perhaps they're all entertaining themselves at my ex-
pense. Why not? Katya never really loved me. All she had to do
was go to a palace ball, dance with Alexis and presto! they're engaged. He shook his head angrily.

"No, no, Alexis. The Revenge Rider is no myth, no silly couple on their way home from a night in a haystack, and no peasant
behind a mule. He is one man. We know it. And he is in Kiev.
That is an absolute fact. And you, who approve of his brand of
justice, are hiding his identity." He looked quickly around the
room.

Boris, the Tartar, looked positively benign. Julie, the delightful slip of a girl, was listening so raptly her lips were parted.
Ronya and Katya shared an expression of boredom. The consen-

sus, he could not escape it, was that he was being exceedingly boorish. Stolypin turned to Julie.

"Surely you know," he said to her, "that it's better to turn Igor over to me than let the police capture him? I'll find some way to save him if you tell me where he is."

Ronya prayed silently, dear God, don't let Boris interfere. Katya, a room's length away from her brother-in-law, tried to will his silence. Don't be a fool, Boris, keep your mouth shut, Alexis said, but not aloud. When they realized that Boris was going to let Julie answer Stolypin, an almost audible sigh of relief ran around the room.

Little Julie gazed up at the big bearded man, surprised. If she was acting, it was consummate acting. "Gospodin Stolypin, Your Excellency, my husband Igor is the Ukraine's champion rider. He is a great war hero. Everyone knows his face. If he were in Kiev, you would have him. Police on horseback, police in carriages, police on foot with dogs have searched everywhere and not found him because Igor was traveling in the Orient. Now he is visiting his brother Georgi in California. It seems to me easy for you to prove this, too. Don't we have an ambassador in America who acts as the Tsar's representative? I'll give you Igor's address—I write him every day. Perhaps the ambassador could send someone to see his passport and whether it matches his face. Then he could write the Tsar. You see, Igor von Glasman Pirov simply *can't* be the Revenge Rider."

For her family, Julie's little speech was pure pleasure, for the Premier of Russia, unqualified embarrassment. Day after day he had considered checking through the Russian consul in San Francisco but, convinced beyond a doubt that Boris, not his son, was the Revenge Rider, had not bothered. Now he had tried to trap the girl and she'd made a fool of him.

Peter Stolypin was not, however, Premier of Russia for nothing. He saved face by blaming himself and added, "Julie, you've spared the ambassador a bit of a nuisance. So now we can all settle down and devote ourselves to finding the real Revenge Rider."

There they had it, inescapably. The Tsar must have his victim to appease the Black Hundreds, and Stolypin was prepared to

305

wield the knife and shed the blood of an innocent man to force Boris to sell out the Ukraine. Boris, in his chair, stretched lazily. "Wait!" he called to Ronya, who had announced she was ready for bed. "I'll finish my drink and go up with you."

Her voice floated back, "I want to tell the girls in the kitchen they needn't finish till morning. It's been a long day." Katya now rose. "I'm exhausted, too. Don't stay up all night talking, Alexis." When Julie asked to be excused, Stolypin said, "I'm being deserted! Give me a song before you go. Katya, I know, can manage to play one more piece."

The two women turned helplessly toward Boris. Unruffled, he picked up his glass and drained it. "Neither Katya nor Julie, I gather from the signals, are in a performing mood any more, and I'm a touch anxious about old Tromokov. I've seen him consume vodka and never before seen it consume him." He got to his feet and followed the women without a backward glance.

"Another brandy?" Alexis said.

Nodding dismally, Stolypin sat down. "Please."

"I think," Alexis remarked, "that you, my distinguished friend, are a double-barreled jackass."

There was no argument. Alexis could hardly have thought less highly of Peter than Peter thought of himself. Now he tried not to excuse but to explain. "I wanted some sign from Boris or Ronya and when there wasn't any I grabbed at the straw of Igor. Alexis, I've got to have the name of a traitor or my talks with Boris will get nowhere. Someone has to be shot for the Tsar and, incidentally, for the Ukraine.

"Why in the devil won't the Pirovs help me? They insist that I nail myself to the cross by clearing Beilis and publicly refuting the cry of ritual murder. Yet they take a negative stand when it comes to crimes against true Russians. Each fire weakens my position with the Tsar. I'm disturbed by the change in his attitude toward me of late. All this business here is undermining his confidence, Alexis."

Alexis screwed up his eyes. The effect was far from friendly. "Can't say that I have much confidence in you either, Peter," he said brutally. "Mendel Beilis is an innocent man. Ritual murder is a barbaric crime. Why should Boris and Ronya collabo-

306

rate with you by informing against the man who seeks to avenge him if, as you aver, there is such a man?"

With a growing sense of personal injury Peter looked angrily at Alexis. "I'll tell you why. Because Boris Pirov is the Revenge Rider. That's why!"

Alexis sat unmoving. Strange, he mused, a gifted politician and in some ways a statesman—certainly the man best suited to the job—but he lets his tongue run away with him. Lurking conviction is one thing, but open threats violate the rules of the game. And tip the scales in favor of the Ukraine. "Your proof?" he said.

"I haven't a kopek's worth of proof," Peter admitted, sounding old and exhausted. "I confess that at first I believed it was Igor. I wanted him to be the Revenge Rider. With Igor in my net I'd have Boris on his knees. My police force turned Kiev inside out looking for him. Then I went over his war record, found out what he'd done to that sergeant. But I couldn't see him as willing to die for the Jews even so. His father? That's another matter. He'd take the chance. The boy hasn't that kind of character. It has to be Boris."

"Indeed!" Alexis said evenly. "And if you can pin the evidence on him, can you hand Boris over to the Tsar?"

Stolypin resisted a temptation to say yes. "A year ago I would have put my own son in front of a firing squad if he'd been the Revenge Rider. Now I need the Ukraine so desperately I'll make any kind of deal."

Alexis was moved by Peter's gray face. The man was, after all, his friend. "We've known each other more than a quarter of a century," he said, "and understood each other all that time. Your coming to the attention of the Tsar was no accident, you know. In all honesty my interest in you was not just friendship. We have an identical concept of government. But what you suggest is monstrous, an offense against everything you and I believe in. How can you allow Nicholas to incite you to what, let's face it, amounts to murder? Persuade him that country bumpkins and town hoodlums are the arsonists."

"I can't."

"What haven't you told me, Peter?"

Stolypin's voice sank to a hoarse whisper. "Rasputin, too, has settled on Boris as the Revenge Rider." The monk had pricked Peter with questions—Who rides like Boris Pirov? Who is nowhere to be found when he doesn't want to be found? Who gets out of the bed of a Jewess and is worshiped by Tartar and Cossack, Mongol and *moujik?* Who? Who? Who?

"The Tsar has made me personally responsible for the capture of the Revenge Rider. Failing that, I must clear Boris of suspicion."

"I see," said Alexis. "Look, Peter, it's long past midnight. You must get to bed. I'll mull it over. Your tour with the Tsar gives us time. When you speak to Nicholas, sound confident—and vague. With Boris be honest and vigorous in pursuit of your high ideals.

"Stay in bed late and ring for breakfast whenever you're ready. The meeting isn't scheduled until two and Ronya's cabin is only about half an hour off. Good night, Peter." Stolypin's eyes were veiled as the two men parted.

Ronya was very much awake. On the small sofa in his attic room she sat beside the Blond One. The only light came from a full moon. Still she could see his bowed head. "I never thought I'd hit a priest, ever," he said disconsolately, "especially not Father Tromokov, who's been my friend all my life. But I did, Ronya! Deliberately and with all my strength. It was like—hitting a child. He was so unprepared for my fist on his jaw and he went down with such a woebegone expression, sagging onto his knees just long enough for me to tie him to the foot of the bed with sheets. He'll do no revenge riding tonight."

Ronya reached out and touched the Blond One's face. "I'm very proud of you, and grateful. Tell me the whole business. You have your father's habit of leaving out the choicest bits."

Because it was so late, the Blond One raced through the story. On his way to his own room he saw a light under Igor's door and went in. There he found Father Tromokov, very excited. "Stolypin saw me weak kneed from vodka," he crowed. "Tonight I'm going to remove Boris from his list of suspects." Of late Tromokov had not been riding. The others would not let him since his church's decision: Death to him who laughs at us with fire! The Blond One reminded him of the double penalty he risked, but the older man wasn't even listening. "I've been saving Leo Gorsky for myself," he said, rubbing his hands together. "He oozes evil, that bastard robs, destroys, even wastes his own land. Now he's got his dirty yellow teeth into Mischuk. Wants him transferred to the provinces because our honest chief of police is fighting to get Beilis acquitted. Look! You can see a corner of his land from this window!"

The Blond One had protested that the guards, both Tartar and Cossack, would leap onto their horses when they saw the flames and Tromokov would never make it back to the house.

The priest chuckled slyly. "What's to prevent me from joining them in their search?"

"You're handing Stolypin a length of rope to tie around your neck," the Blond One told him, and the padre said, "If Stolypin doesn't like my brand of religion, let him drink the urine of a holy cow. And believe me I'll set no pukey little fire, son. The afterglow will outshine the sunrise."

That was when the Blond One hit him.

Ronya's delight was enough to erase the boy's sense of guilt. "But you know," she said, "he's absolutely right. Somebody's got to ride tonight, shortly before morning." She held fast to his hand. "Not you. The Tsar and Stolypin would like nothing better than to sacrifice one of Boris' sons.

"Nothing has really changed between your mother and me, nothing at all. We still fight—we always did and we're still hopelessly loyal to each other. She's the only one who can do tonight's work. The camp is unguarded. Tamara rides like a demon and that's what we need. Tell her how desperately we're defending ourselves. Unless Stolypin can say to his Tsar, 'As God is my witness, Boris Pirov was by my side when flames rose to the sky,' an innocent man will be arrested, questioned, beaten and, when he can stand no more, made to confess to any crime for a few hours' peace."

The Blond One drew a deep breath. "The Gorsky place?"

"Yes. Aside from its nearness, he's given plenty of cause. Tell Tamara not to strike until about five and that no life is to be

lost. Not even *his*. Then you come right home. Make sure Stolypin sees you. Take pains to be the one who knocks at his door.
You can tell him that in this house you are responsible for his
safety. Act worried about our fields and woods. Ask your father's
permission to send some of our men as fire-fighters."

The Blond One had put one leg over the windowsill and vanished into the darkness almost before Ronya finished speaking.

When she walked into Father Tromokov's room and turned
up the lamp, he reared like a horse trying to break his bonds.
"You're only tightening the knots," Ronya remarked.

"Damn it, Ronya! The impudence of that pup!"

She looked at the sheets around his arms and legs. "He did a
good job."

Tromokov's indignation was boundless. "Boris was here. He
tested the knots, yanked them tighter and walked out laughing
like a simpleton.

"Don't stand there, woman! Get me loose!"

Ronya sat down. "What's the rush? You're not going anywhere." She kicked off her shoes.

Raging, Tromokov cursed and Ronya took no notice of him.
Her impertinence began to undo him and all at once he started
to laugh.

"Give up?"

"Oh, hell, Ronya, get me a bottle of vodka. I might as well
pass out."

"But, my dear, what will you use for hands? I certainly won't
come an inch closer until you promise—priest's honor—to behave yourself. Besides, all your heroics are silly. Tamara rides.
Tonight she is Tsar Peter's ghost and hooks Premier Peter." His
laughter was thunderous.

"Ivan, shut up! Peter will hear you."

"His misfortune. I'm drunk. Come on, Ronya, untie me."

She knelt down and dove into one of his pockets, from which
she extracted a number of odd items, among them a pocketknife.
With it she freed Tromokov in far less time than it had taken to
truss him up. Stretching his long arms and legs, the priest muttered, "I'm one immense cramp. Tell that young scoundrel the
next time he sees me he'd better get out of my way. Fast."

"May God bless him," Ronya said tenderly. Then, still in

stocking feet, she reached as high up as she could and kissed Ivan Tromokov, abruptly turned, and ran.

The lights in her room were high, her bed empty. Very much needing the comfort of Boris' arms, she took a quick, perfumed bath, brushed and braided her hair, put on nightgown and robe and tiptoed to his room, noting with pleasure that his windows, like Stolypin's, faced east toward Gorsky land.

Boris growled from sleep, "Where've you been?" She answered only by brushing his lips with hers. Boris drew her close and in the circle of his arms, Ronya slept.

Through the warm dawn, church bells sounded the alarm. Horses hooves sprayed gravel from the driveway; a voice shouted, "God almighty, what a fire!" to be answered by, "No mistake, it's the Revenge Rider."

Stolypin, instantly awake, sprang to his feet and crossed the carpeted floor to the window.

Julie ran to Rachel.

Father Tromokov hummed happily and tried to wedge his enormous feet into Ronya's tiny slippers. Since the shoes resisted his efforts, he looked further, found his own and put them on. Arrayed in a long red nightshirt, he departed for Stolypin's room.

The Blond One belted on his gun and felt for his dagger. From the attic he went downstairs and continued along the bedroom hall. At the Premier's door he stopped, straightened and knocked. "Your Excellency, are you all right?"

Father Tromokov answered. "Come in, my boy. My vision being impaired by chicory coffee, I can't make out if the fire is jumping to our trees."

"No," said Stolypin from the window, "they look safe so far."

Lydia heaved herself up off her bed, splashed cold water on her face and dressed, as Stolypin would expect of Ronya's housekeeper, in style. She ran through the servants' quarters calling out to sleepy maids, "Stop hanging out the windows. Do you imagine you'll catch a glimpse of the phantom rider? Hurry, there's a big breakfast to get."

Katya and Alexis exchanged whispers.

"Who, Alexis, and why?"

"Your sister is a genius, my love."

311

"Who could she trust?"

"Tamara. . . . The rest of us are all in the house. I must get myself to Peter's room."

Boris opened one eye and squinted at Ronya, six inches away.

"Go to Stolypin, my darling," she said.

"Right!"

When he arrived, Stolypin was looking years younger than he had the night before. "How serious is the fire?" he inquired of the Blond One.

The Blond One stood at attention. "A few acres and Gorsky's summer pavilion by the lake is my guess, sir. Unless it spreads. But there doesn't seem to be any wind."

Boris crossed the room jauntily, like a man without a care in the world, and took a position at the window, saying to the Blond One, "Send whatever help you think is needed."

Peter Stolypin's relief was so evident that Boris' good humor faded. He said, in a low, savage tone, "If you were considering indicting *him*, you can forget it now!" He was astonished at his own vehemence.

They watched the Premier then, Tromokov and Brusilov overtly. His future relations with Boris depended on how he replied.

"To me," he said, "that boy looks not one bit like the ghost of Peter the Great." Quick smiles lit two faces. "I shall have to report to Nicholas that neither Boris Pirov nor anyone else closely connected with his household is the Revenge Rider."

Boris stood stubbornly by his guns. "Tell him this, too. It is you, or men like Trotsky and Lenin. And if the head of Louis XVI could roll, so can the head of Nicholas II."

If his intention was to provoke a quarrel, Stolypin turned it aside adroitly. "Boris," he said, "do you honestly consider the radical Socialists a formidable threat?"

"Good God, yes!"

"Ah, my friend, happily I disagree with you. My land reforms will make the peasants into small capitalists. Heavy industry is starting to return dividends. And legislation against official anti-Semitism and a guarantee allowing Jews who wish to remain distinctively Jews, all rob the Bolsheviks of the support of the intelligentsia." He looked once more out the window, saw the flames dwindling and moved to a chair.

"Look what we're doing—improving and allowing new freedom for public education. A whole generation of young people will adore the Tsar. Let's not forget that the Bolsheviks are hopelessly divided among themselves so they're no political threat. Reform disarms them."

A manservant arrived with tea and the morning seemed to have swung into its accustomed round but Boris remained intransigent. "Paper reforms! What of the unemployment in Moscow? What of the foreign debt? What of the nationalist resistance here in the Ukraine? And in Georgia? And among the Moslem Tartars?"

Alexis could not stand by and allow Boris to wreck his own hour of triumph. "Father Tromokov," he said, "must go to mass. Ronya may sleep until noon. Katya's alone. Let's have breakfast with her in her sitting room in about an hour. Then Peter and I will take up your gauntlet, Boris."

"I'm sorry, Peter," Boris said. "I'm a poor host. I meant you to enjoy this morning and have a quiet walk while it's still cool, not a smoky sky and a hot argument."

"The sky doesn't depress me," Stolypin said. "Nor do your opinions. Everything augurs well for the meeting. Before that I shall take time to write a report of this morning's affair to my master, Nicholas. Can you spare a courier to ride with it post-haste?"

"With pleasure," said Count Alexis Brusilov.

Later that day, at the cabin, there were passionate espousals of opposing points of view and Alexis feared that Boris was showing his hand too rapidly, too strongly. At one point, in an access of bravado, he said, "So you had me pegged as the Revenge Rider? So I am. And I came to it naturally. My people burned Moscow to the ground in 1381. Now, as husband to a Jewess, I burn at what you do to the Jews. I ride against the savages who torture her people and make her so afraid she sends her sons away from the country she once loved."

And since Boris had established a climate of dangerous honesty, Stolypin too spoke of grave matters with frankness. "I recoil in disgust—in repugnance from the Tsarina. My undivided loyalty to Tsarism has nothing whatsoever to do with my private opinion of the Tsar or my disappointment in the pitiful, hemophilic Tsarevitch. Yet I dedicate myself to preserving the monarchy."

And again, less openly, he became the politician. When Boris asked, "Why should Ronya's peasants apply for government loans to buy government land when Ronya put them on a percentage basis long ago?" he stirred, not pleased, and said, "This I neither knew nor like. In our program for the peasants we must avoid colliding with the interest of the large landowners or we will forfeit their support."

There were moments of unbridled fury, in one of which Boris said, "I repudiate you, Peter Stolypin. You worm your way in and out of compromises. Appease the Tsarina, appease the peasants, appease the Jews, appease private wealth—mortgage Russia to France. You proclaim that you hate murder and rape and at the same time profess to love the Tsar."

Cunning Stolypin chose when to defend himself; shrewdly he pointed out flaws in Boris' arguments. And Alexis stepped in and eloquently explained the two adversaries to one another.

Stripped to fundamentals, Boris spoke from the heart when he asked, "What do I tell Ronya?" and they were all moved. Stolypin sighed then and said ruefully, "What a lot of trouble you are, Boris!" and for the first time they all laughed.

Alexis pleaded for sanity. "No country is pure and perfect. We will, God willing, reduce injustice and abolish insult. We will institute a balance of power and render the Tsarina impotent as an influence. What we are striving for is fair laws and a decent standard for all. Bring home your sons, Boris. Let them share their country's victory over itself."

Stolypin swore, "I shall abolish the Black Hundreds, outlaw pogroms, guarantee complete and full citizenship, including freedom of movement, to all Russians. There will be a free press and Mendel Beilis will be acquitted—so help me God!"

And Boris pledged, "I will, to the utmost of my power, persuade the members of the Ukrainian party that our good is one with Mother Russia's. I promise the Ukraine's wheat to the com-

314

mon granary. I shall publicly denounce the madness of revenge and the feebleness of retaliation."

And Alexis promised, "I shall serve."

The vodka splashed into glasses and toasts were drunk to the Dowager Empress, to the sons of Ronya and Boris, to truth and freedom, and to Peter Stolypin, Premier of Russia.

XXXV

CONVERSATION was intimate, unstrained, as the wine was poured. Everyone laughed when Rachel drank, clutching the goblet in one hand and the stem in the other so as not to spill. She explained to her new uncle, "We are having a party because Igor, my father, is coming home from America, and so is my Uncle Georgi."

The guest of honor turned to his host. "Have you sent the cable?"

Boris replied cheerfully, "Ever since the Tsar arrived, Kiev has been celebrating. No one has any time for work. It will have to wait until after he leaves."

Then it happened. Shortly before Boris' departure, an hour ahead of the others, to take up his night's duties, Ronya made a graceful little speech.

"Peter, it will be difficult to get you alone later. May I thank you now, and confess I had not dared to hope that you would earn our gratitude or the trust and affection we now feel for you?"

Stolypin, a trifle flustered, made a light response—to Julie. "And you, my dear, are you pleased with me, too?"

Tears welled in Julie's eyes. "All the heaven I ever dreamed of is here in this house. There were times when I thought I'd rather die than leave it. Now Igor and Georgi are coming back and I'm not frightened anymore. Oh, I do thank you, Gospodin Stolypin, your Excellency."

There was no mistaking the Premier's pleasure. This girl had given him his strongest lever for moving Boris—her devotion to the mansion and the land might even outweigh Ronya's revulsion against the Tsar. Fumbling, and finding no words, he instead unhooked the tunic of his uniform and reached for tangible proof. Around his neck was a small gold cross on a thread of a gold chain, which he had worn for many years. Now he took it off, his fingers lingering affectionately on the holy talisman.

"Rachel," he said, "come here."

The air was electric with shock. Even orthodox Catholic Father Tromokov prayed, in heaven's name, do not break the ancient law! Ronya's and the Brusilovs' faces were unbelieving masks. But Stolypin did not look, did not see. As Rachel stepped obediently forward, Julie's hand shot out in a reflex that sent the cross sailing across the room.

No one moved but Ronya, who rescued the Premier and the moment.

"Dear Peter," she said, "our daughter means no dishonor to you. Julie was raised in orthodoxy and though, since she came to us, she has rid herself of many prejudices and superstitions, the pull of tradition is strong. Her motive is good, her behavior deplorable. We all ask you to forgive us."

Boris picked the cross up, fastened the chain around Rachel's neck and put his arm around Julie, who cried out tearfully, "If Rachel wears a cross, how will she know she is a Jewess?"

It was Stolypin who answered, looking directly at Katya. "Little Julie, some young fool will tell her. He will say, 'Rachel, I love you but I am ambitious for high office and titles and it just isn't sensible to marry a Jewess.'" Katya moistened her dry lips with the tip of her tongue.

From Rachel's point of view the episode had been mysterious and silly. A present was meant to be taken with a thank-you or a kiss. If she had been Julie's mother, she'd have sent her straight to her own room. And now Uncle Peter had said something strange and no one was replying.

"Why?" said Rachel.

The only answer was the rustle of Katya's ball gown as she fled the room.

Boris rode with an easy heart. The large, handsome square in front of the opera house was thronged with people who loved a spectacle. Tsar Nicholas II of Russia and his royal daughters, with glorious pomp and panoply, would drive through the square and up to the classic marble portico of the theater. All along the route of royalty's procession the police kept order and the crowds happily cheered every carriage that passed and threw their hats in the air at sight of an occasional "sport" in a motor-car. When at last the Imperial entourage drove up, and officials bowed and ladies in their grandest toilettes curtsied to the floor, there was a wild bellying-out of the cordons of uniformed men who, hands joined, tried to hold the crowd in check.

By the time Boris took his place between Ronya and Julie in the front row, the last strains of the national anthem had sounded and the audience was settling back in its seats, attention focused on the royal box. When the lights dimmed for the over-ture, all the women were intent on studying the young faces and demure white dresses of the Tsar's daughters, the costumes of the ladies-in-waiting and the handsome face of their ruler, with sweeping moustache and geometrically clipped beard. What fol-lowed, when the curtains parted, the social leaders of Kiev suf-fered in boredom, and to Boris the long first act, sung by a third-rate company, was pure torture. He fought drowsiness.

Poor Pushkin, he thought, what a mockery the librettist has made of your "Tsar Saltan"! But Julie, he noticed, was en-tranced. Ronya, on his other hand, looked as if she might, for the one and only time in her life, faint from the heat and he laid a comforting hand on hers. Oh, hell, unless this bloody house burns down, I'm stuck, he conceded, and closed his eyes. But though the desire to sleep tempted him almost beyond endur-ance, he tried to keep awake by dwelling on his victory of yes-terday.

Boris heard Ronya whisper, "Applaud," and opened his eyes to see the curtain coming down.

Righteously convinced that he had earned a vodka by endur-

317

ing the first act and that he would need it to live through the second, Boris made his way to the lobby. True, it meant deserting Stolypin, but that gentleman was encircled by ladies of such ultra-respectability it was hard to conceive of their harboring murderous intentions. Officers, soldiers and police ringed the group so closely they formed a living barricade. He signaled to Ronya his plan to go to the buffet on the mezzanine and started upstairs.

If the first act had been a bore, the second was an outrage. Boris wondered irritably why theater seats had all, obviously, been designed for midgets, and squirmed until Ronya laid a restraining hand on his knee.

Only those who were closest heard the crack of the two shots. The curtain had just descended and there was a hubbub of cheers and bravos, as if to honor not the stage Tsar but the real Tsar—whose favorite opera this was said to be.

Boris had heard, however, and knew the sound for what it was. He threw his body across Ronya's. From his seat, Stolypin rose, rocking crazily, and the big, bearded man whom Kievians now loved and trusted drew their attention from the footlights and the royal loge. "Long live Stolypin!" rang out here and there.

Ronya, crushed and half-suffocated under the weight of Boris, was stunned. "I'm all right," she managed to say. "Get off me." She pushed at him, anxious about Julie, who was moaning piteously, "Tamara told me: Death on a warm night. Tamara saw it! Igor will never come home!"

Stolypin was gazing at the royal box and Katya, beside him, clutched the white chiffon of her dress on which a red stain was spreading, her face blank with horror. Raising his left hand, Peter Stolypin made the sign of the cross, then slumped into his seat, but Katya saw none of this. She had fainted.

For a second Ronya blocked Boris' way to the aisle, and in the confusion other hands than his helped the wounded man toward the exit. Using the space cleared to let him pass, Alexis followed with Katya in his arms.

Boris lunged free of Ronya's grip, hoping to lay hands on the assassin, but a voice boomed from the stage, "His Majesty commands you to stay where you are. The police have taken the prisoner into protective custody." The voice reached Boris' ears but not his understanding, so consumed was he with a single passion —not to protect but to destroy the bastard who had done this thing. When he did succeed in pushing past Ronya to gain the aisle, she and Julie were right behind him. The passage the length of the theater was a passage through purgatory, but when they reached the lobby it was fairly clear.

Alexis was near the door, looking like a sick old man. "I had to let Katya go home in a hired carriage," he said. "It was near the entrance and I wanted to get her out of *this* as fast as possible." His face was lined with pain. "She insisted on my staying, kept saying between sobs that Boris would get himself in trouble trying to do something heroic." Boris was not convinced that Katya, barely revived, had said anything of the sort and swore a great oath which at an ordinary time would have made Julie blush. Now she was far too numb. Catching sight of Krasmikov, he strode across the lobby.

"Whom have you caught?" Boris demanded.

The police chief's face was drawn.

"Man named Dmitri Bogrov, a terrorist. Obscure fellow."

"Not obscure anymore," Boris growled. "How in the devil did he get in?"

Krasmikov drew him out of the range of listeners. "He's in the service of the Tsar, on my payroll, damn it. I gave the order for him to be admitted. There was a request. From higher up." Krasmikov had the decency to look as if he hated himself, and his job. "By the by, Boris, get along home. You could be the next target. Your stallion permitted Mischuk's man to get aboard and he's riding the beast back for you. You'll not be escorting the Tsar any further this evening."

The strains of the national anthem floated through a door which had been opened and when it finished, Olga and Tatiana appeared behind their father, faces frozen. Already a letter to his mother was shaping in Nicholas' mind, and before he went to bed that night he wrote her:

> During the second interval we had just left the box as it was so hot, when we heard two sounds as if something had been dropped. I thought an opera glass might have fallen on somebody's head and ran into the box to look. To the right I saw

a group of officers and other people. They seemed to be dragging something along. Women were shrieking and, directly in front of the stalls, Stolypin was standing; he slowly turned his face toward us and with his left hand made the sign of the cross in the air. Only then did I notice that he was very pale and that his right hand and uniform were bloodstained. He slowly sank into his chair and began to unbutton his tunic. While Stolypin was being helped out of the theater there was a great noise in the corridor near our box; people were trying to lynch the assassin. I am sorry to say the police rescued him and took him to an isolated room for his first examination. . . . Then the theater filled up again, the national anthem was sung, and I left with the girls at eleven. You can imagine with what emotions!

Boris and Mischuk sat on the box of the Pirov carriage. Boris leaped down as Ronya and Julie came up, and explained, "Mischuk sent Benko home on my horse. Thought we'd want to go to the hospital to inquire . . ." His voice trailed off. "I'll take you and Julie home first," he said to his wife.

"That's idiotic," Ronya protested. "We'll all go."

Boris frowned. "Katya's alone."

"Scarcely! With Father Tromokov, the Blond One and Lydia all at the house, and, by now, probably Tamara, too."

Boris lifted her and Julie into the carriage. He held the door for Alexis and waved to Mischuk, "You, too." Mischuk looked inquiringly toward the coachman's seat. "In," said Boris and Mischuk did as he was told.

Across the empty streets of Kiev, with lights burning in every window, Boris drove like a Tartar till the horses were shining wet. Inside the carriage, Alexis was delivering a eulogy. "Everyone respected him, even Trotsky. And Peter was brave. He handled the disorders of 1905 admirably."

"He was a very sensible man," Mischuk said simply. "Very sensible in manner, too."

Ronya was distressed at their funereal use of the past tense. "A strong man doesn't die from a bullet wound in the arm!"

"There were two shots, Ronya, my mother," Julie reminded her.

"That's right," Mischuk said, "and one of them went deep."

Boris' face, when he came out of the hospital, told Ronya

what she had dreaded before he spoke. "Peter is in critical condition. He won't make it."

Julie dissolved in tears—for herself, not Peter Stolypin. Alexis, with his arm around her, spoke comfortingly. "It's not hopeless yet, Julie," though he was convinced that it was.

"Take us home, darling," Ronya said.

There were lights burning all over the estate. The news which Benko had brought when he rode in on the stallion had spread from house to house like wildfire. In Ronya's kitchen Katya sat alone with Father Tromokov, who had been explaining why he had no faith left in his country. "Hear me, Katya," he was saying. "Stolypin made noble noises but his land reform bill wasn't worth a damn. This is how it works: The peasants borrow money from the government to buy a piece of government wasteland. Mortgaging their souls, buying their own coffins. And let me remind you, Rasputin is very much alive. Get ready for that cloven-hoofed devil to return."

"Please, Father, leave me one straw to clutch at."

"I can't," Tromokov boomed. "I feel responsible for you."

Katya rallied sufficiently to ask, "Is it true you're a Socialist? I've been told that."

He considered and realized that the woman drooping across the table from him was far too tired for political hairsplitting. "I care absolutely nothing about labels," he temporized. "If you want to know what I am, I'm a priest who is also a jealous lover of justice."

"I'm sorry, Ivan."

"On Ronya's return from Manchuria," he said, as if in vindication, "I closed my ears to what the outside world thought about us. I believed with all my heart that if the Ukraine were freed, it would be an end of evil. For a long time I defended my stand. It isn't possible anymore, Katya. Now, I ask you to leave Russia. Take your wealth and take refuge. Nicholas will never forgive Alexis for forcing Stolypin on him, for his devotion to Ronya and Boris and for his undertaking to clear Mendel Beilis. Sooner or later Alexis will be destroyed."

"Can you convince Alexis of that?" Katya was heartsick.

"No, Katya, I can't. Neither can the Bishop of Moscow. He's tried." The priest spoke tenderly. "Tell Alexis you refuse to be separated from Ronya. Tell him your life is incomplete without Georgi. Tell him how you adore Rachel."

Tired though she was, Katya's pride was intact. "I will not force a choice on Alexis."

Father Tromokov raised his head. "They're here."

They came into the kitchen as day was dawning. Katya ran to Alexis, alarmed at his pallor, and threw herself into his arms. "Food and scalding tea are ready," she said before she even inquired about Peter.

Ronya arranged for her sister and Alexis to be alone together a few minutes, taking herself off to change, sending Julie to bed, making Father Tromokov responsible for installing Mischuk in Igor's room.

Julie was so clearly exhausted that Boris swung her into his arms and carried her to her room. He laid her on her bed, took off her shoes and kissed her fleetingly, full on the lips.

"Boris, my father, I'm frightened," she said. "It's morning and the birds aren't singing."

"I'll send Lydia up with some warm milk to make you sleep."

"Father," Julie said weakly, "will you come back later, please?"

"I'll come back," he said.

In Rachel's room he stood above the sleeping child who, with her arm thrown back over her head, bore such an amazing resemblance to Ronya. Around her neck he saw that she still wore Stolypin's cross and gently unclasped it. "That's not your heritage, little *krasavitsa*," he said to her so quietly she did not stir. He patted Beljik and went on to his own room where he put the cross in the back of a small drawer, then poured a tall glass brimful of vodka. This he carried to the bay window and stood listening. Julie was right. The morning was unnaturally silent. A premonition, a wave of fear, slid through him. "The hell with it," Boris said aloud and turned away from the window, his glass empty. His boot came away from his swollen foot with difficulty and though a hot bath soaked away much of the pain, his depression remained.

The sun was high, the day already oppressively hot, when he

returned to Julie's room. Boris sat on the edge of her bed. "Why did you ask me to come back, Julie?"

Suddenly she buried her face in the pillows and sobbed. He watched but made no move to comfort her. "We'll talk another time."

"Please don't go." She lifted her head and rubbed her eyes with the back of her hand in a gesture reminiscent of Rachel. "Boris, my father, must we leave this house?"

"Yes, Julie," he said. "You and your mother and Rachel will go. I, too, if it is my destiny. I've promised."

Julie gave him a look he read with astonishment. She had not, he suspected, the slightest intention of going back on the vow she had sworn to herself to stay where she was, giving it precedence over her marriage and over her awe of Ronya. Quite a woman, she was.

"If Georgi became Alexis' son," she said, her eyes never leaving his face, "it would give the Tsar proof of Pirov loyalty."

Boris took Julie's hand. "Listen, child," he said, "the whole idea of a monarch and subjects is wrong. Man is born free."

Again Julie's eyes glistened with tears. "I can't rest, Boris, my father. I keep seeing Igor begging me to come to America. When I said I'd never leave this house, it broke his heart."

"Don't reproach yourself, little Julie. There was more to it than that. Igor was restless before you married him, and the fires of war fed his restlessness and I, too, drove him away."

Julie was not comforted. "I lied to Igor. I lied to everyone," she said. "It wasn't just the house. I couldn't leave you, Boris, my father." She closed her eyes and held her breath. Boris took hold of her arms with his strong, gentle hands and she breathed again.

"Darling Julie, I understand. I never did understand my sons when they were children, but I understand about you and me. I am the father you wanted. You are the daughter I never had. We needed each other."

Peace washed away the trouble in Julie's eyes.

So disordered was the state of Russia, Peter Stolypin was buried before he died. Special interests made special plans, as did special people. Stolypin's adherents wanted Count Vladimir Nicholaievitch Kokovtsov for next Premier. They acted quickly before the opposition had time to gather its forces. As first step they secured the endorsement of the Dowager Queen.

The army had its own interests to serve, as did the navy. The church wanted no man who could be duped, as they saw it, the way Peter Stolypin had been by the Jews. They favored a priest and the news filled pious Alix with joy. Already she was relieved because Stolypin's death would shorten the distance between Siberia and the gardens of Tsarskoye Selo.

Ronya was the most frustrated woman in Russia. Boris had taken himself off to the stables, translating his usual "done is done" to "what will be, will be." But in sight of victory, with every conceivable reason for leaving Russia, every member of her family evidenced ties and loyalties stronger than her persuasiveness. To Julie's village she dispatched the Blond One and to her offer got back one word from Sara, the baker's wife, "No." Politely said and accompanied by a substantial gift of fresh bread and honey. What, it implied, could enrich life more? And, has America something finer?

That zealous patron of liberty, Rabbi Levinsky, said, "No, Ronya. While one Jew remains on Russian soil I stay."

She could not let it go at that and pleaded, "Come with us to a new home. Fight anti-Semitism from a free land."

"My fight is here," he insisted. "What a pity our Tsar is no student of history! From time beyond recorded history, it is the tyrant who loses at last."

Father Tromokov was more succinct but the outcome was the same. "My peasants are enslaved. I'll stay and set them free."

Katya's mind and face were closed. "Of course not, but we'll see each other. Alexis and I plan to spend part of every year abroad."

"Dreamer!" Ronya cried.

For once she got no spate of words from Lydia when she commanded, "Pack at once." The old woman was too astonished to do anything but scuttle out of the room.

Boris shrugged indifferently; he had retired into some private hell of his own.

On the afternoon of September 18, the church bells began to toll. Peter Stolypin was dead.

XXXVI

RONYA stared up at the ceiling. By her side Boris had thrown himself down and lay silent, a stranger, withdrawn and alone. It was a relief when he spoke, though his voice was chilling. She answered his question, "I wanted Rachel to get away for a few days so I sent her with the Blond One to visit Sara and Rhea. They're just as much her family as we are. A house without laughter is no place for a child."

She braced herself for his reaction. There was none, neither surprise nor displeasure. Why, she asked herself, is everything suddenly so wrong between us? Is Boris waiting for some outside force to excuse him from having to take action? And Julie was remote, Katya, mute, Alexis ashamed. Despite a promise he had made Katya, he was back in St. Petersburg with the Tsar, having gone, he said, to support the new Premier, Kokovtsov, until the Tsar should learn, once again, to trust him. "Then," he swore, "I'll retire, so help me God."

Anger took hold of her. She wanted, she realized, to hurt Boris. Physically beating him with tight fists, she cried, "If you don't move or say something, I'll—I'll—"

Ronya got no further. Her body was crushed against Boris and he was whispering, "Oh, my lovely Ronya." His eyes had come alive again.

She laid her hands on his golden head. "Why haven't you taken any notice of me these past three weeks? Why do you ignore Igor's cables to hurry? Why do you avoid the house so that only the woods and the wild animals see you?"

For answer there were quick, hot kisses, long shuddering sighs, two bodies plunging together in perfect union. Then they lay still for an eternity. "Let's go to the cabin, little dove," Boris murmured.

Ronya laughed the lusty laugh of a woman in love and beloved and jumped out of bed. By the time she was dressed in
close-fitting pants and high boots and a tailored shirt, Boris was
ready in a rough shirt and riding breeches. He poured two
drinks into silver tumblers, gave her one and downed his. "Losing everything squeezed me dry. I had to go off by myself, dear
love."

"But, my dear, what we would lose by leaving Russia," she
said, "is nothing compared to what we would gain. You'll have
other stables and build me another cabin on Igor's mountain. I
do want a town house, too, where the grandchildren can live
while they're at school." She raised her tumbler and drank "To
life, my darling."

Boris walked into Ronya's dressing room and returned with a
short fur cape which he threw over her shoulders. For an hour
they walked through mist across Ronya's land, holding hands.
She bade a silent farewell to pastures and ploughed fields, bluffs
and woodlands. It was dark by the time they reached the stream.
There they rested and smoked and for the first time talked.

"This morning I saw Rostovsky," Boris said, "and began negotiating the sale of the stables. He offered a cash down payment
and a mortgage but I told him I'd only take cold cash for the
whole amount. At that, I should make an enormous profit."

Ronya damned herself for not having told him of her promise to Tamara. "That kind of sale takes time and it isn't worth it.
We don't need the money, really. Father taught me that a Jew
always has to be ready to run so I have a fortune in jewels
alone."

He grinned. "Wear your fortune, my pretty, it becomes you."

She moved a shade closer to the truth. "Boris, I just can't bear
to think of the Pirov stables falling into strange hands."

Boris ceased smiling. "And how in hell are we going to avoid
that?'"

Ronya answered almost too glibly, "Easy. Give them to your
second son."

His eyes widened. "Are you suggesting that Georgi come
home?"

"I'm not suggesting anything!" she flared. "I'm asking you to

326

legitimatize the Blond One, adopt him legally and give him your name—Boris Pirov. As to the stables, they *are* his. I told his mother he could have them."

Boris, breathing heavily, said, "You had no earthly right to give him anything of mine."

Ronya whipped back, "You had no earthly right to give him life. But you did! Now call him son."

Boris' cry of "No!" was demented. Ronya jumped up and started to run.

"Come back," he called after her. "You're off the path." She stumbled then and fell. Seeing her sprawled on the ground, Boris sprang after her, unmindful of his crippled leg. He gathered her up anxiously. "Are you hurt, baby?"

"Put me *down!*"

Nevertheless Boris carried her up the slope and across the dirt road to the cabin while she protested, "I am *not* hurt! Put me down."

On the threshold he stopped and his lips brushed her nose.

"The Blond One can have the stables," Boris said. "He's earned them. But don't ask anything more than that. I *cannot* call him son."

They sat down late by candlelight to a delicious meal.

"I know you're a scheming imp, my sweet," Boris said, "so I'm experiencing some trepidation about the price of this enticing supper. . . . I'm pretty tired."

There was no flirtatiousness in her gaze as she looked across the round table. "In exactly a week from today, this being Tuesday," she said, "my ship sails for the port of New York. Are you and Julie and Rachel going to be with me?"

Boris leaned his elbows on the table, chin in the palm of one hand. He spoke mildly, almost affably. "Julie must speak for herself."

"She has," Ronya said.

"What a dutiful daughter," Boris mused.

"And what a rotten wife!" Ronya said. "You would have dragged me away from my father by my hair, if necessary."

"The fault must lie with Igor."

"That's cruel and unfair! Is it all you have to say?"

"No, Ronya, it isn't. You'll not take Rachel away from her mother."

Ronya said in a small voice, "What shall I tell Igor?"

"You'll think of something. You always do."

"Yes," she said tonelessly and rose. "Goodbye, Boris. Please stay here in the cabin until I've left. Lydia will come down from the house every day to look after you. And don't be afraid I'll steal Rachel. Julie has already given her to me."

"Given her to you!" Boris was up and around the table and had raised her to her feet. She made no attempt to free herself from his iron grip—it would have been useless. So she stood docile but unafraid.

"Ronya, can you leave me?"

"Yes," she answered.

"Do you love me?"

"As much as life."

"And trust me?"

"Yes."

"Give me a month." His eyes were pleading.

"No."

As Boris carried her into the bedroom and dumped her onto the bed, Ronya knew that nothing, nothing at all, from tears to conjugal rape, could change her mind. He pulled off her boots and began undressing her while she fortified her determination by remembering that she was saving their lives, maybe even Katya's. He can't live without me, she recited to herself like a litany. He can't cut Igor and Georgi out of his heart.

Boris struggled to pull a long nightgown over her head and drag her limp arms through the sleeves. At last having accomplished this, he was about to ease her under the comforter when Ronya said, "I have to go to the bathroom."

"You don't need a chaperone. Go!"

Ronya said, "You put me to bed. It's your duty to take me. My feet are cold." And Boris sat down on the bed while Ronya climbed onto his shoulders so he could carry her piggyback, arms wound around his neck. In the half dozen steps between bed and bathroom all Boris' resentment evaporated.

Snugly bedded down for the second time, Ronya was pleased

with herself and her world. One minute she was capable of slamming doors and shrieking insults, the next mend the damage by simply being herself. Now, in the stillness of the dark room, she nestled against Boris, stroking his back. Boris knew he was being maneuvered but liked the way she did it. He rolled over and kissed her.

"Oh, Boris," Ronya sighed. "I never for a moment had the least intention of taking Igor his child without his wife—not for his sake, not for Julie's, but for Rachel's. How could I live with myself if I made Julie do to Rachel what Rhea did to her?"

Boris nuzzled his leonine head into the crook of her neck. "You must go, my darling little dove, and I must stay here. I'll reach San Francisco a month or so after you do, with Julie and Rachel."

"Oh, Boris, I've waited so long already!" She was fighting down tears. "Why can't we all go together, next week? I hate to travel alone. Without you the sea will be cold and forbidding."

"I have business in Odessa," he said.

"The devil with it! Give those barren hills to your relatives or will them to the sea gulls. I know in my heart that you shouldn't drag on here."

"It's not the hills, pet. I have to put a cross on my mother's grave. It's an obligation only I can fulfill."

"You mean your mother's grave is unmarked?"

"Yes. I had to postpone meeting Stolypin when Rachel was so sick. I couldn't very well put him off a second time, nor refuse to ride in the Tsar's escort."

Ronya slid down in bed. "Let's get some sleep, darling. If we can, we'll leave for Odessa early tomorrow."

"Raise yourself up on the pillow so I can look at you," Boris said. "I can't leave Kiev now. Within two weeks Mendel Beilis goes on trial. The judge is from St. Petersburg and a vicious anti-Semite. You can be sure the jury will be drawn a hundred percent from the Black Hundreds and the Jewish community will be barred from the courtroom. I have to be there to represent them and support Mischuk and Beilis."

Ronya flung herself on Boris, kissing his eyes and his mouth.

329

Then, half laughing, half crying, she said, "Why didn't you tell me, my honorable Boris? I'll wait, gladly, until you're ready to go to your sons."

"There's something else—"

"What?"

"This cabin, dear love. Stone by stone, plank by plank, the way I built it, I have to take it down. I *must.*"

Ronya ached at the heartbreak in his voice. "Yes, you must. I'll wait."

He forced her awake, cupping her small, triangular face in his hands and his voice sounded almost raucous in the quiet night. "I want you to go!"

"Don't think you can get rid of me, Boris Pirov," she rebelled, "just because I was such an imbecile as to think you were stalling. I'll not be pushed off."

She was his girl again, eighteen, standing imperiously at the head of a staircase saying, "Choose, Boris Pirov!"

"And what will you tell Igor if you don't go to him now?"

"I'll think of something. I always do."

"No," he said wearily, "Igor's borne enough. Have no fear. We will be with you in a few weeks in your promised land." And Ronya knew that she must do what he asked.

The next two days they spent like honeymooners. When they were closing the cabin door for the last time, a late autumn thunderstorm was raging and Boris said a strange thing. "Ronya, wait for the next clap of thunder, then swear to me that you will never take another man."

Lightning forked the sky and to the drumming of the thunder, Ronya said, "I swear it in God's name."

They walked back to the house through the rain.

The station platform was crowded with well-wishers but at this last moment, the family had closed in together for its farewells.

"I bid you a pleasant journey," Alexis was saying. "For the present, *au revoir,* Ronya—still the most beautiful girl in Kiev." He was sobbing.

Katya said, *"Glückliche Reise,"* with tears in her voice.

330

Julie's choking sobs were drowned out by Rachel. "Tell Igor, my father, I want him to get me a pure white colt."

Lydia wrung her hands. "Who am I going to serve for the rest of my life?"

Ronya and the Blond One clung to each other.

"We can delay no longer, Mistress Pirov," the conductor fumed. "Board the train, if you please," but she was whispering to the young man and went on until Boris took his arm and led him away.

It seemed to the harried conductor that the Pirovs were disentangling themselves and he could signal the engineer to depart. His hope died when Tamara sidled out of the crowd leading a small girl dressed in red.

"Say goodbye to your granddaughter," she said insolently, and Boris took a step to put himself between the two women. But Ronya unhesitatingly dropped to her knees and gathered the child into her arms. In full sight of everyone, she looked deep into the little girl's eyes.

"What is my name?" the child asked and Ronya replied immediately, "Your name is Queen."

The conductor shouted desperately, "All abo-a-r-d!" and Rabbi Levinsky's voice was so low it could hardly be heard, "God go with you, Ronya." Boris lifted Ronya up the high step. They did not say goodbye; they never said goodbye. Wordlessly he handed her her whip. "I hope you won't need it, little dove."

"Please, Gospodin Pirov—" the conductor wailed but Ronya did not relax her embrace, Boris did not tear his lips from hers. The conductor semaphored. As the train started to move slowly, family, friends, gypsies fell back, even Boris jumped clear as it picked up speed.

Half-blinded with tears, Ronya groped to her compartment. Standing at the door was a thin, bearded man. "Reuben!" she cried.

"Huang does not like you to travel alone, my lady."

XXXVII

KATYA, just returned from Odessa, where she had gone with Boris, was resting in bed when Lydia appeared with a laden supper tray. "Lydia, you have no business carrying trays," she scolded. "You're puffing."

"It's my feet," Lydia said. She sliced the breast of cold chicken expertly thin, the way the countess preferred it, poured dill dressing into a bowl of raw, shredded cabbage and announced, "I came to talk."

Katya pointed to a chair and Lydia allowed herself to perch on the arm. "Another two weeks gone—just slipped away. What's going to happen to us next?" she said.

"I don't know," Katya sighed. "On our way home from Odessa we stopped a night at an inn. Boris' foot was one swollen mass of flesh and when I winced at the sight of it, he told me not to look at him, said he was no longer Boris.

"But now he seems like his old self, energetic enough, though he does keep changing plans and procrastinating."

"May I be allowed to tell the countess how he lives these days?"

"Of course. Why do you ask?"

"I'm never entirely comfortable with you, my lady," Lydia said in a slightly injured tone. "Even as a child you weren't one to make friends with the gypsies or the children of peasants. Only Ronya did that."

Katya smiled. "That's nonsense, Lydia, and you know it. Now get on with what you came to tell me and drop the 'countess.' From you, old friend, it's a bore."

Lydia smiled, too, satisfied. "Did I tell you, Katya, that he'd had the portrait of Ronya moved out of his room and hung it in hers where he sleeps now? It's on the wall beside the bed."

Katya nodded.

"And that I moved into the old nursery and leave the door open just a crack at night? Yes, I suppose I did. Well, Boris has been acting queer the last three nights. After you go to bed and he says goodnight to Julie, he takes himself to Rachel's room and that's no ordinary visit.

"Sometimes he paces with her in his arms. Sometimes they sit and rock and he tells her stories about Tartar heroes and makes her promise to be proud of her Tartar blood. Then he calls her 'little Ronya' and she says, 'You're all mixed up, Boris, my grandfather. I am Rachel.'

"That tickles him. 'You're a beautiful little dove, that's what you are,' he says. Then he tucks her into bed and goes to Ronya's room to drink. In a little while he begins to talk to her picture, rambling on about how he used to snatch at every pretty girl and damning himself and saying he never loved anyone but her. He weeps and curses. 'My leg is growing cold,' says he. 'Will my loins fail next? Is this my punishment? Tamara was piss on the wind, the Blond One an albatross to my sons.' He carries on like that until the vodka knocks him out, fully dressed, across the bedspread.

"Then I look in and tidy up. He hates to wake to a mess. I open the windows, pull the quilt over him and five or six hours later fetch tea and two glasses. By that time he's all bathed and shaved. For five minutes we drink hot tea, sour with lemon, sweet with sugar. We're just friends. And before I leave he grins and thanks me for taking care of him. When he comes down to breakfast he is Boris, my master, again. I look at that golden eagle and think, Last night I was dreaming. It never happened.

"What do you make of it, Katya?"

"All I can say, Lydia, is come and tell me every morning what's happened the night before. And don't be worried. Boris won't break his word to Ronya and Igor."

Lydia waddled out of Katya's sitting room to the hall, where she stood to deliver a parting shot. "Light a fire under him. He crawls when he should be running. With Ronya gone he has no peace in his soul."

The old servant never knew how well she had succeeded. Katya spent most of the day brooding over what to do about Boris' emotional turmoil. In the afternoon she found Julie happily sorting out treasures she intended to take with her and the idea was born. Katya delivered her blow that evening, after Julie had gone to sing Rachel to sleep. Boris was delighted to have her to himself—Alexis had long since hurried off to Moscow—and said, "Play for me, Katya."

She finished drawing coffee from the porcelain urn, handed him a cup and remarked, "I would prefer to play for my husband."

"Odd that you should say that now, Katya." Boris was not on guard. "After all, he'll be back in a few days."

"Of course." She stirred her coffee. "He comes. He goes. But I am forced to stay here with you and Julie."

"What do you mean 'forced'?"

She looked at him coolly; then her glance fell to the Dresden cup in her hand and she seemed to drift away from him.

"Let's start from the beginning, Katya," Boris sounded severe. "If you want to leave Kiev, why don't you? Fortunately Lydia and the maids are still in service here. We'll manage nicely."

"That's just it, Boris," she sprang her trap. "You *do* manage nicely—*very* nicely indeed. At least with me here as official, if ineffective, chaperone, there can't be any ugly gossip. Because I'm loyal to Ronya, I have to sacrifice Alexis . . . to protect our good name."

Boris cringed. "Please, Katya," he implored, "say you didn't mean that. I can't bear to believe that the thought crossed your mind or that you could bring yourself to say it out loud."

"I meant exactly what I said."

Boris ran his fingers through his hair distractedly, went to make sure the library door was shut and stood listening for Julie's light step.

Katya looked at him affectionately. "Don't you go baring those strong white teeth at me, Boris Pirov," she said. "I'm not Ronya."

"Goddamn it, you're right you're not! Since she left everyone around here has gone crazy. And who's to blame for that? Me! I let her go."

Katya said, "Are you ready to listen to me?"

"If I had any choice"—Boris' expression was wry—"I'd say no."

She went to him and looked full into his face. "Boris dear, I do respect you and love you but—" His right arm shot out and she was in his lap, her long, elegant legs, from under the crispness of her petticoats, dancing in the air.

"Go easy," Boris teased, pulling down her skirts. "We're relatives."

Laughing against her better judgment, Katya could not resist him. "Boris, you make me feel like Rachel and you've driven my lecture right out of my head. I was going to remind you that Julie isn't your daughter biologically, a fact you seem to forget, but an exceedingly pretty young woman who has slept alone too long."

"Don't," he whispered, running his fingers over her mouth. "You von Glasman girls talk too much."

"Please, please, take yourself off to Ronya," Katya pleaded. "And take Julie to Igor—she needs him. She's twenty-five years old, Boris, and not a child anymore."

His lips were against her ear. "Come with us, Katya."

When Julie returned from the nursery, Katya was curled up on the sofa, Boris pacing the floor. Katya reached out to her. "Sing for us, Julie," she begged.

As long as they lived all three of them remembered that song. Father Tromokov, his cassock flapping, burst in on the middle of it. Lydia was right behind him.

"You'd think a priest would have the manners to wait to be announced," she rattled. Tromokov pushed her toward the lacquered chest.

"Get me a drink and stop babbling."

The priest did not sit down but stood to gulp his drink, not in itself exceptional, but Boris detected anxiety in his abrupt movements, even in the firmly shut mouth.

"If the empty glass in your hand," Boris drawled, "prevents you from speaking, Lydia will refill it. Think I'll join you, as a matter of fact."

"All hell's to pay, Boris," Tromokov said in a heavy voice. "The Tsar has dismissed every anti-Rasputin man in the regime, right up to Kokovtsov—*he's* lucky to have gotten away with his life. The workers, about half a million of them, are striking and the fool police are firing on them. The miners are in a particularly grim spot. In some parts of the country the peasants are in open rebellion. In others the Cossacks are on the rampage. And we have plenty of problems without all that, as you know."

"Beilis?"

The priest nodded. "The eternal Jew. Always and forever resented, pursued, destroyed." Tromokov was near tears.

"What's happened?" Boris asked softly.

"Our good Mischuk has been kicked out to a wretched little job in Georgia. Given five days, Boris, *five* days after all his years here! The twenty-two Christian lawyers hired to defend Beilis have been disbarred from the practice of law and are under arrest, charged with conspiracy against the Tsar."

Boris was dumbfounded. "How in God's name could it happen and not a ripple reach us here or in Odessa? I—"

The priest held up his hand. "Wait! There's more. The Revenge Rider has been designated Stolypin's murderer and Dmitri Bogrov is a free man." Automatically he handed Lydia his glass. "Vodka," he said, "refreshes even the most holy palate and I have some distinctly unholy things to tell you still."

Julie interrupted to ask about her village; Katya was frantic for news of Alexis and Lydia wondered about her son Ivan, who had married a girl from Borowsk and lived there.

Boris sat in terrible stillness. All of Huang's warnings, all of Ronya's importunings passed through his mind. He was a fool, a deluded, gutless fool. Out of his nightmare, he roared, "Shut up, all of you!

"What's happened has happened," Boris said more quietly. "We'll put things right as soon as I know whom we have to deal with—the Tsar or Rasputin."

Father Tromokov regarded Boris with a troubled eye, thinking, You can put nothing to rights, my golden friend. Go to Ronya!

Aloud, he said, "Rasputin is not going to be simple to deal with." He clenched his glass. "Rasputin is in fact on his way back from Siberia, and Nicholas has vowed to end Judaism in Russia. Any Jews who refuse to be Russified—by acepting baptism—will die where they are, or die in prison camps slowly."

Boris jeered. "Priest, isn't that God of yours interested in all this? Or is he too holy to pay attention to the affairs of men?"

Tromokov bowed his head. "Believe in him, Boris. Out of grief and suffering, man draws strength."

Boris' grin was sardonic.

"I'm sure what Father Tromokov has told us will change Alexis' plans, Boris," Katya said. "He can't possibly get here in time to say goodbye. But in a way it doesn't matter. What does matter is that with Rasputin back, he'll be leaving St. Petersburg for good. We'll have a great reunion before the summer is over and a celebration to remember."

With terrible frankness, Boris said, "Katya, you know better."

She turned white. "Come, Julie," she said, "you must get some rest. You're leaving Russia tomorrow."

"That decision is up to me," Boris declared. "I shall tell Julie the date and it will not be until after Alexis gets here."

Katya's cheeks flamed. "You made my sister a promise!"

"And I shall keep it, Katya."

"Come to bed, Julie," she said frostily.

Julie hung back. "I want to ask Father Tromokov a question."

"Anything you like, little Julie."

"I have been thinking and thinking. How is it that you know everything? What happens in St. Petersburg and the Summer Palace and Siberia and the mine fields. I can't find a word about it in the paper. Even Tamara, who hears everything, hasn't sent any messages lately."

Tromokov pantomimed applause. "Dear pupil," he said, "if no one had asked that I'd have been dreadfully disappointed." He pulled himself out of his armchair and poured another drink. "Lydia, you pearl among women, bring me food!"

"Not unless I hear the answer first."

"The answer is a great secret which your master will share with you and Julie when you're far from this pagan land." To Katya he said, "I'd like to concentrate on my Sunday sermon. An infidel who can hear individual snowflakes is better off than me trying to think over the creaks and groans of my cottage window frames. I'll stay here tonight."

Julie turned to Boris. "Will you come into my room a little later for your song?"

"No, Julie," he said quietly.

Lydia brought his supper and Father Tromokov blustered, "Meddling old female—out! I'll serve myself. And no dusting the keyhole. You're too fat to squat."

Boris himself led her to the door. "Be comfortable in your own bed, Lydia," he said. "I promise not to get drunk."

She gazed up. "Do you mind if I don't, sir? I like being in the nursery and hearing you breathe."

"Lydia, you're a jewel."

"And that's plain truth," she chuckled.

The priest was stuffing himself with smoked herring, pickled cucumbers and spiced tomatoes, cheeks distended. "Go to Ronya," he said, despite his full mouth. "You're a fish out of water without her."

"I'm glad you stayed on." Boris disregarded his remark. "I wanted a word with you. It may interest you to know that I heard about your fluttering off to Moscow. Did you see Alexis and were you with the archbishop?"

"Yes, and he sent you word to get the hell out of here." The priest smiled. "The wording is strictly mine."

Boris stood silent and a change came over his face. Tromokov thought he had never seen a man look so sad. "Sit down, Boris," he said.

Boris refilled their glasses and took a chair close to the priest's. "The last few nights I've spent in a haze of vodka. Can't seem to sleep with Ronya gone."

"Your leg?"

"That, too."

"Stop punishing yourself, man. Go!"

"I will . . . in a few days."

"Too late," his friend warned. "I'm told the borders are going to be closed so no Jews can escape—barbed wire, soldiers, police dogs. You won't be able to get Julie and Rachel out."

"Russia has no borders for me," Boris mocked. "I know ways in and out the Tsar never heard of. There'll be no patrols on *my* tail."

"Boris," the priest exploded, "you'd try the patience of a

338

saint. Think of the weather, which isn't in your favor, and the fact that you'll be handicapped with two women and a child. What wretched reason have you for delaying? It's murder to drag Julie and Lydia and Rachel through the forest. Leave for the border tomorrow by train."

"There's one thing I have to do. After that we'll leave."

"The cabin?"

Boris nodded.

"Let me and the Blond One help."

"No. It's after midnight now. I'll start at daybreak."

"Well, if that's the way it's got to be, at least get some sleep."

Boris said, "I have the rest of my life for sleep. Don't you abandon me. When I'm alone I'm haunted by—presentiments."

Early in the morning Boris and the Blond One talked in the stable.

"You'll be alone but I'll be within hearing distance of our signal if you need me," Boris said. "You're to keep watch on the wood road to the house but there's no hurry. Father Tromokov is there. Put whoever you think is up to it in charge here. Then load a couple of wagons with guns and ammunition from the camp and send them to Julie's village. The priest there will know what to do with them. If the Cossacks ride I want the peasants armed with more than pitchforks and scythes."

"Expect trouble?"

"No, not yet. The storm won't hit Kiev until after we're gone."

The Blond One's brows went up and Boris was startled—that was Ronya's look.

"Rasputin's back," Boris said, as he mounted his stallion and headed him toward the cabin.

The first hours were torment. Ronya was everywhere. Even physical reminders of her remained—a ribbon with which she tied up her long hair when she bathed, a half-empty box of cigarettes, a crumpled lawn handkerchief on her dressing table, still breathing a ghostly whiff of her perfume. Thinking of her limitless delight in cooking, he walked into the empty kitchen. There was a bottle of vodka on a shelf and he took it down.

What had been built in love and gladness, he began to destroy in sorrow and pain. Boris worked until he was drenched with sweat, stopping briefly to peel off his coat, and later his shirt, at each interruption fortifying himself with a swallow of vodka. By late afternoon he felt unsteady and realized he had not eaten all day or slept the night before. And the cabin was sturdily built; he was a fool to think he could bring it down in a day or two.

Ideas blurred and ran together: Little dove, I'm sick. I need you . . . got to take Julie and Rachel away . . . sent Igor off. Why? . . . Julie go alone? . . . Wild oats . . . Destroy, demolish, wreck, crash, topple, smash! Madness. . . .

Words faded and in their place came pictures. Of Ronya, dark eyes laughing, lips parted, bronze hair glinting, nothing else, no hands, no body and the phantom was two entities, Rachel-Ronya, Ronya-Rachel, one dove.

His mother's icy face appeared and her voice sounded from beyond the grave. "You thought a cross would lock me in." He shook his head—"You're dead." "Neither heaven nor hell can hold me." He took a mighty swing at a strong upright, intoning, "I am stronger than you." "Come with me." "You're dead." "You got lost in the hot jungle of a Jewess' love. Come back to the Tartar womb."

Boris felt a warm presence and his stallion nuzzled his cheek and breathed against the skin like a faithful friend reminding him that it was time to go home. He flung his axe aside, picked up his coat and sprang into the saddle.

His mother's voice followed him. "Death rides a white horse."

Boris screamed, caught his breath and leaned low over the stallion's neck. "We're being followed by a Tartar woman out of hell who rides a horse. Run!" he panted.

His panic was contagious. The horse flung up his head, the long mane tossing, neighed wildly and gave one frenzied jump. Boris knew that he must fall and tried to free his feet from the stirrups, but his right leg was paralyzed with pain. The white stallion fell, his great body rolling onto Boris' agonized leg.

When he regained consciousness the sky was dark, the pine forest darker. His head was clear and his horse was thrashing helplessly. Useless to try to free his leg. His jacket was open and spread out, the pistol lying within reach. Somehow he succeeded in raising it to the stallion's head, he fired and the animal shuddered and lay still.

Again he raised the gun, pointing it toward the sky, and fired. One, two, three times slowly. One, two, fast. It was the signal agreed upon with the Blond One, but had he stationed him too far off to hear? Boris lay still, controlling his breathing.

The Blond One came running lightly along the road. Kneeling beside his father, eyes brimming with tears, he asked, "Are you in pain?"

"Surprisingly little. Get help."

They heard running feet and Tamara, carrying a lantern, burst out of the surrounding darkness. "Run!' She jerked the Blond One to his feet and took his place beside Boris.

"Listen, Boris," she said, her lips against his ear. "I know how to cure your leg with oil from the bark of trees, the juice of downy leaves and magic roots from under the earth. I will kill your hurt and keep your leg alive."

Damn her! She saw her chance to come into Ronya's house, take Ronya's place, even try to get into Ronya's bed! The idea filled Boris with so violent a wave of revulsion that he found strength to speak.

"Listen to *me*, Tamara. Listen well. My Ronya inherited you with her land and for some absurd reason of her own—God knows why—she loves you. To me you are—" His voice faded. "Just leave me," he whispered. "I'd rather be dropped in a limestone pit than—"

In crazy abandon, Tamara took his face between her hands and kissed his eyes and lips.

Boris lifted his head with a groan. "Damn you, you gypsy bitch!"

Tamara rocked back on her heels. "We have broken bread together. We have a son," she cried.

A wave of relief flowed over Boris. There was a sound of galloping horses. By the light of torches the men freed him, lifted him into a wagon and onto a bed of straw, wrapping blankets around his numb body. The Blond One held out the nearly empty bottle of vodka but Boris shook his head.

"Katya and Julie—do they know?"

"I didn't stop at the house. Only took time to bang on Father Tromokov's door. He galloped off at once for the doctor."

Boris beckoned to Tamara. "Ride on ahead and prepare Katya and Julie and don't frighten them. Then fetch men to bury my stallion right here."

"Someone else can attend to that," Tamara flounced. "You'll need me at the house to nurse you."

You dirty whore, he thought. "After my stallion is buried, go to your own house, Tamara. And *stay* there!"

By way of answer she climbed onto the hub of a wheel and leaned far over him. "Don't send me away, Boris. I'll heal you."

Sick with humiliation, the Blond One pulled her down.

"Make up for your lack of pride and pity. My father is hurt. Can't you think of anyone but yourself?"

She got into the saddle of a horse that stood beside the wagon. "When you need me, Boris Pirov," her voice carried far into the woods, "send for me!"

Tamara saw Julie open her mouth to scream and slapped her roundly across the face. "Little fool! All he needs is hysterics." Katya, judging that Tamara had acted wisely, said, "Go, Julie. They won't be here for another ten minutes." But Julie sat down on the edge of Katya's sofa and regained her composure.

In a somber voice she asked Tamara, "How serious is it? Tell us the truth."

"He's lucky, Julie. He can move his leg and he isn't in pain. I doubt if he has a broken bone." They studied her face to learn if she was telling them all she knew and in her expression Katya sensed her torment. Ronya is right, she thought. We're all strangely bound together.

"Don't try to see your father, Julie, until he's been put to bed," Tamara added.

Julie's face clouded, "I'll go if he asks for me."

"By all means," Katya said.

"Walk me to the door." Tamara took Katya's hand and Julie watched them go. She sat alone, waiting, for half an hour. Then the door opened and Katya said, "Come along, dear. He's been bathed and is settled and wants you to sing to him till the doctor arrives."

The seconds it took to get to Boris' door denied Julie her pleasure. The doctor had arrived. Julie and Katya, the Blond One and Father Tromokov clustered beside the partially open door while he made his examination, fragmentary phrases reaching them. ". . . where it hurts." "Good." ". . . flex your foot." And, at last, he called, "Come in."

Clinging to her self-control, Julie entered first. Lydia was pulling the covers over Boris' leg and the doctor announced, "Nothing serious. No broken bones. Except for some contusions I'd say you're fine."

"Does that mean, doctor, that you attach no great importance to his injury?" Katya asked.

"Absolutely, Countess."

"In that case my brother-in-law can leave for America soon?"

"Indeed he can. True, the leg is very cold but in general the color is good. A week, maybe less, in my considered opinion."

"Thank you, doctor."

He bowed. "I shall prescribe for my patient and then I presume the young gentleman will take me home? Unfortunately I did not come in my own carriage—"

Father Tromokov laughed. "My apologies, sir. I was so afraid the accident was lethal I trembled for my friend's soul. The Blond One will give you a gentler ride back. Will you have a drink before you set out?"

"A sip of wine, perhaps." The Blond One brought a decanter and glasses on a tray.

"I want that leg raised on pillows and cold compresses applied around the clock." Reaching into his bag, he took out a small white envelope and gave it to Katya. "If Gospodin Pirov has trouble sleeping, give him a teaspoon of this powder in a glass of hot milk."

He rose. Boris seemed to be lost in thought and said only, "Good night," but the man lingered.

"Your strength must be the envy of the gods," he said grandiloquently. "Even in a youth your physique would be phenomenal. Eat everything you want. Drink as much as you

343

like. Smoke if you wish. I'll look in again. If not tomorrow, the day after."

Father Tromokov followed him across the room, saying, "A restful night to you, Boris. I'll see you tomorrow."

Boris smiled wanly. "Bring Levinsky with you. That way you can convince each other."

"You're wrong, Boris." The priest stopped, momentarily. "I won't bother you now." He regretted having spoken.

"I'll not eat a wafer to save my soul, you can depend on that. Piety is not my natural diet."

Tromokov's lips moved and Julie whispered, "Amen," her tongue reverting to the Hebrew pronunciation.

As soon as they had packed Boris' leg in compresses and raised it on a heap of pillows, the women went to work transforming Ronya's bedroom into a sitting room. They moved in a second sofa, a round table for suppers and everything else that would make visitors comfortable. The sound of their voices and the bustle of activity pleased Boris as he watched them and made suggestions of his own. Finally Lydia bowed herself out, leaving him to Katya and Julie. Knowing Boris' penchant for quiet, they fell silent until he said, "Get some rest, my loves. I can manage by myself. And only one wall separates me from Lydia. She'll hear if I call."

Katya said, "Boris, dear, dear Boris, are you unaware that neither Julie or I can get along without you? One of us will always be here."

He smiled at Julie, already comfortably settled on the far side of the big bed. "Sing to us, daughter, and I'll go to sleep."

Her eyes went to the pile of pillows. "I'm thinking and thinking," she said, "that your doctor is an idiot."

Katya, who had taken her shoes off and was already half-asleep on the sofa, sat up abruptly. "What's come over you, child?"

There was an obstinate look on Julie's face. "Ronya, my mother, taught me: cold is for hot—for a headache. But cold for cold makes no sense. Your leg is like ice, Boris, my father, and the doctor orders more cold. I don't trust him."

Katya was alarmed. "We'll telegraph your uncle in the morning and have him send a consultant from St. Petersburg, just to make certain."

344

"That's good," Julie said, "but I want Ronya, my mother, home. She's the only one who'll know what to do and how to do it."

Boris' voice was like the snap of a whip. "Under no circumstances are you to summon Ronya to Kiev. Is that clear?"

"It's clear, Boris, my father, but it's wrong. If I didn't let her know you'd had an accident, she'd never forgive me."

"I am master here. I make the decisions. And I give the orders," Boris said angrily.

On the verge of tears, Julie reached for his hand. "I didn't mean to upset you. I'm sorry."

Despite his harshness, Boris was delighted with Julie. How wonderfully she had made herself like Ronya! And Katya thought, Julie's instinct is extraordinary.

"I made a promise to your mother and Igor," Boris said. "I never break my word. There's a Bible in the top drawer of that dresser. I set no great store by it, Julie, but I know you do. Get it and swear that you'll not worry anyone and not drag Ronya back here needlessly."

Julie neither moved or answered.

"Julie!" Katya had risen and gone to the foot of the bed. Dazed with fatigue and baffled by her docile niece's independence, she spoke wearily. "By any chance, Julie, have you forgotten the ordeal your father has been through? Give him your promise. There's no reason to frighten the rest of the family. The whole thing will be over in a few days and Boris will be on his way to America, taking you and Lydia and Rachel with him."

Julie mumbled into Boris' shoulder, "I promise."

"Am I safe with you?" Boris asked Katya.

"Of that you may be certain."

"Would you mind putting that in the form of a proper pledge? I've been brought up not to trust women."

"No. How about a dose of that white powder?" Katya asked. "Or are you some sort of miracle man who's learned to live without sleep?"

She drew a winning grin from Boris. "If I had a second chance, I'd still pick you for my one and only sister, beautiful Katya."

"Perhaps we'll all have hot milk," she said.

His grin widened. "Vodka," he said. "Then go to bed. Julie will stay and sing to me."

Katya bent over and kissed him. "Good night, you two. Sweet dreams."

Julie sang then, of Solomon, King of Israel, of brides and horses and luckless fellows and beggars. Her little Yiddish melodies ranged from love to woe to humor. And Boris understood not a word but, warmed by her closeness and her vigil, he slept.

When Lydia tiptoed in to relieve Julie, the girl, her head on Boris' shoulder, was atop the quilts, sleeping as quietly as he. Lydia lowered herself onto the sofa and was soon dozing.

Boris woke, surprised to find himself perfectly comfortable. Daylight was seeping through the shutters. Expecting Katya or Julie, he saw instead Lydia, standing firmly on her flat feet, beaming at him. It was apparent that she was in charge of his person.

"Oh, no," he protested. "You're too young and far too innocent. Send in the Blond One. I'm shy of female nurses."

Lydia continued to beam. "Ring when you're ready for breakfast," she said.

Right after her lunch, Rachel came in with Beljik, climbed on Boris' bed and seated herself on his chest. She looked at him from under long lashes and her eyes were Ronya's, sorrowing. Boris realized that she was grieving not for his hurt but at the loss of the white stallion. He took the child in his arms, hands stroking, eyes caressing her.

"Do you want to ask me something, little Rachel?"

"I am to amuse you and not ask questions," she announced primly. "If I play too hard or crawl under the covers and bounce your leg, I mayn't come to see you by myself again. That's what Katya, my aunt, said."

Boris preserved the gravity of the occasion. "I'm sure, Rachel, that if we talk ver-y quietly, Katya, your aunt, will forgive a few questions."

"I love you best." The little girl flushed with pleasure. "Even more than Beljik."

"Do you want to talk about the white stallion, angel child?"

"He was my second-best friend, Boris, my grandfather. Don't let him be dead."

Boris hugged her.

Tromokov and Levinsky arrived in time for supper at the round table. Until after Lydia and the maids had cleared away, neither one tried to transform Boris into a believer; then they strove passionately for his godless soul. Father Tromokov fired the first shot. He sat and talked. He paced and talked. He went back to his chair and talked. Suddenly he gave up. "Damn it, Boris, you're not even listening!"

"That's right," said Boris cheerfully.

The only possible consolation was in vodka and the priest availed himself of it, muttering, "Numbskull!"

It was Levinsky's turn. Believing that Boris had sucked his mother's paganism in with her milk, he tried a different tack. "Because of you and Ronya," he said, "Ivan the priest and Joseph the rabbi came to know and love each other. To us this is not unnatural. We are both men of God, both orthodox and of the same mind. All that we want is that you make your peace with God."

"Just in case?"

"That's right. Who has a contract? Life vanishes like smoke."

"So," Boris spoke mockingly, "one of you men of God wants the soul of the baptized Arghun and the other wants the husband of the Jewess. Toss a coin, my friends. Winner take me. I'll be six feet underground and not give a fig either way."

Father Tromokov maintained a wrathful silence but Levinsky said, "All I came to say, Boris, is—you have a Jewish wife. Your children are Jews. Be a Jew, too. Because if you're not, your last sleep will not be at the side of Ronya."

The priest pondered. For all he wanted to bring Boris to the arms of Christ, he did not want to remove him from the arms of Ronya. When he spoke, it was from his loving heart.

"Be a Jew, Boris. Joseph has spoken truly."

XXXVIII

BORIS let the book slide onto the counterpane. With the consultant from St. Petersburg downstairs, he could not concentrate. He was excited at the prospect of meeting the man Alexis had described so eloquently. Of a rare breed, Alexis maintained, this doctor's thinking was sufficiently unorthodox to have created a stir among his medical colleagues. Still comparatively young, he was said to have warm, strikingly communicative eyes. To himself Boris admitted the full extent of his worry, which he measured by the impatience with which he listened for the doctor's knock at his door.

When it came, he sang out, "Come in." For a man of action it is difficult to wait, nearly impossible pinned to a bed.

The doctor walked across the room and held out his hand. "I am Sergei Sergeyev. I insisted on coming upstairs alone and introducing myself."

Smaller and slighter than Boris had expected; Alexis had made him sound grand and grandeur was equated in Boris' mind with largeness. But there was something about him, a confidence, almost a radiance, that invited trust. Surprisingly, too, his grip was robust. Conscious that the doctor was reading his thoughts, and noting the sparkle of laughter in his eyes, Boris was delighted.

"Pull up a chair," he said, "and sit down."

The doctor smiled. "I choose my friends on impulse. Do you mind if I call you Boris?"

"It is a compliment, Sergei."

"With your permission, Boris, I will make my first examination immediately," the doctor said.

He took off his jacket, went into the bathroom and washed

his hands, then stripped the blankets off Boris' injured leg. First he lowered his head and smelled the toes, then felt the skin and searched for pulse and temperature. With one finger he pressed the flesh above the blackened area and taking a needle from the lapel of his coat, dotted it lightly along the skin, with each gentle prod asking, "Sharp or dull?" From thigh down he explored, following the path of the major nerves. The same procedure was repeated over the length and breadth of the left leg. He looked at Boris' hands and fingers, felt for the pulse in the groin, listened to heart, lungs and stomach, auscultated the chest, looked into Boris' eyes and ears. Only then did he pull the blanket up over his patient.

Dr. Sergei Sergeyev made no comment but went back to the bathroom and once more washed his hands. Upon his return he pulled up a chair and sat down. Taking up the bottle of vodka from the bedside table, he poured two drinks and gave one to Boris. After the first swallow Boris felt his taut nerves relaxing. Nothing whatever was said until he put down his empty glass. Then Sergei Sergeyev spoke.

"You realize, of course, that your accident is not solely responsible for your condition?"

Boris gave a tight nod.

"How long have you been troubled?"

"Years—on and off."

"And done what?"

"Drunk vodka." Boris sounded defiant.

"Not bad medicine," said Sergei uncritically. "Smoke much?"

"I used to."

"What made you stop?"

"My leg seemed to bother me more when I smoked a lot."

"Did anything besides tobacco increase your discomfort?"

"Yes." Boris looked down at his hands. "It was always worse when my wife—Ronya—was away."

"Any pain in your left leg?"

"I get a tingle now and then."

"Arm?"

"Nothing." Boris winged them out tentatively.

The questions ceased. Boris looked like a man who was debating whether to volunteer information.

"Doctor, in recent years I've lived a life of comparative restraint. Before that my physical excesses were monstrous."

"I see," Sergei was smiling. "So now you're convinced that that's what got you into this—predicament?"

"Is that absurd?"

"On the contrary. If you feel guilt or fear, they're as real handicaps as tumors and can retard your chances of full recovery, perhaps even prevent it."

"Did you say full recovery?" Boris asked. "And could that kind of recovery come in time for me to take my daughter and her child out of Russia? Or will it be too late?"

The doctor sighed. "Boris, my friend, it's my duty to tell you that recovery is for you. Not for your leg."

Hope died in Boris, but not defiance. "Let me tell *you* one thing," he said. "I had a Tartar mother. As soon as I was born she began teaching me to reject weakness. I want the facts."

Heart heavy, Sergei Sergeyev nevertheless maintained his professional calm. "As to facts, I'm afraid that we are going to disagree," he said. "You are concerned with your leg. I am concerned entirely with Boris Pirov the man. Your leg must be amputated. There isn't any pulse behind the knee or in the foot, or feeling in the damaged area. Your foot is black, dry and shriveled and there is no chance of healing because blood can't get to the injured area. Fortunately infection hasn't set in, so your life is not in danger. But the leg must come off and because your circulation is so bad, it must be removed above the knee. I am sorry, Boris, but that's what's got to happen."

The doctor waited for Boris to speak, but what was there to say? He would *not* live a cripple.

Into the pool of silence Sergei tossed an exploratory pebble. "Boris, you rugged, powerful men are ill equipped for physical affliction. But the human animal is a remarkable organism. It adapts."

All Boris could bring himself to utter was a mocking, "Interesting!"

Seeing the man on the bed sitting immobile, as if encased in a carapace of ice, the doctor tried to break through. "This is a time," he said, "that tries men's courage, yours and mine, too.

It's sheer hell to say the word 'amputate.' It makes me feel as though medicine hadn't progressed beyond the Middle Ages.

"Medicine cannot save you from being physically crippled. But that doesn't imply that you will be a psychological cripple. Will you let me help you?"

"How can you?" The voice was surly.

"Would you be willing to tell me what really happened the day of your accident?"

"How in the devil did you guess? And what does it matter now?"

"Like all Russians, Boris, my friend," Sergei said, "I'm something of a mystic, and like any physician, I am a scientist. I believe that the mysteries of the mind can be understood. We have a long way yet to go and so far, here in Russia, except for such rare spirits as Ivan Pavlov, who is doing revolutionary experiments on dogs to establish the nature of what he calls conditioned reflexes, few physicians delve into underlying causes of behavior. We teach our medical students the bones and sinews of their profession, the mechanics of the body, but not the motivations that drive it. And that, coupled with a lack of encouragement to research, makes Russians bad doctors.

"They're far ahead of us in other countries. Vienna has a Jew named Sigmund Freud who says that below the surface of awareness and accessibility, the mind operates like the wind. We can observe what it does but in and of itself it is invisible. Yet it pulls and pushes, builds and destroys. In England a physician called Ernest Jones is also exploring the mind and concludes that human illness stems from mental turmoil."

Boris was no longer thinking about himself and his tension was uncoiling. Sergei took two cigarettes, lit one for himself, the other for Boris, who took it but stamped it out in the ashtray.

"Why not?" the doctor asked, looking at the dead butt. "When a man decides he's beaten, what's one more nail in his coffin?" He lit another and Boris smoked.

"Don't try to go it alone, my friend. You don't have to. That's why I'm here."

"I see what you mean," Boris conceded, "but it's no good. Only my wife can quiet my devil. With her near me I am invincible and unafraid."

"Who is your devil, Boris?"

"Oh, what's the use?" Boris said petulantly. "Will telling you make me whole? Or do you, like my holy friends, want me to see God? To come out of the anesthetic a new man, wise and serene, and the hell with my lost leg so long as I've found my soul? I'm a pretty lucky fellow if I can divine a plan in this stinking mess."

The doctor smiled. "I, myself, find it hard to see God as a sort of little Napoleon, sitting on a throne, judging souls."

Then Boris began to talk, not only of the disastrous night but of the principal people in his life—pouring out his passion for Ronya, his love of Julie, his delight in Rachel. For Igor's guilt he took full blame, passing judgment on himself without mercy.

"Boris," Sergei took advantage of a pause, "tell me more about your mother. Can you remember her before she put you on that wild stallion?"

"No. All my life I've been haunted by memories I can't remember."

"Your father?"

"We were strangers."

He spoke with such finality the doctor, understanding that the curtain obscuring the past had been lowered, asked no more. He studied Ronya's portrait.

"Is it a good likeness?"

"Depends on what you see in it," Boris evaded him.

Smiling, the doctor rose. "I'll come in again soon."

Boris looked up. "Not that it matters now, but I'm curious. If you'd seen me at the time of the accident, instead of nearly five days later, would it have made any difference?"

"No, except that I'd have had you in surgery a day or two sooner."

"How much time have I got before that?"

"No time at all. Every minute now is precious. I'm letting you have early dinner with your family—the ladies got around me and I said yes. Then we're taking you to the hospital. Tomorrow I'll operate."

"Sergei," the film of ice separated them again, "I am not going to be moved out of this bed until Julie and Rachel are on their way to America."

The doctor sat down again. "Boris," he said, "how long since you've seen a newspaper?"

"The tiresome thing about women," Boris fumed, "is the way they swaddle a man in sweetness and silence. Even Rachel is allowed in only if she amuses me. What's happened?"

Sergei gestured to the bottle. "If you want another drink, you're entitled to it."

"That bad?" Boris' eyes narrowed.

"Enough to choke on."

"Shoot! From the hip."

"None of us are going anywhere." The doctor crushed out his cigarette. "At least for the time being. Your son's wife and child aren't going to the United States. I'm not going to London to study with Dr. Jones. It is forbidden to travel out of Russia. Patrols and police ring the borders and are concentrated along the usual escape routes."

The rest was difficult and Sergei hesitated. Boris himself helped. "The drizzle is over, my friend; let's have the rain."

"This house is an armed fortress, at least a hundred men on guard. I'm told a whole platoon of Tartars rode in from Odessa this morning and made camp in the pine grove between the house and stables." Like any decent Russian, he was ashamed to have to admit, "Hatred against the Jews is so vicious by now that even Rasputin is urging that they be let alone."

Boris sank back on the pillows. He looked very tired. "It is indeed a sad day for Russia when Rasputin can be labeled a humanitarian."

His wonderful eyes fixed on Boris, Sergei deliberated. "Like the optimistic lunatic I am, I dare hope some good will come out of this barbarity . . . the foolish Tsar and his crazy wife driven from the throne and monarchy ended. Today's corruption hastens a new era. God grant it may be based on reason and justice!

"At any rate, Count Alexis is bargaining for permission for you to leave Russia—and for me, too. That's my fee, safe conduct across the border. Meanwhile we have enough time to get you well and able to manipulate an artificial leg before you leave. The sooner you do, the sooner you'll be able to resume a normal life."

353

"I'll take that drink now, Sergei. Join me if you will. You're not going to operate tomorrow. Julie and Rachel are my responsibility and they are not going to wait for me. They are leaving now, no matter what the restrictions are. Poor old Lydia will have to stay here but she didn't really want to go and leave her family. I'll need at least twenty-four hours to make arrangements."

Boris in this mood was not a man the doctor wanted to have as an enemy. However, he said with professional crispness, "Not possible. From a medical standpoint—"

"You've had a wearing day. I hope your room is comfortable. And would you present my regrets to the ladies? I'd like to have dinner with Count Alexis."

"Very well," Sergei bowed. "But here are some orders for *you*. Overfatigue or any anxiety that drains your strength will make my job harder and your recovery slower. You're to eat lightly and—"

"Good appetite to you, doctor! I'll see you tomorrow. Not too early. I'll be here!"

Sergei sighed. "You're buying time expensively, Boris." Then he capitulated gracefully. "All right.Twenty-four hours. I have to get you in shape before I operate."

"Thanks, Sergei."

The moment the door closed behind the physician, Boris tugged the bell cord sharply and Lydia scuttled into the room.

"Sit down," he said civilly.

Lydia sat in the chair beside the bed, words streaming from her mouth and tears from her eyes. "Don't blame me. Everyone told me to spare the master, even Tamara, I'll have you know. She's the rose around here. I'm just an old cabbage."

"Blow your nose," Boris said. "Not on your apron, woman!" She wiped it with the back of her hand, complaining, "Easier to manage a sack full of fleas than that Tamara."

Boris exploded into laughter. A little happier, Lydia asked, "What did the big specialist from St. Petersburg say?"

"He enjoyed the muscles in my arms." Boris flexed them and she shrank back dutifully. "Where's Father Tromokov?"

Humor returned to Lydia. "He moved in with Rabbi Levinsky. He's got more stableboys and loyal peasants walking Jewish streets than there are Jews."

"Where's the Blond One? He hasn't been here all day."

"Back. Not more than a quarter of an hour ago. Ever since yesterday afternoon he's been riding from one Cossack chief to another, his saddlebags heavy with gold. He's bought their promise—no pograms around Kiev."

The same rotten nightmare, Boris thought, bribes and intrigue and Rasputin on high. Why didn't I listen to Ronya years ago? My end might have been on a warm summer night, instead of— He shifted in bed and swallowed a lump that was rising in his throat. "Lydia, I want to see Count Alexis. Send supper up as soon as he gets here. And one more thing—I'm afraid it won't be possible for you to go to your mistress with Julie and Rachel. Later, perhaps." Lydia sat looking down at the apron that billowed over her belly.

"I'm glad," she said simply. "I want to see my grandchildren grow up a little so maybe I'll go to live at Borowsk till my mistress comes home."

Better like that, Boris thought. Who would harm old peasants, whatever happened?

Alexis, whom Boris had seen only briefly when he arrived earlier that day, sensed Boris' anger. "I protest, on my honor," he said, "that it was on orders from your medical man."

"Let's not waste time, Alexis," Boris said. He hated to wound his brother-in-law but there was no time for pity. "It's pointless to beat around the bush. I've got to have my leg off." He turned his eyes away, unable to watch the blow go home but could not avert his ears. "For Christ's sake, stop that!" he said.

The sobs slowed. In a faltering voice, Alexis said, "With one leg, Boris, you'll still be more of a man than any other two, including Hercules."

"I'll hang onto that thought."

From the doorway Lydia sang out, "Supper!"

Alexis dallied with the food set before him. "Keep me company and eat," Boris urged. "My job is to stay strong; at least that's what my master, Sergei, says," and Alexis forced himself to swallow a few mouthfuls. Boris' obvious enjoyment of his supper

355

helped to steady him though he was relieved when Lydia removed the last plate and left them alone.

Alexis began to give Boris details of the arrival of the Tartars. "About forty of them came at dawn, Katya tells me, and made camp in the pines, far enough from the house but not too far. No one dreamed they were here till midmorning, when their leader came to pay a formal call. To Katya, he said, 'Countess, news travels fast. We came for our own. You are perfectly safe.' "

He spread his hands helplessly. "Everything would have gone smoothly if Julie hadn't misread the words and panicked. 'Even an animal looks after its own hide,' she apparently screeched. 'They've come to kidnap Boris, my father, and maybe steal Rachel.' That shook even my usually level-headed Katya and the women ran into the house and locked the door. Tamara was sent for and came at a gallop. She and the women held a high-level conference and instructed Lydia that no one was to be admitted and peace had to be maintained around you.

"Then Tamara took to the saddle again and went calling. No one had thought to check on whether Rachel was in the house or not, and she found the young imp and Beljik eating cold chicken and drinking hard cider in the Tartar camp! Tamara got her home fast and Julie put her to bed. She slept like a drunkard all afternoon."

Boris threw back his head and howled with laughter. "You mean she was honestly tipsy?"

"Gloriously," said Alexis. And Boris thought, Now why did Beljik allow that? Perhaps the dog was smarter than any of them.

"Go on." He was in high good humor.

"Tamara was like a whirlwind—everywhere. She rounded up her prettiest girls and sent them along to keep an eye on the Tartars, told 'em to flirt and tell fortunes. That plan misfired. They were met by a sentry with a cold eye and sent packing."

"Did Tamara recognize any of the Tartars?"

"No, Boris. And she studied every face she saw."

Boris' voice was low; his look, undiluted Tartar. "Did they bring a white stallion with them?"

Alexis was immensely tempted to lie, but in the face of Boris' stare his tongue stuck to the roof of his mouth.

"Answer!"

356

Count Alexis Brusilov, the suave and devious diplomat, surrendered. "They brought a young stallion—a big beast and pure white. . . . He could be yours, born all over again."

Strangely, at this moment, the ice that encased Boris thawed, as though certainty were release. Staggered, Alexis cried out, "In heaven's name, Boris, that's too preposterous! You are *not* going to die."

Boris stuck out his lower lip. "Everyone dies. Let's have a drink. Vodka or brandy?"

"Vodka, if I may," said Alexis.

"Forget the Tartars, Alexis." Boris was nursing his drink between steady hands. "I'm sending Julie and Rachel out of Russia with the Blond One."

His plan had been brewing for hours and now he outlined it to Alexis, who was at first skeptical. Then, as he went over the details with Boris, he decided that, while it left a good deal to chance, it was the only way.

Boris felt a slashing pain, like lightning, splitting his head, and rubbed his forehead irritably for a moment, thinking, "God, why didn't I heed Ronya? Me and my grand hopes of Stolypin! What possessed me to risk the lives of the Jews in my family?"

"What can I do to help?" Alexis pulled him back to the present.

"As a starter, answer a question."

"My privilege, Boris."

"How much money did you bring with you?"

"Plenty, and the rest of Katya's jewels."

"Good," said Boris. He lay back. "Please tell Julie and Katya I'd like to see them now. Right away. I'm short on time."

Alexis, on the way to the door, said without turning, "When does the doctor plan to operate?"

In an easy voice, Boris answered, "Don't be frightened. There's no infection. Sergei was in hopes of operating tomorrow. I told him I had to have twenty-four hours and he agreed. He has no misgivings."

After Alexis left, the Blond One came and managed to get Boris to the bathroom with the aid of a crutch, while Lydia made up his bed with fresh sheets and aired the room. They left him as debonair as a god of courage and it was unthinkable that he would never leap in the *gopak* again.

Minutes later Katya, Julie and Alexis arrived, dressed as for a special occasion. Katya looked like a delicious dessert, flambéed with cognac; Julie was a flower, swathed in blue, her hair in a Psyche knot. She went right to Boris and sat on the edge of his big bed. "We finished dinner long ago," she told him, "and we've been talking to the doctor for an hour. I'm not going anywhere except to the hospital with you tomorrow and the Blond One can't go anywhere else, either. You need him, Boris, my father."

Boris was immensely proud of his Julie. "Darling," he said, "there are two reasons for you to leave and one of them is a debt you owe me. Because of what may happen in Russia in the next few months—possibly even civil war—I'll have less to worry about if I know you and Rachel are safe. That's for me. The other is for you. Go to Igor. Start the son you both want."

"No," said Julie flatly. "Igor and I have waited this long. We'll just wait a little longer."

"Listen to me, Julie. I'm—"

She laid her hand on Boris' cheek. "Please, Boris, my father, every reason for my going has already been said. The doctor even grabbed and held me when I tried to run away from Aunt Katya's anger. I'll not go until you're able to travel and we can leave together. I've written Ronya, my mother, to say I have a severe chest cold and a famous doctor from St. Petersburg forbids my making the ocean crossing in winter. We must wait until spring."

Julie dropped her hand and waited for the denunciations she expected from everyone in the room. But there were none, as each person realized how artfully she had made delay possible without bringing Ronya racing home.

"Is that letter posted?" Alexis asked.

"Yes, Uncle Alexis. When the Blond One got back I told him a falsehood. The outer envelope was addressed to Igor. I said, 'Have you time to mail a letter to Igor?' and of course he did."

Lord, thought Boris, a colt learns from its mother. He bent forward and lifted her chin. "I have never asked anything like this of you before."

358

Pale and contained, Julie slewed her eyes around to the clock on the mantel. "Boris, my father," she said, "I think it is time for you to have your hot milk. The doctor said we weren't to stay long, that we could have real talks with you later on."

"What do you say, Alexis?" Boris asked.

"She's a wonder. Katya, my love, tell our astonishing niece that because she lives under its roof, this house is somewhat taller and, indeed, stronger." Katya got up, gave Julie a little hug, then went to the bed smiling her captivating smile, and kissed Boris full on the lips.

"And a kiss from you, little Julie; then I'll keep you no longer."

The Blond One stole into the room about half an hour later to find his father dozing, his face, with his guard down, harrowing to look at. He took a drink of vodka and settled himself in the chair beside the bed to keep watch.

Boris slept and then wakened. The room was full of firelight shadows.

"Been here long?"

"No," the Blond One said.

The young man held out his hand. On the palm lay Rachel's cross, which he had brought from his father's room.

"Put it in that drawer," Boris pointed, "and get me a pad and pencil. I can draw it easier than I can explain."

While Boris sketched a map, the Blond One built up the fire, then sat watching.

"Come closer, son," Boris said. "You recognize this place?"

The younger man nodded; his heart was racing, for Boris had at last called him "son."

"See this cross? That's where you turn off. Then travel east two miles. You'll come to a village and—"

"But why, Boris, my father? I can make it straight to the Polish border and never meet a patrol."

Boris said, "On horseback, yes, but the roads are little more than trails and at this time of year, even if you abandon the sleigh and you and Beljik each pull a sled, it would be too chancy." He dropped the pad and took a firm hold on the Blond One's arm. "We'll get back to that later. First I want to settle something I've never been able to talk about before."

359

He considered his son. "I'll make it brief. Neither of us is much for talk. The truth is I've done something I never meant to. By some ridiculous process I've convinced myself that I got you from somewhere not Tamara."

His eyes had shifted and the Blond One was aware that Boris was looking at Ronya's portrait. A mist came into his eyes.

"She always wanted you for her son, especially after our David died. Well, it's done. Tromokov has the papers that make you legitimate."

Inexplicably, the Blond One felt shattered, like a mirror with the image destroyed. "What's my name?" he said.

"All of mine that's Tartar I bequeath to you, including my mother's family name. Deeds and other legal rigamarole are in my room behind the gold mirror over my dresser." Boris took a long swig from the bottle to avoid being caught up in the Blond One's emotion. "Now let's get back to the village.

"It's a rich village where they don't take kindly to strangers. Find Ivan Vikulov. If he's not there you'll have to manage on your own. Travel east along the railroad tracks all the way, prepared to shift your route if you run into trouble.

"If you're challenged, stop. Bribe your way from patrol to patrol. Travel light but take plenty of oranges for Julie and apples for Rachel. No matter what you have to jettison, hang onto your vodka. It's insurance against frostbite."

The Blond One started to say, "The number of times I've smuggled guns over the border," thought better of it and said only, "I'll get Julie and Rachel to Amsterdam."

"I know that," Boris said. "Then come back. I'm in no shape to see to the stables."

The Blond One picked up Boris' crutch. "I'll get you ready for bed," he said.

"No. Not yet. Fetch me Tamara and tell her to hurry."

"Now?" he cried.

"Now, son."

The Blond One smelled death in the air, as palpable as the aroma of the pine fire.

In a remarkably short time, Tamara came into the bedroom, closing the door quietly behind her. "It's snowing," she said, throwing off her sable coat and removing her boots.

360

"Heavily?"

"It starts and stops, and the wind is bitter. By tomorrow everything will be frozen and the wind will be blowing a gale." When Boris said nothing, she came to him and kissed him full on the lips.

"For Christ's sake!" Boris growled, pushing her away. "Go sit down. Not on the bed!"

"You didn't bring me here in the middle of the night to discuss the weather," Tamara blazed as she flounced to an armchair. "Oh, Boris, listen to me!" She leaned forward, her passionate eyes fixed on his face. "You will be a man in my arms. We rob no one. Ronya has left you—"

Boris' voice rose. "Get the hell out of here!" he bellowed and Tamara burst into tears.

He was almost at the end of his endurance and there was little time left. The Blond One's orders were to return in ten minutes.

"I sent for you, Tamara, because I need you." Despair replaced anger in his voice.

She raised tear-filled eyes. "Pour two brandies," Boris said. Then, as she drank, he asked in a kindlier tone, "All right?"

"You do believe I love you?" she pleaded. "*Really* love you? Not like an animal?"

Wearily, Boris put his glass down. "Please leave, Tamara."

Suddenly she realized that the man on the bed was a shell compounded of sleeplessness, strain and some terrible knowledge. "Forgive me, Boris. What do you want of me?"

When he told her she sprang to her feet and backed away from the bed. "That's odious," she breathed. "It's against God."

"I am not concerned with your judgment—or with God's. I *am* concerned that Ronya remember me as I was, and with the lives of Julie and Rachel."

Humble, Tamara implored, "You do not have to die. You have me."

"No," he said. "Only Ronya."

And Tamara, too, said, "No!" and laughed crazily. "At last I've said no to Boris Pirov."

Boris shrugged. "Suit yourself." He closed his eyes and turned his head away.

361

"You had better not be here when they find me dead."

"How, Boris?"

"I have my pistol."

The wind was rising, rattling the windowpanes, and the room, despite the leaping fire, was icy with the tension of battle. But Boris had won. Tamara had nothing left to fight with.

"You shall have what you want." Her head was bowed.

Boris held out his hand and for a moment she sat on the bed looking fixedly into his eyes, then she leaned forward and said, "It will taste sweet."

"And you'll get it to me within a few hours?"

She nodded. "Sweet," she said. "Even in death you will be beautiful."

At five in the morning, Doctor Sergei Sergeyev gave up trying to sleep. Questions raced through his mind, countered by other questions and arguments. In an anguish of compassion he thought of the heroic man who denounced his mother, scarcely remembered his father, and whose heaven was a black-eyed Jewess named Ronya. The man whose life he could save and, in a sense, destroy. How could he be helped to face that change as courageously as he faced his pain?

The doctor got out of bed, dressed warmly and went out into the piercing cold, past the Tartar tents and along the path that wound toward the gypsy camp. He asked directions of a massive guard who, squatted under a tree, was eating grits off a tin plate.

Tamara herself opened the door. "What brings you out at this hour, doctor?"

"Design."

"Come. Get out of the wind."

Sergei Sergeyev felt vaguely annoyed because Tamara was taller than he, so that he had to look up at her, but look he must. "If it's no inconvenience to you, may we breakfast together and become acquainted over coffee?"

A pretty girl in a bright dirndl appeared wheeling a well-laden table, and Tamara and the doctor sat facing each other. The silver was ornate, the linen hand-embroidered, the china eggshell thin, all as elegant as the appointments in the big house. Tamara saw that the doctor was impressed.

"I am a queen born to quality on the wrong side of the blanket. Does that answer your curiosity?"

The doctor smiled.

"I am less formal at night," Tamara said acidly, "or anytime with an upstanding man."

The doctor met her eyes steadily. "May I call you Tamara?"

"Of course."

From his gold case, he took and lit two cigarettes. When they were smoking he said, "Don't be my enemy, Tamara. I have a favor to ask."

"Ask ahead! I'm an expert on foretelling the future, in reading palms and interpreting dreams."

"As a physician I, too, am interested in dreams. And that brings us to Boris."

Her mood changing completely, Tamara looked at him beseechingly. "How did Boris describe me to you?"

"Boris never mentioned you. He assumed, rightly, that I already knew of your existence."

"Aside from Boris, I am quite sane," she said almost humbly.

"That's why I've come to you. If I am to save Boris, I must understand him. Give me knowledge of him—any scrap of knowledge."

"What's so complicated? He had an accident. You're a fool if you doubt his courage."

"His courage doesn't cheer me. It alarms me."

"Why?"

"Because I believe that his accident was caused by fear—deeply buried fear."

Tamara jumped to her feet. "I can't help you!"

He took her hand and drew her to the sofa. "Please talk, Tamara—talk about Boris and Ronya and you."

She thought: Why not? To talk of them will be to spend another hour with them. And toward the end of that hour she was saying, "Between the time I worked on him at the wedding reception and he came to me and we danced, I fell in love. I thought to myself, 'His world is made up of wild horses, lusty men and loose women. He is not for haughty Ronya.' How wrong I was! But that night I swore I would share the man Ronya slept with."

363

The doctor brooded over this naked revelation. "Just one more question," he said gently. "It is very personal. Do you mind?"

Her head fell back among the cushions. "Boris will fulfill his destiny. The Tartars are already here. They brought the white stallion with them."

"Superstitious legend and coincidence," scoffed the doctor.

"Ask your personal question then."

"When Boris took your virginity, how great was his guilt?"

Tamara's voice was drained of feeling. "Boris did not take my virginity. His father did." Then she scowled and her voice was threatening. "I never told that to anyone but Ronya," she said. "Tell that even to your priest and I'll cut out your tongue and throw you off my land!"

How strange, thought the doctor; of the three women who loved the young Boris, only his wife had remained sane.

"I am a doctor, and your secret is safe," he said gravely. "And now I must go to my patient."

"Will you carry a present to Boris?"

"An icon of a saint who can assuage suffering?"

"Something like that."

"I'll be glad to." Sergei took the neatly wrapped small package. "Thank you for breakfast, Tamara." She turned the moment he stepped out, and shut the door without a word.

Boris' bedroom was flooded with winter sunlight, and his face was serene when the doctor came to his bedside.

"How do you feel, Boris?"

"I have felt better."

"Did you sleep?"

"Some."

The doctor lifted the quilt.

"Leave it, my friend. You've seen rotting flesh before. Let's have a vodka and talk."

"Do you really want to?" Sergei glanced at the clock.

"No." Boris grinned. "I just want to lure you into staying. The stretches between visitors are lonely."

Doctor Sergeyev sat down. "Now that you've made your arrangements and are bored, why don't we go to the hospital

364

straight away? It would be highly desirable from my point of view."

"We made a deal," Boris said stubbornly. "The next few hours are mine."

"Yes, we agreed." The doctor sighed. "By the way, I have here a present for you, sent by Tamara." He handed Boris the small package. "Perhaps that will divert you."

"Perhaps," Boris said indifferently, putting the package on his bedside table. "Now tell me something about yourself. That would divert me."

"You're a disconcerting man."

Boris grimaced. "So I've heard."

Like old friends they sat in silence until Boris noticed that Sergei was frowning. "What's on your mind?"

"All sorts of things."

"Are you married?" Boris asked.

"No. I live alone in a bachelor flat. Your Lydia puts me in mind of my old housekeeper." He opened his cigarette case and thought, I'm like Boris. He didn't want vodka. I don't want a cigarette. We each want a palliative.

Philosophically he inquired of the room at large, "Who can judge a woman's virtue. And what on earth *is* virtue? Is it like truth? Whatever truth is."

There was no comment from the man on the bed.

"You're an intelligent fellow, Boris, and I need to know the truth. What is virtue?"

Boris' eyes softened and he looked at Ronya's portrait. "It's all there," he said. "An honest wife."

Sergei was too good a doctor to tire his patient out. He got up then, saying, "I depend on you to rest," and went to the door, where he found himself confronted by Rachel and Beljik.

"It is my all-alone visiting time, doctor, my uncle," Rachel said gravely. He yearned to make it a foursome but Sergei Sergeyev closed the door behind the little girl and her bodyguard.

"Guess what?" she inquired.

"Little *krasavitsa*, I guess better when you sit on my chest and not my neck."

Rachel slid down. "Can you guess now?"

"It's beyond me."

365

There was little pleasure in instantaneous victory. "Did you *try?*" She examined Boris suspiciously.

"Yes, Rachel, I tried."

She passed her hands over his face.

"Do you hurt?"

"No, my lamb."

"*I* gave the white stallion an apple. He ate it out of my hand. Then I talked to him and he answered me."

"What did he say?"

"I don't know, Boris, my grandfather. I couldn't understand his language."

"Put your head on my shoulder, little one, and I'll tell you what he said." Rachel listened with passionate attention. When he had finished, he moved one arm and reached into the drawer of his night table. His fingers touched the small package Tamara had sent him; reaching further, he came to Stolypin's cross. He lifted it out.

"That's my present from Peter Stolypin, my uncle," she said possessively.

"Yes, Rachel. Do you know what it is?"

Rachel studied the gold cross on its thin chain. "It's my present."

Boris spoke quietly but with penetrating distinctness. "I am going to put your present around your neck, Rachel. If *anyone* at *any* time asks you what you are wearing, you are to say, 'It is my baptismal cross.' Can you remember that?"

"Oh, yes, Boris, my grandfather—it is my baptismal cross."

"Good girl," Boris said. The Blond One was on the threshold. "All set?" Boris asked him. The Blond One nodded.

"I'd like the pad and pencil." The young man brought them. "Stall them, will you?" Again the Blond One nodded.

Boris kissed Rachel and lifted her off the bed to the Blond One, whose eyes were swimming in tears. "Boris, my father?"

"Thank you, son."

The first note was to Sergei Sergeyev:

> My friend,
> You asked me, what is truth? This is my truth because it is my fate.

Understand that Tamara did us all a great favor. She spared me the bullet and all of you the sound of the shot. Promise me that you will not blame yourself.

He wrote briefly to Lydia, added Rabbi Levinsky's name to his letter to Father Tromokov, then composed a long message to Katya and Alexis, ending, "It is now certain that Georgi is to become an American citizen. May I make a suggestion?—and believe me, not impulsively. Perhaps, Alexis, if you try, you can bring yourself to follow suit. It seems to me that today the title of count is as outmoded as that of Tsar. To you both I leave my love." After he had signed his name he added a postscript: "Dear, generous Katya, I never got around to telling you how much your presence softened the vicissitudes of recent years. You are a joy. Don't fret about Julie and Rachel. They're fighters. They'll make it. My one complaint is, we should have played 'Rachel' more often. Your legs are wonderful—simply wonderful."

Boris put down his pencil and poured himself a long drink. He watched the curtains bellying back from the window and was conscious that the wind was rising again. A few snowflakes drifted across the sill. Snow. I go out in white—like a bride. He picked up his pencil again.

Dear little Julie,

You must not be sad. To me, what I do is perfectly natural. I think a man has the right to renounce life if he finds it unendurable. Besides, my dear, the white ambassador from Odessa has come for me. The Golden Ones always ride out on parade. For that we are born.

Rachel is to be allowed to wear the cross I have put on her until my Ronya's hands take it from her. Trust me. And trust the Blond One. You are to obey him to the letter until you embark from Antwerp.

This, my ring, is for Rachel, not Igor nor Igor's son. Tell her she holds it in trust for the first male descendant of her direct line, that an empress gave it to her grandfather as a wedding gift because Ronya von Glasman, the most beautiful girl in all the Russias, wanted him for a husband.

Wherever I went, darling Julie, I heard your song—even before I found you—in the yellow wheat fields, on high green

367

hills, in silvery pools. In the swish of my Ronya's whip I heard your song. Sing in America, Julie.

We've talked about Igor and you know the message I send him. Tell Georgi I am proud of him.

I love you, Julie, my daughter.

Boris
Nov. 13, 1911

Boris lay back on his pillows looking at Ronya on the wall above him. Then he wrote the shortest letter of them all.

Ronya, my love, my exquisite little dove,

Remember me on my white stallion. Remember our laughter and passion and the love that is ours—alone.

Boris, your husband

From the bedside drawer he took out a hand mirror and comb. Like the lusty male he was, Boris set his golden locks in becoming order. He unwrapped Tamara's gift and poured the contents into a glass, to which he added water. With the third finger of his left hand he stirred it, drank, then lay back and, remembering to grin, said: "Farewell, life!"

In the next room Sergei Sergeyev heard him call, "Ronya!"

XXXIX

JULIE beat her fists against the doctor. "Why did you let him die?" she cried, pushed past Katya and flung herself on Boris' chest. "Father, Father, I am half-orphaned again."

368

She subsided onto her knees beside Katya. Together they looked from the still form on the bed to Ronya's face on the wall, while the rabbi chanted:

"And the rib which the Lord had taken from man, he made into a woman and brought her unto the man. And the man said: 'This is now bone of my bone, and flesh of my flesh, she shall be called Woman because she was taken out of Man.' Therefore, shall a man leave his father and his mother, and shall cleave unto his wife, and they shall be one flesh."

No one in the white house slept that night, and all through the dark hours the storm rose and the wind screamed and lashed against the walls and shutters. Yet when the small cortège set out across the ice and snow, the sun shone. Bells tolled high in the crystal air and hot tears ran down rosy cheeks.

Beside the grave in the von Glasman family cemetery, Rabbi Levinsky, head covered with a black yarmulke, delivered a eulogy. Around him clustered Boris' family and a few neighbors; behind were peasants and gypsies. Fringing the edge of the crowd, the Tartars stood, swathed in furs, watching and waiting with an unearthly intensity.

"Boris Pirov," the rabbi intoned, "we lay you to rest in Ronya's land between the grave of your son and the grave of a son's son, innocents who see God." From behind the Tartars a horse neighed.

"In a life bereft of faith you were neither Christian nor Jew. Still, in a measure you were both.

"It will be remembered in heaven that, though in youth you indulged the appetites of the flesh and even in death subscribed to your own will, you did so cherish Ronya, daughter of Judea, that you fought for her people; that you gave to Julie a father's love; and that you called the fruit of your sin, son. To no man did you speak false.

"I, Rabbi Levinsky, therefore declare before God and man that you, Boris Pirov, are worthy of supreme bliss. May the spirits of angels guide you to the heavenly abode."

"Amen," said the Christians. They had loved him.

"Amen," said the Jews. They had trusted him.

The Tartars were silent. Father Tromokov led the Christians

369

to his little church. There he fell on his knees before the altar and prayed, "Heavenly Father, see fit to forgive him his sins and hear our praise. He surpassed us all."

When they came out into the cruel, cold wind, they found Tamara standing beside Boris' grave, holding her adopted daughter by the hand, her gypsies around her. The Tartars drew closer.

Her long hair hung loose over her shoulders and the incessant wind tossed and tangled it and blew black strands like whiplashes across her ashen face. With an enormous effort, Tamara lifted the child in her arms high enough for everyone to see while she turned slowly around once.

"Your name," she said in a hollow, strident voice to the girl, "is Queen and Ronya." She swayed and hands reached out to take the child from her and support her. At their touch a shivering spasm ran through her frame and her lips turned a livid blue. Dr. Sergeyev started to shoulder his way through the crowd but already it was too late. Watching horrified, her people saw their queen topple like a forest tree across the grave. She had reserved for herself half of the strong poison that had killed Boris.

Moaning, the gypsies gathered up their chieftain and passed, too stricken for words, out of the graveyard. The wind played a dirge in the icebound trees.

Into the space around the grave which the gypsies had left, the Tartars slipped stealthily and positions were reversed—family and friends relegated to the outskirts, the alien men of the steppe forming an inner bastion. No signal was given. One moment they were standing monolithically; the next they crouched down and with bare hands began clawing away at the clods of earth. With a gasp, the outsiders realized their intention. Father Tromokov took an angry step forward. Lydia crossed herself and began to pray audibly, "Merciful Father—" Katya groped for Alexis, whose face was almost as white as the snow.

Julie stood alone, stony, straight and strong against the buffeting wind. "No," she said in a voice that rang with authority. Her family looked at her questioningly. "They have come for their own."

When the great marble coffin was cleared of earth, inch by

inch they raised it and, forming a long column, marched at a funeral pace out of the cemetery.

Boris was going home to his Tartar mother.

Julie and Rachel, Katya, Alexis, Sergei Sergeyev, the Blond One, the rabbi and the priest, Lydia, and Ronya's broad-faced peasants, met the Tartars when they stopped on the snow-covered lawn.

Their spokesman addressed Julie. "Embrace us and we spare this house."

Julie's intensity matched his own. "Tear out my eyes! I will still say no!"

He rubbed his chin. "You compare well with the other one, Jewess."

No one stirred.

"Step forward." He pointed to Rachel. "And what did your grandfather tell you, little beauty?"

Rachel's piping voice carried clearly to the throng below the front steps. "I have to go to my father, Igor."

The Black Tartar's voice was the crack of a whip. "Burn!"

The Blond One stepped forward. "Must the curse be accompanied by sacrifice?" he asked. "I was never told so."

"A torch must be set to the house of von Glasman," the Tartar insisted. "The Golden One did not die alone. You have an hour." He withdrew.

Julie went first to the place where she had hidden Boris' ring and this, with her emerald, she gave to Lydia. While Julie wrapped her silver candlesticks, Lydia sewed the great green jewel into the lining of a sable coat, and secured the ring of the royal guard in Rachel's fox-lined ermine. Katya, moving like a ghost, took only the portrait of Ronya.

Then they stood on the lawn, joined in fatalistic acceptance of Boris' own dictum: what will be, will be; done's done. The first smoke drifted through the windows of the glorious old house, and Julie said, with a grandeur that echoed in all their ears forever after, "I see this house burn gladly since Boris, my father, did not die alone. No Tartar grave will hold him when God says, 'It is Ronya's time.'"

Katya, weeping, put her arms around Julie, grown so heroic.

371

"Don't be sad for me," the girl said. "I have Rachel, beautiful like Ronya, brave like Igor. I leave Kiev richer than I came."

Through the early winter twilight, the Blond One drove Julie and Rachel and Beljik away from the burning house into a wilderness of silence. The heavens seemed infinitely remote, and as if they were too far above the earth to send any token through the still, glacial air; no snow fell. In light that faded from blue to mint green, the horses took fright, lost their foothold and the sleigh tumbled amid trees whose twigs glittered with ice in the eerie light.

The Blond One hauled three sleds out of the shattered sleigh and tied Julie, from one of whose cheeks blood trickled, on the first, Rachel on the second and the supplies to the third, entrusting its rope to Julie to drag over the snow-locked earth with one hand. In the other she clutched her candlesticks. Before he harnessed himself to her sled and Beljik to Rachel's, he cut the horses free to find their way back.

For fourteen days they lived a hunted life, forever plodding ahead. Sometimes they emerged from the woods at a small hamlet like Julie's own village and bought food and promises that they would not be pursued. But whenever they could they avoided settlements. They hid by day, traveled by night, stumbling over tree roots, slipping into drifts. Julie walked until she dropped with exhaustion and the Blond One put her on a sled once more.

Close to the border, where Boris had told the Blond One to turn and follow the railroad tracks, their spirits lifted. Freedom was within their grasp.

The moon betrayed them when they were only a few yards away from safety. A patrol suddenly blundered out of a copse so close that there was no chance to slip across the tracks and hide again.

Gun barrels glinted in the moonlight. The order rang out: "Halt or we shoot!" and the Blond One untied Julie and Rachel from the sleds and helped them to their feet. A match flamed and the sergeant in charge peered into the white face and blue eyes of Julie, who was fanned by fumes of vodka on his breath.

In this desolate outpost the soldiers' quarry was escaping Jews—preferably rich Jews. Fortune had perhaps sent them a Jewess who was lusciously pretty as well. The sergeant's brain was foggy but not so fuddled as to rule out the possibility that the three might be aristocrats on the run from peasant uprisings. In that case it would mean a court-martial to interfere with them. The blue eyes? It was puzzling.

His own eyes slits in his great, fair head, the Blond One saw before him a man who could not, like the villagers, be bought. He wanted Julie more than money, if his expression meant anything. Besides, the Blond One had almost no money left, so much had gone into the greedy hands of those who had let them pass.

He might have been Boris, the way he spoke, so easily confident. "Our documents were lost with our personal possessions. However, it does not matter. Take us to your captain. He doubtless has been notified that we have permission to pass."

The sergeant needed no lantern to see that the bearded man stood head and shoulders above him and his three soldiers. He snapped the safety catch off his pistol. "Drop your arms," he said. "If you plan to trick me, you make a big mistake."

The Blond One shrugged and complied. It would be foolhardy to take risks with Julie and Rachel. He said, "Would it be possible for us to take shelter, sergeant? My sister and niece are very cold."

Gun against the Blond One's back, the sergeant said, "March! And no nonsense. You could get shot."

They started to walk toward the outline of a small building when a threatening noise sounded behind the sergeant. He whirled and shot in a single motion. And Beljik, whose business in life had always been to guard Rachel from ugly strangers, paid with his life for a growl.

Rachel stood looking down at her dear friend in frozen silence. Her mother's hand squeezed hers and she followed the sergeant without a tear or a word. Her sorrow was too deep.

When they entered a rickety hut, two more soldiers were sitting close to a small stove, tin cups in their hands. Boredom vanished from the tiny room and cups clattered down at sight of

373

Julie, her fair skin roughened and pink from the wind, her gleaming black hair falling loose from under a fur turban. The color in her cheeks deepened but she kept a firm hold on herself and her candlesticks.

"The devil knows when our captain is coming back—if ever," the sergeant said maliciously to the Blond One. "Your—uh—sister is without identification? A pity!" He rolled his eyes toward the ceiling and thrust out his lower lip. "We shall have to detain her, of course. For quite some time." The men around him stirred, delightedly. "As to you," his voice was oily, "how much are you prepared to pay for your own skin? We'll throw in the black-eyed sparrow."

The Blond One had the sangfroid to grin. "You set the odds. If any of you survives the fight, we can discuss it later."

The sergeant moved with unexpected speed. Knocking over a packing box, he seized Julie, pinioning her arms to her sides.

"Rope the bastard," he said to his men.

With a show of rage worthy of her father, Rachel's mittened fists shot out at the brutal sergeant with sufficient impact to send Julie's package hurtling to the floor of rotting boards.

The paper wrappings around the ritual candlesticks burst open. Every man in the room jumped at the Blond One. He was fair game. This little party was made up of escaping Jews.

While his men tried to hold the blond giant, the sergeant cocked his sweat-streaked face in Julie's and said, "Be sociable and I'll give you a drink first." But he figured without Rachel, who had gone to the aid of the Blond One. She broke a bottle of vodka over the head of one man, who slumped to the floor and remained there. As a soldier knocked her aside and the furious child struggled to get up, the captain entered. He called a thundering halt to the fight and commanded, "Take your hands off the lady!"

The sergeant leered. "After you, my captain. They're Jews. We caught them trying to escape."

The officer's fists rose. "I said to take your hands off the lady."

"See those Jew candlesticks?" the sergeant bleated.

"I see them, swine. Now get out and take your patrol with you. You're on duty." He busied himself with rolling a cigarette while four of the men followed the sergeant out into the snow.

374

"Who did that?" asked the captain, looking at the man Rachel had downed.

"I did," Rachel announced firmly. "I am not sorry."

With a smile he reached out for her. "You're a tiger cub," he said, picking her up. Rachel's coat had fallen open and the light of the lantern glinted on the chain around her neck. The captain regarded it intently. With his right hand he lifted it off over her head.

"That's mine," she said. "Give it back to me."

He did not respond, nor put the child down, but continued to study the object in his hand, then turned his attention to Julie. How, he wondered, does one distinguish a blue-eyed Jewess from any other pretty girl—especially in Russia? And the blond fellow. If he's a Jew! The child? Perhaps, perhaps not. He completed the circle, his eyes again on Rachel. It's the eyes, he decided; only Jewesses have eyes like that.

"What is this, little one?" He held the cross out to Rachel and she took it from his hand. Julie shivered; the Blond One's fists clenched.

"That," said Rachel, "is my baptismal cross. I have to wear it." She spoke with such naturalness that not even the Blond One could be sure she had been rehearsed.

"Thank you, small pigeon," the captain said and set her down and put the chain back around her neck. Rachel picked up Julie's candlesticks and gravely handed them to her mother.

"Let's sit down and talk things over," the officer said and led Julie to the only chair in the shack. He and the Blond One and Rachel sat on boxes.

"All passports are void," he said. "Have you identity cards?"

"No, sir," said the Blond One.

"You are escaping from Russia?"

"That was our intention, sir."

"It's a serious offense," the captain said mildly.

The Blond One countered, "Let them go and keep me as a hostage."

"And can you buy your freedom? Are you talking gold?"

The Blond One grinned engagingly, "*Yes*, sir."

"That, too, is serious—a capital offense, offering a bribe. Mmmm—much of it?"

"The accumulation of generations of gold," said the young man, "the finest stables in Russia and countless hills in Odessa."

"I am a reasonable man, and practical. I enjoy spending money," said the captain ruefully. "And a captain's pay—"

"I pledge you a fortune."

"You pledge your life, my friend. And what security can you give me?"

"Trust me," the Blond One implored. "You'll have no trouble finding me. My name is Boris Godinov and my sister is Madame Kozny. I belong to the Odessa Tartars, and Count Brusilov in St. Petersburg will vouch for me."

The captain whistled. "That's a hell of a long reach and by the time I find out whether you're telling the truth your sister"—Was she? he wondered, and decided not, but let it pass—"will be a long way from here."

In despair, the Blond One looked at Julie.

"May I have a knife, please, captain?" she asked evenly.

He pulled one out of his pocket, puzzled. Julie took it, leaned down and ripped open the hem of her coat. When she stood up she had the emerald in her hand. She held it out to the officer.

"Stolen?" he asked.

"No," she said. "My engagement ring. It will be redeemed." He believed her and took it.

"Let's make our arrangements, tall man," he said to the Blond One. "You're quite a responsibility. The patrol will be back before the train pulls out. Say goodbye to your sister quickly." He reached out for the child. "We'll start up to the station, little Rachel Kozny," he said. "You're a brave little lion, you can tell your father that."

Rachel stared at him. "My name is Rachel von Glasman Pirov," she said.

"My God!" the man took a startled step back and stared at Julie. "Are you Igor's Julie?"

"You know my Igor?"

"Hell, yes!" he roared. "All this trouble for—" Suddenly he changed his mind. He was a kind man, even sentimental on occasion. But! A man who likes to spend money must be practical. He put the jewel in his pocket.

376

"Ronya Pirov saved my life in Manchuria years ago," he said, and took Rachel, too tired to protest, from the Blond One. "We'll wait outside. Please hurry."

Julie kissed the Blond One. "Because of you, Boris, my brother, I will lie in Igor's arms again. Our first son will be named Boris, partly for our father, partly for you."

The Blond One was not sure how far he could trust his voice, or his heart, so he limited himself to saying, "Give them my love."

"I will," said Julie and walked out of the shack.

In the small shelter that served as a station, the captain all but emptied his pockets of rubles for Julie and they came to more than the train fare. "We have a few minutes to wait. While we do, would you answer one question?"

Her hands were shaking with the cold; her eyes, when she turned them on him, were tear-filled, and he had not the heart to press her. "Never mind," he said. "You're too exhausted to talk."

Julie shook her head. "You've been very kind, captain. Please ask."

"It's this." He considered. "I can't help wondering. . . . You carry candlesticks, symbol of the Jewish Sabbath. Your daughter wears the cross of Christendom. To put it simply, I just don't understand."

Julie's smile was wistful. "I've been thinking and thinking about that, too," she said, "and I don't understand it either."

A whistle sounded, high and lonely, through the cold night and the captain, carrying Rachel, led Julie out onto the crude wooden platform.

The train was slowing down. "Turn your head, Igor's Julie," he said "and take a last look at Russia."

By the thin yellow beams of the conductor's lantern Julie saw steam drifting from the engine. A wrack of clouds was beginning to obscure the moon. On all sides the bleak, snowy landscape stretched away. The conductor took Rachel from the captain. "God go with you both," said the officer, and walked off into the stillness.

Julie and Rachel followed the conductor down the dusty aisle,

377

and under their feet the floor reverberated to turning wheels. He found them seats and they sat huddling in their fur coats, Julie with her candlesticks still in her arms, unaware that tears were falling on them.

"Lead us to the free land," she prayed silently.

Rachel's small hand found her cross. Her head fell back. She was asleep.